When The Light Gets In

David A Dunlop

Cover design and Photography
David A Dunlop & M-C Bretherton
(With a little assistance from Chatgpt)

Published by Kindle Direct Publishing

Copyright © 2024 David A Dunlop

All rights reserved.

ISBN
9798861496599

For Valma

While this novel was inspired by a true story, all characters, events and places are wholly fictional. Any resemblance to actual people, happenings or locations is entirely accidental.

No. 17
CASTLECUINN

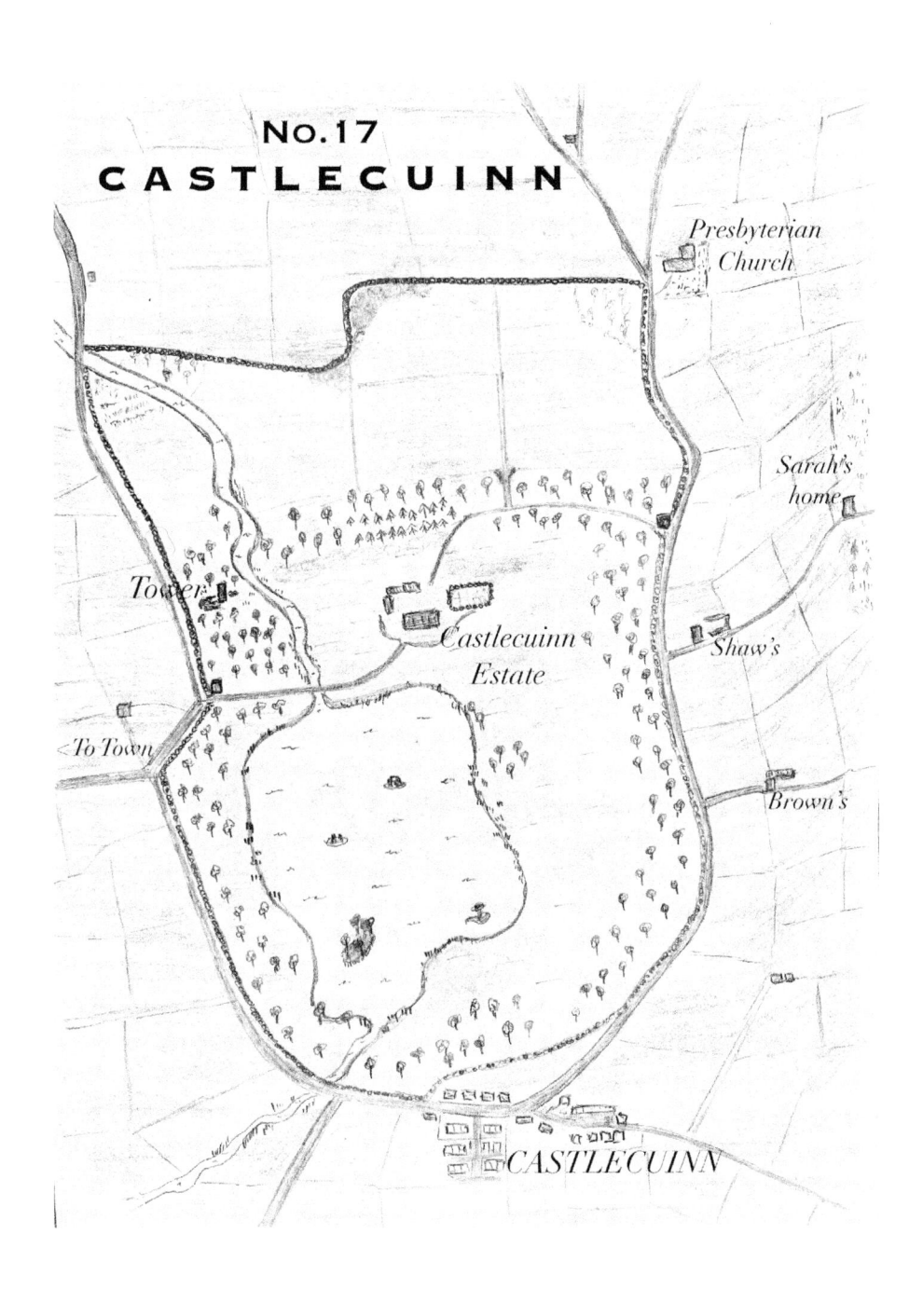

Presbyterian Church

Sarah's home

Tower

Castlecuinn Estate

Shaw's

To Town

Brown's

CASTLECUINN

'Ring the bells that still can ring,
Forget your perfect offering,
There is a crack, a crack in everything,
That's how the light gets in'

'Anthem' - Leonard Cohen

When The Light Gets In

Chapter 1

Wake

My eldest brother's wake, and my life takes an unexpected lurch into uncertainty.

As if his untimely passing at the age of sixty-seven isn't bad enough. Liver disease, like death itself, is no respecter of persons. He had reached the end of his mortal coil far too quickly. Each of the visiting mourners to our sorrowing family home in Castlecuinn acknowledge that reality.

A litany of sincerely meant platitudes. Variations on a theme.

"He was far too young to be taken."

My response is sorrowful appreciation, followed by pious resignation to Divine will. On repeat.

"The heavenly Father knows best."

Then a careless comment from someone that I haven't spoken to in ages lodges in my head, and begins to worm its way into my grieving soul. A comment that will haunt me, change my life.

Against the background of cooing wake-chat, that gentle blend of reflection and banality, so many awkward silences in the mumbled consolations of visitors.

The 'sorry for your trouble' part is easy on the ear; easy to give and to receive; but the absence of 'he's in a better place' lies heavy on the heart. Neighbours, clergy, friends, relations, anybody with spiritual insight who knows anything about my brother would be fairly confident that he's not.

It is going to be a very difficult funeral service, particularly for our minister. His instinct and training will of course prompt him to bury my brother with hope. He will do his best; he will preach the gospel, the resurrection of the body, the hope of eternal salvation. He will not 'miss them', as my father would often have pronounced with quiet approval after a particularly evangelistic funeral address. But there will not be the ring of triumph and certainty in this sermon that I remember so well at father's service. My father was ready to go. His faith was strong and steadfast, as was my mother's. My poor brother had lost his many years ago; I could never understand what had happened to him to entice him to backslide, to choose the path of the outsider, turning his back on his God, on his father and his church family.

His life-style left a lot to be desired, we all know that…which makes it very difficult for the solid Presbyterian folk of our community to say much about him. I understand their reticence, even as they take my soft hand firmly between their rough ones, as they meet my eye fleetingly before passing on to my twin brother beside me in the hall.

We have our certainties. Not a soul who visits us in our old homestead of grief is going to embarrass us with references to the after-life. My brother's hollowed-out body is for the dank, dark earth of the churchyard; his never-dying soul…well, that doesn't bear thinking about. Certainly not talking about.

Lukewarm condolences dry on lips; downcast glances rise sheepishly to try to identify someone to talk to in rooms to right and left; somber mourners shuffle in the direction of refreshments; these, as our tradition demands, consist of tidy, triangular sandwiches, red-cherried tray-bakes, and tea in cups of Wedgwood china.

I see a familiar figure peer shyly in at the hall door.

He must be well over eighty now, our old farmhand. The 'servant man', as my father would have referred to him. I always thought that was a term that reeked of slavery. Jimmy was no slave; before he retired he was every bit as vital to the prosperity of our farm as either my father or brother had been. Over fifty years he had laboured on our land, in our farmyard. He has known me from my infancy. I cannot recall a time when he wasn't working for us. Well, actually now that I think about it, there were some blips in his service, but they were brief; few and far between. I wouldn't want to give the impression that he was a drunkard or anything, but occasionally he would succumb to the temptation of the demon drink and disappear for a few days.

"Ah wus on the tear," he would confess apologetically, albeit with the hint of a lopsided smile about his thin, crimson lips. It would make my father mad. My brother, though, had a soft spot for him; he always brought him back in. Final warnings had been quickly forgotten when set beside the value of Jimmy's labour. He knew the farm inside out, better than any of us. There was no better cattle handler in the countryside, nor better tractor man. He was never beaten by a recalcitrant animal, nor by a mechanical failure. He could work eleven hours in the day, five days a week with a half-day on the Saturday, and never a complaint out of him. He knew us all so well into the bargain.

I watch his face as he limps towards me down the hall, his crumpled little wife in his wake. Mrs McGrath, (her Christian name slips my mind for the moment, such is my inner frazzle), can't be more than six or seven stone. Her wee face is the picture of misery, God love her; about to burst into tears, you would think. Her man is well slowed down now; he slipes his gammy leg behind him like it's an uncooperative paling-stab that he'd have used for fencing. He sets his blackthorn stick against the hall-stand, tugs the threadbare cloth cap off his balding head, then runs a crooked hand across the top where he imagines there may still be a few strands of stubborn hair.

That face, wrinkled like a dried out seed potato, not much different in colour either; the grey stubble of his beard testifying to yet another shambolic attempt at shaving. Those eyes, still incredibly alive for a man of his age; they always had a light in them that shone out from the crevasse between his tufted eyebrows and high, ruddied cheekbones. I always loved his eyes; I will forever have the memory of them, twinkling like shards of blue glass through curls of Woodbine smoke as he rested in the feed-house during lunch-break. He would raise his dirt-tracked hand to his mouth, dragging a whiff of tobacco from the stubby cigarette, with a wink in my direction. Then he'd nick the glowing ember from the point of the fag with gnarled, nicotine-stained fingers, and tuck the remaining butt behind his ear for later use.

Now he takes my hand, holds on tightly, the longest grip of the night. He meets my gaze without a flinch of embarrassment. His voice is the dry, low-down rasp of a smoker, but none the less sincere for that.

"I am so sorry, lass," he says...he always called me 'lass'. "He was a fine man. Many a good turn he did me. Fine man to work for. It's just a shame he's gone before his time, but yous can all be proud of him, you hear me now? Proud of him."

I thank him. I know I am going to cry now, despite my attempts at stoic self-control. I cannot help it. I reach forward to hug him, and, God bless him, he hugs me back, so tightly for such a feeble frame. There's not much to him now. Those wiry arms that pulled calves from panicking heifers and fought with stubborn bulls. All the memories of the fun we used to have around the farm, the fields, the byre, the sheds, come flooding back to me.

I show him into the sitting room where the open coffin rests in front of the dormant fireplace, and where a straggle of neighbours have already turned their backs to the corpse, now discussing how bad the harvest weather had been. I stand there briefly beside my old friend. We are wordless now. He is studying my brother's face as if to draw a final nod of connection.

"Not like himself at all," he whispers. "Poor Jack."

Indeed. The pallor is smoke-grey, my brother's features ugly, clay-like, as if carelessly sculpted by someone who had never known the earlier man. I am glad I had the sense to ask the undertaker to trim his hair, shave off his stubble. He's a bit more Protestant looking now than in those final few weeks of descent; the white shirt, the red and blue striped tie, the navy suit that I only ever saw him wear at funerals. Fitting, I think; one last time.

I take Jimmy's elbow in my hand, a brief squeeze of affection as he continues to stare at that face, the shake of his grizzled head faintly noticeable. Leaving him there I slip away, back to the greeting hall.

His wife is waiting for me there, too shy to follow in with her man. So withered, she is, now late seventies, I imagine. She crosses herself, being of the other religion. It's an inappropriate gesture; she should have known that. I forgive her though; it's just her custom; deeply ingrained and hard to unlearn, I suppose.

But it's what she says that so upsets me!

The poor woman, so mixed up. How could she say something like that, make that mistake?

I hadn't realised until now that she had deteriorated so much, and so quickly. My own mother had had dementia at the end, but I hadn't realised that our workman's wife had started to dote as well.

She passes on to speak to my twin; I try to listen to her high-pitched voice, like an out-of-tune flute. I wonder will she say anything daft to him, and I strain to hear. I fail though, for a cousin I haven't set eyes on for half a life time is grabbing me in an awkward bear hug, and the moment passes.

Moments pass, don't they!

Except that Mrs McGrath's *faux pas* has now lodged in my head, a ghosting shadow of self-doubt.

The Castlecuinn Young Farmers Club is saddened to hear of the death of one of its founder members, Mr Jack Shaw of 16 Church Rd, Castlecuinn. Jack was a stalwart of the club in its early years, a long-time committee member and participant in all its activities. His expertise as a judge of cattle at agricultural shows, both locally and at Balmoral, was greatly valued. A good friend to all who knew him, he will be sadly missed. Our sincerest condolences to all the members of the Shaw family.

Chapter 2

Funeral

We kick our way through a thick carpet of leaves; their curl and rustle has survived last night's October shower. A yellowed fragment of fallen sycamore sticks briefly to the toe of my shiny black boot. It's slippery underfoot. Hopefully no-one falls. The undertaker recognises this danger. With both hands he steadies the shouldered coffin at the back, and murmurs monotone guidance to the six bearers.

"Slow and steady, now. Slow and steady."

My twin brother in his long, coal-dark funeral coat is at the front, his arm grasped around the broad back of a stocky gentleman, Wally Brown, a good friend of our family whose farm is just across the march ditch from ours. These two are about the same height, if quite different in age and bearing. Behind them, my husband and nineteen year old son, Jonathan, make up the middle rank of bearers, followed by a couple of my cousins. The undertaker's custom seems to be to have the tallest men at the rear, but this convention leads to the coffin being in some danger of sliding forward as the cortege descends the gentle slope of our concreted lane. It's not a long carry though, the length of a stubbled field from our yard down to the road.

Smokey fumes drift up from the hearse's exhaust, catching in my throat, making me want to cough. In the somber circumstance, I generate and swallow as much saliva as I can, and just about manage to stifle the urge. The soft purr of the Daimler's engine is soon being drowned out by the swirling choir of crows that rises inevitably from the plantation opposite. I can risk a few soft coughs now, thanks to the cover of their cacophony. Black-robed and possessive of the feeding space around their wooded territory, their toneless symphony has been an incessant drone in the musical score of my life. My former bedroom window looked directly across our front meadow to their nesting colony. There was not a day in life when I did not suffer their tone-deaf canticle. Is it too much to imagine that they might have taken a respectful day off for this funeral? In death, as in life, they circle above him, and rasp their husky tribute.

Safely to the bottom of the lane, and into the sombre shade of the forest, we turn right towards our church and graveyard, a mile and so many memories to the north. The hearse pauses on the narrow, single-track road, still puffing gentle wreaths of carbon at us, while my brother's coffin is manoeuvred inside. Relief for the bearers, I imagine… but we will walk the entire route behind him, in respect to what he might have wished. This was his town-land, his territory. Nowhere and nothing on planet earth was of greater importance to my eldest brother than this landscape.

He loved every inch of this locality, particularly the forest we now walk beside. Our farm lies in the shadow of the Colonel's estate, literally as well as figuratively. Its two-hundred year old trees tower protectively over us to the west; from March to October each year their rich foliage blocks out our view of the setting sun. Then in winter we watch it winking coldly at us, as if from between boney fingers, our ration of sunlight filtered through the pale, skeletal limbs of leafless ash trees. In my childhood I remember feeling that the Colonel's forest was forever glaring at us across our front meadow; there was a malevolence about its constant gaze, its oppressively persistent presence. We lived under its frown. As I grew up I slowly came to understand that its purpose, of course, and that of the high stone wall that surrounded the whole estate, was to veil and protect the privilege that the Colonel and folk of his class felt entitled to.

Our land had been bought out from the Colonel's ancestor landlord back in 1925, I believe. I can't quite recall how much my father had said it cost our grand-father, but I do know that it was only finally paid off in 1960, the year that twin and I arrived on the scene. No more paying rent to the well-heeled landlords with their English, public-school accents and military medals; the farm was now ours, and how my brother loved it, loved it to the point of worship, I fear.

To be fair, he also had a great affection for the Colonel's estate, the landscape itself, rather than the system that this ongoing anachronism embodied. He would never have been a forelock-tugger, in terms of his opinion of this kind of place, or these kind of people. Respect maybe, but seasoned with a dusting of scorn. He loved sneaking around in the shadowy woodland there, staying out of sight of the big house, a clandestine re-coloniser of the less trodden backwoods.

I have the happiest memories of when I was small, and Jack would take me exploring in that forbidden territory. It was a different world, an almost magical kingdom; he knew every inch of it. We would have to scale the wall, climbing up an old, bent alder tree that had been allowed to grow beside it, conveniently so for us. I remember that my brother told me this was a 'famine wall', built generations ago during the 'great hunger', paid for by public funds, and using local labour. Seems the peasants, tenants of whatever landlord was in residence at the time, were compelled to work here for months, creating this protective edifice for the aristocracy. The irony! The exploitation of their poverty, just so they could earn oatmeal rations to make gruel to feed their families.

Their families? Our family! The Shaws as well, for I am quite sure my ancestors were among those labourers, grafting their guts out just to survive. It didn't bear thinking about how bad things were away back then when the potato crop kept failing. The wall remained, a hundred and sixty years later, a sort of unintended monument to those destitute people, the stones of dark basalt as harshly formidable now as when they had been put in place.

We used to clamber over this wall without much of a thought about its origins. We would drop down on to the soft grass beyond, then explore among the trees and the labyrinths of endless rhododendron bushes that seemed to have overwhelmed the area, staying well out of sight of the Manor House itself. Sometimes twin would be with us, like when he wanted to visit the great horse chestnut tree to collect those golden-brown conkers for his duels in school. But twin was harder for our eldest brother to manage; he would yelp and scurry about like a terrier dog let off the lead. So, more often than not, it was just Jack and me. I loved those adventures with him; I felt like I had entered the world of 'Swallows and Amazons', or 'The Lion, the Witch and the Wardrobe.' It was all so mystical, so mysterious. He was a great brother to me then, my idol really. I saw no wrong in him, not a hint of anything untoward. He used to catch delicious brown trout, and sometimes even salmon, in the river that wove its lethargic way through the estate. He had a very special privilege in that, for I do recall hearing about local boys who were caught poaching there and finished up in court…the Colonel had no mercy on trespassers and interlopers.

How then did he permit my brother to have the run of the place?

It turned out that, in his mid-teens, Jack had been given a Saturday job in there. The Colonel had kindly invited him to assist the groundsman in maintaining the place; so in exchange for being allowed to fish the river, he would have the job of mowing the huge lawn, trimming hedges, pruning trees, draining wet areas, raking up leaves and so on.

'We could be doing with him today,' I think to myself as a gust of wind stirs the stand of trees beyond the wall, sending a diagonal drift of leaves our way, a kind of confetti, mottled and irreverent, falling on the slow procession of be-suited mourners.

As the cortege shuffles slowly forward, I am recalling a summertime visit with Jack to the far side of the estate, beyond the big house. The Colonel and his family must have been away on vacation or something, for my brother marched me proudly across the gravelled turning circle in front of the entrance door as if he owned the place.

There was a statue standing in the middle there, some sort of Greek or Roman figure in cloud-grey marble, looking very out of place. Such a thing should have been left in whatever warm country it had been brought from, not stuck here in the damp chill of rural Ulster…not least because the poor fellow was completely naked, apart from the large leaf he was holding to hide his uncomely parts. Thankfully the leaf did its job effectively, but shame on him nevertheless! I remember that that day Jack did an extravagant pose beside the figure, as if he himself was modelling for the sculptor.

The building was magnificent, to my childish eye. Two storied, a huge square-shaped structure that spoke volumes about the solidity and status of this family. I counted ten rectangular windows on its front facade, each with twelve panes of glass. The walls were built of a lovely tan shade of sandstone, very unlike the usual dark rock in this part of the world, so no doubt it had to be brought in from miles away. I lost count of the number of chimneys sticking up from the slated roof. A balcony sat proudly on a pillared porch which framed the front entrance. We stood briefly on the steps, another moment of arrogance by my risk-taking brother, as if daring someone to discover him.

From that position we could see a long way to the south, over the lawn, and across a very picturesque, tree-framed stretch of water. A couple of feeding swans bobbed in the shallows close to the shore, and a little flotilla of richly coloured ducks paddled carefully away from us. There seemed to be some more statues standing on a small island in the middle of the lake, their forms reflected on the smooth surface of the water; beyond that, clumps of trees were elegantly placed here and there on the parkland, and sheep grazed in contentment. It was idyllic, like a classical painting.

Then to the walled garden; I remember being amazed at the colours, the order, the symmetry of that place. Everything was so well planned and laid out. Somebody had taken great pride in creating this hidden jewel of flowers and bushes. What pleasure the Colonel's children must have experienced playing here, their own real-life 'Secret Garden', the icing on the cake of privilege.

But it hadn't been the 'highlight' of that particular day for me.

We had passed further to the west, along the curving drive towards the main gate that opened on to the road to the nearby town. A few hundred yards later Jack took my hand and pulled me through between mounds of bushes and what seemed to be even older trees, native elder and berried rowan, as I recall it. We arrived at a clearing, and I couldn't believe my eyes. In front of me, across a marshy area of rushes and shrubby bushes, stood the remains of a very dilapidated castle of some sort. Most of it appeared to be in ruin, but three uneven walls were still standing. An ancient tower remained, as if in defiance against the passage of time, I thought. It was maybe twice the height of our farmhouse, crumbled and uneven at the top like a lonely, broken tooth.

"This was the castle of the O'Cuinn clan," he told me. "They were the original people who lived here."

"What happened to them then?" I asked.

"They got driven off."

"Driven off? How did that happen? If it was theirs, like?"

I remember he looked hard and long at me then before answering. "I suppose they must have rebelled against the English," he said. "But they lost, didn't they."

"So the Colonel's army defeated them and took the land?"

"Maybe not quite as simple as that," he told me, leading me carefully by the hand from dry spot to dry spot across the watery surface. "You see, the present Colonel comes from a long line of Majors and Generals and military men. This land would have been given to our Colonel's ancestors by the King, likely as a reward for leading his army and beating the Irish rebels. That's why the castle is a ruin; but then the Colonel's folk would have built their own mansion to replace it."

"How long ago was that?" I asked.

"Not sure," he said. "Could've been after the Battle of the Boyne, Siege of Derry and all that…or maybe later. Maybe 1798… there was the rising of the United Irishmen that year. There have been a few rebellions. Thank God all that is past."

I remember those words well, for the following reason. It must have been around 1968 or 69 at that time; the early Civil Rights marches would have been in the news; people marching in various parts of the province, Londonderry especially, demanding better housing and things like 'One man, one vote'. We didn't know it then of-course, but another period of trouble was just about to break out to disrupt the peace of our wee country.

One of the things that sticks in my mind from that day is that my brother took me to a room down under that castle…a 'secret cellar', he called it. Yet again it felt as if I had walked into one of CS Lewis' magical kingdoms, such was the eerie feeling around it. We clambered down a steep set of moss-carpeted stone stairs. There was a heavy wooden door blocking our way, its hinges very rusty and the hint of paint on it almost all flaked off. He put his shoulder to it, pushing it open so we could go inside. He had to sweep away a whole curtain of dead ivy and cobwebs. The only light down there was from the stairwell, so I couldn't actually see very much at the start.

My brother took out a silver lighter and clicked it a few times until a small flicker of flame rose up from it. That was the first time that I ever saw a cigarette lighter. I didn't know what it was, nor what it was for. Our farmhand always struck a match and cupped his hand around his cigarette when he stopped in the field for a quick smoke. I was so innocent back then. It was only later that the dread of realisation dawned on me that if Jack had a cigarette lighter he was most probably a smoker too. Smoking was such a terrible sin to my family. Did my parents know he was a smoker? Should I tell them? It put me in a horribly conflicted position as a nine year old. I lay awake for nights after that, wondering what I should do, praying that it wasn't true, praying for Jack not to be such a silly sinner. It wasn't so bad for Jimmy McGrath to smoke for he wasn't 'saved', I thought. But my brother!! He was supposed to be.

The flame of his lighter showed me little, just some bare stone walls, a few old bottles, no furniture, a partition that divided the room in two and a low platform covered with what might have been hay or straw in an earlier life. I couldn't wait to get out of the place and turned to clamber back up the steps.

"It's alright," he called after me. "It's safe, honestly. It's a great wee hideout if you ever need to escape."

"If I need to escape I will never come here," I told him.

How well I recall that day, that conversation, still clear in my mind. There was an emotion stirred deeply in me that I couldn't fathom. A darkness that transcended the excitement of this furtive adventure. An aura of something inexplicable, like an invisible imprint somehow echoing through from the ancient history of the place. Had this cellar been a prison where unspeakable things had happened?

I think it was possibly the first time I had been disappointed in my eldest brother, and while I forgave him for it, the experience stayed with me. Fear entered my soul that day away back then, but walking behind his coffin now I forgive him again. No point in holding on to disappointments, resentments. They only become woodworm to your soul, burrowing into your peace of mind; that's what I heard some preacher say anyhow.

We continue to stride at a better pace towards the church, the road now further narrowed, hemmed in between the famine wall and an even older dry-stone dyke on our right. Halfway there we pass the eastern gate-lodge at the back entrance into the Colonel's estate, the huge iron gates closed against intrusion. Waiting outside is Jimmy McGrath and his wife, their frail bodies unable to commit to the procession. This gate-lodge has been their home for maybe sixty years, a small four-roomed dwelling with its strangely hipped roof; here they had raised their brood of children. Far too many wains for such a tiny house, I always thought, but that was their way. I have been inside a few times back in the day; I remember the shock of the untidiness of everything, the lack of space, the mustiness of the atmosphere. For all that I will always think well of him; what a lovely man he was, our old workman. I watch him now, his eyes fixed on the coffin through the glass-sided hearse. He grapples to remove his cloth cap again while his other hand rises to his chest as my brother's remains come adjacent to him, and I see him bless himself. Their custom again. His wife does the same.

I wince inside at the memory of her insensitivity at the wake. I must forgive her, put it from my mind. I smile in their direction, and raise my hand in the smallest of acknowledgements. Just what is appropriate.

Another half-mile to the church. How often have I walked this road? In childhood sometimes three times on a Sunday. I know every black stone in the wall, every five-barred gate. There is the rose tree that we used to rob, taking the rose-hips home for our mother to turn into pink, sickly-sweet syrup. And here is the old, humpback bridge over the burn where we often stopped to skip stones on the flat pond above the weir. But for every time I trod these furlongs my late brother must have done so hundreds more. Cows to be followed to the rented far-field when grass nearer home was exhausted. The bull to be led back from the neighbour's herd, contented after 'services rendered'. Himself, ash-plant in hand, following patiently behind a slow-moving group of springin' heifers, or trotting after a scattering of fattened bullocks, their fresh skitter greening their rumps and glistening the tarmac; twin and myself, and the collie dog of course, would be darting here and there in front to guard the open gaps in the hedgerows… 'slaps' we called them.

I can still hear my father's tense voice. 'Kep them slaps!"

Such a flow of memories. For a moment's diversion I look forward over the hearse to the spread of sky ahead of us. The Divine weather-maker has spilled a slew of porridge-grey clouds from here to the line of rounded hills on the horizon, completely blocking out any semblance of sunlight today.

It matches my mood perfectly. Life has slipped into a minor key in the past while, and what grace notes there are are melancholy.

Chapter 3

Service

They don't want me to play the organ at the funeral, but I do. After all, it was mainly Jack who had encouraged twin and I in music all those years ago. It was he who set me on this course of life that was to lead to me being the church organist here, and, for so many years now, the music teacher in the secondary school in town. Music was very much my identity; it still is who I am. The twin brother less so. He packed it in after a few years. Jack tried to persuade him to keep at it; a waste of time, for he was never going to change his mind; 'stubborn as a Border ram' as my father said.

"Sure let somebody else play today," they said. "It's hardly right for you to play at your own brother's funeral? You'll maybe not be fit for it."

Fit for it? I have endured much more trauma in my life than this.

I have had to play at the tragic funeral of one of my brother's colleagues, blown up by an IRA car-bomb in the mid nineties. A devastating experience that took a terrible toll on him and left him with a legacy of trauma, and a depression that has stayed with him for years. The troubles had made their first horrible incursion into our family environment, but it could just as easily have been ourselves that suffered devastating loss at that time.

Anyhow, I can handle this. Initially, though, a former pupil of mine is playing piano at the front of the church, soothing us with gentle renditions of modern praise songs while I sit with family. She's so good too. It gives me time to compose myself, and I close my eyes briefly in a settling prayer. When I open them to the familiar scene before me it strikes me how ordered and symmetrical everything is in this wee country 'kirk' of ours, as if conceived by someone with mild OCD.

The pulpit stands unambiguously as the focus of all our attention; the 'Word' is central, our clergyman strategically elevated above the congregation as he preaches. My father, when in critical mode back in the day, would sometimes have referred to the minister as being 'up there in his pulpit, six feet above contradiction'. I could see his point. Despite the democratic foundations of the denomination, those somberly dark-suited clergy tended to rule the roost.

The central lectern, on which rests the heavy, black Bible, is covered with a hanging pulpit-fall in Presbyterian blue. Embroidered there is the symbol of our denomination, a golden motif of the 'Burning Bush'.

Our Communion Table is a much less elaborate affair than altars I have seen in Anglican and Catholic churches. It's basic in design, light oak to match everything else in the place. It has no religious carvings or symbols; in fact it's closer to a grand dining room table than to the ornate works of art in some churches. I suppose that in the origins of non-conformist traditions like our own there was a backlash against the ostentatious grandeur of church furnishings; everything had to be plain so as not to detract from the spiritual glories contained in the sermons and singing.

To the right, an upright piano, mirrored on the left by the organ.

The symmetry is completed by two stained glass windows, one on either side of the pulpit. The one on the left portrays the Good Shepherd, reminding us of the gentle, caring nature of our Lord…except that I have always felt that this particular shepherd's eyes had an icy glint about them that was less than welcoming. On the other side we have a version of Holman Hunt's 'The Light of the World', with Jesus, lamp in hand, knocking at a door. Those windows are the only concession to visual art in the building. Everything else is as basic as possible. We are a simple people after all.

The minister parades solemnly from his vestry hide-out to ascend the pulpit steps. I rise and slip across to the organ console. My friend's piano rendition of "The Londonderry Air" reaches its climax. Strangely enough, this was the one tune my brother had requested to be played at his funeral. Not being a 'sacred' piece of music, it had raised a doubtful eyebrow on our clergyman's face until I pointed out that the hymn, "I cannot tell why he whom angels worship", is sung to that great tune.

"It was my brother's only request," I told him. He conceded.

The hymns are all traditional choices. "The Lord's my Shepherd" to Crimond, and "In Christ Alone", a fairly new anthem that the church has learned recently. The singing is enthusiastic as usual and, even as I play, I can make out twin's fine baritone voice from behind me in the left-side pew, a touch of defiance about it, I think. It crosses my mind that he is trying to make up for a glaring, if forgivable, absence.

Obviously it was impossible for our middle brother, Isaac, to fly home from another continent for the funeral. Apart from anything else, even if he'd wanted to, how would his surgery have coped without him? He had sent an email tribute to be read out at the service.

As Rev Waterman starts to read it, I am so glad that I have had the opportunity to check the email first. The last thing we need today is for its contents to add to the pain of our misgivings about Jack's eternal destiny. Thankfully Isaac has shown some tact and wisdom about how he put things in this missive.

Isaac Shaw 23 October 2007 at 15.37
Re: Funeral Service Tribute
To: Derek Waterman

It was with great sadness that we received the news of the passing of my dear brother Jack yesterday. It is extremely difficult, as you will understand, to be so far from home at a time like this, but needs must. Our work here in the hospital is relentless just at the moment, and our staff is over-stretched due to some recent changes of personnel. So, while our thoughts, indeed our hearts, are with you all in the church there today, we must apologise that we cannot be with you in the flesh.

We knew, of course, that Jack's health had been deteriorating of late; nevertheless his death comes as a great shock, and is well nigh impossible to process. 'It is appointed unto man once to die', as we all know, but when such an event visits one's close sibling the reality comes into sharp focus.

Let me quote from the letter of James in the New Testament. "For what is your life? It is even a vapour, that appeareth for a little time, and then vanisheth away." How true and how poignant.

My memories of Jack, in childhood and in youth, are chiefly of his capacity for hard work, his love of the farm, his constancy and dependability. These were the qualities I admired in him. He was, as all of you who knew him understand, a complex character; at times a person of great humour and fun, at other times he would be very seriously minded, a man who enjoyed his own company, happier to be out among his animals than to be in social society. Lisa and I have at times joked that Jack would have felt very at home around here; our neighbours also hold the cow to be sacred. He would have understood that veneration, up to a point…the point of divergence being, of course, that here it is illegal to kill a cow, except for sacrifice to the gods. That wouldn't have sat so well with our Jack!

What a great success he has made of the farm; our father would surely have been proud of that aspect of Jack's life, were he still with us. After dad's passing, he cared so well for our mother for as long as he could, as he did for our dear unfortunate sister, Miriam. (We think about her today, in her silent state, and pray God's blessing on her there in the care home.)

Jack's financial support for our mission hospital here in India has been invaluable, indeed we could not have maintained our level of care over these many years had it not been for Jack's constant and generous giving. We, and indeed the many patients we care for, owe him so much in that respect.

We look forward to being with you all in Castlecuinn in the near future, as it is our intention to retire from the work here in the new year. After 35 years, we feel it is time to hand the reins over to the next generation, and the mission is currently putting in place good visionary leadership.

Thank you for being present today to pay your tributes to my brother.
Isaac and Lisa

The tribute was perfectly weighted. Its tone could raise no hackles from any quarter. Indeed his clever reference to the 'sacred cows' of India, and how Jack would have felt at home in that culture, has brought a mild ripple of laughter, lightening the mood. There may be a subconscious barb in the comment; of course it is in there, but there is an element of truth too. Not much had been more important to our late brother than his cattle, sadly so. No question he inherited that from our father, but at least father had his priorities right.

To be fair, the letter does pay tribute to the fact that Jack had sent a great deal of financial aid to support the medical ministry. What most people present will not realise is that, since our father's passing twenty-two years ago, back in 1985, half the annual profits of the farm went straight to the mission.

Isaac had always been the star of the family. Academically he had been head and shoulders above any of the rest of us. His diligence and his love of study were legendary. Being so much younger than him, I had not really known him in his childhood or his youth…he was already fifteen when I came into the world.

My middle brother was a sportsman, playing rugby for the school first XV and then for one of the teams at Queen's, his university in our capital city. From what I gathered in family chat, his studies and his sport always came ahead of any of his duties on the farm. I suppose he must have felt that that was the domain of the elder brother, and that his efforts on the farm weren't really needed. He would have helped out in the afternoons in our shop in the village, but never at weekends; on Saturday he'd always be away for a match somewhere, and, of course, there was never any work on Sundays; 'Somber-day', as Jack called it with his trade-mark irreverence. The shop did not open on the Lord's Day.

When Isaac was about eighteen, just about to leave the grammar school in our local town, his life changed dramatically. He'd felt the call of God to be a medical missionary in some far off land. My parents had been delighted. It seems that it had always been their prayerful ambition that one of their children should go to the mission field. They proudly supported his decision. They encouraged him in his studies, and took great delight in his various graduations as he qualified to be a doctor.

I vaguely remember his wedding; the brightness of everything, the joy of Isaac marrying this beautiful lady from the city. I must have been seven or eight at the time, delighted to be a flower girl in that grand church for the wedding. My brother was marrying Lisa, a cultured city girl whose accent was so refined, so different from our culchie country talk.

Thinking back on it all now, and as I stare at the mahogany veneer of this coffin, I cannot help but wonder if the success of the middle brother somehow soured the elder one. Was there a sense of jealousy?

"Here he is, the family star, the smart one, the sporty one... and yet again he is out-doing me? I am stuck on a milking stool at the rear end of a cow while he scores tries for fun. He pulls a glam girl from 'the big smoke', while I haven't even time to go looking for one!"

A strange thought strikes me as our clergyman launches into his sermon. He has just read from the gospel of Luke...the famous story of the Prodigal Son. In our family, the prodigal is the elder one, the one who stayed home, the one lying in this coffin in front of me. The black sheep. Not the one in the far-away country, for he is the hero of our family story. Sixty-three now and nearing the end of his ministry away there in the steamy east. Thinking of returning to his inheritance, to take over the family farm.

After the benediction I follow the coffin to the leaf-strewn graveyard, my arms around the shoulders of my two children. My daughter, Christine, twenty-one and home from England for the funeral, sniffles slightly. By the graveside Jonathan puts his arm around me, pulls me gently into the shelter of his shoulder against the rising breeze. It is a moment of uncharacteristic empathy from him which I will always appreciate.

As the minister's voice drones on I am reading the inscriptions on the family tombstone.

> Jacob Boyd Shaw
> Departed this life 7th Sept 1985
> Also His Wife
> Isabella (Bella) Shaw
> 17th Feb 1999

At the bottom the inscription, "Gone to be with the Lord". I wish I could believe that this is true for Jack.

He is laid to rest, his coffin on top of those of father and mother. Whatever enmities there had been between them in life, whatever resentment my brother had harboured, whatever the depth of disappointment that father had felt concerning his firstborn...these feelings will get shovelled into oblivion with the loamy earth of this our town-land.

A burial of tensions, unspoken and unresolved.

I focus on the clergyman's homily. I hear him read, "For the fates of both men and beasts are the same: As one dies, so dies the other—they all have the same breath. Man has no advantage over the animals, since everything is futile."

Goodness, I think, what a troubling thought. Is it in the Bible at all? Must be, I suppose…but has the minister chosen this verse specifically for the final moments of my brother's existence, before the light closes on him and he descends into endless darkness?

Is this what we are meant to shake hands on now? A sort of pact of dismissal, an underlining of finality? Our hands are washed of this sinner, for he turned his back on us? Is that the underlying message here?

It is yet another huge challenge to my fragile peace of mind. I shudder with the bleakness of the moment.

The futility indeed!

I compose myself, and try to re-fix that pleasant smile of Christian piety as the first of the winding queue of mourners comes to take my hand beside the open grave, to the sound of stifled coughs, of shovelled soil, and the grating craw of distant crows.

Chapter 4

Photograph

Traditionally guests at one of our funerals will be entertained in the church hall after the burial, the buffet-style meal served by members of the local branch of Presbyterian Women. Much more sensible than going to a hotel; it's cheaper for one thing, and there's less chance of people over-indulging themselves. No alcohol in sight, just tea or coffee in a saucered cup, a smorgasbord of crinkle-cut crisps, golden-brown sausage rolls, mushroom vol-a-vents, salmon sandwiches, (precisely cut, their crusts tastefully cropped and discarded of course); then there are the ubiquitous tray-bakes, the currant squares and fifteens, and a slice of sponge cake if you're fortunate. It gives a wonderful opportunity for folks who have travelled from a distance to relax, eat, meet the family and chat. Some of these are strangers to me; hopefully they are friends of my twin and his in-laws; some are possibly connected to us through farming or business. One or two, however, may be what we would term 'habitual mourners'; these are generally older men who either have some sort of fascination with the whole culture that surrounds death and burial, or are simply partial to the bounteous free food that is served afterwards. "I never miss a good funeral," as one of our neighbours was reported to have confessed without shame. Apparently he travelled all over the country, mourning folks he had only the slightest knowledge of, all so he could join the feast after the burial!

The funeral is a significant social occasion here, not just for the support of the bereaved family, but for the community more generally. You can almost feel the bonds of neighbourhood and kinship being reinforced during the hum of conversation in the hall as the community shakes hands with itself.

A few other guests I recognise as semi-distant family. In some of these cases, I have insisted that they call at the farmhouse this evening, before they return to their far-flung homes. It is always good to have cousins back in the home of their grandparents, possibly for the final time. You never know what the missionary brother will do with this homestead, indeed this farm, when he eventually comes back to us.

So it is that I find myself back in our farmstead home, in the centre of a huddle around a coffee table in the sitting room, holding nostalgic court as we leaf through old photograph albums.

The "Ohs" and "Ahs", and "See how well your mother looked in her young days!" And "Wasn't he the handsomest fellow you ever saw!"

"There's your father with that prize bull at the show. Isn't that the one that nearly killed him?" And it was! He had been very fortunate to have survived being dragged across a field and tossed over a hawthorn hedge by that beast, and him a man in his late sixties at the time. For all we know the damage he suffered to his ribs then may have hastened his death. Nobody could ever prove that one way or the other.

"Look at this one. Seems like your mother managed to get a bunch of you to the seaside for a day."

Indeed she had. Neither twin nor I were present in the black and white photograph though; it was well before we had arrived in the family, and apparently well before the advent of colour film in our neck of the woods. Mother stood with the grey sea behind her, Jack to the right looking like he might be fifteen, his hair greased up in what would have been a modern style at the time.

"He was a bit of a spiv, wasn't he?"

"He always tried to look like one of the Everly Brothers, can't remember which one. Would you look at the tight jeans he has on him. Drainpipes, they were called, weren't they?"

"Aye, drainpipes! And winkle-picker shoes! He was some catch!"

A slightly embarrassed silence after this comment. The elder brother never did get 'caught'. I was never aware of him having a steady relationship with a woman, not in all my time; I suspected maybe just an odd fling on those infrequent occasions when he disappeared for a weekend. He was too busy farming, I imagined. Just once or twice over the years it entered my head to wonder if he might have been….you know, a bit 'different' in that area, but, for all his issues, there was never any evidence that he was that way inclined. Jack was a very hot-blooded male, the epitome of masculinity, good-looking in a rugged-farmery sort of way.

To break the moment of quietness one of the cousins throws in the comment, "Sure he never grew out of the teddy-boy phase, did he?"

There is truth in this, I believe. Even up until his decline in recent years he had swept his hair up in that fifties style, conceited about the fact that he still had a good head of it, wistful for the Brylcreemed teenager he had been. He must have been in his fifties before he left off wearing that old brown leather jacket he so prized. Trapped in some sort of time-warp, I always felt.

On the left of the picture was Isaac, looking serious, as might befit what was later to become his religious vocation. He must have been about ten in this photograph, boyishly attractive with his high cheekbones and well-set eyes, but grumpy in this particular shot. Maybe he had dropped his ice-cream on the Portrush sand, I think, for the others had cones in their hands whereas his were empty.

My mother's hands rested on the wheel-chair of my only sister. Miriam, the special one. Younger than the two brothers in the picture, she had been born with a severe handicap, a complicated version of cerebral palsy.

"The poor wee darling," someone says.

Poor darling indeed. Innocent as the day she came into the world. A terrible cross for my parents to have to bear, mother especially. How she was loved, the special one. How many sacrifices did my mother make for her before it all became too much for her.

"Yous didn't think of bringing her today?" someone asks.

Insensitivity personified! I take a deep breath.

"We did, but it would have been impossible. The home advised against it. Said it would only upset her routine. She wouldn't have had a clue what was going on anyway, would she?" I say, a touch drily I think. To smooth the topic I add, "We went to see her yesterday in the nursing home...we did tell her, but...well, no reaction, as you'd expect."

"So you go to see her fairly often?"

"'Course we do, every week, either me or him," I say, nodding at my twin who stands at the sitting room window, staring blankly into the dark curtain of the Colonel's forest across the meadow.

"And is she in good enough form?"

"She is, thank God. It's always so hard to know. I'm sure she misses mother, but that's only me guessing, maybe me reading into her what I hope she is feeling. Who knows what goes on in her poor mind."

"Her mother was a great woman, wasn't she? She gave herself so completely to looking after..."

"She did," someone agrees. "Her mother was an absolute saint."

Yes indeed, my mother had been a saint. She ran the house, she ran our father, she ran the family, she even ran our wee shop in the village for a time...and of course she cared for my sister so tenderly for so long, until it became impossible for her to do everything. On top of that, she'd endured the ongoing worry of a wayward son. She came so close to having a complete nervous breakdown that eventually the horrible decision had to be made to put sister into the care of a nursing home for people with severe physical and learning difficulties. Nobody could fault my mother for that decision...she had given blood for my sister, for all of us. I have no doubt that it shortened her own life. It certainly contributed to her quick decline after father passed away, her memory loss and slowly developing dementia.

There was no hint of what lay ahead for her in these photographs though. Her shy, contented smile was there in every picture, her serenity so clear to see. How at odds with the manic worry and regret that seemed to take over her poor head in those last few years. As the girders of her mind had begun to rust away, you could see her self-awareness crumbling slowly towards dust.

I have many memories of harrowing visits to the care home to be with her then. The repetition of questions, of her 'go-to' phrases.

"What time are they coming?"

"Will they not be here soon?"

"Is mammy not here yet? What's keeping her?"

There was no point in trying to talk sense to her at that stage; it only antagonised her, added to her upset. It was just a case of humouring her. She was living away in her childhood, I think. She had even forgotten who I was. She would be talking about her own sisters, both no longer with us. She might even call me by the name of the younger one. I would have to explain that, no...I wasn't her sister, I was her daughter.

"You're no daughter of mine," she would say.

Now that should have hurt, but there was truth in what she said, of course there was. Twin and I had been adopted, so while in her normal mental health she would never have dreamt of saying such a thing, this was not a normal time. She did not mean it to be hurtful, anymore than any of the other ramblings.

I would have to go over the names of the five children for her. As like as not she would reply that she had far more than five children, and I would have to pretend to go along with that. Actually, she was, in a sense, correct in that as well. I was aware that she had had the trauma of at least two miscarriages before our adoption, so she had a point...but it was no use me arguing, or trying to clarify the family history for her. Where I could, I did talk about her younger days before she met my father; she liked that, and sometimes would throw in some snippet of knowledge or some strange happening that I knew nothing about. These had to be taken with a pinch of salt of course.

She seemed to have had a special place in her heart for her middle son. It was weird to me that she would ask about him, as if she was aware of his role in a place very far away, as if she was awaiting his return. She gave the impression of being worried about him, certainly more so than being concerned for either her handicapped daughter or her oldest child. They seemed to have been blanked out of her sub-consciousness somehow. Same with my twin. If I introduced him into the conversation she would just look blank, make some ridiculous and unconnected comment. This, despite the fact that, from my jealous observations in earlier times, she had doted on him; she had been beside herself with worry when he joined the RUC back in 78. There had been no history of police or military involvement in our family. Nobody, so far as I was aware, had joined up in either war; nobody had been in the 'B' Specials back in the day. So it was a shock to the parents when, the week after he finished school, twin had announced that he had his forms in to join the police. Her understandable concern grew into a fixation that he would be killed. When his friend was murdered, she'd had to have tranquillisers prescribed by the GP. She improved only after twin took a package and resigned from the force, following the reforms brought about by the Patten report. But all that stress and worry seemed to have been obliterated from her poor mind by the Alzheimers. She had forgotten him entirely, so far as I could work out.

It was all very strange, very taxing, and I'd come away from those visits feeling like I needed a walk on the seashore, or a cup of good strong coffee with a friend who could help me straighten my head out again.

But yes, my mother had indeed been an absolute saint. That is the way to remember her; I must never let the latter days of her life taint the memory of the person she had been. To some extent, a lesser extent, I admit, that would be true of the brother we have just laid to rest today.

Chapter 5

Origins

We twins were eleven when the parents sat us down in the sitting room on a Sunday afternoon to tell us we were adopted. They brought our whole family together for the announcement, even though both brothers were aware of the fact anyhow. Maybe they wanted their moral support; I can understand that. I suppose one of the reasons for the timing of the announcement was that Isaac had finished his training and was just about to leave to go abroad to the mission. And, of course, it was the year that we were leaving the local Primary School and about to begin education in 'big school', the Grammar School in the town.

That dark day of disclosure! It is all a bit clouded in my memory now, but you can never forget the absolute shock of hearing those fateful words.

"We have to tell yous a big secret. You two are adopted; your mother and I adopted you into our family when you were tiny babies."

The stagnant slur of silence between us then, accentuating the impertinent tick-tock of the Westminster chiming clock. Its big, round eye glaring down at us from the mantlepiece above the coal fire, not a trace of sympathy about it. Suddenly the thumping of my heart in my chest was matching its rhythm.

The stares between us. Eyes bouncing off each other like marbles in a game, desperate for a giggle to signify that this was all just a bad joke.

Mother's head down on her chest, her shoulders heaving.

Then the growing weight of apprehension in the gut.

They were serious!

I had just been chain-sawed off at the knees, emotionally speaking.

The tears that squeezed themselves out through my screwed-up eyelids without permission started to course down my cheeks.

The assurances that bubbled up in an eruption of words from all four of the adults, amid hugs and kisses, them taking it in turn to cuddle us, hold us tightly against the shock, the uncertainty, the questions. Trying to crowd comfortingly into the new-born emptiness in us both.

I had never seen this degree of unity amongst my folks…these 'pretenders' who were my family, these 'parents' and 'brothers' who were now suddenly strangers. And poor, silent Miriam, rocking back and forward and moaning in her chair, her pitiful face distended and twisted even more than usual, as if she could empathise with our shock. They were all spilling over each other to assure us that we were every bit as much loved as if we had been from my mother's womb. The togetherness even seemed to have swept away the cold stone-wall of bad feeling that usually stood between father and Jack.

Much of that afternoon is a blur. What I do recall is that we went to the church service that evening, because the meeting was a special one, a valedictory service for Isaac. It was a sort of farewell for him and his wife, a commissioning where hands were laid on him and prayers offered for his work. Once again he was the heroic brother. It made me feel even more of an outcast, a second class child. At least our brother would always be able to consider himself legitimate. Now I couldn't, not any longer. It was during that service that the sudden realisation hit me that I was most probably born out of wedlock; the two of us were bastard wains! The shame of it. The shame of that woman who had borne us, whoever she was. A shame that stained my very soul, like an invisible birth-mark, but a shame to which I had been oblivious up until today. And the childish question, does the fact that we are adopted over-ride, and somehow blot out, that tag of illegitimacy? How does that all work? It was so perplexing. I heard little of Isaac's big moment of valediction.

I think I cried more or less all through the service. Several members of the congregation must have noticed, and came to give me little hugs of support afterwards, imagining that my tears were to do with the emotion of brother leaving home for a few years. It had nothing to do with him, other than the coincidence of timing. How could they have guessed that I was just beginning to face up to the existential question of my identity? I was a child of eleven years. It wasn't fair.

Who was I? Who was my twin brother?

Where have we come from? Were we even twins at all?

Who was our birth mother? Who was our real father?

Are we allowed to know that? Should we even ask the question? Would it annoy our father and mother to be asking these kinds of questions? Should we even continue to call them father and mother? Was continuing to do that not a white lie? Or if not white, some other colour of lie?

That night Isaac came up to my bedroom. He wanted to say my prayers with me, he told me. It was probably the first time that I could recall him doing that, and it was to be the last, because he was to be gone by the end of the week. He was very kind that night. He listened so well to all my fears and confusions. He was a good listener; he let me talk. I struggled to put words around the emotions I was feeling; it was all too sudden, too deep, too confusing. I couldn't bring myself to allow the word 'bastard' to cross my lips, so that imponderable remained in the vault of my heart for many years thereafter.

Why did such a thing happen to me, I asked him. Why me? Why now? Could it not have waited? Or why couldn't they have told me when I was very young, like four or five? It wouldn't have hurt so bad then…I could have grown up gently with the knowledge of being adopted, knowing that our new mum and dad loved us enough to take us in and care for us just like their three real children.

"They likely love you more than they love us! You're a real son, we are just adopted," I threw at him.

He insisted that that was absolutely not true. He made me look at him in the eye and repeat after him some words to that effect, that we were loved every bit as much as the others. He went over all the good things mum and dad had done for us, all the things they gave us, how good our father was at providing everything we needed.

"Yeah," I said, "But my real mother and father could have done that too, just as well."

"Maybe not though," he said. "Maybe they weren't able to, and that's why they put yous up for adoption. Maybe they were poor…"

"Put us up for!" I interrupted. "Like we were being 'put up' for the night? Or like… 'put up' for sale! It's just not fair. I want to know who they were, my real mum and dad."

He told me that that was impossible. I shouldn't even think of such a thing. After all that mummy and daddy had done for us, didn't I see it would be very hurtful to them for me to be even thinking about who my real parents were, or wanting to try to find out? Anyway, he told me, it's impossible.

I remember asking about our birth certificates. How precocious was I as an eleven year old. I think I only knew about birth certificates because recently the new school had requested to see them for our enrolment in a few weeks. Maybe that was the reason why we had to be told now about the adoption thing…they didn't want us to find out by accident if we happened to read the birth certificate. I suggested this suspicion to Isaac. Surely our birth certificates would have the names of our real mother and father?

He told me very calmly that the documents we had now were adoption certificates, not birth certificates.

"But we must have had birth certificates at the start?" I argued.

"Yeah, most likely you had. I think everybody has, but your original birth certificate would have been replaced by an adoption certificate," he told me.

"But does this adoption certificate not say who my real mother was?"

"It doesn't, I'm sorry. You see, she might not want you to ever find out. She may have had very good reasons for that. Maybe she was very ill, or not able to look after you two. But you have been blessed by being adopted into this home where we all love you; even your sister who can't tell you… she loves you too, doesn't she?"

I shed some more tears and he waited. Then he had another point to make. "You are doubly blest," he said, "because you have not only been adopted into our family, you have also been adopted into God's family. Just think about that. How special you are, aren't you? Adopted twice."

I knew what he was trying to do. I knew I was supposed to be filled with grateful joy about everything. Twin and I were so lucky, weren't we? Of course we were. I wasn't going to deny that. But it didn't dull the shock. And it certainly did not quell the curiosity about our true origins. Nor did it come anywhere close to stabilising what now felt for me a very unstable foundation. All was shaken in my little life.

A knock at my bedroom door and Jack was standing there. "Can we swap over?" he said, and they did. Isaac went to twin in his new room in the attic. I so wished twin and I could be back together again in the same bedroom, as we had been up until a few months ago; at least we could have talked about it all, as the two central victims in this drama.

Jack wasn't so good with words; I was just about talked out anyhow. So I cried, and he held me so strongly that I thought my ribs would crack. He just kept saying, "Sorry", and rocking me back and forward like a child, until I found myself going to sleep in his arms.

I woke up the next morning, and for a few minutes I thought it had all been the weirdest and worst dream of my entire life.

****

It wasn't long afterwards that I found myself sitting in the middle of thirty other first year pupils in my new school. It was my first Grammar School roll call, and I wasn't to forget it in a hurry.

My uniform felt too new; it wasn't the best of a fit on me, maybe a size or two too large; it was all too stiff of itself, like it had been meant for someone else. I was an imposter here among all these sophisticated townies with their bobbed hair and Donny Osmond pencil cases. Other girls were chattering away, probably knowing each other from previous schools. Boys were already eyeing up the strangers. I knew no-one in the class, not a soul. Twin had been put in another class; I wasn't sure if that was because he was smarter than me or the other way around.

A gruff teacher swept into the classroom. Straight away you could see that his nose looked a few sizes too big for his pasty face. He waited for quiet, then introduced himself, but I couldn't make out what he said his name was. Instinctively I did not warm to him, the sort of man you imagined hadn't smiled since Christmas. He was to be our form tutor this year, and we were going to get on 'smashingly', so long as we kept our noses clean and didn't give him any trouble.

'Our noses clean?' I thought, smiling inside. 'Must be a full-time job with that hooter of his.'

If we had any problems we were to come to him, he told us. I couldn't envisage that. Then he began to call out our names, ticking away in his register with great zest.

A chorus of 'Present sir', 'Present sir', 'Present sir'.

Sometimes he would stop and look long and hard at the child who had just answered; then there would be some comment like, "Ah, I think you are Roberta's sister, aren't you?" Smiles and nods. She is known, the pedigree recognised and accepted. On one occasion it was, "Good grief, Samuel Blair, you must be a son of Uel. You are the dead spit of him. Tell him I was asking for him. It's years since he was in my class. I hope you're as good at rugby as he was, eh?"

It went through my mind that he wasn't going to be telling me that I was like anybody in my family, was he? There would be no welcoming recognition for an adoptee like me, no little nostalgic links to any of his past pupils. I began to think about that. Was I like my mother at all? Would I ever know?

To be fair, I was listening to him at the start as he droned through this list. I heard all these interesting names. Some I had never heard of before. Maybe townie names. Mine was boring. It wasn't even my real name. Maybe my real name was just like one of these other kids in the class. Something refined maybe, or, better still, something exotic, cool. Sabrina or Francesca or….

Then I noticed there was a silence. My classmates were looking around. The teacher was scanning the class with the look of a curious jackdaw on his face, his 'beak' pointing inquisitively here and there.

Then he spoke again.

I heard my name. My name!

He had been calling my name and I hadn't noticed.

What to do now? Pretend I didn't have that name? After all it wasn't my real name. Could I not just make up a name, ignore the fact of this arbitrary one that he had on his register…it had nothing to do with me, had it? Who was I anyway? As all this was going through my head I heard him speak again. A dubious tone this time, almost disappointed. My name, once more.

I did the stupidest thing I have ever done!

I said, "Absent."

And, believe me, I really, really wished I was!

There was a split second of absolute silence. Sixty-plus eyes were upon me, disbelieving eyes. Then the roar of laughter. The teacher had great trouble getting everything calmed down again. When he did he made a short speech, at my expense. I was completely mortified.

"So maybe you wish you were absent. Maybe your little brain had gone to sleep and, in truth, your mind was in fact absent, but from what I can see, unless you are impersonating someone else, you are actually here and present…am I right?"

I don't think I ever really lived that first experience down. The form tutor would jokingly double-check with me during future roll calls.

"Are you sure now? Definitely present?"

My brother laughed his head off at me when I told him. He succeeded in reducing me to tears yet again, until he saw how deeply the whole thing was affecting me, then he backed off. I did find it hard to talk to him about the adoption though. His reaction was very different to mine. Being a boy, I suppose, he kept things locked up inside himself. With me it was all out there, and I struggled for a long time to come to terms with it. But he and I didn't connect on the issue, not then anyhow.

He stopped going to piano lessons after that fateful day in the sitting room. I often wondered if the two things were related. He was making a statement of stubbornness, of individuality. He wouldn't be entirely moulded into the image of our family. The rebel in him had a new authenticity, and he would be his own man from now on.

I have had a secret theory that the knowledge of his adoption was what lay behind his desire to join the police. I think he may have hoped to find acceptance in the camaraderie of the force, the uniform giving him an identity which couldn't be challenged by some contrary piece of intelligence coming at him from left field. The force became a surrogate family to him. The risks he was prepared to take spoke of a cavalier attitude to life. He would prove to himself his own validity as a man, an individual, and it didn't matter what his origins were. It mattered much more who he was becoming.

I share, to some extent, that quest of 'becoming'. Like Bunyan's Pilgrim, we are all on a journey. We are all being changed as we progress in our lives. Hopefully it is to be better people than when we were struggling in the 'slough of despond', swamped by sin and guilt and self-doubt.

Reactions to that surreal discovery have occurred at regular intervals over the years. The feeling of dislocation never really leaves you, in my experience anyhow; the wondering about who you really are, the mystery of origin. I remember that in those first few months of the new reality I had sudden, inexplicable bouts of anger; these waves of resentment were mainly triggered by memories of occasions in the past where opportunities were missed to explain our status to us at what would have been a much better age.

One thing that had happened a few times really bugged me.

We would be with our father at some hall or tent mission halfway across the county, maybe even in another county altogether. He would be taking the service for some para-church group; mother would be there as well, maybe Isaac too, but never Jack. How well I remember those drab events, the dullness of the lighting, the hiss and stench of the old Super Ser gas heaters, the cold ache of bone-hard timber forms against my hips, the half-hour-long roaring sermon to a couple of dozen drowsy listeners in slate-grey suits and stiff white collars.

Inevitably we would be invited to have a meal before the service at the nearby home of whoever was the key figure at the mission, generally a complete stranger to us. We'd be pushing tasteless mushrooms around our plates, that or an unwanted element of some exotic salad, under the invasive gaze of the woman of the house, her beaming smile matching the generosity of the spread before us.

Then, after a period of observation, she would point to me… usually it was me.

"I think this one takes after you," she would say to my mother. Father would try to change the subject, but there were one or two instances where the host and hostess would have a mild disagreement about which of us took after our mother, and which was 'the spit of his father'. We'd be sitting there looking from one to the other, ten years of age and totally oblivious of the fact of our actual origin, innocently agreeing or disagreeing with the verdict, unconscious of the reality that our parents were living a lie at that point in time. Maybe they justified it by thinking, 'Isn't it just as well the twins don't yet know they are adopted? We got away with one there! No embarrassing 'owning-up' required…as yet anyhow. Now… let's go and preach the truth of the gospel.'

The truth about me hadn't seemed important to them.

I have struggled with these feelings over the years. Only through much meditation and prayer have I come to the place where I can say that I have forgiven my folks for the imprint of their unnecessary silence, and its undermining impact on my personal development. I have found that it is possible to be successful in my profession, to have a strong faith and be respected in my role in the church and community, to be the mother of two fine kids, and hopefully a good spouse…and yet to harbour, in the deepest recesses of my soul, feelings of incompleteness, the suspicion of being a bit of an imposter, a smiling fraud. I have struggled with that all my life…certainly since the age of eleven. It is something that colours every prayer I breathe.

Application No. 237160-2

Caution- There are offences relating to falsifying or altering a certificate and using or possessing a false certificate

Certified Copy of an Entry

1. No of Entry- xbk14925	
2. Date 25th April 1960 and	Registration District Edinburgh
Country of birth of child	Scotland.
3. Name and surname of child	Sarah Shaw
4. Sex of child.	Female
5. Name and surname Address	Mr Jacob Shaw (farmer) 16 Church Rd. Castlecuinn N Ireland
and occupation. of adopter or adopters	Mrs Isabella Shaw (housewife) of the same address
6. Date of Adoption Order 26th April 1960 and description of court by which made	Edinburgh Sheriff's Court
7. Date of Entry	3rd May 1960
8. Signature of officer deputed by Register General to attest the entry	Robert J. Fox

Chapter 6

Videos

My brother has arrived at my home with an armful of old video tapes. It is a couple of weeks after the funeral. I have a sinking feeling; I fear we may be in for a night of slow viewing; a heavy-limbed tramp through the labyrinth of family memories. I'll be cross-eyed from nostalgia before this is over, probably damp-eyed as well.

He'd found them in a chest in Jack's bedroom, he tells me.

"What were you doing in there?" I ask him.

An unnecessary question. He looks at me before replying.

"Why shouldn't I be? Somebody will have to clean the place out at some stage."

"Aye, of course…and I promise I will soon…I just don't feel ready for it yet."

"I get that, but we shouldn't leave it too long. You never know when…"

"I do know when, as a matter of fact," I tell him. "I had an email today. He says he'll be home in the new year. Maybe February or March."

"Goodness, that's quicker than I expected," he says. "How will the place do without him? Well, we'd better get a move on. The room needs a good airing. It has the smell of death about it."

"I know, I know; I'll get to it. I have a man coming to shift the piano up to us, if he ever gets round to it. I'll have to take a bunch of his stuff to some charity shop. You don't want any of his clothes do you?"

"You must be joking! Wouldn't be seen dead…Sorry, that wasn't very clever, was it?"

"Certainly wasn't," I tell him, sticking the first tape into our ancient VCR player. "Let's see what's on this one… if it even works at all."

"To be honest," he continues, "you might have more joy giving his gear to some fifties or sixties theme shop…or donating them to the school for their drama wardrobe. They'd be useful if anybody was putting on 'Grease'."

"'Little Shop of Horrors' more like. Ah no, that's unfair," I correct myself. "He's not here to defend himself, dear love him."

We watch some Christmas clips, badly shot by a very shakily held Super 8 cine-camera, way back in the day. My father must have bought that machine somewhere, second hand no doubt. Then at a later stage somebody, maybe Jack himself, had transferred the footage on to video. Had he done this manually, the cheaper way, or had he taken the old cine films to some professional outfit to be copied? It does strike me that someone now needs to take the videos to yet another expert who could digitise the material so it can be handed down to yet another generation. How time makes a mockery of our technological advances!

Sometimes the camera had been taken outside to the farm; in the first clip, this seems to have been to catch the last few rows of silage being cut. We see the final load being drawn up the lane by a shiny, new-looking Massey Ferguson 65 tractor and dumped into the pit.

There is footage of our father with his bull at the local agricultural fair, his pride in this fine, pedigree Friesian specimen as evident in his body language as if he'd just received a knighthood. It is interesting to speculate who was behind the camera in each clip. Sometimes Jack would feature in the shot; my initial reaction to those pictures is to realise just how carefree and jolly, idiotic even, he seemed to be. This, when I reflected on it, was something that jarred with me, shocked me. It was not the person I had known during most of my childhood, but then these were images from the time before I was even born. He was maybe in his late teens in some of these clips. And yes, he was a handsome devil, I have to admit.

Amazingly, there are several brief clips of our father playing his bagpipes in a Twelfth of July parade. We both sit forward on the settee when this appears…neither of us have any memory of this period. By the time we arrived in the house father had abandoned this tradition. I was aware he had been in the junior Orange Order himself, up until his conversion led him away from it. I recall his little sash still hanging gloomily in the upstairs cloakroom, an abandoned piece of nostalgia from his youth. He had remained in the local pipe band, however. That was mainly to do with the music, the heart-call skirl of Highland pipes, all part of his deep identification with Scottish culture. And of course, it was the custom that this band was invited to lead the local lodge to 'the field' on the Twelfth, and later in the marching season, around the streets of Londonderry for the Apprentice Boys parade in the city.

Our father had had a very complex, and indeed contradictory attitude, to the Orange. Part of him applauded their stated objective to protect freedom of worship, to promote the Scriptures and the Protestant faith. Indeed, in his role as a lay-preacher he frequently took services which would have been held in local halls around the country. At the same time, he despised the hypocrisy of many of the members, particularly the failure of the masters of the lodges to put an end to the huge drinking culture associated with the parades. He ranted about this so often, both in his public sermons and within the household. What a blow it must have been to him when his oldest son turned away from his father's teetotalism, and embraced the drinking culture that he had castigated so vociferously.

Next on the screen an even more astounding vision appears; we see Jack also playing pipes, alongside his father. He looks about sixteen, maybe seventeen. In this latter shot both are marching up and down on our yard, both kitted out in kilts, sporrans, the full regalia except for the feather bonnet. They march in step with each other, across the yard, down the lane, turn around and march back up. Isaac is there too, but he is just a wee lad…so we are guessing that father persuaded mother to do the filming.

What a shame there was no sound on those old cine films! I would have loved to hear how well they played together. Twin sort of stole that thought out of my head, a more than frequent occurrence.

"I'm sure if there was sound with this we would be hearing the cattle roaring in protest," he says. "Or maybe anticipation."

"How come?"

"I can imagine some wee heifer thinking they were piping in a Highland bull, eager to do the business."

His weird sense of humour always got me.

"I had forgotten about him playing pipes," I say. "I wonder why he didn't stick with them?"

"I have no idea. Another part of the enigma, isn't it? They look as if they are both enjoying it in this footage, both pretty happy with each other," he says.

And he is right. There is absolutely no sign of any of the animosity that we can recall from our childhood days in the sixties and seventies, those days when we were caught in the crossfire between the two men.

"You wonder what happened to sour things between them."

"I also wonder why he never tried to get you into the bagpipes," I say. "They had been such a big part of him, away back then. He must have been so hurt that nobody in the family was keeping the thing going."

"Yeah, but he did try to get us into music surely?"

"The piano? That wasn't really him though, was it? It was more…"

Twin nods. Those music lessons seemed to have been Jack's idea. I have no recollection of father ever encouraging us in that; if anything he seemed to be grumpily against it, this despite his love of music.

On the screen, a small car can be seen driving quickly along our narrow road, the Colonel's plantation rich with forty shades of vegetation behind it. It turns into our lane. Cut to the yard; the car is stationary beside the milking parlour, its fern-green paint standing out beautifully against the white-washed wall behind it, like a picture from a magazine advertisement. Our leather-jacketed brother steps out and looks straight into the camera, trying not to smile, but failing in his attempt at nonchalance.

"Goodness, must be his first car. So that's what rock 'n roll looked like in the fifties! A beat-up Morris Minor!"

"He always loved his cars," I reply. "I suppose he had to start somewhere."

"I wonder how much he paid for that yoke? And where he got the cash? He can't be much more than twenty. I thought those were supposed to be hard times."

"Likely trying to impress somebody," I say.

"She must have been easy impressed."

"What will we do with his Saab?"

Twin looks at me a bit blankly. Jack had told us that his prized 1980 Saab 900 was not to be passed on to anyone but us two; yes, Isaac could keep the farm jeep, but we were to keep the Saab.

"I don't really want it."

"Me neither. Should we not just pass it on…?"

"That's not what he wanted," he says, reading my mind. "Maybe just put it in Auto Trader sometime. See what we get for it."

I would love to keep it, for sentimental reasons; but we are already a two-car family, and I can't see husband being too keen on me having to maintain and tax and insure another one. So I agree with him.

"Stick it in the bottom shed in the meantime sure."

The video progresses, now showing footage of what looks like a Harvest Thanksgiving display in our church, heaps of carefully arranged fruit and vegetables, little tidy stooks of barley and the like. A close up shot of a remarkable miniature corn-stack that somebody had fashioned using actual oats. Had our mother made it?

I fast forward, losing interest, thinking of what I have to do tomorrow, and how I'd love to quit this.

"Don't you wonder why he never got into a serious relationship though?" he says. "Like, he had so much going for him, didn't he? He woulda been some catch for any of those farmers' daughters in his days in the Young Farmers."

"On the surface, aye, but he had that twist in his nature, that temper, the bitterness. He'd have been hard to live with, don't you think?"

"Of course, but it's a catch twenty-two. Maybe that's why he was as he was. Maybe if he'd found a girl and gotten married he would have been….you know….a bit more normal."

There's a moment of awkwardness at this observation…silence, because anything else is too difficult to verbalise.

"Something we'll never know now, I suppose. Here, could we stop this now and look through them later? I have stuff to be doing."

He leaves me with a brief hug at the door. I watch as he swings the black BMW out of the drive and accelerates down our long tarmac lane. My twin and I are close, thankfully, even though he comes across as very self-contained, aloof even, at times. He's been a rock to me, and I have needed that. We look nothing like each other and have very different perspectives on life, but he's a good, sound brother.

Chapter 7

Neighbour

We have always had great support from our neighbour. Walter Brown, (no-one ever calls him that…he's Wally), farms the land beside ours, to the south. Whereas it would be fair to say that farmers can be a competitive lot, maybe even jealous of others in the locality, Wally has been more than decent. He is a friend rather than a rival. His generosity has been something we have all depended on, maybe even taken for granted.

If help was needed with an animal in trouble, he'd be there. If we were short of anything on the farm he could be relied on to see us through. If any of us, in our rashness, managed to get a tractor stuck in the soft, peaty soil of the lower bog, he would be there in his beat-up old Land-rover to winch us to safety. He had been a very dependable mainstay to our Jack when illness began to encroach on his ability to work the farm. He'd helped him manage a gradual winding-down of the business, taking cattle off his hands and making sure things kept ticking over, but with a much reduced intensity. He even rented a few of our fields that were going to be lying fallow this past eighteen months, land he probably didn't need. Now that Jack had been laid to rest, the neighbour is still around the place, making sure that our temporary farm-hand is on top of things. Together with my twin, they are going to try to keep the farm operational for a few months until Isaac gets back to take over.

Wally's generosity, however, did not stop at the practical. He prided himself on his local knowledge, his insights into why things were as they were, his understanding of the history of our town-land…and others, for miles around! He knew everything there was to know about the story of our family and farm, as far back as you would care to ask him. And he didn't mind sharing this knowledge, at length, at any time of the day or evening. He used to sit in our house talking to my father into the wee, small hours. The household myth was that my father used to fall asleep on his big armchair, and when he woke up Wally would be still telling a story. Audience aware he was not.

When Jack had found himself as the sole listener to this neighbour, he claimed that his only way of getting rid of him was to stand up and say, "I'm away to bed now. Will you turn off the light and pull the door after you when you're going!" I'm not sure of the truth of this claim, but I wouldn't put it past him.

Wally had a very interesting appearance; a big, round tuba of a body, with a voice to match, a deep, sonorous bass. His facial features always gave me the impression of having been quarried, the angular slabs of flesh, granite-grey and unyielding. His brush of white hair stuck up in the style of a clump of faded rushes, and a thin line of moustache adorned his longish upper lip, looking as if it had been imported from another cultural epoch. Most noticeable of all, however, were his eyebrows, the greatest set in the country; eyebrows that acted like they had a mind of their own. So bristling and dominant were they that my brother used to joke that the poor man had to follow them wherever they decided to take him. Wally walked with the gait of a man who was holding himself back from throwing a punch, shoulders always hunched in on himself; it was a false impression, he was a most affable man.

The sad thing about our neighbour, though, is that for all his goodness and for all his going to church, he still isn't what we would call a born again Christian. He is still outside the fold, for he hasn't taken the vital step of faith. Maybe someday he will; I pray so.

I am sitting at the old piano in the farmhouse; I am in wistful mood, playing a very stately version of *'Prelude in E Minor'*, pensive in the extreme. It's hard to beat a bit of Chopin when you are in morose mood, and this tune means almost as much to me as the piano itself. The fact that the old instrument is wildly out of tune now seems to add to the melancholy of my performance, and to this reflective moment. I should have arranged for the tuner to come and have another go at getting it up to pitch long ago. It deserves better than to be allowed to descend into such discordancy. I should really have insisted that it come with me to the new house when we built nearly twenty years ago, but my husband contended that it didn't fit with the modern style of the new build, its decor and ambience. He would buy a brand new one, he promised, maybe even a baby grand…eventually. So the piano that Jack had bought me when I was very young, maybe seven or eight, if I can recall correctly, stayed in the farmhouse with him, and decayed…like everything else about him. In some ways I still prefer the deep richness of its timbre, its Germanic confidence and warmth, to the brightly vibrant sound of the gleaming Yamaha we ended up with…and it is no baby grand either; the standard upright was all we could afford at the end up. I look forward to this one being reconditioned, and joining me up at my home when I get the chance.

I am just reaching the final section of the piece when, out of the corner of my eye, I sense a shadow cross the window. A knock at the back door, but long before I can get anywhere close to it, the burly figure of our good neighbour has landed in the kitchen, and has stuck his ample rump against the front bar of the Aga cooker.

I greet him by warning that the fire is freshly on.

"You'll get burned if you stay there too long," I tell him.

That is the signal for him to park his bum on the settee, remove his cloth cap, put his hands behind his head, stretch out his legs and cross one foot over the other, a little ritual of self-comforting I have seen so many times over the years. My heart sinks a little, yet again.

I feel it is only right and proper to tell him once more how much we appreciate everything he has been doing for us over the past while. Before I get too far into this wee speech he interrupts, as ever.

"Agh, would you stop, daughter. Look, six years ago I'd have been bankrupt if it hadn't been for your brother helping me out. Least I can do to help yous now in your time of trouble."

The foot and mouth crisis of 2001 had indeed been a terrible trial for everyone in the farming community. It was gut-wrenching for people to have to watch their livestock being incinerated in the very fields they had been grazing, the billowing, black smoke rising like a sacrificial signal to heaven. 'God have mercy on our poor cattle'. We had somehow come out of it all fairly unscathed, merely sniffing the air for the aroma of roast beef from across the fields, so it was nice to hear that my lost-sheep brother had been a good shepherd to his neighbour in need during that emergency, whatever he had been able to do.

The 'conversation', for want of a more accurate word, is maybe half an hour old when I hear us getting into the subject of this farm of ours, and its backstory. How the train of thought has ended up there I don't know, but I listen anyhow, and, to be fair to him, I am learning things I never knew before.

For example, (and I don't have a clue how he knows this little nugget of information), back in the year before Jack was born our father had bought an adjoining farm, thus almost doubling the size of his holding. This is of personal interest because father had bequeathed to me the old dwelling house on that land, a derelict wreck of a place that had been unoccupied for ages. The point was that it included a half-acre site which boasted a brilliant view out over the lower countryside, including the spread of the Colonel's grand estate. Not long after my marriage we had applied for planning permission to build there. We had knocked down the old rickle of a cottage, and built our two-story home.

In contrast to the tree-darkened farmhouse I was reared in, we had an incredible view right out over the forest, across the sweep of low country to the hills beyond. Below us, the bog was like a water-colour painting, variegated brown and beige in autumn and winter, but vibrant greens during the warmer months, a tartaned landscape that changed clan with the season. We could trace the inky-grey river as it threaded its way from the mountains in the south, through the spread of the valley and onwards to the town. A line of rounded hills arranged themselves lazily on the other side of the narrow plain, like a tired man stretching himself out for a rest. This was a 'beaded-esker', according to what I was taught in geography lessons back in school. What a vista we had from up at our new home; in the summer evenings the sun, setting behind those hills in the west, flooded us with wonderful horizontal light, as vibrantly orange as my father's old sash. In the mornings, the sun shone directly on the sides of those same uplands; it always looked to me like someone had cut little patches, in a variety of colours and shades, and stitched them randomly on the slopes.

Wally knows all about our treasured site, of course, but it's what he tells me about the original purchase of this second farm that intrigues me.

"You see, your father was likely afraid some stranger would come in behind him there, maybe some boy that kicks with the other foot, you know what I mean."

I do know what he means.

"I am sure that wouldn't have bothered him," I say defensively, but, for all my outward protestation, I know that Wally may not be far off the mark. "Anyway, the land lay in to ours, so it was a chance he couldn't miss…I'm sure that was it."

"Aye, 'course," he says, "but the thing was, it was 1939, and no sooner had he put a bid on it than the war broke out. We were going to be fighting the Germans, and suddenly the money dried up."

"How do you mean?" I ask. "Did he not have the money?"

"No, and nobody else in the country had money either; nor could they get the bank to advance any more. You have to remember that we were all still in debt up to our ears buying our farms out from the landlord."

"But…so how did my father get the money?"

"Well that's the thing. He was still a very young man at the time, maybe mid twenties. Must have been a feisty one even then. He went to a law firm in the town. Only lawyer in the place worth a damn…sorry for swearing, but it's true. An able man; Catholic man too."

He leans over on one hip, another of his idiosyncratic gestures, the purpose of which I am completely aware of, but just hope the result doesn't completely overwhelm my nostrils.

"And?"

"And what? Oh aye!" he says, recalling what he is about to tell me. "Your father went to him to ask advice; likely to pull out of the deal, for the bank had told him there's no chance of more money. He told me this himself. He was nearly in tears telling the story of it."

"Told you what?"

"Told me the solicitor lent him the money."

"The solicitor? Why? What did he do that for?"

"I think he saw that he could help somebody that deserved helping. Maybe he had knowledge about your family in earlier times, how they had stood up for his people in the land wars."

I have no idea what he is talking about with this comment, and I'm about to ask, but he continues.

"I haven't told you the best bit. The solicitor said it was interest free; it was to be paid back only when he could afford it."

"Unbelievable," I say, and it is. It must have been such a different time then, well before we had any of the recent troubles. "I wonder how long…or when my father got it paid off?"

"That I don't know, daughter," he tells me, "but I have no doubt your father had him paid off as soon as was humanly possible."

I make him a cup of tea; as much as anything else it is to give me the time to digest this piece of family news that I never knew before. Here we are in 2007, and the troubles seem to have died down since the Good Friday Agreement, former sworn enemies seem to be bosom pals now, laughing together all friendly-like, and sharing power in Stormont…but I cannot imagine anything like what I have just been told happening so spontaneously in the present times. Maybe I am wrong. Maybe there are still examples of good people with generous hearts in this country. Maybe this new dispensation of peace will bring about a healing that will lead to more acts of generosity. I am saying as much to my squatter neighbour who shows no sign that this is the only piece of information he has to share with me tonight.

"Your family, ya see," he says. "What you likely don't know about your own folk is… yous were always known as being a bit different from the normal run of people around here. Maybe the solicitor knew that, do ya see?"

I don't see! I don't have a clue what he is on about.

"Go on," I hear myself tell him. What am I saying? Go on! Go on home, it should be. "How do you mean 'different'?"

"Well, during all the trouble about the land, you know, the Land League, the fight for tenants' rights, land reform and all that…well, your great-grandfather…aye, that would be right, wouldn't it? The late eighteen hundreds, your father's father and maybe his grandfather too, I don't know for sure. They were active."

"What do you mean, 'they were active'?"

"Well, I mean…what they called 'agitation'; holding meetings to put pressure on the authorities, giving out pamphlets, blocking roads, just causing a fuss to draw attention to the fact that the bulk of the land still belonged to the high up folk, the aristocracy. Fifty years after the famine, the same boys that had been responsible for it still owned the land. Ordinary people like your ancestors, my ancestors too, they still didn't own their own wee bits of farms; they were still paying rents to the landlord. It was all wrong. But the thing was that your folk stood up for the rights of the tenants, all of them, no matter what religion they were, Catholic or Presbyterian. They took a lot of stick for it; even the papers and the high and mighty around the place were down on them. But they stuck at it. And eventually we got our farms. So you can be proud of that."

"I had no idea about any of this," I say.

"No, I'm sure you hadn't. There was even a Presbyterian minister not far from here who was a leading light in the Tenants' Rights campaign. These things get forgotten, unless somebody keeps the memory alive."

"Indeed," I say, getting up so as to signal that maybe he should too. But he wasn't finished yet.

"Another thing."

"What other thing?" I ask reluctantly.

"You have likely never known that your folk were supposed to be United Irishmen. I heard this bit of your family history from Jacob's father…it had been passed down to him a long time back."

"What do you mean, United Irishmen?"

"The 1798 Rebellion. You know about that? A lot of Presbyterians were caught up in it; they joined with the Catholics against the English. Again, some of our own ministers were involved, so they were. Presbyterian clergymen were hung for being part of it. Dozens were arrested and did prison. Some had to leave for America to escape the authorities. Ordinary Presbyterian men were hung outside the Courthouse in the town, some of them buried in the same graveyard as the judge that hung them."

I have a vague memory of hearing something about this before. I don't think it was in a school context, maybe just some passing reference in family folk lore, uttered behind hands in self-conscious whispers. Anyhow, history was never one of my strong points. I gave it up as a subject before O Levels; it was either it or music, so there was no chance of me choosing history.

"How do you know all this?" I ask him.

He smiles. "Just a big interest of mine. Always was. I read a lot, but I also pick up stories and rumours here and there."

"So what you say about my family may be just rumours? There may be no truth in it at all?"

The smile develops to a dry laugh. "Ah now, my dear," he says, becoming serious again. "I think if you dig into it you'll find there's a good deal of truth in what I'm telling you. I can lend you books on it if you like."

I don't give him any encouragement on this idea. I have enough on my plate.

"Your Jack would have been a great reader, you know. Me and him was always talking about stuff like that."

"Really? I didn't know that," I tell him.

"Oh aye. Jack was a clever chap, so he was."

It's nice to hear his opinion of my brother, but I say nothing. We have chatted long enough. I glance up at the clock. Wally isn't quite finished though.

"And listen daughter, you should never be afraid of the truth. Not only that...you should be proud of your heritage, and the folks before you that stood up for what was right at the time. It couldn't always have been easy for them, going against the weight of opinion, against a lot of the local folk. The church too, and the authorities. But back then the Shaws were strong people. They had backbone, whether you agree with what they were doing or not."

"Well, be that as it may, the rest of that story will have to wait for another night," I tell him with a smile. "I would need to be getting back up to my own house, or there will be a rebellion closer to home."

He takes the hint, but before he leaves he is up the yard to check on a sick heifer. What would we do without good neighbours? A kind-hearted man, Wally. Just a pity he isn't a Christian. Not yet anyways.

Chapter 8

Girlfriend

Tonight I lie awake for several hours. The proverbial tossing, the turning, the remembering, the unanswered questions, the tears, the loneliness of doubt.

Perhaps as a result of what our neighbour had been saying to me earlier, I am thinking about my own experience of people of the Roman Catholic faith. More likely though, my trend of thought is because this morning I had a sympathy card from a very good friend from my university days. I had let her know of my brother's passing, and she had sent the card. Actually it's a Mass card, the first one of those I've ever seen, I believe…so I'm not all that sure what to do with it. I placed it on the dining room table with all the other cards…at the back. It was very good of her to send it; I really appreciate the wee note she wrote inside.

The schools I attended in childhood had been state schools; almost all of the pupils in these schools had been Protestant. That is just how it is in this country, of course; it is an unfortunate system which reflects, but also tends to perpetuate, the division that runs down the middle of us like a treacherous river. I wouldn't profess to know or understand the history of the system, but I am fairly sure of where the blame lies. But as we say around these parts, whatever you say, say nothing.

Looking back, I think there were three or four families from foreign countries in my school in the seventies; these students may have been of a different faith; they did not have to attend Religious Education classes with the rest of us; they could stand outside the hall when we had assemblies. At the end of the religious part they would be fetched in, like errant strays; they'd have to stand at the back to listen to important announcements, or receive awards and the like. They had to survive the gaze of a few hundred of their peers, as heads turned to stare. We may have had a couple of Catholic families as well over the years; they did exactly as the others of a different faith did. It couldn't have been easy for them.

I do recall that there had been a debate about integrated education in the Grammar School's debating society. I stayed after school for it, and was happy to vote for the motion that day; it had read something like 'This house believes that children of all faiths should be educated together." I was pleased, too, that the motion had been carried with a huge majority. There had been, now that I think about it, an Integrated Primary School established in the town some years before, but I gathered that numbers were still small, and that it was unlikely there would be a Secondary school of that type set up. That was probably a relief, for my school and the one up the street beside the Chapel.

So, unbelievable as it may sound, when I went to University in 1978 I had never had a decent conversation with a Catholic of my own age; not a proper chat anyhow. On our bus I had, of course, met kids wearing the green or black uniform of St Whoever's school, and had sometimes made conversation with a couple of them…the journey was little more than fifteen minutes, so the chats were brief, strained even, especially after some of the terrible atrocities that had been carried out by the IRA or loyalist terror groups in those days during the seventies. There had even been fist fights at the back of the bus following some massacre or other, though generally we put up with each other's dirty looks and under-the-breath insults. It was mainly all about male bravado anyhow; sometimes I would deliberately seek out one of the more civilised girls in green or black for an oil-on-water sort of conversation. I was, after all, a prefect in my school; I had to set an example, and build little bridges.

The first day in the University Lecture Theatre I found myself sitting beside a stranger who, it turned out, was taking the same units as me in the education course. We were talking almost at once. Her personality was just so warm and open. She was hoping to be a music teacher in a post-primary school, same as I was. We introduced ourselves to each other. That was where the first problem emerged. I had never met anyone with her first name before…in fact, I don't think I'd even heard of the name until it landed awkwardly on the table between us that day.

"Seer-shaa," she said; at least that's what I heard.

"Sorry, what?"

She repeated. I asked her to spell it. That only made it worse. I felt like an idiot.

"It means 'Freedom' in Irish," she told me.

"Freedom?"

"Yeah, freedom…you know…?"

Things weren't getting any better.

"Mine means 'Noble-woman,'" I countered.

"Noble-woman?"

"Yeah."

Our eyes seemed to bounce away from each other. It wasn't a promising beginning.

But then she giggled, and I joined in, and the ice was well and truly cracked open by the hilarity that followed as we both realised that we had just lived through a quintessentially Ulster moment. Now that we knew where we both stood we could have a decent conversation.

We became best of friends. From then on, if ever I was getting above myself in a seminar or something, she would bring me down to earth with a whispered, "Come on now, get off your high horse, 'noblewoman'!" It got to the stage where all she had to do was make that clicking sound out of the side of her mouth, the 'kk' tongue-against-gum sucking noise that horses all over the world seem to understand as "Gee up!" All I could do was laugh at her wind-up. I could always take that from her, for some reason. I suppose I liked her, trusted her, as she did me, I believe. I found it difficult to think what I admired about her. Perhaps it was what we colloquially call her 'ready humour', that plus the fact that she had a refreshing randomness in her persona. She just had that air of the whimsical about her, an aura of uncertainty. Even her walk was a bit arbitrary, like a leaf caught in a swirl of wind at the corner of one of her city alleyways.

When I told them at home about this friendship father seemed to be worried. He didn't say much, but I could tell he thought that this girl, with her irreverent humour and such free spirit, was somehow influencing me. He would drop wee hints, subtle as a bulldozer, about how I needed to be sharing my testimony with her, bring her to faith in Christ alone… he was apparently concerned that she would draw me away to some ecumenical cause or questionable lifestyle. Even when I went to her wedding in Londonderry, many years later, he was counselling me about staying out of the Mass, telling me, "It's an abomination. It will contaminate your soul!" I told him not to worry, that I'd be sitting at the back and I wouldn't be parading up with the others, not even for a blessing from the priest.

I think he was also concerned that I would be exposed to her political views. My father was easily stressed, to be fair; for all his deep-rooted confidence in God, he didn't seem to be able to trust the Heavenly Father to keep me safe and secure in my beliefs.

We did talk about religion at times, my friend and I. I recall that, on one occasion when she came to stay over the weekend with me on the farm, we had probably our most serious argument about churches and beliefs. It was in early July. She came to church with me, mainly because I had just taken on the role of organist.

I remember she had been taken aback by the wee doors at the end of each pew. She looked hard at me as I left her in our family seat, pushed the low door closed behind her and snibbed it.

"What are the doors for?" she asked with a quiet snigger. "To keep me in or to keep sinners out?"

I had to shush her, for sanctimonious heads were starting to turn, and a few admonishing stares were bearing down on us; there wouldn't really have been a place for 'the giggle' in our order of service.

She had been happy enough to come to church though, 'to hear me play, for the craic', as she put it. That part was no problem. What was a problem was that our clergyman announced the Orange Service to be held in the church the following Sunday. She hit the roof about that afterwards. Thankfully she calmed down until we had finished the Sunday dinner, so my father didn't get involved in the argument. Lunch that day was probably the most silent and awkward meal our kitchen had ever hosted.

We went for a walk up the back lane afterwards, and she let fly. I had never seen the whole thing about the Orange Order from a Catholic's viewpoint before. It was an education. Even though I tried to explain that we were not an Orange family, we were separate from all that, we didn't even go to the Twelfth any more… the fact that 'a sectarian, secret club of bigots', (her words), 'can have a divine service in a Presbyterian church' meant that we were all complicit. It took some effort to get her calmed down. I tried to explain that there were many decent men in the Orange who were only carrying on the tradition that had been passed on to them from their fathers. Many of them had, in my opinion and experience, no great animosity to people of her faith. She just shook her head at this, and did a John McEnroe.

"You cannot be serious! The reason the Orange exists is to keep you lot on top, and keep people like me in our place."

I argued back. I told her nobody wanted to 'keep her in her place', or keep the Protestants on top. I told her she was over-reacting.

"Maybe it's not the same where you come from," I told her, "but around here people are fair to their Catholic neighbours."

"You think? How do you know? What's your evidence? You are only looking at it from a Protestant point of view, the same way your folks see it."

I thought about that; she had a point, and for once she was expressing herself quite forcefully, but I argued back. I told her about the fact that my father employed a Catholic labourer on the farm, had done so for ages, and he had had a Catholic working in the shop in the village for a while. That brought more head-shaking and wry laughter.

"That was big of him," she said.

Later that evening we had a long discussion, maybe even could qualify as an argument. I remember that she joked that I was like a tethered goat; my circle of life was so tight and I couldn't see outside of it. I found myself promising to let her 'broaden it out a bit' by taking me to her home city to walk around the streets and areas that I had only ever heard of on the news. She would show me how it felt to be a 'victim of the whole sectarian culture of this society.' I wasn't sure what I had let myself in for, but I trusted her, and liked her enough to promise to do that.

The visit was an experience that will always stay with me. I took the train over later that same summer. The journey was a unique experience in itself. I have so many little memories of it, perhaps because of the intensity of my emotions that day, the nervousness and, yes, probably the fear. The track at one stage ran alongside the broad river Bann; for a short time I had a close-up view from my window seat of two beautiful swans as they seemed to try to keep pace with the train, their long necks stretching out in eager optimism as they followed the course of the river. A golf course to the right, some garishly-coloured players trying to compensate for their poor form by out-scoring their competitors in the fashion stakes. A brief stop in the seaside village of Castlerock, then the sudden darkness as we burrowed through a tunnel under Mussenden Temple, emerging to a very different prospect across the long, curving rib of strand at Downhill. Over the flattest of landscapes, Magilligan point to our right, we passed through a tiny station at Bellarena. Beyond the stretch of water known as Lough Foyle, I could look across to County Donegal in the Irish Republic, a place I looked forward to visiting, if ever I got the chance.

I had been on this train journey once before. I suppose I must have been around ten on that first visit when my parents took us to Londonderry, so it would have been 1970. On that occasion, we had visited a relation on the eastern side of the Foyle river, the Waterside, as it is known. We had, however, travelled across the Craigavon Bridge to the city itself, and walked right around its famous walls. I well remember looking down into the shambles of narrow streets that was the Bogside, and having some sympathy for the people who had to live in those tiny, cramped-up houses. In my opinion then, however, nothing could excuse their rioting.

Now, as a young adult, I was back in the city, this time down in the Bogside, standing, with thumping heart, at a wall which had some significance to the people around here. They called it Free Derry corner. I read the huge black letters painted on this lonely, white gable; "YOU ARE NOW ENTERING FREE DERRY". It did not mean much to me, but my friend spoke of it as if it was a hallowed shrine. I was looking up at those imposing city walls that towered sternly above us. Both edifices spoke of defiance in their own way. One was all about defence and dominance; the other said, "We'll see about that!" What a difference between the two structures, each sacred in its own way to its congregation.

If I'm being honest, I have to admit to being as nervous as a kitten in that environment; my friend read aloud the names on the Bloody Sunday Memorial, her strong Derry accent infused with something between sorrow and anger. Hearing her talk about people she knew whose brothers had been shot that day was so difficult for me to listen to.

"They were innocent lads," she said, "out on a march to protest about internment. Even your great leader Paisley was against interning people without a proper trial!"

"What was it all for?" I said, rhetorically.

She was ready with an answer for that one.

"It was for civil rights. It was for justice. Same as what they marched for in 69. Your clergymen ever make sermons about that? About human rights?"

That was a strange question I thought. I couldn't think of an answer that would satisfy her, so I just said, "I wouldn't think so. They just preach the gospel."

She just shook her head. We said no more about it, sensing that the subject was going to be too divisive, and that we were talking at cross purposes anyway.

Still, that was an unforgettable day for me.

A few months later that visit wouldn't have been possible.

The country had been thrown into an even more divisive period when Republican prisoners in the Maze prison had gone on hunger strike. Quite a few of them died too; we found it hard to countenance that young men would be prepared to die for their cause, and for the principle of political status. To us they were just common criminals. There was a lot of mocking sarcasm in the Protestant community about it. 'We will never forget you, Jimmy Sands', some loyalist student had scrolled on a college wall. But for once I was able to see the issue in a more balanced way, through the eyes of my girlfriend. I will never forget her tears of pure joy and relief on the night when it was announced that the hunger strike had been called off. We were at some play in the theatre; at final curtain one of the actors came rushing back on to the stage.

"It's over! It's over! The hunger strike is over!"

He was elated, laughing and crying at the same time. My friend was the same, except that for the first time she was hugging me, bawling her eyes out, jigging up and down like a child. Half the audience were the same, delirious! The other half watched in bemusement, clearly relieved and glad of the news, but not able to feel its visceral impact as their fellow audience members were. It was a revelation to me. That moment was this country of ours in microcosm.

When my friend and I talked about beliefs and faith, I really struggled. We were so far apart in our thinking most of the time, and yet I cannot deny that she had a love for her faith; she had a very clear and strong belief system. It did involve the Virgin Mary, it did have saints in there, but Jesus was in there too. No matter how I tried to get her to see the truth she would just laugh at me, and tell me to 'wise up'.

"What makes you think you are right?" she would ask. "Have you ever found a Catholic trying to convert you?"

I had to admit that I hadn't.

"You see! We are content to let you choose how you think. But you lot…you are all so arrogant. You are 'the people'! Always right! You cannot allow other people to have their point of view. What gives you the right to try to convert me to Protestantism? Look, my faith had been around for fifteen hundred years before some dirty English king switched to Protestantism just so he could bed his wife's lady-in-waiting and divorce his queen."

I often wonder how, after the vitriol of these arguments, we managed to stay friends. I have to say that eventually I backed off; I even apologised for myself, and tried to explain that I had been reared with this idea of the 'evangel', that I had to spread God's word, bring others into the faith. She thanked me for that apology, very graciously so; said she understood…but that I needed to relax, enjoy the breadth of difference in the world, rather than see everything through 'orange-tinted glasses', as she put it, and trying to drag everybody into the same straight-jacket that I was in. She was wrong about that though…I did not have an orange-tinted view of the world.

In uni she tried her best to get me to come to events with her, many of which did not sit right with me at all. While she was going to things in the Irish club, I was to be found at Christian Union meetings. We were both big music fans of course, and, although our tastes in music weren't always the same, there were lots of great gigs to be going to. But, while I didn't mind going to some of these concerts with her, and I loved them as much as she did, I would never let her tempt me into going to clubs or discos or pub events. That was outside the pale for me, given how I had been brought up. My father would have taken me out of university if he thought I'd be indulging in strong drink and dancing. Both were very worldly pursuits in the way of thinking of our family and church. How my friend pulled my leg about that.

"Come on, ye square oul prod! How will the noble-woman ever find a noble-man if she doesn't let her hair down once in a while?"

I have to admit that, on a few occasions towards the end of my final years of study, I did accompany her to parties and events that my folks would not have been happy about. I told myself it was alright, because I had just met a fellow, and he was coming with me…so I was safe.

My brother Jack only met my uni girlfriend on that one occasion when she came to the farm. I was really quite surprised by how he had taken to her. He was joking away with her in no time, and she seemed to respond to it. I couldn't believe what I was seeing. As we were going to bed that Saturday night I commented on this to her. I said something like, "Hey, I'm watching you…flirting away with my brother in front of my eyes!"

She just laughed. "He's not bad looking, is he…to be a brother of yours like? Anyway, he's an old man, so content yourself."

And he was, of course. I suppose he was twice her age at that time, somewhere around the forty.

My twin brother wasn't home then. Maybe just as well. He had a particular worry about our friendship. With him being in the RUC at the time, and stationed not a million miles away from the Maiden City, I had to listen to him lecturing me that I must never ever say what his job was. I must always say that he was a civil servant, which was true of course. This is what I did, faithfully.

"She may be the nicest person in the world, but you never can be sure that whatever information you let slip about me, or about us, won't find its way to the Provos. They're crawling in that place," he told me.

I understood his fears. All during his career in the RUC he was so careful, checking his car for booby-trap bombs, taking different routes to and from our farm, dressing like a farmer when leaving the house and so on. During his whole twenty-two years in the RUC I would say he probably lived in constant fear. He covered it with typical flippancy, and a fatalism that I found ridiculous. Something like that leaves a huge mark on you whether you like to admit it or not, there can be no doubt about that. It didn't help that he lost that friend and colleague back in the mid 90ies.

While everyone else in our family welcomed the peace that came with the Belfast Agreement, he was the only one who was against it. To his mind, far too much was being given to those men who had terrorised the country for thirty years, paramilitaries from both sides who were now going to be walking free. Many of their victims did not have that luxury; many had deep scars, both physically and mentally. My twin was not immune to those deep psychological wounds either. I have always felt a massive burden of responsibility for him, as the brother who shared the womb of our phantom mother, and as his closest friend, to be sensitive to his vulnerabilities, and to be an ear and a shoulder for him whenever he needed it.

As I lie awake tonight, just thinking back over our lives, I sort of pledge myself again to continue to do that, and I say a prayer for help in fulfilling that desire.

I also have the strange thought that, after what our good neighbour has told me earlier this evening, I would love a good chat with my friend from university days, to tell her about the deep history of my family that I had known nothing of. I wonder how she would react to the notion that my dissenting Presbyterian ancestors had been to the forefront of the struggle for land rights back in the day. Would there be a spark of connection arcing across the cultural space between us? Perhaps there is a subconscious need in me to identify with that intriguing quality she had, a quality which is so well summed up in her Irish name, that 'freedom' vibe that she so embodies.

Dear Sarah,

I am so sorry to hear about Jack. Thank you for letting me know. I would love to have been able to get over to the funeral but you know how strict schools are now about getting out. So this card will have to do. . . I hope you don't mind.

Poor Jack. And poor you. It is very tragic that he got this illness at the start of what should have been his chance to take it easy and enjoy life, when your other brother returns. Now he doesn't get the chance. I only met him a couple of times, of course, but he always struck me as a very interesting and independent sort of person, quietly courageous in his own way and that bit different from the run of the mill. He seemed, way back then, to be very civil, open-minded and a real handsome charmer. I am sure the funeral was a sober affair, but you can be proud of him and hold close to your heart the good memories you had with him.

I hope we can meet up again soon; it's been far too long. Derry is still in the same place, if you fancy coming across that Peace Bridge for a catch up. We're a lot more civilised over here now since Martin McGuinness and Paisley kissed and made up. Wonders never cease, do they?

May your dear brother rest in peace.

Love, Saoirse

Chapter 9

Piano Teacher

We were a music-loving family. That being the case, I suppose it was inevitable that at least one of the children would eventually be sacrificed to a random piano teacher, some Mozart-worshipping high-priestess of keyboard instruction with a fixation for sight-reading. I am not sure how our two older brothers had managed to escape from that altar. Our poor sister had a fair excuse. No such luck for the twins.

While we began going to piano lessons together at about seven or eight years of age, the headstrong boy somehow broke free after a few years. He had 'talent and aptitude, but no stickability'…that was what was written below his final report from the lady in question. Actually, he was a much better player than I was; his natural ear was far superior. He could hear 'Hey Jude' once, then go away and make a really good stab at playing it, including the bass notes. But he just hated the discipline of having to be bothered trying to make sense of the 'birds on the wires', the musical notation. He particularly disliked the whole business of using the proper fingers when practising a scale.

So I was left on my own, much to the piano teacher's disappointment. I thought she was going to cry when the brother chickened out, leaving it to me to be the one to tell her that he wasn't going to be coming back.

"But he could be so good. This is a terrible waste of talent," she moaned that day. "Will you not persuade him to reconsider? What is it? Does he not like me? Is it how I am teaching him?"

"I don't think so," I believe I said. "It's not you, Miss…it's just him. He's thick."

I remember that that comment annoyed her.

"Don't ever call your brother thick," she chided. "Maybe if he could be taken to another teacher? A man this time perhaps? Will you suggest that at home?"

I didn't bother doing so, for I knew it would be a waste of time. Twin was listening surreptitiously to pop on the radio. There weren't many pianos in the songs he was hearing. Guitars ruled his world in the late sixties and early seventies. It would be no time until he'd be begging father for a red Fender Strat. Good luck with that, I remember thinking.

So I was left with the piano lady for the next twelve years or so, right up until I did my letters. For all her faults, she was an excellent teacher, and I valued what I had absorbed from her, all the technical stuff, but more so the appreciation of such a wide range of music. She was a phenomenal musician herself. She loved the music of the romantic era. Sometimes I could persuade her to play a bit of Brahms or Schumann, two favourite composers that she seemed to be fascinated by. But she had wider tastes. I remember one day she was in a strangely exuberant mood and played me a section of *'Rhapsody in Blue'*. I recall being shocked by that; it seemed out of character for her. The first movement of *'Moonlight Sonata'* was a go-to piece, eventually for me as well. It was one of the first proper compositions that I felt I had mastered.

However, it wasn't only the straight classical repertoire that she encouraged me to play. She introduced me to the theme music from the film *'Love Story'*; that was another of our favourite performance pieces. I adored playing it, but my teacher had it at a different level; she could make you cry with the atmosphere she created playing that tune. She had such a feel for it, full of emotion, great delicacy of touch. It helped me get over her oddnesses. Actually, it is a tune that I frequently find running around in my head even now, more than thirty years later.

I have a vivid memory of when Jack first drove twin and I to lessons at the teacher's home. It always seemed to fall to him to deliver us to her mansion of a house, out in the suburbs above the town. My lasting impression was of the awkwardness of it all. He left us at the gate; we walked, with some trepidation, along a sweeping drive lined with the most gorgeous, sweet-smelling rose bushes and elegant lupins. A fairytale avenue in pinks, reds, whites and yellows. I remember having to reach up to a brass door-bell, because twin wouldn't. He was all for hiding until Jack returned to collect us.

On the way home I remember him asking the question, "How come that woman is so rich?"

"How do you know she is rich?" Jack asked.

"She must be loaded. Sure look at the house she lives in. Have you ever been inside? It's full of old antique stuff, like a palace or something."

"Maybe her daddy was very rich, maybe he had a big, important job or something. I don't know."

The house was indeed the grandest place I had ever been in. The ceilings were high, with plaster carvings around the light-fittings. The decor was tasteful in an archaic sort of way, crimsons and purples, cream and rusty colours; here and there, however, there were signs of paint peeling, places that could have done with a new coat. Expensive-looking oil-paintings of landscapes and seascapes, each in a heavy gilt frame, hung in the hall and in the piano room itself, the 'sanctuary' as I came to think of it. Tall, dark-wood furniture, mahogany panelling everywhere. A very ornate staircase right in the middle of the entrance hall. All that was fine, but what really caught our attention were the statues and holy pictures. The Virgin Mary was everywhere in that house. Our Lord Jesus as well, staring down sorrowfully at us, his blood-red heart gleaming on the outside of his chest, inappropriately so, I thought…it seemed a bit gruesome to my squeamish Presbyterian eyes. Some sort of porcelain water bowl stuck on the wall just inside the door, a couple of colourful necklaces hanging to it. It was only much later I learned that this was a holy water font, and that the necklaces were rosary beads.

It all felt so alien to us. You might as well have been in a convent, I imagined.

Actually that was one of the first impressions of the teacher as well. When I looked at her, she had the sort of face you see in illustrated Bibles or holy pictures, the sort of countenance you might imagine on a nun, or on the mother of Jesus herself, reverent, placid. Her skin was clear, pale, without blemish or freckle. Her fox-coloured hair was tied tightly back, maybe in a bun or a roll or something. In all my time going to her I never saw her with her hair down, natural-like. Her choice of clothes told me something too; they were always so dark. Skirts of chocolate-brown corduroy; long, charcoal-coloured dresses; dull purple cardigans that her mother or grandmother likely knit for her…twenty years behind the times, I thought. This was the sixties and seventies. Had she never looked at a magazine, or noticed the pretty pinks and blues that girls were wearing in the streets? I couldn't imagine her in a mini-skirt though. She was no Mary Quant.

Speaking of her mother, I never saw another female in the house; actually, I never saw anyone else in the house. I had the impression that the teacher lived alone, which was strange, as this was a much larger house and property than most others in the town. I thought then that perhaps she had lost her parents; that might explain the aura of melancholy about the place.

In total contrast to the bustle of my home, this was a strangely quiet house. There were displays of photographs, which I suppose must have been of her kin; I didn't ever get time to study these, but just once, after she had left the room in something of a hurry, I did notice a picture of her as a teenager, I am guessing, standing in front of this grand home. She was looking down at some sort of trophy in her hands; I remember thinking that she had managed to look shy, proud and pretty at the same time.

I would have struggled to guess her age during that period when I was her pupil. As a child, of course, everyone older than me was regarded as 'adult'. 'Adult' was a homogenous group to the young; after 'adult' came 'elderly', grandparent-aged people. The music teacher was in that adult group, but I couldn't have told you what decade she belonged to. She was certainly a lot younger than my parents. They had wrinkles and looked permanently worried; she was serene, with the sedateness of a plastic doll. And she always wore the same perfume, a faint, floral scent… like from a very delicate flower, honeysuckle or some such. My brother hated it especially, but I thought it fitted with the person she was, fragile and sweet, all at the same time, just a bit old-fashioned in a way that maybe made her seem older than she was.

How she presented herself always put me in mind of an oil painting from a different era; her shape, her bearing, was what you might see on the cover of a Jane Austin novel. She struck me as being a bit out of time, a bit startled by being caught here in this modern century with its fast cars and electricity and loud music. Her defence seemed to be this air of constant detachment. Tranquil was her default mode.

Having said that, there were a couple of occasions when her composure did falter a little. Sometimes towards the end of the half-hour lesson she seemed to get frustrated. Her concentration wavered, and she would turn her head away from me, as if she was exhausted, or fed up with my inadequacies on the piano. I felt I had disappointed her. I recall once apologising to her, tearfully, I believe. I said something like, "I'm sorry for disappointing you, Miss. I'll practice harder for next week." She kept her face turned from me and muttered, "You don't disappoint me, dear. Just keep doing your best."

Well, I was doing my best. She did continue to encourage me, but I couldn't help the feeling that I was not living up to her expectations, that I could be much better. So I did increase my practicing…it became a compulsion to me to the extent that my mother actually told me not to take it all so seriously. Mother would have been the least musically inclined in our family. Maybe her house-bound life-style and work load precluded her from taking time to appreciate what the rest of us enjoyed. Maybe she thought of music as frivolous, a non-productive waste of time and money; whatever the reasons, she paid little attention to my pieces and my practising. My father was more interested, the piper in him connecting with the melodies I was learning, especially those with a traditional feel, and particularly those of Scottish origin. I remember his excitement when I had to learn *'The Skye Boat Song'*; it wasn't long before he had resurrected the pipes from their storeroom crypt, dusted them down, and was trying to play along. I had little patience for the duet though; the whine of the drone annoyed me, and the tuning of the bagpipes was an issue as I tried to come to terms with the elaborate arrangement on the sheet in front of me.

Father was particularly pleased when I became competent enough to play hymns. He would take me with him on a Sunday evening when he had been invited to take a meeting in one of the many mission halls he frequented. If there was a piano, a keyboard, or even, as in one case, an old pedal organ in the place, I would have to come along and play for the singing. It wasn't something I particularly enjoyed, but I did appreciate his pride in me. I might have been ten or eleven when that all began; it lasted until I was maybe fifteen. By that age I'd had enough of the condescending compliments of the meeting-goers, and wanted to spend the evening before Monday school engrossed in a novel, or surreptitiously finishing a homework in the privacy of my bedroom.

I lost touch with my piano teacher after I did my letters. I remember her emotion when I brought her a present to say thanks for all she had done for me. It was a brooch that I thought she would like, a very pretty piece in the form of a grand piano, carved and crafted using ebony and ivory. She seemed to appreciate it, and we parted with a handshake which turned into a hug halfway through, all a bit out of character for her, I thought.

I left Miss Quinn to her holy pictures, her sonatas and her loneliness. I haven't seen her since.

Chapter 10

The Servant Man

Our old farm labourer was a loveable rogue in many ways. He was the source of much consternation to me in my growing-up years. There were times when I had such a sense of remorse that I felt so enthralled by him. I shouldn't have…he was a bad influence, but such a character.

I loved Jimmy's company. I loved his humour, his mickey-taking. For all his scruffily decrepit appearance, he was always optimistic, never seeing the worst in people, and never complaining about things. He had such a strange slant on life, so different from the serious perspectives of my folks. There was nothing that couldn't be lightened, no circumstance that couldn't be made better, if only he could come up with a funny anecdote or saying to take the grimness out of it. How many stories did I hear from him over the years, often more than once?

"I likely toul you this wan before, but…" he would begin. It did not matter whether or not he had, of course, you had to hear it again… and again. The tale could begin in this town-land, but, by the time it was finished, it could be in a different county altogether. And I loved it.

He was such a divil. His language could sometimes be very crude, but he would always apologise for it afterwards, especially if he forgot himself, and a swear word slipped out through his nicotine-stained teeth. His stories sometime strayed into the vulgar before he would realise his audience and clean up the tale as best he could. He smoked so many cigarettes over the course of a day, with all the associated coughing and spluttering, that I was certain he'd die off with cancer. My father, the model Christian gentleman who never touched strong liquor nor smoked a cigarette in his entire life, dead and gone half a life time ago, yet this 'oul' sinner is still cheating the grim reaper, and with a derisive smile on his face. Aye, such a rogue he was, and so unrepentant. But I adored him in those childhood days, and could never understand why, for he was almost exactly the opposite of what a good Christian role model should be. Hence my feelings of guilt.

Over the years, he never changed one iota. The same shabby flat-cap, sweat-welded to his skull; the soil-stained stump of a half-smoked fag wedged above his 'lug'; the creased face, like a medieval relief map of Ireland; the boiler-suit, tattered and clay-caked, fresh patches stitched untidily over any rips in the original navy-blue cloth; the crumpled jacket, held together with lengths of binder twine in the absence of long-lost buttons; the black Wellington boots, decorated with splodges of avocado-coloured calf skitter. He was the animated version of a Van Gogh portrait.

He used to get his wife to shave him once or twice a week. She would also have the job of cutting what was left of his thinning hair. Poor woman, she was no expert in either department. The number of times I saw him arrive at the breakfast table with a plaster on his cheek, or a razor scratch still oozing red on his upper lip!

"Aye, she notched me again this morning, lass," he would say, fingering a scarlet wound on his earlobe. "When she worked her way 'roun' to the ither side, I toul her it didn't matter whether the two sides matched or naw, just to leave this ear alone."

His accent was that bit different to ours, a broader vibe to most words and expressions; his colloquialisms made us all smile at times. He was from a different part of the country, away to the north. I had the impression that he even laughed in that dialect. And he laughed a lot! When he wasn't laughing, he would be whistling some old tune. I say whistling, but that is a very loose description. The sound was a sort of blending of contralto vocal and a sighing noise, not unlike the wind blowing through a keyhole. Two sounds for the price of one really. I often wished I could have recorded it for my college friends to hear. His tunes were bright and folksy, likely Irish dance tunes, I imagined. Never any words, just occasional repetitions of sounds in some of his performances, like, 'toura-lur-i-ay, toura-lur-i-oh', and others phrases that I couldn't decipher. He told me he was 'lilting'.

"Whatever you say," I assured him.

I remember once when I walked in on him urinating in the byre. I was maybe about ten at the time, and would have had chores to do around the yard, feeding the farmyard fowl, lifting eggs and the like. I came into the byre to leave a bucket or something. There he was, his legs wide apart, one arm akimbo on his haunch, the other doing whatever it was doing, his back to me, thankfully, and the sound of water splashing in and around the gutter that drained away such fluids. He looked over his shoulder, cigarette between his teeth, eyes half-closed against the curl of grey tobacco reek, but still sparkling, though not with any suspicion of embarrassment.

"Agh, Lord bless us! Hang on there lass till I nick this," he said. Then under his breath, "Can a man naw ha'e a quiet pish in peace?"

I got back at him though. I don't know how I thought of this, or where I got the nerve to say it.

"Sorry," I said, "I heard the sound... I just thought it was a cow!"

"Ha ha, you're a funny wan," he laughed.

He had brought me down to his level, and I was secretly delighted. Even more delighted that he got things put back in place and the buttons mastered before he turned round.

To some extent, I blamed his Catholic upbringing for this lack of reverence in him. The flippancy, the blasé snigger, the lack of awareness of how and when to take things seriously…I found it so attractive, and yet at the same time I was horrified by it.

To add to this ambivalent feeling, I must recognise that I learned so many life lessons from him. He taught me to value things that maybe other people took for granted; he taught me the local names of flora and fauna, like 'peeweep' for lapwing and 'whitrick' for weasel; he encouraged me to love our homely tastes and smells, the bitter tang of buttermilk, the sweet sugariness of the molasses we used to add to our cattle feed, the rich scent of soil-covered potatoes, wholesome as porridge.

"Sniff that, lass," he would whisper almost confidentially, holding a handful of freshly dug spuds up to my nose. "If that's not the smell o' heaven then I might have to content myself with the other place."

While I winced at his sacrilegious bravado, I would always oblige him. I breathed in that evocative, earthy aroma and, yes, the whiff of soil and new-born potato… the very essence of my existence here on this land of ours.

"You know what kind they are?"

I didn't.

"Here, brush the soil aff and luk at the colour o' them. Ye see there's blues, and pinks, and whites."

These ones just looked dirty to me. I said nothing. He took the spud from me, spat liberally on it and rubbed the skin.

"Do ye see? It's sorta rosey. It's a Kerr's Pink," he pronounced. "Now if it was a bluey colour it would be an Aran Victor, a blue. And if it was white it might be an Irish Queen."

"An Irish Queen?" I said, eyebrows raised.

"Well, if you were listening to my folks it would be an Irish Queen, but here yous call it a British Queen."

He giggled to himself.

"Even the spuds have to take sides in this neck o' the woods."

He made me aware of the cries of various birds, those around our farm, and those who frequented the forest over the road from us. The difference between the songs of the thrush and the blackbird, the harsh whistle of the curlew, and the unique piping tune of the dunnock. The curious, clacking racket that arose from the many magpies around the place, like an ensemble of castanets. The screeching pheasants that strayed across to our land from the Colonel's estate were my favourites. The sheer excitement of their colour combinations got me. Their shawl, speckled ginger and copper, with a dusting of tawny browns, separated from the rich emerald sheen of their neck by that thin, silvery necklace, the scarlet seal stamped royally on their heads. I remember he tried to tell me that in an earlier life they had been beautiful Irish princesses. It was enticing, this mythological idea, but I never allowed myself to agree with him. I am not even sure if his religion allowed him to believe in reincarnation, but it wasn't something we read in the Bible, so I couldn't countenance it. Anyhow, when you think about it, it was the male pheasant that looked so stunningly colourful; the females were a bit more plain of themselves; if the tale of the princesses was true you would have expected the hens to be more attractive than the cocks. I just told him God painted the feathers on the pheasant, and we should be thanking him for being such a great artist, not wondering about stupid mythology.

Some of my first lessons in biology came from him. Being brought up on a farm ensured plenty of opportunity for this. I remember when he would take me for a springtime walk across a few of our fields to where a slow-flowing burn separated us from the next door farm. Beyond the stream, we could look across at the neighbour's newly planted potato drills, so perfect and precise, narrowing away in the low distance, like the bellows of a gigantic accordion. From the sluggish brown water he would help me collect guey frog spawn in an old tin bucket, a translucent splurge that always reminded me of mother's tapioca puddings. I would hide this in some shaded corner of the farmyard. Over the weeks I would keep watch, waiting for the squirming little commas to emerge from their glutinous womb, turn into wiggling tadpoles, and eventually reach full frog-hood state, with all its potential for amphibian devilment.

"No sign of those wee black lads growing any legs yet?" His every day refrain during this wait. "Shouldn't be lang now."

He used to annoy my mother with one of his tricks; I had to be his accomplice. She had a pet hate, a phobia about these very same animals. She detested frogs. So, any chance he had, he would catch one or two, put them in a basin for me, and my role was to release them in the kitchen when we were having our dinner in the evening. We would have a screaming mother climbing up on a chair when these slimy green visitors would start hopping around the floor tiles.

As a child I was aware that quite a few neighbouring farmers would occasionally arrive in our yard towing a rusty cattle trailer behind their jeep or tractor. Inevitably a heifer or cow would emerge from this trailer, a rope halter around its head, the farmer holding tightly to it against the frolicking of the animal.

I would catch snippets of the conversation between this farmer and my father, or sometimes with my eldest brother.

Something about a 'service', if my ears didn't mistake me.

"But services are what happens in church, surely? And this is only a

Thursday?" I would be thinking. It was all very confusing.

My father and maybe Jimmy McGrath would then accompany the visitors up the back lane, for what purpose I knew not. On these occasions twin and I were always told to "Go in the house till we come back!" Generally we obeyed; our mother saw to that…but curiosity grew. What was this 'service' that required such secrecy? Twin had a theory. It was a ridiculous notion, I thought, the stupidest idea you could ever imagine. But such theories need checking out.

So it was that, when an opportunity presented itself, the two of us made the call to investigate, to test twin's wild hypothesis. We couldn't have been more than eight or nine at the time. My mother and father were away to a wedding in the town, Jack was over in the Colonel's estate, and nobody but our workman about the place. Wally, our neighbour, arrived in the yard, a frisky roan heifer in tow, and his eyebrows clearly delighted to be out for a walk in the sunshine, for it was a gloriously bright day. A calm morning had had its face scrubbed clean by overnight squalls of rain and wind, and now our sloping fields seemed to stretch themselves out as if to sunbathe while this spell of bright weather lasted. The heifer, though, was agitated, tugging at the halter, wide-eyed and moaning, its hooves skittering over the dippled concrete surface of our yard as it tried to break free from Wally's firm grip of the halter.

The two men chatted on, sharing countryside gossip. The nervous heifer was still refusing to settle. Twin and I looked at it, and then at each other. He put his finger to his lips, sneakily as if plotting, and nodded towards the hay-shed. I scooted after him, knowing full well that he had a secret plan, and fairly sure I knew what it was.

"Give them a minute to get up the lane a bit," he said.

"Are we going to follow them?"

He didn't need to reply; I could sense the mischief in his eyes.

As the two men led the eager heifer up the back lane, we two followed on the field side of the stone wall. I say 'led', but in truth the heifer was doing the leading. She seemed to know the way, or at least have a fair idea where she was going, and what she was going to be getting up to. At one point, our workman looked over his shoulders for a second. I could read his mind.

'Where did those two scallywags disappear to? They were in the yard a minute ago.'

But he didn't see us, not at that point. At least I don't think he did. I am not sure what he'd have done if he'd spied us peering curiously over the ditch. Maybe nothing at all.

We hunkered along, sometimes crawling through long summer grass, purple-topped thistles, broad-leafed docks and yellow-headed ben-weeds. No nettles, thank God, although I did get jagged by a thorn sticking up from a severed sprig of hawthorn. We had almost caught up on the trio by the time they reached the five-barred gate at the end of the lane. We heard the rusty hinges creak, and the gate bang shut behind them. I could smell the tobacco smoke wafting over the wall from Jimmy's cigarette. 'He wouldn't be smoking that if my father was here,' I thought.

"Here he comes now," I heard him say. "I'll take the heifer. Stand you well back, for he doesn't know you."

"He's a powerful baste, isn't he! A powerful baste," was Wally's observation.

Our heads peeped up over the wall, and we watched as our massive Friesian bull thundered down the field through the whin bushes, clods of dark, peaty soil churning into the air behind him as if from a potato digger. He was moving much quicker than usual; I'd never seen him run like this, so eager, so alive, the froth flying from his mouth, in anger maybe, or in excitement. You couldn't even see the brass ring in his nose for slevers and foam. I was suddenly concerned for our workman. This bawing bull was out of control, an avalanche of bone, muscle and snorting terror. It could do anything to the two men over there on the wrong side of the gate.

I needn't have worried. The bull was not in a bother about two puny humans; it didn't even seem to notice them. It had eyes only for the roan heifer. Eyes, and nose, and very soon other parts as well.

Twin and I were engrossed. We were completely out of our depth here, but transfixed. So much so we had forgotten that we were not meant to be there, that we should be staying hidden from the adults. Just as the black and white monster leapt hungrily on to the poor heifer's back, I was horrified to notice that Jimmy's gaze was fixed, not on the bull's amorous antics, but on my wide-eyed face popped up above the stone ditch. To be fair, he was pretty wide-eyed as well. From that distance, I couldn't work out if they were still twinkling, those mischievous eyes of his, but I had a feeling they weren't.

In an instant I had pulled twin down beside me behind the shelter of the wall. We had seen enough. We couldn't un-see what we had seen. Worst of all, we had been seen doing the seeing. That wouldn't be unseen either, I suspected.

We scarpered back home like a pair of startled rabbits, wordless, heart-scared, but sometimes giggling at what we had witnessed. The big fear in our heads was that our parents would be told. Would my friend spill the beans on us?

I needn't have worried. After the neighbour had marched away down the lane with his happy heifer, Jimmy came dandering across the yard to us. The twinkle was back in his eyes, his mouth a lopsided grin.

"Well, you two monkeys," he said. "Yous got a bit of an education today, didn't yous! That was a better lesson than the frog spawn and the tadpoles. A bit more exciting, wasn't it?"

"Don't be telling on us," I begged in a small, penitent voice.

"Sure yous can explain it all yourselves to them. You'll be wanting to tell your mother what you saw surely?" he taunted, mischief leaping out of his eyes!

"I will not!"

"Sure…yous can ask your father for some explanation."

"Please! Please don't be telling them!"

He was grinning at me like a halloween turnip.

"Not a word, lass! Sure ampt I as good as a priest at keeping secrets. Silent as the grave," he said putting a dirt-hacked finger to his lips. "Anyways, I wouldn't know where to start, would I?"

I don't see so much of him nowadays. He used to walk up to the farm for a yarn with my brother Jack; he did that long after he had finished working for us. I'm not sure he has the legs for it any more; that long-standing limp of his seemed to have become much worse when I saw him at the wake. I wonder how he spends his days now. He wouldn't be a reader, like Wally Brown; I don't recall him ever having any pastimes or hobbies; farm labouring was the sum total of what he was about. I don't think he and the wife see much of their brood of wains; most of them are abroad, from what Jack had told me.

I picture him and her on their sofa, watching daytime TV most of the time, maybe playing draughts or cards…that's if she is able for such games, given how confused she seemed to be when I talked to her at the wake. I can't get that out of my head, the comment she made then. I should call in soon for a chat, just to see if there's anything I can do for them.

Chapter 11

Husband

When I was a student at university, I had met the young man who was to become my life partner, and the father of my two children. We had flirted, then courted more seriously for a good few months before becoming engaged. I had gone through a low patch in my life around that time of change to university living, feeling very insecure and exposed in my new life there. I suppose I'd had a very protected existence up until then, narrow, rural and shielded from much of the mores and popular culture of the seventies; there was a depth of vulnerability in me that I had not ever realised before, never mind confronted. Everything was such a challenge. What attracted me to this boy was that he seemed so calm, secure in himself. I started to shelter under his convictions. He made me feel significant and safe. I was loved for who I was; it was a step-up from those shaken emotions I had had to live with after the news of adoption…back then, coincidental with the fragility that accompanied entry to puberty, I had suspected that the affection I received from my folks had a tinge of duty about it. But this young man did not have any of that back-story to contaminate his regard for me. I was anchored in his devotion.

He was studying maths; its certainties and predictabilities appealed to his personality. His tastes in many things were quite different from mine, more conservative and safe, despite my background insularity. This was most noticeable in his musical inclinations; all very basic and predictable. He had a fondness for country and western songs, for song-writers such as John Prine. Mainly, though, he was into brass music, the big band sound of Duke Ellington, Glenn Miller and the like. He also adored songs from the musicals. As a joke I used to call him 'Roger Hammerstein'; he didn't always laugh either. To him, there was nothing to beat the rousing songs from such shows as *'Oklahoma'* and *'The Sound of Music';* he loved the emotional call to greatness of *'Climb Every Mountain'* and similar anthems. But that was about the height of it…well, the breadth of it.

I recall that one evening after we were married when, in a sour mood, he told me he never wanted to hear me play another Scott Joplin tune…ever. I couldn't believe it. Initially I thought he was joking, then I looked at his face. He was serious. I was so shocked I walked away from the piano.

"What on earth do you have against Scott Joplin tunes?" I asked him.

"Nothing but voodoo music," he grumped from behind his Telegraph. "Shallow, syncopated, flippant, ragtime nonsense."

Hard to redeem it after that critique, I thought, but I forgave him for his narrowness. It was the form he was in.

Nevertheless, such differences in taste were not going to derail our courtship back in the day. He was the man for me.

My father had had doubts about my relationship; my brother Jack was vehemently opposed to the guy. This was very strange to me; I had imagined they would get on well, as both had a love of fishing. The main reasons, so far as I could work out, were to do with the fact that my fiancé was a city boy, with hints of the accent and vernacular of Belfast. That was certainly the case so far as my dad was concerned. On his very first visit to our house in the late spring of 81, my boyfriend had made a remark that my father never forgot, never forgave him for. It was right in the middle of the muck-spreading season. The rich, acrid smell of rotten farmyard manure pervaded not only the countryside, but also every room in the house. My boyfriend got out of his second hand Austin Metro holding his nose, and didn't let go of it until my father gave him a frown that was a lot longer than the handshake.

"How can you live in that stench?" the boyfriend asked. "It's ratt'n!"

Not the most auspicious beginning to a father/son-in-law relationship.

"Likely the same way you can live in the dirty smoke of the city," my father said below his breath as he turned away.

With Jack the dislike was more for religious reasons. Given that he had turned away from his faith many years earlier, and was disinterested in all matters theological and ecclesiastic, it bugged him to the core that my fiancé could not respect his antipathy. Instead he would try to engage my brother in serious discourse about everything from the subject of child baptism to his favourite topic, the sovereignty of God. It eventually came to a head when, a few months after we were married, Jack told him in the most colourful language imaginable to stop such conversations once and for all, or face having the dogs set on him. That was not a pleasant night in our relationship.

When we first met and got to know each other in university, I was quickly aware that he was interested in doctrine. Interested? More like 'fixated'. He knew the ins and outs of every denomination, what they stood for, their founders and histories, their practices and creeds. He himself was Baptist by background, but he knew the subtle distinctions between Reformed Presbyterian, Free Presbyterian, Evangelical Presbyterian and our own branch, the Irish Presbyterian Church. He knew where all these denominations were in error, including mine of course. I suppose I must have imagined that this obsession was something he would tire of, or at least grow out of; after all, many people go through philosophical or ideological phases during those heady university days. He was a really able guy; he had an appealing personality, I thought, and could be really charming. He was certainly good-looking. He seemed to be everything I was looking for in a relationship. We were very much in love from the start.

After we were married, he came with me a couple of times to my church up the road. He wasn't happy. Children were being baptised; 'in clear contradiction of the scriptures'! So he started to visit the town every Sunday, trying out the various denominations available there. He attended the Methodists for a while, until they had a baptism service for a squealing infant. Then it was the Plymouth Brethren; they baptised only faith-confessing adults, but there was something wrong with their view of the Second Coming. He even sampled the Pentecostal Elim church for a couple of weeks. At least they didn't baptise babies; but soon the exuberance and 'speaking in tongues' put him off and he didn't go back. So none of these churches could meet with his approval. And there was no Baptist church within twenty miles. I suggested to him, tongue in cheek, that he try the local Church of Ireland in the village. I might as well have mentioned a mosque. He gave me a lecture about Anglican history, how it was the church of the ruling classes, and had colluded with the state in oppressing non-subscribing people in past centuries. Having tried all the other alternatives, Church of Ireland was a box he was not going to tick.

As our marriage progressed, and the initial thrills of intimate life together began to wear off, I started to realise that these boxes, these categories of people, were of increasingly intense importance to him. I tried to argue that we were all the same as Christians, 'all one in Christ'. For a while I thought I was winning that argument.

Then we had our first child, Christine. The duet of our married life was about to lose its sense of harmony. The grating cello and the lilting violin were clearly playing in different modes. He had gone all monotone, whereas I, on a complete hormonal high with my beautiful baby girl in my arms, was exuberantly tuneful.

The obvious issue that arose immediately was…to baptise or not to baptise the baby. The discord became so intense that it led to an early diminuendo in our relationship. In the end, I had little choice other than to accede to his wishes, and not go through with the planned baptism in our local church. The minister was more than disappointed, taking it all as a personal insult, and letting us know how deeply this had hurt him. My parents were mad about it too, father being a leading elder. What would the congregation think of him, of our family, of me?

Maybe I should have seen all this coming in those early days at uni.

I often recalled the laughter of my Catholic girlfriend, Saoirse, when I told her who I was going out with.

"Him?" she laughed hysterically, mentioning his name. "You can't seriously be going out with a guy called that?"

"Why not? What's wrong with him?"

"Nothing wrong with him, hopefully. But with a name like that he sounds like he's just landed in from the time of the Reformation."

But I was going out with Calvin Moore. And I married him. He believed it was all in God's plan, from the beginning of time. It's hard to argue with that degree of certitude.

He wasn't on for inviting my friend to the wedding either, so we didn't. She would have had to switch to calling her city 'Londonderry' for the day.

The whole thing about God predestining everything was what ordered my husband's life. So when father died, that was all grand, 'cause it was God's time. I didn't disagree; how could I? The next controversy to arise in the family was our father's will, with all its complications. That was all in God's plan as well, in his considered opinion. Again, that was hard to argue with.

"And I was meant to have been adopted? Right from the beginning?"

Of course. Otherwise it would never have happened. Was I not glad to have been given up for adoption? I hadn't been separated from my twin. We had been placed together in a Christian family, given the best of everything, taught the true faith. I should be eternally grateful.

I was, of course.

It hadn't stopped me wondering, though. It hadn't stopped me thinking about who I was when I arrived in this world. It hadn't stopped me trying to find out about my origins. The 'eternal gratefulness' didn't really trump eternal curiosity. Who was my birth mother, my actual father? Where had we come from, and what was the whole process of how we had been placed in this family? Our adoption certificates indicated that our place of registration had been Edinburgh. That was as far as we could get.

We had made early enquiries back when we were still in our teens. We'd kept this secret from our folks. It led us nowhere. There did not seem to have been any adoption agency involved, as would apparently have been the norm in most adoptions. So how had things been arranged for us to be adopted into a Northern Irish family rather than one in Scotland? What was the process? How had those two Scottish-born twins been 'put up' for adoption? Had there been some form of advertisement?

We met a brick wall at that stage. The channels were secret; such information could not be divulged from the authorities in Scotland. It was all very frustrating…and, of course, we couldn't let anyone in our close-knit adoptive family know that we were researching this. My brother and I agreed to drop the subject until we were older.

Many years later I went out on a limb; without telling anyone, I wrote to the National Records of Scotland Adoption Unit, asking for information about my birth. I was delighted to see a reply arrive in the post; however, the information was disappointing. The actual records regarding my birth and adoption were not available. The reason seemed to be that these records were sealed and held for twenty five years in some body called the Edinburgh Sheriff Court. I should write to this organisation, they said. So I did, and waited eagerly for their response.

Unfortunately it was Calvin who found the reply. One morning as he picked up our mail he became curious about an official-looking item that had arrived from Scotland. I remember the sour face that evening when he presented me with this letter. He insisted I open it in his presence. In fact, all that the letter said was that I would have to go to Edinburgh and show proof of identity in order to have my actual birth certificate released. It was a possibility.

My spouse, however, was very displeased with me....so displeased that he took the opportunity to ingratiate himself with my brother Jack, by sharing with him my secret quest.

That betrayal, for that was what it was, set the cat among the pigeons.

Jack immediately phoned my innocent twin, demanding that we call to see him, the two of us together. So, after he closed the shop that evening, twin drove to my house, demanding to know what this was all about. He was not best pleased with the admission of my independent inquiry, to say the least, feeling a bit abandoned. I had to eat dirt, apologising profusely for leaving him out of the loop. Gradually he calmed down, and we managed to put on a united front as we drove down to the farmhouse.

It was a strange feeling, like we were back as children, having to come into the old kitchen for a naughty-step reprimand, and this when we were adults, our adoptive father dead and gone, and our mother sitting in a care home with hardly an ounce of wit left in her poor head.

I felt a wave of sadness for our brother as he dragged himself in from the milking that evening. I watched the bend of his back, the slump of his shoulders as he washed himself in the utility room, soapy water splashing everywhere. He wasn't in good form. His head was then hidden by the drying towel as he seemed to take ages, like he was delaying this conversation as long as he could. Then his face! He looked so tired, so eroded for a man in his fifties, the weight of the world on his shoulders, and nobody to help him carry the load, no wife to comfort him, no children to be passing things on to. He didn't know then that these were early signs of the bad health he was to battle with later.

He came slowly into the kitchen, slipping off the shoulder straps of his old, oily dungarees, and sticking his feet into a pair of slippers, so worn that his fungus-deformed toenails stuck out grotesquely at the front. He turned a chair around from the table and sat.

"Yer man was telling me," he began, addressing me specifically. A deep breath. "Telling me you have been trying to…to pry into where yous came from."

Twin came instantly to my rescue. "It's not just her fault. We are both curious. You can say what you have to say to me too, whatever it is."

A long silence, eyes to the terracotta tiles which suddenly seemed of interest to all three of us. Strangely, I missed mother in that fearful pause. She would have had some quiet little piece of wisdom, a time-worn adage to dispel the tension. That was Bella!

"You don't think it's a bit of an insult to…to our mother and father?"

'Our' mother and father, I thought! He could have phrased that better in the circumstances. But I let it pass.

"How is it an insult to them? Daddy's dead and gone. And mother knows nothing anymore."

"That's the point. It doesn't say much about your respect for them, or their memory… that yous go digging into all that, does it?"

"I don't see how it is disrespectful to them that we are interested in how we came to be adopted by them," I said. "We intend no disrespect whatsoever."

After a long pause he resumed. "I just think it's bad form. They would be very hurt if they knew yous were going down this road."

"Why would they be hurt?" I asked. "Mother and father have been brilliant parents to us; we love them, but do you not think we have a right to know who our real parents were?"

"Maybe," he said, getting up abruptly and going to fill the kettle.

"Here, let me make you tea," I said, going to help. He watched me take over, studying my every move in a distracted sort of way, sightless, miles away and so weary.

"Aye, maybe I would be curious too if I was in your shoes," he conceded in a whisper.

"I think you would."

"But I just wish you would let it sit. What does he think about it?" he said, a twitch of his head in the direction of our house up the hill behind.

"It doesn't really matter what my husband thinks. This is about us two," I said. "Look, all we have been able to find out so far…for everything seems so difficult, like we were asking for state secrets or something…all we have is that we were registered in Edinburgh, and that there was no adoption agency involved. If there had been we could maybe trace our mother, just to see who she was, and why she needed to put us up for adoption. But up until now we can't trace her. We don't even get the option of whether to try to find her or not."

He thought about that, eyes half closed like he'd prefer to stretch out on the sofa for a sleep. He gave me a long stare before beginning again.

"Well, maybe that is what she wanted. Leave no trace. That must have been what was in her head," he said quietly, stirring his tea.

"But why Scotland? If mother and father had wanted to adopt, why not in Northern Ireland?" I asked.

"What's wrong with Scotland? Sure most of us came from there originally," he said, now with a flippant tone which annoyed me.

"You know what I mean," I replied. "And why adopt twins? What was behind that?"

My brother beside me pretended annoyance at that comment. "Why not twins? What's wrong with twins? You saying you'd rather have been on your own? That's a bit rich."

It took some of the tension out of the conversation, and maybe that was a good thing.

The last thing I recall Jack saying that night was something not unlike what my husband had said. It was an uncharacteristically long speech too...he was a man of few words, and only necessary ones.

"My advice to yous...what I think you should do... is...just leave it. Be thankful for this family, for it is your family, right? Be glad of the love mother and father gave you. Manys a child would be delighted with the care and love you two have had all through your lives. Look at you with a business in the village. Look at you with a great teaching career, and a lovely house up on the hill, and two wains and a husband to take care of you. You should thank your God for that.... everyday you should thank him, you hear me! You have no notion....Look Sarah. Don't take this any further, please."

And I remember he turned away at that point, just as his voice became brittle, like he was already regretting what he had said; we stared at his broad back in a silence of revelation, our mouths open, our eyes flicking to each other as if to say, 'Did he just say that? 'Thank our God?" Our apparently cold and godless brother had a deep well of softness in him; a calm well whose smooth surface we had troubled. Maybe down in that well there lived some sort of hurting ghost that we could never understand.

I talked about it all evening with my husband. He had no answers, other than the one obvious one. It was all meant to be. Our birth, our adoption to this family, this place, our journey through life to this point... it was all in the Master's Eternal Plan. So just accept it.

I asked the question, "Is it not possible that our curiosity is part of that plan too? That our attempts at investigating the whole saga is part of God's plan? And if it is, do I have a choice about whether to continue it?"

His answer was not really understandable to me, and anyhow, by that stage of the matter I was beginning to see flaws in the theology he was living by.

I remember disputing the Troubles with him. It may have been just after the Enniskillen bombing, I think. If everything was happening in accordance with God's will, then you had to accept the fact of the violence, of a terrible injustice like the Remembrance Day massacre. He seemed to say that logically that was the case. All of human history was 'under God's sovereign will', he argued.

"So, in your view, Hitler and all that…that was all part of God's will?" I asked.

"Absolutely," he said. "World War Two and the holocaust had to happen so that the Jews, God's chosen people after all, could return to their homeland back in Israel. It was all prophesied by the Old Testament prophets."

"So he didn't mind wiping out six million innocent people to achieve that? Is that how it works?"

Yes, that was how it worked.

I was furious at this callousness in him.

Our relationship never really recovered properly from that disagreement.

Some years later, when it came to him resigning from his job over some minor financial oversight, I was supposed to accept that this was all part of God's plan as well, to purify him through adversity, or some such notion. I should see this as a divinely-inspired 'accidental' in the grand score written for his life before time began; I should value it as a one-off black note which would easily resolve itself, and leave him a more sanctified person.

I didn't though. And wouldn't.

However, out of respect for our parents, and in response to the passion with which Jack had appealed to us that evening, I agreed to abandon the search for knowledge of our birth mother.

Now the river has moved on, sweeping Jack away with it. The swirl of uncertainty around his passing has stirred my curiosity again. The old questions are being dredged up from the under-bed of my consciousness, and I can see myself making a trip to those offices in Edinburgh as soon as I get the opportunity.

Chapter 12

Wills

I have often thought that my father lived his life with an eye to the size of his funeral.

When that sad event came, back in 1985, there can be little doubt that he would have been very gratified, and not by the volume of attendees alone. He had been a very popular man; gregarious was his middle name; he was widely known and respected, both near and far. Whereas a lot of people are known for one particular identifier, it would be hard to say which of many would be most associated with my father. As the clergyman said, "Father, husband, farmer, businessman, preacher, church elder, Sunday school superintendent, musician and friend to many."

He had been 'a big man' in so many senses. Physically, he was well over six feet in height, and in his prime probably sixteen stone plus. Given his physique it was almost inevitable that he should be such a dominant figure, although perhaps not so inevitable that he could be so domineering. He wasn't a man to put up with ideas that were alternative to his view of the world, a view completely determined by his strong, evangelical faith. Challenge to his authority was either dismissively ignored or verbally swatted away, usually with an appropriate text of Scripture to underscore his pronouncement. So, while my quiet, underplayed mother was the meek resin that bound the family together, there was no doubt as to who was the figurehead. When mother lacked the words to say what she might have needed or wanted to say, he filled the space with edicts of his own. Many of these were his efforts at humour, stories from his past, tales he had heard in the marketplace of his life. In frequent cases he might have been better having a think before he uttered them, but mostly we forgave him for that.

He was the proverbial 'big man' in our locality, even if he didn't have a lot of time for the country's more famous 'big man'. In my father's opinion, Dr Paisley should have stuck to his role in preaching, and left secular politics to others. There were many who disagreed with him on this, even within our church, but he felt that it was all a bit too contaminating. He did not appreciate the angry, 'rabble-rousing' speeches that frequently characterised the DUP leader's style.

"Can you imagine Jesus speaking like that at a rally? He's a poor advertisement for the gospel," was his usual response. That is not to say that he wasn't as loyal a Unionist as the next man, and as horrified by the wanton death and destruction that the IRA were causing in Northern Ireland.

"They're trying to ruin our wee country," he would often have said, following yet another atrocity.

In terms of business, he had done very well. His hard work ethic and his nose for commercial opportunity had raised our family from a small farm mentality to what you might call a more middle class status. He had invested in land, doubling the size of our original holding. Then he had bought a small, run-down shop in the village that had been there for generations, and was on its last legs. With a bit of vision and good management, he had turned it into a profitable business. At the start it was a great outlet for our farm produce, everything from vegetables and fresh eggs to mother's baking and meat products; by the eighties it had reached the level of a small supermarket. Villagers and people from the surrounding town-lands didn't have to drive to the town any longer for what they needed; they could buy almost everything in our shop. I worked there on Saturdays myself in my teens, as did my twin. It was a great way to gain social confidence in handling the public, and to get to know the wider community outside of our church family.

Not long after father's home-call to heaven, the family gathered in the solicitor's office in town to hear the reading of his last will and testament. We were all there, all except Miriam, of course. Mother was between my two chalk and cheese brothers, sat in front of a grand mahogany desk; twin and I had to make do with a pair of folding chairs hastily set up at the side. The meeting had been arranged rather quickly so that Isaac could be present. He had travelled home in the week before father's death, once it had become clear that no recovery could be expected from that series of heart attacks, so his timing had been good. Now though, he was itching to get back to his post in the far-away tropics. You could tell in his countenance, bronzed but bored, as he shifted from one hip to the other on his seat. His body language spoke of impatience. 'Get this over with till I get away to the airport.'

The solicitor, a more than handsome lad who looked like he should be sitting his A Levels rather than dealing with matters probate, addressed us in a nervous, high-pitched voice. His tone seemed to me to be at odds with his appearance, incongruous, like a rugged rugby player singing falsetto in a choir. Perhaps this was his first time in this particular role. It probably did not do his confidence any good that portraits of no less than six of his illustrious predecessors glared down over his shoulder in solemn sepia tones from the vermillion wallpaper behind him, their names and qualifications etched on brass plaques underneath.

None of us had ever been in this situation before. We tried to understand the legal-speak, and pretended we did; we probably should have asked more questions because, when we discussed things afterwards, it became clear that we had all heard different messages. The lack of clarity only served to add further layers to the tension that already existed between my two older brothers. But in the office that morning, when the young lawyer had looked up from his documents and squeaked, "That's it folks. Any questions?" there was a disbelieving and frankly horrible silence.

From what I could understand of the will, Jack, the one who had been farming the land since he left school nearly thirty years ago, seemed to have come out of matters very poorly. The farm had been left jointly to him and Isaac.

We found this difficult to take in. I think we had all expected that, as the one who had lived, breathed, slept and eaten the land, the eldest would inherit the farm. Now he was going to have to somehow share it with Isaac! How was that going to work?

To be clear and complete, my twin had been left the business in the village; that made sense...he had been keeping an eye on it, even though he was in the police. I had been bequeathed a good sum of money and a very valuable site. Father and I had already discussed this, and he had obtained building permission for a replacement dwelling house on the second farm for my husband and I. Our sister in the nursing home had been looked after too, her upkeep promised jointly from the profits of farm and business. Mother was to be guaranteed full use of the farmhouse her day. However, when she passed away in the future, the house would belong to both brothers. That was just strange. How were they going to manage that, when they had found it hard to manage the relationship up until now, and them living a few thousand miles apart?

To be fair to Jack, while he had every right to resent the will back then, he had made a go of it over the intervening twenty-two years before his own death. He would have been entitled to grumble that his hard work on the farm during that period, not to mention the earlier years, was going unrewarded. He was only receiving half of what he was earning, less if you consider the amount needed to provide for our sister in the home. The other half was going to Isaac who, for all his charitable heart, had never done a hand's turn around the farm. I suppose my father's intention was to support the great medical work that was going on out there and, to his credit, I never once heard Jack complain about the arrangement. The big worry would have been what would happen when the missionary career was over, and the two brothers were going to be back in the old farmhouse together. How would that have worked out, Isaac retired, his wife with him, his children and grandchildren having access to the house, and Jack farming away as he had always done?

The issue never arose, of course. Jack's passing was not without blessing in disguise.

That was my husband's opinion anyhow. To me, though, it seemed that he was siding with father against my back-slidden brother, that there was an element of punishment in how the will was organised so as to partially disinherit Jack in favour of Isaac.

Could it have been because Jack had no children to be passing the farm on to, whereas Isaac had two, including a son who might just want to farm? Or might the decision have been a final judgement on Jack's sinful lifestyle, at worst a revenge for his abandonment of the family faith and practice?

I hoped not.

But one result of our father's decision about inheritance was that now, all these years later, there was a clearer and less contentious set of transactions after Jack's passing. With him gone, everything to do with the farm basically passed to the soon-to-return missionary brother.

Simple.

Simple, except that as I nursed Jack through his final few weeks on earth he made a few special requests of me.

Chapter 13

Passing

The final months of Jack's life have been difficult beyond words. We knew, as he knew, that his liver disease was incurable. But neither he nor any of us expected the end to come so quickly, so cruelly. Infection after infection had ravaged his failing body, poisoning him in a matter of a few weeks.

During the past summer I was available to be with him, being off school. In the autumn, however, I have had to take leave as it became apparent he wasn't going to make it through to Christmas. I didn't mind. Twin and I were all he had; we took it in turns to sit with the patient in his bedroom.

There was the farm to manage as well. My twin did his best, with neighbour Wally's advice, and my son did try to help when he was home. Jonathan's study in Belfast was all-consuming, however, so his assistance was patchy. My husband did try to lend a hand, undertaking some menial tasks at times, but, not being a country man, he struggled to know what needed doing…and I didn't like to be his foreman. The farm had been wound down to make it manageable, a number of animals sold, for example, as there wasn't going to be enough silage saved for winter feeding.

It had been my brother's wish to see out his final days at home, in his own place, rather than be in a hospice situation. There was nothing hospital or the medical profession could do for him, other than visit periodically to check if we needed anything. They were very good; the medications did their job, and Jack's pain levels were well managed with morphine patches and occasional injections. During that final ten days I was by his bedside more or less constantly. It was an incredibly challenging and, at the same time, a very special period for me. Sometimes twin was by my side, just watching sorrowfully, seldom speaking. He found it all over-whelming, seeing his robust brother so dramatically diminished.

I held my patient's hand, whether he was awake or asleep, conscious or out of it. I talked to him frequently, just general chat about memories of growing up on the farm with him, stories from the area and from our experience, sometimes asking him about his earlier life, the twenty-year period before twin and I arrived. He didn't say very much; he couldn't, but he did listen well to my waffling, for long periods his eyes never leaving my face. His speech wasn't great towards the end, very slow and slurred as the toxins built up in his system, seeming to stiffen his tongue. His eyes got more and more heavy. He was shrivelling up into the shell of himself, a metamorphosis in reverse.

A couple of days before he drifted into unconsciousness, he had a period one afternoon when he became quite animated. I have a theory that something prompted his realisation that this was it, that the angel of death was waiting just on the other side of this encroaching darkness. He squeezed my hand more tightly than ever, trying to turn over in the bed towards me. I struggled to hear his words initially, his voice a thin rasping wheeze, but he appeared to get strength from somewhere to communicate with me. It seemed to be very vital to him to get me to hear certain things.

He pointed to the dressing table.

"Open...top drawer...no, the other..."

He was pointing. I did as he bade me.

"There...two..."

"Alright," I said, "two envelopes, is that what you want me to bring you?"

He nodded. I did as he requested.

"Read..."

I looked at the scribble. His hand, shaky but clear enough. My name on one. Twin's on the other.

"Open!"

I opened my envelope, gentled out a slip of paper...no, a cheque. I read. Payable to Sarah Moore. Fifteen thousand pounds. My eyes widened. I looked at him, eye to eye.

"Him too," he said.

"Ok, thank you. I'll make sure to give this to him," I said, the big tears welling, blurring his yellowed face.

I was realising that this was his final will; he was bequeathing to the two of us in a private manner, no solicitor involved, no legal niceties. Maybe his experience after my father's death had made him think, 'I can do this just as well myself. No need to be paying a lawyer.'

"Lodge it....tomor...before I go. Him...too," he insisted hoarsely.

"Oh Jack, don't say that..."

"The piano," he whispered.

"The piano....downstairs? The one you bought me?"

"Aye." He winced and shifted his position on the pillow, pain etched on his gauntly jaundiced features.

"What about it? What do you want me to do with it?"

"Play it, for God's..." he seemed to smile, as if that was the obvious thing to be doing with a piano. "Take it up...up..." he nodded towards the hill.

"Take it to my house, you mean? But maybe it will be needed... maybe Isaac would like it left..."

He raised his hand, abruptly, almost agitatedly. "No...it's yours..."

"Ok," I said. "Thank you; I love it; always have. That other one up there...it's so tinny by comparison. It can take the high road."

Another tiny nod of the head.

"Do you wa...want...the pipes?" he asked painfully.

"I don't know, maybe one of the kids would like them, even as a keepsake," I answered. I couldn't see them being much use in our house, but I could understand what he was doing here; it was heirloom-type thinking; something that had been heart-valuable to the previous generation, something that, although he had never shown any interest in playing himself after whatever estranged him from his father, might be sentimentally valuable to the next generation. An artefact of lineage.

"Fishing...st...?" He pointed to a corner of the room between wardrobe and wall.

"You want me to take your fishing rods and all?"

"Aye...maybe the..."

"Yeah, sure," I agreed, with the unspoken idea. "Might be useful to some of the young ones. I wonder will the new generation across in the estate be as obliging regarding fishing in their stretch of the river as before."

A shake of the head, barely noticeable. He was tiring fast, sinking visibly into the pillow again.

"They'd need to have a lot better luck than you," I joked. "The big ones always got away, didn't they."

A weak smile that turned into a grimace halfway through. "Aye, always...got...away," he mouthed.

I thought that was it. I thought he was exhausted, that I had possibly heard his last words, but no...there was something else.

He was pointing, pointing across the room, to a painting hanging opposite his bed. The image he went to sleep looking at every night, and woke to every morning. A painting of the old castle tower in the Colonel's estate.

It was not a very attractive piece of art; dark, dusty, repressive. The monument itself was shrouded in a cold, blueish haze which seemed to resent the single splurge of sunlight that had somehow managed to penetrate through one of tower's 'eyes'; a glowering, crimson-tinged sky beyond guardian columns of leafless trees; thickly textured blobs of grey disfiguring the ancient edifice, looking like they might flake off from the canvas, break the glass and land on the carpet at any moment.

Was the artist just trying to use up a few tubes of colours that he or she couldn't get rid of any other way? I could never understand what my brother saw in the composition. It was a heavily framed piece of art that apparently he had picked up in an auction house somewhere when he had been in the habit of attending such sales. There was one very noticeable thing about this painting; uniquely, it was not adorned by a verse of scripture, unlike most of the other pictures left behind by my parents. The significance of this omission was not lost on any of us; it had often crossed my mind that this was his statement of independent thought, in his private domain, his bedroom.

"You take…"

"You want me to take the painting, is it?"

"Aye, but…" he reached for my hand, sort of stroking it. There was emotion in it. He was fading.

"Do you know who painted it? The signature isn't very clear."

A slight shake of the head. "No…idea," he breathed. Its significance was not artist-related then.

The door opened and twin came in. He joined us at the side of the bed, looking down at his brother with so much anguish on his face that I wished he would try to hide it a bit.

"How's things now?"

What a stupid and unnecessary question, but I let it pass.

"He's telling me about the painting," I said, for want of anything better to say. "He wants me to take it."

"Take it to the skip," twin said softly, trying to be jokey to hide his suffering.

Our brother reacted to the comment with a jerk of energy and agitation that surprised us both. We looked at each other.

"What is it?" I asked. "What is it you want me to do with the painting?"

"You, Sarah…you keep…it…always," he said, as much passion in his voice as he could muster.

"Ok, I will keep it, I promise. I won't throw it away," I told him. He squeezed my hand again; that was confirmation. Then he went on.

"Clean it…ok? It's all…filthy…full of dust. You take it…give it… good clean….inside 'specially."

This was a strange instruction, but I promised him I would do exactly that. He seemed to be exhausted by all this instructing he had been doing, but at least he had got off his chest what he wanted to say.

"The Saab…," he said. "Where is…?"

"It's safe. Down in the shed, covered over with that tarpaulin to keep the dust off."

How proud he had been of that great old car, maintaining it like it was a true vintage machine, rather than a mere twenty-something years old.

"Should we not leave the car for him to drive?" I asked.

He shook his head.

"Not him," he said. "The jeep…give him…the jeep. Yous…the … car."

I had no idea what we would be wanting with his car, but this was no time to argue.

"We'll look after the car," I told him, thinking that we might at least sell it on to some collector who would value it.

I still had the envelopes in my hand. I turned to twin and showed him.

"He's given us a cheque each," I told him. "Very generous."

"Lovely," he said. "Thank you very much. You shouldn't…"

Then he caught himself on; broke down briefly. The daft things you say when 'normal' is another country. But our dying brother was opening his eyes again, struggling up from under whatever wave of venom was trying to finally drown him, like a swimmer surging up for his last gasp of air. I took one hand, twin the other.

"You two…love yous."

"We love you too," we both said in unison.

"I…am…sorry…" A long pause, a quick flicker of a glance between twin and I. Then he whispered, "Please…forgive…..me."

A slow exhalation of breath. I thought he had gone. I was wrong. It was just exhaustion.

"We don't have to forgive you," twin said. "You haven't done anything that we have to forgive you for."

"But please," I begged him, "Please ask God to forgive you. You don't have to say it out loud. Just breathe it to Him in your heart."

A tiny shake of the head…or was it a nod? I cannot say, and I was there watching as closely as you can imagine. Did he pray? I don't know, but he still wanted to communicate with us, even though his eyes had closed for the last time. His two hands pressed on ours, and he whispered in the thinnest breath.

"You… two…"

Those were his final words.

I turned to look at his precious painting; I could no longer see it. Everything was a blur of darkened emptiness.

Thirty-six hours later it was all over.

Chapter 14

Painting

A couple of wintery months have passed since the funeral.

Mist swaddles the valley below, variable in density and thickest above the river and lake. I stand for too long, staring across its spread to the rounded hills in the west, lost in memories and imponderables. This is a frequent pose of late, I realise. What is wrong with me? Where has the in-charge, coping woman hidden herself?

I have had to talk myself into going back down to the empty farmhouse to begin sorting out my brother's things. I've put it off for too long, but Isaac's imminent return forces me into action. This will be a lonely job, a slow one too, despite the limited number of possessions Jack had accumulated over the years. I can imagine myself getting sidetracked and distracted by what I find in his wardrobe and cupboards. I tell myself to take my time, don't be feeling that I have to rush through the process. Let whatever emotions it stirs in me take their course; it's only fair to his memory, tough and all as this dismantling of his personal world will be.

His bedroom again. A sombre space, dull and shadowy in the dim light of the low wattage bulb. It had been his private cave, and it really had missed a woman's touch. I had aired the room, tidied everything up, and vacuumed the carpet thoroughly, just before he had finally succumbed to his weakness and taken to his bed. Now the windows need opening again to suck the mustiness out, maybe to let the sadness and regret escape as well. The clothing will need a good wash…I've put this off too long.

Sorting his clothes is straight-forward enough. He doesn't seem to have had much of a wardrobe, although I am surprised by some of the items I find; there are a few jackets, shirts and trousers that I am quite sure I have never seen him wear. Everything that looks like it wouldn't be welcomed in a charity shop goes into one set of black plastic bags. If I think that some item wouldn't look out of place in such a shop, it goes into a white bag. How well organised am I, I smile to myself. Black bags for the skip, white for the Christian Aid or Oxfam shops in town.

I check all the pockets, trousers, jackets, overcoats. I don't find very much of interest. A well-folded twenty pound note in the breast pocket of a beige-checked sports jacket, a sale docket from an auctioneer, a folded Alliance party flyer from the last election, and a receipt for the payment of a load of fertiliser.

At the back of his wardrobe, I find his famous leather jacket, grubbily brown, jaded looking. It reminds me of an ageing tiger, the original tan-coloured suede streaked with dark creases. No shame for it; the thing must be nearly fifty years old. In the pocket there is a cigarette lighter, and a cinema ticket for a movie called "The Land That Time Forgot". It flashes through my mind, momentarily and without welcome, that my brother may himself quickly become exactly that, the man that time forgot. I wonder what year this film was in the cinema. Might that have been the last time he wore this jacket? Why on earth had he kept it so long? It should have gone to a charity shop years ago. I am about to pop it into the black bag for the skip, but on a whim I change my mind, and put it with the charity shop consignment. You never know who might want it, maybe for a show or a fancy dress thing.

Next I tackle his book case; that slows me down even more, as I find myself browsing the titles. Many of these he has kept since childhood, the Biggles paperbacks, the Sherlock Holmes stories. A pile of fairly tattered war comics. I flick one open, out of curiosity. 'Boom!!' 'Wham!!' 'Blast!!' 'Grrrrr!!' 'Gotya!!' Thumbs up from a square-jawed, goggle-eyed pilot as 'Another Hun hits the drink!' Good grief, what richly descriptive language those writers used back then, I don't think.

Into a cardboard box everything goes; maybe a collector will find them, if I can get a second-hand bookshop to accept them. A different box, actually two boxes, for his collection of more serious novels, the A J Cronin books, Hemingway, Dickens and so on. Most of these I have never read, and I wonder if I should be keeping a few of these classics for future reading. I'm not sure, though, that my husband would appreciate several boxes of dusty books to add to the hoards that already clutter his space.

I am reluctant to cart boxes of these favoured books to a charity shop. To my mind, such places are the cemeteries of unloved stories…the sad shelves where words go down to die.

It crosses my mind to wonder how my brother was such an avid reader. He would have quit his schooling at fifteen; in his case, second-level education had consisted of a few years of practical training in the local Technical College, but somehow he had developed a love of literature. Then again, how did he ever get the time to read all these books, given how busy he and my father always seemed to be on the farm? I am forgetting, of course, that in his early days there wasn't the distraction of television in the house, so, if you needed your mind stimulated, reading was the only way to provide entry to those wonderful, imaginary worlds. I do recall from my childhood that in the evenings, after he had come in from the farm and had his dinner, he would disappear to his bedroom. If I ever had reason to go in to him there, inevitably he would be stretched out on his bed reading; he would hardly notice me enter, so engrossed was he.

The case containing father's bagpipes. I pull this leather-covered box out from below his bed. It really is a dusty relic of a different era, and that's before I open it to examine the cantankerous old instrument itself. I run a hand-hoover over it before leaving it out in my car. I'll take it back up home with me, maybe tell husband that I am intending to learn to play the bagpipes. That will give him some pause for thought. Maybe I'll tell him it's all in 'the plan' for this next phase of my life. Time to emulate my father. Awaken the inner lowland Scot in me.

The fishing gear I will keep for twin, or maybe for my husband. I swither about what to do with boxfuls of tattered farming magazines that he has hoarded, the Irish Farming Journals and Farmweeks. I could bin them, take them to the neighbour who might want them, but I think I will leave them for the returning brother. He might learn something from them. Like how to run the farm.

His watch I will keep as a memento, there can be no harm in that. 'Keeping an eye on the time' was always one of his noticeable little idiosyncrasies. He was a great watch-checker. Now that life is behind him, I wonder about 'time' on the other side of death. Eternity doesn't sound like it will be made up of tiny slices, like days and hours, let alone minutes and seconds, does it?

All the medications from his illness I put in a cardboard box. I will return these to the Health Centre in case they are of any use. Shaving kit and aftershave I will leave for brother. I open a bottle and sniff it. The scent is very evocative of a pine forest, I think, spruce or some such, but I don't recall ever smelling it on him. The bottle is pretty full, so I am guessing he seldom used it, maybe just on those rare and secretive occasions when he disappeared somewhere for an overnight stay.

When I have filled up my car with bags of clothes and boxes of books, I return to the room for a final look around.

The painting.

It scowls down at me accusingly. Had I forgotten? No, but I had put off taking it down from the wall until now. I am not sure I want this piece of art; I am not sure if it even merits the name 'art'. I nearly wish I had asked twin to store it in some out-of-sight place where its dismal presence could not annoy me. I stand at the bed, arms folded after my busyness. I study the thing. It really has collected a coat of cobwebs and grime over the years it's been hanging here. The substantial frame will need careful cleaning with some powerful detergent; the glass as well, on both sides by the look of it. Afterwards I will see if that measled staining on the canvas itself is mildew, or actually part of the texture of the art.

I take it down, resentfully, almost angrily, from its wall mounting. It is heavier than I anticipated, the wooden frame must be of good quality hardwood. I lay it face down on brother's abandoned bed. The rear panel of the thing, a rectangle of bland hardboard, actually feels less threatening than the composition of the painting itself. I should wait until I have it on my kitchen table back at home, but my fingers seem to have developed a will of their own.

The little swivel fasteners on the back turn surprisingly easily, all eight of them. I gently prise the back up from its bed, and remove it from the frame.

My heart lurches in my chest.

I'm still holding the panel. What is this underneath? What am I seeing here? I am freaked out by…oh-my-good-grief!

I am looking at a secret store; the space between panel and canvas is filled with…with envelopes, white ones, buff coloured ones. Most, I notice, have addresses. A few have just my brother's Christian name. 'Jack'. There are random little notes, some scribbled verses on ragged pages torn from who knows what. And there's an old dog-eared notebook, hard-backed, faded royal blue, like from school days.

These are all jammed inside, in this Aladdin's Cave of mysteries.

My mind is in a turmoil, my hand at my mouth, my heart a butterfly fluttering in my chest. I am hugely curious, but there is also a shudder of trepidation coursing through me.

What have I uncovered?

It strikes me, even at this early stage, that this is what my dying brother was on about when he was so irrationally insistent on me taking this painting…and especially his instruction about cleaning it.

What had he said? 'Give it a good clean…inside'?

This is what he intended. He is speaking from beyond the grave. Time may be of no account in eternity, but communication clearly is. Reputation may not matter where he is now, but self-explanation certainly seems to be echoing from the other side of the curtain.

I am shaking in anticipation as I lift out one of the envelopes. I study the address.

Mr Jack Shaw
C/O Mr James McGrath
East Gate Lodge
27 Church Rd
Castlecuinn

A letter to my brother, but 'care of' a James McGrath? Who is this James? Of East Gate Lodge, Church Road? Suddenly I realise…, of course, it's Jimmy, Jimmy McGrath, our old workman on the farm. This is the most bizarre thing ever. Why would a letter to my brother be sent to Jimmy, and to that address when it could have just as easily have been addressed to him at our farm, less than a mile distant?

The answer is fairly obvious, just as the secreting away of all this material is obvious. It was not meant to be seen by anyone here at home, not during brother's lifetime anyhow. But now I seem to have been chosen to be the recipient of this intelligence, of this hidden world.

I replace the envelope in its exact place. I dare not open it yet, despite my curiosity as to who it is from. Instead I lift one of the torn-out pages, and read the short verse on there. A poem, of sorts. My brother had written a poem? Maybe many poems, now coming into the light of day after he has departed into the darkness of eternal night.

I read it slowly.

Eve and the apple did for me
The apple that fell too far from the tree
Sweet to begin with, bitter as gall
An old rotten apple due to the Fall

Incredible. The man was a tortured soul, that is for sure. What had he meant by this? That he was different, that he felt himself to be rotten? He is clearly referencing that old Ulster adage, 'the apple didn't fall far from the tree', meaning that someone takes after their father or mother. Is he saying that he has been the antithesis of that? I can see that he might easily have thought this; he may have looked a bit like our father in his prime, but he was entirely the opposite in his lifestyle and values. In that sense, yes…he had ended up far from the tree of his parents.

And the whole apple analogy? The Eve reference? Was he talking about temptation?

It is totally intriguing. My brother, a writer, as well as being such a reader?

I put the page back in the frame.

The notebook. On the front cover I read his name, faded though it is.

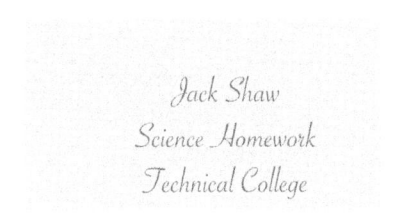

Jack Shaw
Science Homework
Technical College

I look inside. Clearly a fistful of pages have been ripped out, maybe half of the original contents. Presumably there wasn't much homework handed out in his College Science class in the mid 1950ies. There were plenty of pages left for him to use. And use them he has. The thing is filled with entries, more or less in the form of a diary, maybe even a scrapbook. Certainly a record of….well, of what exactly?

I sit on his old bed, and start at the beginning.

This is the brother I had never known. Had not been allowed to know.

This is his heart.

It's a sacred commission he has given me; a commission to try to understand him and his other world. The secret kingdom where he was himself, where he hid away from his parents, his siblings.

I begin at the beginning. The first page of his old notebook. The letters can wait, despite the curiosity raging inside as to their author, their contents.

My heart is a kango now, hammering in my ribcage, pulsing my bloodstream, thumping in my ears.

Chapter 15

Journal

To whoever uncovers this archive and reads this account, I make this explanation.

Throughout my life, a very ordinary and mundane one I think, I kept a brief diary. I suppose it was a way of trying to add some significance to the hum-drum routine of my days. A diary for every year, a Christmas gift from Anderson's Farm Feeds. If you were to read these you would find details of that great day when I bought my first car, the day my Kerry Blue cow calved, the week when the corn was sown in 1965, who won the 'best bull' at the Balmoral Show that year. Nobody needs to read these details.

But some events need a more full description, for reasons that will become clear. I have used my diary to help me, all these years later, to write about the one and only love of my life. So it is a tale of two people. I could write a chronological account of our relationship, telling the bare bones of the story. I am afraid that such a dry account of events might bore a person to death, therefore the skeleton will have flesh and blood, pleasure and pain, dialogue and dreams. So, while this may not be the 'novel' that tells the story of my life, it will most likely be the only record of those special moments which gave meaning to my lonely existence.

Let me take you back to my late teenage years.

28th March 1959

Today, the beginning of something beyond me, I think. I hope.
During my afternoon shift in the estate two unusual things happened; the first

was that a curious young robin perched on my fork, studying me for ages with an angled stare. It had no fear of me, and almost seemed to want to have a conversation. Soon after it left me I heard an unusual sound, one that jarred against the forest's chittering birdsong.

The rattle and crunch of bicycle wheels on the gravel.

I paused my scything for a second. Looked out through the branches of rhododendron.

I was right. A black bike. It was being ridden by a girl. She pedalled slowly toward me from the direction of the Manor House.

Below the noise of her transport I caught another sound, faint, sweet, melodic. She was singing. Maybe humming is a better word, for there were no words with her tune.

And as she came adjacent to me I noticed her face.

No words for her face either. I couldn't take my eyes off it.

I am no expert connoisseur of the features of the human female face. I'd have more experience judging the best Friesian cow from a line up in an agricultural show, to be honest. But straight away I felt that this girl's face is a really beautiful one. Very, very pretty, in a perfectly proportioned sort of way, fine features, not over the top, not exaggerated with a smearing of lipstick or the like, just naturally lovely. A face that is not unlike a certain film star whose picture I have seen on posters and advertisements... I can't remember the name of that actress though.

What struck me most about this cycling girl was her smile.

She wasn't smiling at me, at anyone; a smile to herself. It made an instant impression. It said, 'I am complete. I am fulfilled. I am happy from the inside out, for I know who I am and what I am about'.

She rode on past, towards the main gate. She didn't see me, secluded behind a bush, only my head staring out through its curtain. I was glad of its cover, for I could stare at her face and form without embarrassment or guilt.

As her back receded I took mental note of her clothes; a light blue jacket, some sort of knitted Tam O'Shanter hat pulled down tightly on her head so that I could not see much of her hair, a longish, dark skirt, flapping around, not really all that suitable for cycling.

Age? Hard to tell in that brief moment. Around my age, I was guessing. Maybe anywhere between 16 and 20.

Was she from the big house? I had never seen her before, not in all my time working here. Might she be a new worker in the place, a chamber maid, or kitchen girl? I didn't think so, not from that first look. The bicycle looked shiny new. She had an air about her that spoke of class, of security in her status. Maybe she was a visitor, but why on a bike?

My wonderings continued as the swinging scythe rhythm began again. Swish. Swish. And the memory of her song. Her face.

An Easter Saturday treat for me. I will enjoy this memory. Perhaps I will see her again. Perhaps not.

4th April 1959

I have seen her again. A repeat performance of a week ago, during my Saturday shift in the Colonel's garden. Subconsciously, perhaps, I had found myself staying as close to the main drive as possible, in case she should reappear. When I had reason to go to the tool shed or to another part of the estate I did so quickly, and returned as soon as possible. If she came again I didn't want to miss her, I was thinking.

Sure enough, my diligence was rewarded. I heard the same sound as before. A blackbird rose from the driveway, its strident alarm call ringing out above the other bird noises. I glanced in its direction. There she was, pedalling rhythmically towards me. This time she was riding from the entrance gate towards the big house. I was taken a little by surprise. I stopped my work and stood staring unashamedly, taking her all in. That same carefree face, relaxed, content in herself. No song this time though. Maybe she'd quenched it when she saw me observing.

I was only a matter of a few yards to the side of the drive. A rustic statue, motionless, fork in hand. Did she notice me at all?

The merest of glances, a sideways flick of her eyes without any pause or turn of the head. She by-passed me in a second and disappeared around a bend.

Where had she gone? What was she doing here? I thought I should investigate further. As soon as my immediate task was finished I decided my fork needed to go back to the shed. I could have taken the straight-forward route as usual. Instead I headed towards the Colonel's house, my eyes peeled for any sign of this mystery girl. Sure enough, I saw her bike propped against the ivy-covered wall near a side entrance to the mansion.

So she was inside? What would she be doing in there? She obviously rides here on a Saturday afternoon for some reason. She must live fairly close, certainly close enough for a bicycle journey. Yet I have never seen her before, not in school, not at any of our Young Farmer's Club functions, not at our church or any of its meetings. She is a complete stranger to me.

When would she be reappearing? Could I get another look at her?

I uttered a prayer to God that I would.

Is she as pretty as I thought, based on those brief glances from the patchy semi-shadows?

Unfortunately I wasn't able to stay in the vicinity of the drive during the remainder of the afternoon. The head groundsman found me loitering behind one of the statues in front of the house and chased me to the greenhouse behind.

"Watering to be done!" he told me. "You're slowing up"

So I went a-watering and missed my chance to see her again.

I won't give up though. I pray to God that she will return. I ask Him, beg Him, for a chance to speak to her. I cannot imagine how that will come about. I am too shy to step out into her path as she rides past. What would I say anyhow?

18th April 1959

Late afternoon, and she had not appeared.

Same as last week, when she didn't show up; no sign of a girl on a bicycle. I was almost convinced that I had made her up in my mind, just for someone to fantasise about when I lie awake at night. Can't be thinking about cattle all the time, nor counting imaginary sheep to get to sleep.

I gave up waiting and watching. I was wheeling a barrowful of weeds across the wide space of the turning circle in front of the house when I heard someone call. A small voice from behind.

"Hello. Hello. Can you help me please?"

I turned my head, wheelbarrow still in hand. She was there, standing still where the drive meets the yard. She was holding her bicycle, leaning it against her body, sort of tiredly, awkwardly. I put down the barrow and went to her, thinking all the time, 'This is it. My prayer has been answered. She has spoken to me. Thank you God.'

"Do you know how to put a chain back on?"

Her eyes fell away from mine to study her bike. Eyes that seemed to be naturally very bright of themselves. Not so joyful looking today. Worried, tired. Blue eyes, I think. She had wonderfully clear skin; there was a sheen that seemed to shine off it, putting me in mind of the smooth surface of a still pond. All this I took in as I approached her.

"No bother," I said.

It wasn't much, I know, but I had actually spoken to her.

I reached for the bike handles.

"Thank you," she said. "I am so late. Lady will be annoyed at me, after I missed last week."

"Aye, I saw you missed last week," I said.

What was I saying that for? She gave me a quick look.

"If I go on up to the house, do you think you could fix this? Please? I don't want to keep her waiting any longer."

She began to walk away from me, gradually quickening her step. I followed, wheeling the bicycle.

"No bother," I repeated. So articulate, I was! "I'll leave it there where you usually put it... after I've fixed it, like."

Another look over her shoulder, her feet scrunching on the gravel as she turned. She was giving me a faint grin now, curious, the mood changed.

"Are you spying on me then?"

"No, no! I just happened to see....I wasn't even looking..."

Ahead of us the front door opened, interrupting my stuttering denial. The lady of the house appeared, fussing, flapping her way toward us in her grand, flowing gown.

"There you are, Josephine dear. I was starting to wonder if perhaps you hadn't recovered from your influenza, but...splendid! Here you are. And I see Jack is helping you....what happened? Ah, your chain came off. Well, I'm sure Jack will have it fixed for you in no time at all," she said, the accent so English, so BBC Home Service. The Colonel's missus.

They disappeared inside, leaving me more than happy to be turning the bike upside down, then rethreading the chain on to the teeth of the front ring...it was easy enough. I've done it hundreds of times before, but never with such task enjoyment, never with such anticipation. The job was complete in a matter of seconds. I placed the bike against the wall where she'd left it before.

I should have left and gone back to my work, but it was difficult. I didn't want to miss the chance to connect with her again. I eventually dragged myself away with my wheelbarrow and dumped the weeds.

I was thinking, 'There must be something I can do along the driveway. If not I'll make some work for myself. How long will she be? It is much later today than on those previous times, so perhaps she will be out of there quite soon.'

So I wandered around the area between the house and the main gate. I brushed and raked moss off the drive; some of it was actually there, rather than just imagined. I hung around that area a whole half hour after I was supposed to be finished. It wasn't that I had forgotten about the milking, nor the fact that our workman only worked half day on a Saturday. My father, I thought, can manage the start of it this evening on his own. I would come up with some excuse, if only I could chat to her again, this Josephine.

Suddenly she was there, pedalling furiously, as if making up for lost time. I straightened up as she went flying past me.

After all that waiting, she had ignored me, disappearing around the bend, feet whirling like a dervish, long strands of auburn hair blowing out behind her like a horse's mane. She'd forgotten her strange wee hat. To say I was gutted would be a massive understatement. I threw down the shovel I'd been propping myself on in disgust, put my hands behind my head and complained aloud, "What happened there, God?"

But I was too quick to judge the situation.

As I picked up the shovel and turned towards the sheds I heard once more the sound I wanted to hear… tyres on gravel. There she was again! Was she pulling my leg?

No, no sense of that, no smile on her face. More apologetic, if anything.

"I'm sorry Jack," she said. "Very selfish of me. I should have stopped to say thank you for helping me."

She had called me by my name? She was acting so normally now, so sweetly. Where had the panic gone?

"No bother," I said....yet another time. "How'd you know my name?"

"Same way you know mine," she said. I didn't understand. She must have seen the bewilderment on my face. "Sure didn't her ladyship call you Jack. Anyhow, she was telling me all about you."

Goodness, I thought.

"Telling you what?"

"Telling me how good you are, how kind, how hardworking...how handsome....all that sort of stuff."

This time there was a bit of mickey-taking in those eyes of hers. A definite twinkle of fun. I couldn't help but laugh in response.

"Ok, Josephine," I said, a bit of playful snark in my tone. "But it's not exactly very fair, for I know nothing about you, except that you don't know how to fix a bike chain....that and your first name."

"Well, don't call me Josephine for a start," she told me. "Just Josie."

So Josie is what I will call her. We talked a bit more, but I was conscious of her wanting to get back on the road as she was running later than usual. She told me she lives in the town, (that maybe explains why I have never come across her before), and she rides out here most Saturdays for singing lessons. The Colonel's wife had heard her sing at some festival, and thought she could benefit from formal coaching. I found out all that in a matter of a few minutes, then she was on her way again, pedalling down the drive as ardently as before, but not before I had plucked up the courage to say one more thing to her.

"Well, stop and talk a bit longer the next time, all right?"

"I might," she said with a sideways smile.

Chapter 16

Young Love

Tempted and all as I am to continue, I have to end my reading there for the time being. Things to be done at my own place. I pack the notebook into the frame again, neatly cosied with those intriguing letters. What a different complexion this painting has just taken on. To think I ever considered giving it to twin, or, worse still, sending it to a charity shop, or the skip! What a terrible mistake that would have been. What an unexpected privilege to have found these documents, to have been so cleverly guided to them, to be allowed this confidential insight into Jack's early life. I look long at the painting again. Now it is as if I have a Picasso on my hands, or a long-lost Rembrandt that had been hiding in plain sight, a priceless masterpiece that no amount of money could prise away from me.

This is the brother I never knew; the young romantic. It is the brother of the fifties, of the time before I was born, of the Don Everly hairstyle, the man I only knew of from black and white photographs.

I leave the boxes for another day, but not this precious painting. It may not be easy on the eye, but I cannot allow it out of my sight. Carefully, I carry it downstairs, put it in the boot of my car.

As I drive back home, I cannot help but wonder how on earth Jack ever became influenced by pop culture. Television was banned in our family way back then, and even in my sixties childhood. It was thought to be too much of a two-way window; yes, we could see what was happening in the big world, but we would be led astray by all the evil influences out there. The immoral Hollywood films; the rock and roll music with its suggestive dance; the disgusting fashion trends; the smutty humour. According to my father, and, to be fair, according to all the preachers we ever listened to on the mission-hall circuit, the television was Satan's eye in the living room corner. I think it must have been 1970 before our father bowed to pressure, and bought a tiny, second-hand, black and white TV. 'The Adventures of Rupert Bear' sticks in my mind as my first essential television viewing; the poor bear had to make do with faded grey clothing back then, rather than the bright reds and checked yellows of the Christmas Annual. Our childhood wasn't so much sheltered as incarcerated.

I suppose my brothers had access to the wireless back in the fifties, and so would have heard the likes of Buddy Holly, and Elvis, and the beloved Everly Brothers. I can't imagine that they had any sort of sound system back then; maybe they had, but if so they would have had to play their LPs at very low volume so that father wouldn't hear. No devil's music in his house.

I do have a recollection of a record player at some stage in my childhood; seems it could only play sacred music. Hymns and spiritual songs, and the odd album of Scottish pipe music which had somehow slipped past the censor.

No doubt that, for my older brothers growing up in the fifties, newspapers and magazines had been their main access to the world of pop culture, to modern styles of clothing and hair. From the early photos of my eldest brother, it was plain to see that he had really bought into those styles. I have to admit that he looked like a really 'with-it' teenager. The mystery had always been around why, with his good looks, he had never seemed to have a lady in his life. Now that mystery may be about to be solved, or at least turned into myth.

He had had, at very least, a strong infatuation with this Josephine girl, she of the blue eyes, the translucent skin, and the noisy, black bicycle. This forty-eight year old diary seems to have the evidence, if that is what it is, a diary, and not a piece of fanciful creative writing on his part. That suspicion flits briefly across my mind, but it doesn't survive the realisation that there are letters in the frame as well. More documentary evidence which surely he could not have forged. Presumably these are from Josephine? I can barely wait to check that out.

I start to wonder as well if there are any photographs of her inside the picture frame. What did she look like? Yes, I know about the hair, the luminous complexion, the playful smile, but I really want to see her for myself. Surely, if this relationship developed, as the trail of letters seems to suggest, he will have had a picture of her? My fingers are crossed up to my elbows that there will be. I can barely wait to investigate further, once I get the man of the house fed and back up to his study out of my hair, so I can open up the frame again.

25th April 1959

I could hardly contain myself all during this past week. Sleeping was difficult; the anticipation of our conversation on Saturday coloured every waking moment; work was such a pleasure. My father asked me some awkward questions about what was giving me so much joy. Had I had some Divine revelation in my life? Found a new purpose in living? The answer, of course, was a clear 'Yes', but I couldn't be admitting that to him. He would only have pried into it, trying to find the truth. I have learned to only let him see the bits of me that I want to disclose, keep the rest well hidden. I know he wants the best for me and all that, but he really does slam down on most things that give me a bit of excitement, so…no! He won't be finding out about this girl, not yet, not for a good long time.

Our conversation today. I will treasure it always, even if, when I think back over it, not much of any significance was said.

She had ridden her bike past me on the drive, pretending to ignore me again. Such a tease of a girl. Then she had stopped further along the gravel and shouted back to me. Something like, "I'll only be an hour or so. Wait for me at the gate, if you can drag yourself away from those marigolds."

It was hard to judge her mood. She was unusual in that respect, always doing the unexpected, an impetuous streak in her leaving me continually puzzled. At least I knew that she wanted to talk, after she had finished her lesson, or rehearsal, or whatever she was doing in there with the Colonel's wife.

I waited just inside the gate as she had suggested, a bunch of those beautiful orange flowers held behind my back. The gate lodge on this side of the estate is unoccupied at present, unlike the one on the east side where our workman lives. I had spent the time pulling weeds from around the old place, just in case the groundsman, or the Colonel himself, should happen to see me there. I had a great pile of docks and grass dumped behind the wall by the time she appeared, so I hadn't wasted my time. She took the marigolds from me with a sweet smile and a slightly facetious "Thank you, kind sir".

What did we talk about? She had lots of questions about me, to be honest. For a while I didn't think I was going to find out much more about her, such a relentlessly questioning conversationalist. Why did I become a farmer? Did I enjoy it? Every bit of it? Was I always going to be a farmer? What did I enjoy most about it, machinery or cattle? Where had I gone to school?

All easy enough to answer; the last one gave me the chance to ask her where she had gone to school. Turned out she was still at school. She laughed at me for thinking she was old enough to have left school already, but I don't think that was fair. After all, she is just about to do her Senior Certificate in some school in Belfast where she is a boarder, she says. I didn't catch the school's name if she said it.

"If you are boarding at a school in Belfast, how come you are here on Saturdays?" I asked, logically enough.

"I come home every Friday night on the bus," she told me. "My daddy likes me home at weekends. He's lonely, on his own."

"On his own?"

"My mother passed away," she told me. "I never really knew her. She was only thirty five when she died; it was just after having me. She had married my father when she was twenty nine; he was a lot older than her. He heard her sing in an opera in Belfast, and fell in love at first sight."

Gosh, that took the wind out of my sails.

I didn't know what to say to her, other than mutter something like, "I'm very sorry about that, Josephine."

"Josie," she said.

"Josie," I obeyed.

Imagine never knowing your mother though! I felt so sorry for her, but she seemed quite blasé about it. Maybe that was just a front she has had to learn to put on. I am sure that, deeper under the surface of her happy personality, she hurts about it.

"So your father must be loaded if he can send you to school in Belfast?" I asked. Not a suitable question for our first real chat, but she was ok with it. Just passed it off as a bit of a joke.

"Yeah, sure we live in a castle, with a moat and a guard dog. Keep out any fellas that come looking for his daughter!"

"Really?" I replied, playing along. "It's just as well nobody's going to be coming looking about her any time soon."

I got a playful slap on the shoulder for that, but managed to catch her hand for a second or two. She didn't object too much, allowing me to hold on until I got embarrassed and let it go.

"Talking about castles," she said, "Daddy tells me that there is some ancient ruin in the grounds of this estate, a fortress that used to belong to his clan, way back in history. Do you know it?"

Another surprise from her. I know about this place, of course I do. My father told me a bit about it, and I've had a look around the ruins after I started to work here.

I volunteered to show it to her there and then, but she looked at her wrist watch and frowned.

"That would be great, but I need to be going," she said. "Maybe another time?"

Absolutely another time. Like next week?

So we fixed our first date. She will tell her father that she is having extra time with the Colonel's wife next Saturday. I will finish work early, so I can go home, do the milking, and be back to meet her about half six or seven o'clock. Hopefully I'll have time for a quick wash and change of clothes. I don't want the smell of cow dung to be putting her off, although judging by that glow in her eyes as she left me to cycle home, I don't think anything is going to put her off. She looks as happy, and as hooked, as I am.

Goodness. My brother!! Such a romantic. And to be writing all this down, as if he's some sort of early day Adrian Mole, but aged eighteen and three-quarters. For a brief moment I wonder if, when he was recording the progress of this affair, he had any notion that someone else would one day be reading it. Of course he did; he had virtually pointed me in the direction of this account. He was not writing this simply for himself, I am sure. He wanted us to read it.

Had he any sense of a wider audience, beyond family? Was he writing it as a sort of cathartic experience, in some strange way to help him process what was happening to him, this first love of his? Is this his attempt to give a commentary on his emergence from teenage shyness into adulthood? Had he also perhaps written a diary so as to consider his next steps in the relationship, a reflective prompt?

It strikes me that, even if this wasn't the writing of my enigmatic late brother, I would still be captivated by the story.

I would love to be leafing through those envelopes still lying undisturbed in their time capsule, to see what this Josie is finding to write so many letters about. His story is fascinating so far; I'm sure her take on the relationship won't disappoint either, but it will have to wait.

Chapter 17

The Cellar

2nd May 1959

Today has been even more special than I could ever have imagined.

She was waiting for me by the entrance gate. More pretty looking than ever, in a short black jacket and light blue denim jeans. I hadn't seen her in trousers before; my parents wouldn't have approved of them, I am quite sure. Much too suggestive! Why had she not worn jeans for her cycling earlier? She really suited them, I thought. I couldn't take my eyes off her, so shapely, so attractive. She came straight away to meet me, came so close to me that I got a full whiff of her perfume. I was finding this all so hard to believe; it was all I could do to hold myself back from taking her in my arms right there and then, whether we were being watched or not, whether or not we were only in the early stages of getting to know each other, whether she wanted me to or not...and I found that last bit hard to judge. I didn't want to misunderstand her, to rush her beyond what she expected, what she wanted.

Neither of us said anything. It didn't seem necessary to speak. Our eyes were doing all the talking. It wasn't really an awkward silence either, it just seemed quite natural, full of mutual realisation of what was happening here. She blushed a little bit I noticed, probably taken aback by my wide-eyed stare.

"Come and see this castle," I said, and started leading the way along the inside of the tall boundary wall, in the glade between it and the first stand of moss-sheathed trees. She caught up with me in a second and slipped her hand into the crook of my arm. Maybe it was to steady herself on the uneven ground, but it

was like an electric shock to me; she had made the first move of physical connection, of affection. She was saying, 'We are a couple.' Inside I was screaming with joy, but I played it nice and calm, as if this was exactly what I expected, exactly the right thing to do. I gave her a wee smile of appreciation. Still no actual words from her. Didn't really need to be. The closeness of her body was doing all the talking.

It took us ten minutes to reach the old ruin. She stopped to stare from a distance. I studied her eyes; the dappled light through the rustling leaves above was making strange wee patterns on her face. She seemed disappointed.

"Doesn't look like much. Just a pile of rubble trapped in an ivy cage."

I didn't know what she had expected.

"What did you say about your father's clan?"

"Just that he told me about this place. Hundreds of years ago this was the castle of the O'Cuinn clan. They ruled this part of the world. It was their territory before Plantation."

"Oh right," I said, not knowing much about what she was talking about. "Not a lot left of it. Just that tower and a few bits of walls. And the cellar."

"What cellar?"

I told her. She wanted to see it. So we climbed down the crumbled flagstone steps. I gave the door a good thump with my shoulder. It opened fine. I stepped forward...but my face immediately encountered an invisible obstacle. A regiment of spiders had strung a whole web of defences across the space. My head jerked back in surprise, like I'd encountered a taut elastic band across my eyes; I wasn't ever a big fan of spiders. Josie laughed at my squeamish reaction. Bravely I swallowed my phobia, picked up a nearby sycamore branch and slashed my way inside through the gossamer curtain. She followed me. It was very dark, just a thin shaft of wintery evening light following us shyly, angling down from above. She shuddered against me, as if cold. Or maybe scared.

Either way, my arm went around her, all very naturally. She turned into me. My other arm joined in. Hers too, one hand reaching up to my face, touching my cheek, inviting. And then we were kissing. Nibbling at the start, like two donkeys, then all in, wet-mouthed. Pulling tightly against each other. I never felt a girl's breasts against me before. Exciting beyond belief. Like that for ages.

"Josie, is this what you wanted?"

"What do you think?"

"But... why?"

"What do you mean, why?" she asked.

"I mean...why me?"

"Why not you?"

I was loving our closeness, but I had so many questions. This was a whole new experience for me, but maybe not for her. Maybe I was just the latest one of a number of boys, the one who happened to be around at the minute. It all seemed to come so naturally to her, whereas I was still in some kind of shock. Yes, the prayers that I had so often sent up to heaven were being answered, and in a way far above what I could ever have imagined, but I was reminding myself that I didn't really know this girl yet. She didn't know me much either.

"Alright, don't get me wrong...but I need to know if..." I couldn't finish this sentence.

"You need to know what?"

"If you ...if you do this a lot? Like, if you have had a whole string of boyfriends?"

She pulled away a little bit, still holding me, but at arm's length, to study me, weigh me up.

"You don't think that's a sort of insulting question to be asking me?"

"I didn't mean it to be insulting. I am sorry if it sounded that way. But with you being away at school in Belfast, you know? For all I know you could have had....Look, I am just a farmer boy, stuck out here in the country. You must see that I am confused."

Now she was laughing at me, a touch derisively.

"I could ask you the same thing. You've only talked to me a couple of times and here you are kissing me in the dark. How many other girls have you had down here...or anywhere, for that matter?"

"That's easy, Josie. You would be the first girl I ever kissed. And if you are the last I will be perfectly happy."

She came straight back into my arms at that. More kissing. Then she pulled away just far enough to answer my queries.

"You want to know about Belfast, about my school. For a start it's all girls. Not even a male caretaker. Not a boy in sight. Any boy that came near the school would be taking his life in his hands. Our nuns are a fearsome bunch of women, for all their piety."

A pause. A pause in which I probably gulped and thought, 'What? Nuns?!? Wait now...'

"Nuns?"

She looked at me, gauging my surprise I suppose. Maybe surprised herself at whatever shock she read in my reaction.

"Yeah, nuns...women in long black dresses and..."

I didn't quite pick up on her sarcasm straight away. "I know what nuns are, it just never dawned on me that you are..."

A little moment of Ulster-flavoured silence.

"That I am Catholic? Always have been. Why? Is that a problem for you?"

"No, no problem...not for me. You could be a Hindu and it wouldn't make any difference to me...it just never occurred to me, that's all."

"Good, for it doesn't make any difference to me either that you are...whatever you are. What are you anyway?"

"Presbyterian."

"Presbyterian? You'll have to explain all that sometime…when we run out of things to talk about."

"I can't see that ever happening," I told her. She came back into my embrace. I heard her mumbling against my chest.

"And by the way, we are even."

"How do you mean, we are even?"

"I mean you are my first boy as well."

"Are you serious?" I said. "You can't be telling the truth… you're too pretty to never have had a boyfriend."

She laughed again.

"Sometimes you know how to say the right things," she told me. "There have been a few fellas that I have liked, but I never really had the chance to connect with them. And I was always curious how it would be when…when I met a boy I really liked, when I fell in love for the first time."

"And are you still wondering?" I asked, mischievously.

"Maybe," she smiled, "and maybe not."

When she pulled away it was slowly, reluctantly.

"The time," she said. "I should likely be going."

I walked her back out to where she had hidden her bike behind the disused gate lodge, and watched her ride away. A final turn, and wave, and she disappeared around the twist of a bend.

My run home along the inside of the boundary wall was the most exhilarating of my whole life, punctuated by mad leaps of delight, every step full of the best memories, every breath an expectation of next week's meeting with her.

I have a plan as well; to come back before then, clean up the cellar a bit, smuggle some old blankets to it, maybe a couple of candles, make the place more welcoming, homely. Our secret place.

Chapter 18

Fear

So many things are running through my head after this read. My thoughts are all in a jumble. I need to take time, straighten them out.

Fear!

Fear is my main reaction. I feel the same overwhelming dread that I recall so clearly from that occasion in my childhood when Jack took me down into that same cellar at the castle ruins. I think that experience has also tainted my opinion of his painting, now staring me out across the space of my bedroom from its new position. There is a hint of triumphalism on the face of the old tower, in its gaping eyes, those irregular embrasures beneath its jagged battlements. I have propped it against the mirror of my dressing table. At the moment, its presence seems to suck the light out of the room. I take a second to turn the image around so it faces the other direction; it can have the benefit of bouncing its depressing glare back and forward between canvas and glass. The sense of foreboding remains with me, however. I cannot explain it, this recurrence of earlier feelings, except to say that I can sense no good ending to this story of my brother.

Here he is, writing with such vitality and enthusiasm about a girl he has only just met. A girl who is Catholic. From those final words about 'our secret place', the cleaning up, the blankets, the candles, it doesn't take much imagination to realise that some instinct is kicking off in him. A primeval urge to provide a home, however basic and temporal, for his new girl? The creation of a love-nest, in a place of seclusion, of darkness? And underground? His dream world.

This could become a tomb for whatever faith he still had at that point. I do not sense any check in his spirit about the course he is embarking on with this girl. Yes, she sounds lovely, very sweet, far too affirming of him, but I don't have to read too fancifully between the lines to sense her seductive charms, whether conscious or not. Is his naivety drowning out any alarm bells that should surely be ringing in the ears of his conscience? Even apart from the whole physical temptation he was placing himself in, why was he not conscious of the folly of falling for a girl from the other side? This was 1959. It was double jeopardy back then surely. Even now there are parts of our province where such a relationship would be frowned on, and worse. Back then, and given his strict upbringing, what he was getting into was absolutely no-go territory, long before the expression was used regarding our political ghettoes.

I am feeling such trepidation already, and I am only a few pages into this revelation. It is beginning to read like a testimony to temptation, the very antithesis of the type of stories both he and I have heard so often in the missions and conventions, those thrilling 'testimonies' of redemption, of those whose lives had been turned around through coming to faith. He is playing with fire, drawn to it like a moth to a flame, where he should be running away from it. Different if I could foresee him leading this girl to faith; she could have become a cause célèbre in the mission halls. The testimony of a 'converted Catholic' always brought the crowds in. But that doesn't seem to have been on his radar at all.

That this is my brother speaking to me from 'the other side' is deeply disturbing. I am alone in this dungeon of dread; maybe I should be showing this account to twin, just to share the impact. I don't know how he will react, although I have a fair idea that he will not be impressed. His prejudices will be triggered, I am quite sure.

The other thing that is bugging me is the sheer raunchiness of the writing so far. One part of me is completely engrossed by his account, and by the style in which he has chosen to tell his story. I had never imagined my brother to have this kind of creative gift. It is as if he was writing a script for a movie or for a play. I almost expect some stage or lighting directions. To include all that dialogue between him and his lady, as if he had recorded it, is incredible. Did he really remember all that detail of their chat, or could he be simply making up how he wished the conversation had gone? The same goes for the detail of this blossoming intimacy between him and this Josie. Is it mere wishful thinking, the fantasies of a repressed teenager?

So on one level it is an intriguing account of his experience, especially of his thought processes as he falls in love for the first time. On a completely different level, however, my current reaction is this premonition of disaster. I do not want to be turning a page and reading graphic details of what may come soon in this relationship. It is strange territory for me to be walking in; the excitement of this discovery is breath-taking, the fear of the temptation equally heart-stopping.

I cannot help wondering how my father and mother would have reacted to this account, indeed if they had ever had any knowledge of this double life their son was leading. Perhaps they had; perhaps this has been the source of the many rows…

Suddenly I am remembering.

A time-travelling flash-back to the mid seventies. I am listening at the kitchen door. Twin and I together. In our pyjamas. We must have been fifteen at the time. It was an unforgettable row, a shouting match downstairs that had awakened both of us from our sleep.

As I recall, it was immediately after St Patrick's Day, so a bleak March night, and, yes, I remember the cold of the corridor tiles on my bare feet...but nothing was going to drag me from that drama.

Jack had been away for the weekend. There wasn't anything abnormal in that. He took trips away maybe three or four times a year, even the odd summer-holiday break on the north coast, or in County Down. He liked to walk and climb in the Mournes. Sometimes it would have been a fishing weekend, or some Young Farmers' Club outing to the South. The farm was fine on those occasions, our father was still in his prime as a fifty-something year old, and anyhow, our man, Jimmy McGrath, was available for milking duties, being so close at hand to the farm. We had no idea, most of the time, where Jack disappeared to. There were no mobile phones in those days; we had no way of getting in touch with him, unless he happened to phone to ask about an animal or something. He frequently would have done that on his excursions. There had never been any issue.

To be fair to him, on this occasion he had told the parents exactly where he was going beforehand. He planned to climb some mountain in Co Mayo called Croagh Patrick. That had caused an argument before he even set off. My father was not happy with him crossing the Border, and driving so far into the Irish Republic, just to climb a particular mountain. His point was that things were not safe anywhere at that time in the country. The troubles were at their worst. There had been terrible violence in South Armagh just a couple of months previous to this trip of his. Six ordinary Catholics had been killed there, and the following day ten Protestant workmen had been taken from their minibus and shot in cold blood at a place called Kingsmill. My father's point had been strongly argued. Even apart from the risk of running into trouble, what would be wrong with staying in Northern Ireland and climbing Slieve Donard again? A mountain is a mountain. No point driving all that way just to climb what Catholic people thought was a holy mountain. Who could prove that St Patrick was ever anywhere near it anyhow? And, if that aspect was all-important, why not climb Slemish much closer to home, a mountain where Patrick definitely had been? Didn't he mind sheep there?

But Jack had been determined, and nothing could stop him. The fishing was good in Mayo. He had headed away to the west.

What was really different about this time, though, was that he had been seen down there.

From what we were able to piece together from the fragments of shouted debate, an uncle and aunt of ours had been in the area for some sort of charity conference; by unbelievable coincidence they had walked around a corner in Westport, and bumped straight into our brother.

And he hadn't been alone. He had a lady on his arm!

I can imagine the shock of all three of them. The woman, whoever she was, wouldn't have been phased by it of course, because she wouldn't have known these relatives, but Jack must have been mortified. I hate to think what their conversation was like, them standing there on the street looking at each other awkwardly. Introductions? No, from what I gathered none had been forthcoming. It had been brief, rude even, according to what our father was saying to Jack.

"So who was she, this floosy?"

Jack was not for saying. It was none of daddy's business.

But it most certainly was our father's business. A son bringing disgrace upon disgrace on this God-fearing family. Had he no shame, no sense of right and wrong? Had he not learned his lesson, after all this time?

"I have nothing to be ashamed of." That was Jack's line. "I am my own man. I am thirty-five years of age. You cannot be telling me what to do or how to live my life. It is literally none of your business."

Our father was incensed by this. "While you are in my house you will honour me as the Scripture commands!" He was really shouting. And so it went on.

"Are you going to throw me out?" Jack demanded.

Our mother intervened, begging them to stop it, to step back, leave it to the morning when their tempers had settled down; they were going to waken the wains and so on. Little did she know the wains were behind the door, ears, eyes, mouths wide open.

"Was it her again?" our father wanted to know.

"Her?" Jack said. "I don't know any 'hers'."

"You know who I mean. If I thought for one minute that you had gone back to… like a dog to its vomit, I would…"

"What would you do? Would you throw me out of the house again? Disown me? Disinherit me? Would you?"

"Don't be talking like that," mother pleaded.

Our father settled himself a bit it seemed. He took a different tack, a sort of preachy angle, more reconciliatory. Surely Jack could see the sinfulness of his ways? The hurt he was causing to the family, to his mother, to God Himself? The damage he was doing to the family's reputation? How could he, our father, hold his head up in the community? In the church? How could he preach another sermon in the mission hall when he couldn't stand over the actions of his own son?

"What I do in my own time is no reflection on you, daddy."

That was Jack's answer.

"Don't you see that God will hold you accountable for your sin? Don't you fear that He will visit vengeance on you for your immorality?"

"I don't see it that way."

"Well you need to see it that way! You will suffer for this. Don't come crying to me when some calamity strikes you. God will not be mocked. He will punish you and very soon!"

There was a bit of a pause at that point. I thought our brother was going to give in, make an apology, ask for forgiveness. Instead he said something he would probably always regret thereafter.

"So daddy, let me ask you this, talking about punishments and all that. What was the terrible big sin that you committed that God punished you for… by making Miriam handicapped the way she is? What was that punishment all about?"

Twin and I looked at each other then. I could not believe Jack had stooped so low in his argument. As we turned to flee up the stairs the last thing we heard was our mother crying like her heart would break. All we could hope for was that our brother would see how cruel he had been, and say sorry.

I have no idea whether he did or not.

Chapter 19

Destiny

9th May 1959

Our conversation today was all about life and destiny.
In the sense that we both felt we had been meant to meet the way we did. Sometimes we disagreed on who or what was behind this. Was it blind chance? Was it written in our stars? Was it God who willed this for us, Divine Providence, as Josie called it? Was the 'Moirae' behind us meeting as we did? I had never heard of this, the ancient Greek goddesses of fate, but Josie had studied about them in school. She didn't hold with it herself, just some old mythology, she said.
Was it maybe a combination of all of these ideas? We settled on that because, at the end of the day, who can prove it one way or the other. We were just so happy to have found each other that it didn't matter. I did tell her, a bit sheepishly, that I had prayed for God to send me someone special.
"And you think that's me?" she laughed.
"Yip. I have no doubt. You're pretty special, in my opinion."
She asked me if I had ever read any of Thomas Hardy's novels. I was really pleased to say that I had, 'Far From the Madding Crowd' and 'The Mayor of Casterbridge'. I had found those books very much to my taste. She had read them as well, among others, and was a big fan. 'Tess of the d'Urbervilles' was her favourite, and I must read it. She said it was the whole thing about fate in Hardy's writing that fascinated her, the sadness of opportunities missed through strange twists of fortune. I had to admit that I had maybe missed that point,

being more drawn to the agricultural setting of the books, the rustic and nostalgic feel of them. She laughed at me about this; called me 'Farmer Boy'. I pretended annoyance, but it was really just an excuse to grab her and tickle her into retracting the nickname. Then in a more secretive, mischievous tone she asked if I'd ever read 'Lady Chatterly's Lover'; I hadn't. I had heard of it, yes, but would never have contemplated reading it. Far too controversial for me, the whole immorality of it. She had been given it by a friend in boarding school; she'd been terrified that the nuns would find her with it, so, after reading it in secret she had dropped it in a bin somewhere.

"It's all about a posh lady falling in love with her gardener," she told me, "and the stuff they get up to."

"Sort of like you and me," I teased her.

She protested that we were not 'getting up to any such stuff', that anyhow, she was not posh, she was no lady... and I was no gardener either. I was a proper farmer. But when I pushed her to tell me about her background she had to admit that she was from a well-off family. Her father had his own business in the town and, more than that, he was very active in the Catholic church, a very respected member of the 'laity', whatever that was. Maybe similar to our elders, like my father.

"So he wouldn't have been too happy with you reading what Lady Chatterly was doing with her workman."

"Indeed he wouldn't. I think if I'd been found out with it in my possession in school I'd have been sent home to him. Doesn't bear thinking about!"

"And how would he feel about you lying here in the arms of a Protestant?"

She just held me tighter at that point. Didn't reply. She didn't need to.

"Likely the same as your father would feel if he knew you'd fallen for a wee Fenian," she said quietly. "Can we change the subject please?"

We did.

We talked about what we thought during those first glimpses of each other. Sometimes we laughed at the incongruity of the thing; her making such an unholy racket, peddling that rickety bike of hers, but at the same time singing as if she hadn't a care in the world; me standing like one of the Colonel's marble statues, propped up by my garden fork.

"When are these big exams of yours?" I asked.

"Next month. Don't spoil today though."

"This is your escapism talking."

"No, this is my therapy talking," she said.

I asked her what about after the exams, next year, the future. I was dreading the answer to that question and it probably showed in my tone, just that wee quiver of uncertainty. She drew herself away from me, sat up on the makeshift couch I had fashioned, her arms locked around her knees, and looked away into the curling candle smoke. I knew straight away it wasn't going to be good news. She took ages before answering too, making it worse.

"I'm going to Glasgow," she said.

Silence. I couldn't think of a thing to say. This make-believe world I had been creating was a mere mirage. It was about to shimmer into nothingness.

"I am to train in music at the Royal Scottish Academy," she said, "but I will be back at the end of every term."

I still couldn't speak.

"You'll wait for me, won't you Jack?.... Please say something."

"Sorry, it is just a shock, I suppose. But I should have seen it coming. You're smart. You have to go to college, of course you have. I wouldn't ever want to hold you back. I just hoped maybe…it would be here in Belfast or something."

"I know. But it was all settled before I ever met you. And also, it's not fully settled yet. I have to pass my exams first."

"You'll pass your exams, no fear of that," I tell her. "You're too brainy to fail.

You'll be gone in no time."

"Don't say that. We have the whole summer, from now to September."

"And then you'll disappear and forget me."

"Not a chance of that. I could never forget you."

It was a lovely time after that, until she had to go.

A last kiss. She left me.

Alone, I sat there thinking for ages.

I had the strangest sensation inside my chest; just an intense feeling of elation, something I'd never experienced before. It was beautiful and painful at the same time.

Eventually I folded up the blankets and stuffed them in the bag I'd brought, so as to stay dry for next time. All the time contemplating life, destiny.

I snuffed out the candles and closed the door behind me.

Chapter 20

Hepburn

It is very difficult to set this diary down. It has me spellbound. But things need to be done in the here and now, the real world. I need to be getting my mind readjusted to my responsibilities here in 2008.

I replace the notebook in the back of the frame. I am about to seal it all back up when I am overcome by the temptation to open one of the envelopes, just one. I have time to read one surely? But which one? Random pick? Or has the brother placed these communications in a chronological order? Perhaps he has, I think, because they seem to be sellotaped to the back of the canvas in straight lines…not like him to be so organised. The first row of envelopes have the single word, 'Jack', written on the front in handwriting that looks stylish and neat, kind of old-fashioned. The others have our workman's address, as I've said, bizarrely so, I think.

I pull the top envelope from its sticky anchor. It comes off with a small rasping sound, almost resentful, I imagine, at being ripped untimely from its secure bed; my fingers seem to shake with anticipation, as if, in the opening of it, the writer herself will materialise out of the ether.

Nothing of the sort happens. Inside is a single sheet of light blue writing-pad paper. My first instinct is to examine the signature. For some subliminal significance, I suppose. Nothing, other than

All my love
Josie XXX

No surname; I'm still waiting for that clue. There is also no date on this letter, so I will be trying to piece it into the timeline of brother's diary as best I can.

Dear Jack, she begins, simply enough, *I cannot begin to tell you how delighted I am to have found you, my dream guy, and to feel you return my love in the way you do. I am head over heels, (sorry about the dumb cliché). It feels so good. There you are, I've*

put it on paper for you!

That is one reason for writing this letter, so you can read those words when we are not together, just to remind yourself.

The other reason is to try to explain some things that I find it hard to say when we are together, partly because you are forever kissing me so that it's hard to speak, (ha ha), but partly also because I need time to formulate what I want or need to say.

So, for example, you asked me about being a Catholic. I think you said, "How important is your faith to you?" I have never been asked that question before, so I found it hard to come up with an answer. I didn't know what you expected me to say. I presume you meant, am I a committed Catholic, or just a sort of casual one, a nominal Christian?

Well, when I think about this question, it actually helps me to work out my own feelings about it, not something I have often done before, as I say. I have always just taken church and its sacraments and beliefs for granted, without giving it much thought. I suppose being in a Catholic school has just sort of cushioned me into a secure box of accepting everything that the church teaches me, about beliefs, and about our rituals. So, yes, I would say that I am a fairly loyal Catholic. I do say my prayers, most nights. I pray to God, and to our Blessed Lady, and to the Saints, especially St Anthony, for I need all the wisdom I can get, and to St Patrick because I am Christian due to the fact that he came to Ireland. I also like St Brigid, and I pray to her when I feel inadequate, which is quite often. But above all of these it is really Our Lord who is the centre of my beliefs and faith. From what you said last week, I think you are the same as me on that. Confession? Yes, I do go to talk to my priest every week, as we are expected to do. I don't seem to have much of significance to be telling him so far. I haven't confessed to our secret affair as yet. To me it is not a sin, so why would I confess it. Maybe I am a coward in this, just like I am unable to tell my father why I seem to be smiling all the time these days.

Different subject, but you asked me who is the film star, (the one you think I look like, ha ha!) the one in the advertisement for Lux soap. I couldn't remember at the time, but it's Audrey Hepburn, and I don't look like her at all. She is gorgeous, but thank you for the compliment anyhow. By the way, I can't believe you have never been to the cinema! You must come with me sometime. I would love that. We could even go to see a movie with your beautiful Audrey in it; you would enjoy that, wouldn't you? You could compare us. We should go to see her in 'The Nun's Story' when it comes out later this year. That would be fun, my Presbyterian boy holding my hand while watching a film about a woman in Holy Orders! Ah, I know we can't be seen together around here, so maybe it's impossible. But we could sneak away, and meet in Belfast if you want an adventure. We would never be seen there. (And you wouldn't have to confess it to your minister afterwards, so you're 'on the pig's back'…as you once said to me. What a lovely country expression.)

Can't wait until I see you again on Saturday, when I will watch your face as you read this.

God love her, she's well smitten with him, I think. And, to be fair, she sounds like a nice girl in this letter. Thank God it never came to anything though. It would never have worked, the mixed marriage thing. Two people have to be agreed about faith, the most important foundation of life and of marriage, I always think. My own situation is warning enough, and I am married to one of my own kind, albeit from a different denomination. The tensions we have faced, and continue to face, have driven us to separate bedrooms. Which reminds me, as I pack up this secret trove of memoirs, to make sure I never give opportunity for my husband to find out what I am doing when I am reading Jack's diary, and these letters. He would make a huge song and dance about the saga; he'd probably have some weird theory about it. I don't need any more of those. Hard enough to process the information without a theological commentary from him.

I do have to consider, though, how and when I will bring my twin into the knowledge of this affair. I am finding it hard to read him just now; I don't know how he is processing his grief, or if he is at all curious about those final words and instructions before Jack's passing. I have not seen him now for a few days as he is back running the business full time.

He is probably taking solace in keeping busy. Maybe he doesn't need to know about this Josie person, or of the growing relationship in the castle dungeon all those years ago. The same goes for Isaac, when he finally arrives back from India and moves into the farm. What they don't know won't do either of them any harm. I can maybe just keep it as a skeleton in the cupboard of my mind, and deal with it all there on my own terms.

In some ways, the disclosure of Jack's secret past has kindled some thoughts, perhaps even fears, about the love life of my own two children. While I have been going through this grief over Jack's passing, and now this fascinating trip into his diaries, it is easy to forget that my own two might well be having issues of their own. Both have been supportive throughout this period; there is a fairly constant stream of texts, from Christine in particular. Jonathan, if he is not home at the weekend, phones every week at some stage from Belfast.

My daughter, having gone to Bath to do Spanish and Business, has found herself an English boyfriend…inevitably, I suppose. She has the personality and the looks. The two of them seem very settled, both in their final year of study, and moving towards marriage. Christine will join the inexorable 'brain-drain' that seems to disproportionately affect my community. It's a big question…why so many young Protestants leave here at eighteen, never to return. Is it about opportunity, or is there something in our society that they are glad to be shot of?

Jonathan, my quiet introvert, is a more concerning conundrum. At the A Level stage he seemed to be going down a science route. I had hoped he'd choose a course in medicine, and for that reason sent him to spend a summer with Isaac and Lisa in India, family-holiday-visit meets work-experience sort of idea. If anything, that whole adventure seemed to divert him, and in more ways than one. He has been a changed boy ever since. Jonathan was always a deep thinker, ever the antagonist, the alternative-seeker. He switched direction entirely after India, forsook the sciences and ended up doing the Philosophy and Sociology course at Queen's. Now that he's completed first year, he wears a crust of cynicism that both I and his father find very challenging. While I argue blithely that this is just a phase he is going through, that all eighteen year olds have to process their doubts, in my heart of hearts I worry that the 'Jack-syndrome', the turning away, will repeat itself in him. Thankfully though, so far as I am aware, he does not seem to have developed any emotional entanglements in Belfast. No secret Josie… but then, would I ever know?

Chapter 21

Proposal

I have a free hour on a Sunday evening before tomorrow's return to the classroom. So I pick up my brother's story again as the two lovebirds progress through May, and into the critical examination month of June. I want to scream at Josie to forget about him for a few weeks, concentrate on her revision, the farmer boy can wait. I want to tell him to have a bit of sense, a bit of compassion and understanding for the girl. For all her apparent *joie de vivre,* and her relaxed attitude about the tests ahead, she must be concerned. Concerned that this delusional escapism with my brother is not doing her grade prospects any good. Being the self-preoccupied boy that he is, that he was, he will hardly have noticed such anxiety in her. His drivenness, his need for affirmation, indeed his lust for her, will outweigh any awareness of what would be good for her.

As I read these pages of thoughts and memories, it doesn't take me to have psychic powers to grasp that their relationship is heading towards a level of intimacy that will lead them into serious trouble if nothing happens to prevent it. For all the Christian values they have expressed to each other, I cannot help but feel they are on a very slippery slope.

I have read several more entries. It's all very sweet; his sense of romance, his absolute adoration of this girl, his care to make sure that that dank old cellar is as like a proper wee palace as possible for his princess. He takes her food; lemonade, bags of crisps, sweets and chocolate, apples galore. There's a fair bit of banter about the apples.

"Shouldn't it be you offering me an apple?" I asked her.

She didn't seem to get what I meant.

"You know, Eve and the apple? Adam in the garden of Eden?"

She just laughed. Told me she had no need to be offering me an apple from what she could read of me.

I wasn't sure what she meant by that and was about to ask, but she stopped my mouth at that point with another kiss.

It crosses my mind that his little verse about the apple falling far from the tree must have been written around this point in the relationship. What was that line?

Sweet to begin with, bitter as gall

Oh my! We are still in the sweet stage of the story, of course, but I cannot help wonder about the ominous flavour of the second phrase. What is the sting in the tail?

There are a few weeks when they don't get to meet because Josie, thankfully, is concentrating on her exam revision; the Colonel's wife has told her to take the month of June off from any singing, so she stayed home on those Saturdays. After the exams, however, in July the thing takes off again with a vengeance on the wasted month, it seems to me. They had missed each other so much.

"That was only one month," I told her, "and it felt like hell. We need to have some way of communicating with each other when we are apart."

We talked about this. No way can I send her a letter to her home. Her father would have a fit. Even worse if she tried to get a message to me at the farm.

"We need a system," she said.

I had the idea of finding a place where we could both leave any letters we wanted to send. Like in a hollow tree stump or something. We had a search around the disused gate lodge, and I found a loose capstone on the outside wall, with a perfect wee slot underneath.

I showed it to Josie.

"Ideal," she said. "If I want to send you a message I can leave it here for you."

"And vice versa."

We agreed this was our best plan, but she remembered that she won't be able to use this system when she is in Scotland. We joked about the address.

'Jack Shaw,

Gap Below Cap-stone,

Wall near Western Gate Lodge,

Castlecuinn Estate'.

We don't have an answer to that problem yet. It is going to be so tough for both of us.

"I will miss you every day," she said, more than once.

"What is it not going to be like waiting for you coming home from Glasgow?"

"You could plan to come and see me," she suggested.

Oh Lord, what is she thinking? My brother escape the farm, escape my father, to go off to be with his wee girlfriend for a romantic weekend in Scotland? I cannot see that that was ever going to happen.

Then another one of brother's entries has them talking seriously about marriage. Was he crazy altogether? They were both far too young to be thinking of such a thing. He had known the girl a matter of weeks, eight or nine at most, and here they were discussing what their future together will look like.

I asked her if she could see herself married to a Castlecuinn farmer? Especially after the sophisticated cultural experience she is going to be enjoying in the Royal Academy.

"As long as that farmer boy is you," she told me.

I said something like, "I know you are only eighteen, but…what I am asking is…can we consider ourselves engaged? Even if it's unofficially engaged, I mean?"

"I don't want to be with anybody but you," she told me.

"All right, I'll take that as a 'Yes'," I said, "but how about your father? How is it going to be for us, with me being Protestant?"

"I don't know the answer to that. I'm sure there have been others who have married across… we could find out from somebody else how to work it out."

"As long as you know I would never ask you to convert to be a Protestant, unless you wanted to?" I told her. "I am happy for you to be Catholic and go to Mass and all, if you are happy that I don't."

She smiled and said, "Sure isn't that the way we are now? Why should we change it if we were married?"

"And if we have kids?"

"Well, in my religion they are supposed to be brought up as Catholic. My father would likely try to insist on that, but we could think of a fair solution."

"Like what?"

"Like...alternatively. The first one goes with you, the next one with me...and so on. Or the boys with you, the girls with me."

I liked that answer. It showed she was not dogmatic about her faith and its demands on family. I told her that my folks would probably struggle with the idea of us being married, but we'd just have to work through it.

My word! At their age, to be talking like this. This is puppy love, a typical teenage infatuation. It will never last. Two very naive young folk. Have they not realised they are living in Northern Ireland? Even if it was back in 1959, wasn't there some sort of IRA campaign around the Border at that time? It wasn't as if the two communities had buried their traditional hatchets at that stage, and found themselves in an era of tranquility. Had Jack and his girl never heard of people being disowned because they married outside the tribe? Disowned and much worse!

I cannot imagine that my parents would ever have come around to agreeing with this arrangement, not in a hundred years. Her father too, if he is as heavily involved in the church as she spoke about earlier, is hardly going to welcome this. There's not just the religious divide, there's the class aspect of it too, the country-town thing as well; and, on top of that, this is his only daughter, his only pride and joy, all he has left in the world, and she is about to go to study at a prestigious college like the Royal Scottish Academy, probably end up in a top job as a result... yet here she is getting mixed up in a relationship with a local farmer who smells of stale cow dung, and likely even staler body odour! Utterly nuts, but there he is, my brother, chatting seriously to the poor girl with such blind innocence. I have no doubt he is in earnest; I have no suspicion of ulterior motive, that this might be a ploy to take the relationship into areas of physicality that she maybe hasn't reckoned on. No, he is completely bamboozled by her, and heading for a very serious fall when the parents get to hear about it.

I can hardly wait to read what happens if and when they do.

Chapter 22

Holiday

Sunday 12th July 1959

I had hoped to see Josie yesterday, but she didn't show up at the Estate. No idea why; no explanation. I hope she didn't think that I would be taken up with the Twelfth celebrations. Surely she should know me well enough by now not to think that. No, I can only guess that her ladyship had telephoned to cancel the singing engagement. Josie couldn't let me know, of course. I can accept that, even if the missing of her is so difficult. Feels like we have only had a couple of meetings since the exile of her exam month.

As it happens, everything has worked out for the best. My father has been demanding that I pack in the part-time work in the Colonel's garden. Two reasons for that. One is that this is the haymaking season, always busy and fraught, as we try to beat the rain and have the hay saved as dry as possible. The second reason is a more upsetting one.

Jimmy, our servant man, has been behaving badly for a while now, and my father has come to the end of his tether with him. Mainly it is to do with Jimmy's unreliability, a problem caused by his drinking. Jimmy went on a bit of a bender a week or two ago. He didn't show up for work for three days. When he eventually did, he was in foul form and couldn't be talked to. Then he missed a few mornings; he said he had slept in. No use to us, an excuse like that, when he should have been there to do the milking. So my father laid him off... permanently. Not the first time. I miss him around the place, not only his banter, but the fact that he does so much work with a minimum of fuss. Without *him there my father tends to be much more on edge. It couldn't have happened at a worse time. Now it will be all hands on deck to get the hay saved.*

This being Sunday, however, there was no haymaking on the farm. Instead I took the opportunity after church to ride into the town; I didn't tell the parents; they wouldn't have approved of me 'gallivanting' on the Sabbath. I was just going for 'a quick ride around the roads'. They seemed all right with that. Little did they know my motivation. . . to see if I could find Josie in the town!

I tried to find her house, based on her description of where it was and how it looked. I failed miserably. I suppose I had some vague dream that I would 'accidentally' meet her somewhere in the street. It didn't happen. My dream fizzled out and I turned to ride home. On a whim, however, I decided to go past the west gate of the estate, and to check under the loose stone, just in case she'd had time to bring a message for me. It was a good decision, even if I don't exactly like the news I get in the note she'd left there for me.

I am back on a roll with this tale; it has totally taken over my life, my every waking moment, and quite a few of those when I should be asleep. I found my mind wandering in the staff meeting in school today; not a good look to hear my name mentioned from the front by the Principal, and to jerk so noticeably to attention. I sensed a few surreptitious glances from colleagues. Over the past few weeks I have felt somehow distanced from the kindly support being offered by well-meaning friends in the staffroom. At times I could barely contain my impatience to be in the sanctuary of my own classroom again, away from all the trite banalities.

    I survived the day, falling back on some of my best pre-prepared lessons, and keeping the children as busy as possible. Then to the car, sharp on the bell at 3.30, uncharacteristically so, joining the queue of parents and other early-escaping colleagues to get out of the car park, into the home-crawl of traffic.

    Now back in my house again, a strong coffee in hand, I am once more on the trail of wayward brother. He may be at his rest, so to speak, but he has no intention of letting me rest, that is for sure.

    I have my bedroom door firmly closed, locked against intrusion. Thankfully, Calvin does keep to his own office where he spends hours on end on his new 'professions'.

    After he lost his job, he turned what had been a compulsive hobby into a career. He had always spent hours on end tying colourful flies; mostly he used these himself, fishing in various rivers across the country, but some he sold for a few pounds to fellow fishing addicts. More recently he had developed an online business to market these flies. It wasn't lucrative, but it kept him busy, and out of my orbit. Back in the day he would enter these specialist flies in competitions here and there. He would go through grumpy periods afterwards, due to the fact that he never brought home any prizes. I always consoled him that it must not have been in the Divine plan for him to win; that never seemed to comfort him, but it didn't stop me cooing on about it; of course it didn't.

As well as the fly-tying thing, he reviews religious books and writes articles on theological subjects for a magazine; I confess I haven't read any more after that first one. He's in his small corner, I'm in mine in this marriage. I hope that he stays there just now; I do not want him to see me sitting here cross-legged and morose, scraps of paper scattered randomly about me on my bed, this formerly despised oil-painting dissected, and spread out before me like a gutted fish.

This is an isolating experience, I have to admit. It is only making the distance between me and husband worse. He must feel even more ostracised than I intend him to be at the minute, but I cannot share this intensely personal discovery trail with him. I can imagine his self-righteous reaction to my brother's disclosures. The wise-owl syndrome would rise in him; he'd be preening his judgemental feathers in no time. I would resent the inevitable Scriptures he would have primed and ready to slash me with. I fear the smug, clichéd comforts he would try to smear over my pain.

On the other hand, I continue to have a sense of guilt that I haven't been able to say anything to my twin about this uncovering. I keep telling myself, 'All in good time! I will share the saga with him when I get my own head around it, and when I have more of an idea where the relationship ends up. There are too many unanswered questions as yet, too many loose ends. If I am honest with myself, however, there may be a holding back on my part, a reluctance to allow this intimacy with Jack's private world to become a shared legacy. At the moment it is me and him. I am enjoying the confidentiality, the trust he is placing in me, the closeness I am feeling for him in all his vulnerabilities, a teenage boy finding love for the first time.

Once again the suspicion flits through my mind that Jack was the way he was in later life as a result of the failure of this relationship. Might it have ruined him for all other courtships? Soured and scarred him for ever? I have an internal dialogue going on between the Jack I knew and this earlier version, this romantic man whose diary I am reading; an ongoing conversation between 'dour Jack' and the fulfilled Jack he might have been had he been successful in a love relationship.

My coffee finished, I wonder if I can find this note from Josie among those stuck inside the frame. Perhaps he has positioned it below that first one so as to make this whole saga progress in a chronological manner. Has he made my detective's quest as easy as that? I rip off the next envelope; another with the one word *Jack* written on the front.

Sat 11th July
My Darling Jack,
I am so sorry that I missed you today. There was no lesson, as the Colonel's wife has decided she can no longer afford me the time. I can understand and forgive her, for she has been very generous to me this past year. But I so missed seeing you.
I have other news, which is why I will ride out to Castlecuinn tonight and leave this note for you. My father has decided to take me on an unexpected two-week holiday to Killarney and other parts of Co Kerry. While I appreciate his kindness I am sorry to be missing you for these two weeks. Killarney is important to him as it was the place of his honeymoon. I know he wants to show it to me before I move on with my life and go to University. No doubt he wants to revisit good memories of his time down there with my mother.
We will return north on Sat 25th July, which is good because, as I recall, your birthday is the following day. Would you like to meet secretly at the castle on the afternoon of that Sunday? I would love it if you can…that way I can give you your surprise birthday present. (You won't be able to say 'No' after that promise.) I can make the excuse of going for a bike ride, as I often do. Being a Sunday, you will most likely be free. I only have a few weeks after that before I leave for Scotland, so our time is limited. I miss you so much. I need to have those strong arms of yours around me, holding me against the fear of the unknown future, bringing me a sense of being loved and needed as you always do. I can barely wait for your kiss. I know you cannot answer this letter, other than by leaving a similar note in our hiding place, which would be pointless on this occasion. But I just hope you will be able to meet me in our secret

cellar on that Sunday afternoon, say around 3pm.
I love you, now and always,
Josie xxx

Chapter 23

Making Hay

July 1959

The two weeks passed quickly and, at the same time, far too slowly. There was hardly a minute when I was working at the hay that I wasn't thinking about Josie. I imagined her running along beside the tractor as I drove around the fields, cutting the great summer crop, her laughing and skipping and leaping in the tall green grass, her skirts pulled up to her thighs, her long legs fine and bronzed. I breathed her in every time I raised a handful of drying hay to my nose, the most wholesome of all farm aromas. I tasted her lips in every mug of sweet tea that mother carried out to the field for our lunch. The soda bread and cheese sandwiches have never been more welcome, the zest of the freshly peeled oranges never more evocative. Josie was in every summer scent, every butterfly and dragonfly that flitted between the glinting ricks of drying hay; every blackbird and thrush that we could hear serenading us from the hedgerows when the chugging engine stopped. Her presence walked beside me on the stubble, her soft hand cool against the furnace of my back, slipping under the sweat-heavy shirt, caressing me towards quitting time.

This has been, by a million miles, the most lovingly saved crop of hay in the history of Castlecuinn. Our cows are going to cherish every bite of it in the coming winter. They won't need the usual molasses, for the fodder will be sweet enough. In my head, and only in my head, I am calling it 'Josie's harvest'.

It is only right and proper that she gets to enjoy it too, so I will fill a bagful of the driest hay for our comfort on the Sunday when she returns.

Goodness, brother! The poetry of hay-making! I cannot believe this is the same person who could struggle to answer a straight forward question from a visitor. Didn't he used to avoid conversations in the house, always giving the impression that he either had nothing to say, or couldn't be bothered saying it. Here he is waxing lyrical about saving a field of hay. The poor girl is going to be lucky if she can avoid having to eat a mouthful of this precious crop, he's so proud of it.

Sunday 26th 1959

I will never forget my 19th birthday, should I live to be 100!
Josie arrived in our cellar just after I had completed my preparations, the candles lit and positioned safely, the hay carefully spread on our makeshift bed and covered with a blanket. She was in my arms straight away; there was laughter and tears. Tears of relief, or joy, or love, or something. We are meant for each other, and today proved that beyond any doubting. She was looking amazing; clothes I hadn't seen before, a light, summery-styled skirt, some sort of blue-patterned blouse which showed off her figure perfectly, and a jumper hung loosely around her neck.
She'd come on her bike, and had hidden it behind the gate lodge as usual; nobody had seen her arrive, she thought. We are lucky that this part of the estate is so private. It's a perfect place for hiding, with its sprawling trees, all those thick rhododendron bushes and overgrown thickets...the most neglected part of this massive spread of property. Not a soul ever seems to come near the old castle. She gave me more than one birthday present!
First was a silver chain, more of a bracelet, with both our names inscribed on the inside of a little plate. This was precious to me, the fact that I could look at our names kind of joined together and, beside them, the little heart that she had had engraved. Then she produced a cross necklace thing with an emerald stone in the centre...she said it was a Celtic cross. She had found it in a shop in Killarney,

and thought it would be perfect for me. When I looked a bit doubtful about it, and said that I would have to make sure my parents never saw it, she seemed a bit confused.

"You would never wear it then?" She sounded disappointed.

"Of course I will, just not when my folks can see it," I assured her.

"But it's Christian," she argued.

"I know that, and you know that, but they are just a bit weird about anything that looks...you know....Catholic."

This saddened her for a few moments, I noticed. I took her in my arms, and told her that it didn't matter, that the only thing that mattered was that we loved each other.

"Can I put the cross around your neck?" Her idea. Of course she could. Her arms were up around me as she fiddled with the clasp behind my head. Somehow, in that moment, with her perfume enchanting me, her little breasts firm, pressing against my chest, then her lips on mine...it began.

And ended quite some time later on my bed of hay. Her third birthday gift.

The urge had been irresistible. We both felt that.

We lay there together, euphoric, fulfilled, content...yet confused, wordless, and yes, maybe a bit terrified at what we had just done.

She sat up suddenly, strands of hay tangled in her hair, her naked back picking up the flickering shadows from the stump of candle.

She said my name, over and over again. Held my hand so tightly, as if in pain.

I could not find any words to say what I wanted, needed to say.

Eventually, I told her I was sorry.

"Don't say that, Jack," she said. "You aren't to blame, so don't say sorry. Especially if you are not really sorry."

"Are you sorry?" I asked her. "Are you sure you're ok?"

She turned back around to stare at me, so much love spilling out of those softly *smiling eyes. Then a small shake of her head.*

"There is no point in being sorry now," she said. "It was quite sore at the start but... anyhow, it is too late for apologies. As long as you don't think less of me for it..."

"How could I think less of you for it? That is the best thing that ever happened to me; you are the best thing that ever happened to me or ever could happen to me. I could never think less of you," I told her.

We lay in each other's arms a long time after that, before she suddenly realised that time was passing, and she needed to be getting home.

"Can we meet again next Sunday?" We both spoke at the same time, then laughed.

I pulled strands of hay from her tousled hair as I helped her dress. I kissed silent tears away from her eyes, tears of joy, I think, tears of realisation at how we were forever belonging to each other now, tears of fear about how we will survive her going away, and how we will negotiate our future together, given the thought that I'd have to hide her gifts from the very people who loved me most in all the world. She disappeared up the stone steps, the sound of her footsteps fading to silence. I sat a long time on my hay-bed. Just thinking. Just worshipping the memory.

My worst fears confirmed. No matter how wonderfully my brother has described this his first experience of love, I am horrified by his recklessness. I can see no good come of this, only disaster.

What am I saying? Of course no good will come of it! No good did come of it! They are not together. Never have been together. Never could be together. Why, oh why did he allow himself to get into this situation, to fall into this intense temptation that nobody, nobody could have resisted? Surely he could have foreseen what might happen? Surely he had some modicum of self-awareness, of self-control? He could have ruined this poor girl's life forever! The idiot that he was!

How is he going to extricate himself from this dilemma? That is my question. I am desperately curious, yet again, but I am equally dreading what lies ahead in the next chapter of this confession…for confession is what it is increasingly turning out to be.

My eye falls on another scrap of paper which has fallen loose from Jack's notebook. It has a very short four-line verse, scribbled in dark pencil, the letters tall and aggressive, the words scored angrily, impatiently on the page.

> *I was a bull at her garden gate*
> *She didn't deny me, she didn't say 'Wait'*
> *I've tasted her body, no honey more sweet*
> *But I've trampled her flower under my feet*

He knows, doesn't he!

Chapter 24

Regret

Sat 1st August 1959
Dear Jack,

I am so sorry that I cannot come to see you tomorrow. It is a situation beyond my control. Some relatives of my mother are in the area; having heard that my father isn't well, they have invited themselves to our house to see him on Sunday afternoon. My father insists, obviously, that I be there to entertain them. They are not relatives that I know very well, given that they have not been as close to our family as they might have been, had my mother not passed away. They will presumably want to see me at my best, as mother would have wished, hear me sing and play and show off what a fine father I have had in the meantime.

This is not ideal. I will miss you dreadfully, especially after the joys of last week. Please do not imagine that I am hesitant about spending another afternoon with you in our love-nest. That is absolutely not the case. I love you. If you ever feel like doubting that, just remember last week.

Having said all that, I do have something I want to say to you, and I hope you will not misunderstand, or think any less of me for it. It is easier for me to write it than speak it to you face to face, you understand.

What we did together was wonderful, and I will never forget it. I don't think you planned it, neither did I…it just sort of happened. But afterwards I started to think. You see, in my religion it is a very grievous sin to do what we did. Fornication is a mortal sin. This means that I am in a very embarrassing position. I must confess it to my priest before I next take Holy Communion. I am sure that, as it was my first and only time to have sex, he will absolve me....he will be angry and I will have to do some penance, and he will warn me against doing it again...but he will give me absolution, I am sure. For me as a Catholic, this is important.

I am so sorry to drag you into this. If he asks me who my partner was I will try to refuse to tell him. I will simply say it was a boy from another parish. This is not a lie. You are from another parish, (I will not admit that you are not even a Catholic...that might make him even more mad and complicate matters.)

What does this mean for you and me? Only this, my darling Jack. That I will always be yours, that I will stay faithful to you when I am in Scotland, that you and I can and will be together as much as we possibly can...but that we should promise each other not to fall into that temptation again. I will lie in your arms, I will kiss you as always, I will be everything to you that you need and want, short of making love. Can you understand this request? Please, please do not be annoyed by it. It does not mean I love you any less. In fact my love and respect for you will deepen even more if you can trust yourself, and if you can respect me enough not to ask me to make love again...until.... I know you didn't ask me last week, and it just sort of happened, in a most loving and natural way. We can think of other ways to show each other our love and devotion, can't we? But please please do not hate me or despise me for this, my darling Jack. I love you too much to lose you now.

I will leave this note in our usual hiding place. Can we please meet next week, Sun 9th, at the castle? I hope so. Please!!!! See you then.

Love you

Josie

What a sensible girl, so mature of her to respond the way she has. I admire her for it, and I hope my brother did as well....indeed I hope and pray that he honoured her wishes. One mistake like that can be forgiven, and can be learned from, for sure.

I fold this precious letter of hers, place it back in its envelope, and re-attach it, with fresh sellotape, in its sequence behind the painting. I should be going downstairs now to prepare dinner. The temptation is too strong, however, and I find myself picking up my brother's journal account again. I suppose I am wondering how he will react to this girl's modesty. Will he regard it as rejection, or will he have the wisdom to deny himself and respect the good sense of her request?

In the event, I read of an even more dramatic occurrence, one which will twist the narrative in ways no-one could have foreseen.

Chapter 25

Uncovered

Sunday 9th August 1959

Today has put a massive spanner in the works.

Not a soul on this planet could have foreseen this turn of events. Shakespeare himself couldn't have woven a more tangled web than the one we find ourselves in after today. It would be comic if it wasn't so potentially tragic. And, above all, so full of the most cruel irony.

We met as usual by the gate lodge. I had ridden around the estate myself, telling my parents I was going for a long spin on my bike again. Josie eventually arrived. I thought she looked a shade tentative as she wheeled her bicycle past me to the rear of the building, giving me a sideways glance that had the tiniest trace of doubt in it...smiling yes, but with a query, with some sort of holding back. I could hardly wait to get her to the cellar to find out what was behind it, taking her hand, and almost dragging her through the undergrowth to our castle sanctuary.

We held each other, and kissed as passionately as before; then I held her at arms length and asked, "What is it Jo? Why are you fearful? Everything is alright, surely?"

There were big, soft tears welling up in her eyes. "I was scared you would hate me for the letter," she said.

I should have guessed that would be her worry. She shouldn't have feared. I told her that I totally respected her wishes. I actually got down on one knee, as if proposing to her....and in a sense I was. What I said was something like,

"Josie, I respect what you said in your letter. I would never hurt you, I will never again do anything with you that you are not happy about. That is my promise. I'll never presume anything from you, like what we did last time. I can't say I am sorry we did, for that would be hypocritical, and I loved it too much to tell a lie...but I respect you, and your rights to say no. So stop worrying. Your letter was absolutely fine. We have to be able to trust each other, especially with you going..."

She pulled me back up from my crouch, and led me to the hay-bed. We lay together, cuddled and talked, kissed and comforted each other. We were both feeling the dread of the oncoming separation; there were periods of silence between us as both of us, I am sure, were conscious of the wrench that this parting was going to be. It was going to have to be a completely private grief, one we couldn't share with anyone else.

Then she wanted to know about what my church taught regarding what she called 'fornication'. That big word again.

"They wouldn't be on for it," I joked.

She smiled of course, but wanted more explanation. "Are your clergy as firm against it as the Catholic Church is?"

I explained that I had not heard many sermons about it, but that the Protestant church would be equally adamant that there should be no sex outside of marriage. The mission hall preachers would be very strong in their teaching about it, I told her, more fired up and more dogmatic than you would ever hear in the more toned-down church services. Even then, there was a lot of stuff talked about in a sort of coded language; it was too debauched, too wicked, to be talked about explicitly in a public service with men and women present.

"But you...you still did it with me? Do you not agree with them? With your church?"

This made me pause. "If you are asking me did I feel guilty afterwards...

then, yes, I suppose I did... but the temptation was just too strong, and it all felt so natural. I think we had missed each other so much during your exams in June, and then again during that two weeks when you were away with your dad, that the desire had welled up in us both....and then the dam burst, kind of, when you were hanging that cross around my neck... and you were just feeling so lovely to me."

"Ironic, isn't it?" she said. "There I am one minute, putting the cross of Christ around your neck, and the next minute I'm letting you take my clothes off. I don't think he would have been too pleased with me, nor his holy mother either."

That made me think about the differences between us.

"What does his holy mother have to do with it?" I asked.

She stared up into my eyes for a second before answering, probably remembering that Jesus' mother wasn't such a big deal to Presbyterians.

"Well, she was a virgin when she had Jesus, wasn't she? And she would be wanting Catholic girls like me to be pure until the time of our marriage."

"Oh right," I said.

"Tell me," she said hesitantly, "is it true that... well, I've heard some of the girls talking in school, saying that... well, saying that it's a big deal for a Protestant boy to deflower a Catholic girl. Like... he gets extra merit points for it or something? Maybe that's a Belfast thing?"

"It must be, if it's true at all," I told her. "I've never heard of it. Likely just a sectarian myth dreamt up in the back streets of the city to create fear between..."

What was that noise?

A scraping of footsteps on the stone steps. Descending slowly, deliberately.

We both heard it. Froze. Staring at the door.

Someone was pushing at the door.

Who? The Colonel? My father? Her father? The gardener?

Our candle flickered as a draught wafted into the cellar. The door edged open with a creak. We saw a dark figure silhouetted against the downward shaft of sunlight. A man. He had a flashlight in his hand. The beam swept across the floor and up around the walls, then settled on us. Two scared rabbits caught in the torch-light. A moment of silence. Surprise. Disbelief.

"Holy Mary, mother of God!"

Her again!

The voice. I knew the voice. I even recognised the oath.

Jimmy. Jimmy McGrath. Our labourer. Or, to be more exact, our recently fired labourer.

Josie and I seemed to be frozen, speechless, transfixed in the sudden glare of light. Thankfully both fully clothed.

'Now if that had happened two weeks ago,' I thought. Horrendous.

His voice again.

"Jack, is that you? What under heaven are you...? Jack Shaw, be-god!"

"Aye, it's me, Jimmy."

"And a lassie with you?"

"I have."

"Well that bates everythin'! Ah never thought you had it in ye, son," he said.

There was something about his voice. It was slow, deliberate, just a wee bit slurred. And something in his hand. He took a step or two towards us, towards the candlelight. The flame reflected briefly on the tall, amber bottle in his grasp.

Of course! Jimmy was, to use his own expression, 'on the tear'. He had got himself a fresh bottle of whiskey and this was to be his private shebeen for the next while.

Except that we were here first.

"Jimmy," I began, "this is a bit awkward. Do you think you could maybe..." I paused, not wanting to be too brutal with him in this state.

"Think I could maybe...maybe go again and give yees peace to be at the courtin', if ye like?"

"Aye, please, if you don't mind."

"Ah will. Go and give yees peace...but wait a minute there, son. Wait a minute now. This lassie o' yours. Is she...does yer feather know...naw, what am I sayin'. Your feather will hardly know, will he? An' the two o' yees stuck down here in this dungeon, an' at it like a pair o' rabbits!"

"No, we are not at anything, Jimmy. And you are right, my father doesn't know, and I'd be glad if you don't tell him either, if you don't mind."

Josie was clinging to my arm as we sat together on the bed, trying to disappear herself behind my shoulder.

"That's all right, son," Jimmy said. "I ha'e no intention o' betraying you."

A leering grin at us, the candlelight distorting his unshaven face, casting deep, dark shadows and giving him the countenance of some sort of ugly gargoyle.

"But here, let me ha'e a luk at this lassie o' yours, tae see what sort o' a woman she is. Would she be local, maybe? Let me see if I know her."

Josie was totally hiding behind me by this stage, determined not to be seen. My duty was to protect her, especially her identity.

"She's not from around here," I told him. "From the town."

"The town? An' what would bring a town lassie all the way oot here tae court a farmer's boy, eh?"

"Look Jimmy, can you please just go and leave us alone. We just need a bit of privacy. Josie is going away soon and we were just saying goodbye to each other."

"Ah, I'm sorry son. I'm getting badly in yer road. You work away there an' I'll go on, give yous peace, you and yer Josie."

With that, he turned towards the steps.

"Aye, you and your Josie. Who is she, this Josie?" he mumbled to himself as he stumbled into the slanting sunlight, and began to climb the steps as best as his half-drunken legs would allow him to.

"You shouldn't have told him my name," Josie whispered.

"I know. It just sort of slipped out. But he will never figure out who you are. He'll likely forget it after he's finished that bottle of whiskey anyhow."

"Why does he seem familiar to me? How would I know him?"

"What do you mean? You couldn't know him, surely?"

Josie paused, thinking, racking her brain.

"Is he a Catholic, by any chance?"

"He is. Not a very good one, but yeah, he goes to the chapel."

"That's where I've seen him," she said confidently. "At Mass. He and my father would know each other a bit, I think."

"Oh no, that's all we need. He knows both our fathers. And he doesn't like mine at the minute."

"Thanks be to God he didn't see me. What's he like anyway?" Josie asked.

"He's not a bad spud, just a bit crude. Great worker, but my father sacked him for drinking and being late. Not the first time either."

"What if he tells your father?"

I had thought about that possibility. It did scare me a bit, but I doubted if he would, especially after their fall-out. And, just in case, I was already forming a plan to make sure he wouldn't.

"I don't think he'll do that, but just leave it with me," I told her. "But right now I need to follow him and talk to him. And I need to catch him before he has guzzled that bottle. He's still half sober at the minute, and I think I can appeal to his better side."

So we left it at that. It was getting late anyhow. We agreed to meet next Sunday, the 16th, unless any other weird interventions got in the way.

Chapter 26

Schemes

So, I think to myself, that is how Jimmy McGrath enters the story. I had been so puzzled as to how and why letters for my brother had been addressed to Jimmy at his gate lodge home. Presumably Jack had sweet-talked the workman into being his go-between. That was clever of him.

I want to know how he did that, how he worked his way around this issue. I turn the page in brother's journal, hoping to see a reference to their meeting. Nothing! No mention of it, as yet anyhow. Reading on, the next entry is a straightforward account of the following Sunday's meeting with Josie. No further surprises, no more crises, no repeat performances of the earlier love scene. I am almost proud of him; certainly I am admiring of how his girl had calmed his passions, for the moment at least.

The tone of this entry is so sad by contrast, so resigned to the inevitable separation that, in my brother's words, is 'coming at us like a runaway train'. It is likely that they will have only one further 'date' before her father drives her away to the ferry, and on to her new life in Glasgow.

At the very end of this entry there appears the only mention of Jimmy McGrath.

I gave Josie an address so that she can send letters to me from Scotland. She was really surprised, and puzzled, to see that the name and address was that of Jimmy who had interrupted us last week. She wanted to know how I had managed to come up with that scheme, but I was keeping that a secret. I teased her that she didn't need to know, but just to trust me that this would work out, otherwise how were we going to stay in touch? Jimmy would definitely pass on her letters to me.

"But might he read them too?" she wanted to know. "Maybe he will open the envelope out of curiosity?"

"I doubt it, but maybe he will, or maybe his wife will, so just don't put anything in there that you wouldn't want someone else to read."

"That is going to be so hard," she said.

I understand that, but it is better than not being able to communicate at all.

I have to speak to Jimmy about this. I have to know what blackmail my brother used to bring him into the plot. This cannot wait a day longer; my curiosity is insatiable.

On my way back from school I stop at Jimmy's home. As I enter through the open side gate, I am fortunate to see him a distance along the drive, beyond his gate-lodge home. In the evening shadow-cover of the trees he appears to be walking away from me. This is good; it suits me much better to talk to him privately, away from his wife, especially as the memory of her *faux pas* at the wake is still fairly fresh in my mind. I don't think she needs to know about my present quest.

I hurry after Jimmy, catching him easily as he limps along, blackthorn walking stick in hand, over the thin covering of moss that has been allowed to infest this back entrance to the estate. I call out to him, and he turns to wait. He is surprised to see me, clearly. We don't often meet, and not since the funeral.

"Agh, it's yourself, lass," he says. "What brings you over here?"

No point in beating about the bush with small talk, but I do ask how he is, and he tells me of 'oul pains here and there', and 'expectin' nothin' else wi' the age o' me'. He wants to know how am I getting over things?

Nice of him to ask. As the dark crows screigh down at us from above, I launch in.

"I was getting on all right, Jimmy," I tell him, "but something has come up… about my brother's past. I need you to help me to understand…maybe explain some strange things that I'm struggling to get my head around."

"Oh dear!" he whispers. His body half-turns away from me, his head droops forward, and I sense a closing in on himself. The black-thorn stick takes an involuntary swipe at a clump of ferns beside the path.

"Ye wouldn't need to be askin' o'er much, lass, for me memory isn't the best, ye know."

"That's all right," I tell him. "I am not expecting you to try to remember all the details of this, but you and I have always been great friends, so I am hoping you can maybe answer this one question, please Jimmy?"

"Just the one?" he says. "Well, fire away if it's just the one an' I'll see if I can answer it."

I begin. "I was going through some of Jack's things, you know, sorting out his affairs…and I found a bunch of letters that had been sent to him in the post. The thing is they all had your address on the front. Do you remember anything about that? I couldn't make head nor tail of it."

The point of his stick gets to tracing out some sort of lines on the green carpet by his feet, and he studies the pattern silently for a bit.

"How much do you know about this?"

"Not much," I cover, not wanting to spook him into silence.

"Like, do you know who was sending these letters? Have you read any of them?"

I don't have to lie about this answer. As yet I haven't read any of the letters that had been sent to his address. That pleasure is ahead of me.

"I haven't read them," I tell him, "although I would be lying if I told you that I don't know who sent them. I know they are love letters."

"So you know who wrote them?"

I nod. "I know her first name, that's all."

"And you know the problem Jack had?"

"I can guess he didn't want my parents knowing about his friendship," I tell him.

"And you know why he didn't want your folks to know about her?"

"I think so."

"The lassie…you see, the lassie was a Catholic, like myself."

"I sort of worked that out," I say, "but how did you get involved in the thing, like how did you become his middle man?"

"Middle man," he laughed. "Never was called that before. But I suppose maybe I was, caught in the middle. The way it came about was this. I came on him and her one day in the oul castle. Courtin' like, not up to anything bad, not then anyway."

"I see. Go on."

He has paused, as if to try to recall the details.

"Far as I mine," he continues, "I had a fall oot wi' your feather. He had given me my cards, so I was outa a job. I was on the drink a brave bit at that time, mind you. Anyway, young Jack promised to get me my job back, if I would do him a favour."

"And the favour was for this girl to be able to write to him using your address?"

"That's the long and short o' it. She was goin' away, you see. I wasn't going to agree to it, though, but then he toul me who his lassie was. It turned out that I knew her folk. I knew her feather. He was a big man in the town back then, the chapel as weel. I knew he wouldn't be on for his daughter getting mixed up with a Protestant."

"Goodness! You knew all that, but you still agreed to help our Jack? How come? I thought you were a good, loyal Catholic yourself, Jimmy?"

"And I am, Sarah, I am! I just didn't like the idea that this lassie should be kept away from the fella she loved, especially when that fella was one of the best lads in the countryside. Your Jack was a grand chap, you know. I toul you that before. He was always very good to you two, and to your poor sister. I would have done anything for him."

"So you came back to work at the farm?"

"I did surely. He got me my job back. I never looked behind me after that. I stayed on the wagon for years. Well, maybe just the odd wee wobble, but Jack always got me through it. Fine fella, Jack. It was a shame what happened."

"What do you mean? What happened?"

"Well now, if you don't know anything about that, lass….I am afraid I can't be the one to be telling you your family's business. I'm sorry, but I'm sayin' no more. Maybe said too much already."

"But you know why they didn't get together in the end?"

He looks at me as if I'm stupid; that pursed-lip, head-wobble thing.

"Agh…sure you know yourself…"

I wait.

He hesitates, or maybe that was to be the end of the explanation; that default escape clause in these parts. Nothing more ever needs to be added to our age-old stock phrase. The ambiguous, Ulster cover-all. 'You know yourself.'

But I am not satisfied by its vagueness this time. I stare him in the eyes, demanding more. He half-turns away again. But he speaks, his tone something between resignation and bitterness.

"Everybody in this bloody country knows why they didn't get together in the end, lass. Too much silly religion! That's the truth of it."

Chapter 27

Return

My reading has been interrupted by the excitement of the return of my brother and his family from the mission field. I say 'excitement', but to be honest their arrival and welcome has been a muted affair.

The only thing that hasn't been in any sense 'muted' is the wintery storm that has been raging over the countryside on these first couple of days since his arrival. The unseasonal gale has howled down from the hills in the west, relentlessly so, for a couple of days. Reaching the forest opposite, its voice screeched in the swaying branches like the sound of violent wind through the taut strings of an out-of-tune harp. The noise rose in waves to demented crescendos, falling away to wounded moans in a way that put me in mind of a Wagnerian opera.

Several huge trees have been uprooted in the Colonel's estate, including a mighty elm which crashed down across the famine wall, blocking our road. It has taken a few council workers a whole day to chainsaw it into submission so as to reopen the thoroughfare, their yellow, high-vis jackets and flashing orange lights bringing the only trace of colour in the greyness of the weather and the dark shadow of the forest. I have felt sorry for the line of Leylandii cypress trees that we had planted several years ago along our lane. The wind seems to be trying to bend them over into abeyance. Branches and all sorts of debris have been scattered everywhere. Hail has battered the window panes of our homes with devilish force. We have been fortunate though. Jimmy has lost a bunch of slates from his roof, and has ended up with a flooded living room. The worst that has happened on the farm has been the loss of some time-worn asbestos roofing from a disused shed.

So it has not exactly been the sort of 'warm' welcome home that Isaac and his wife might have hoped for. Apart from a special service in the church hall, moderately well attended by members of the congregation, and with the customary supper afterwards, there has been no great sense of fanfare. Yes, it was a case of 'Well done, thou good and faithful servant', as our clergyman intoned, and yes, there has been a short report in the local paper, with photographs of Isaac at work in his clinic, but it isn't too difficult to detect a slight trace of disappointment in his spirit.

"A feeling of anticlimax".

That is how he puts it to twin and myself the night after the service.

We have gathered in the home place for a chat with him and Lisa, making sure the new residents are feeling all right, and that no loose ends need tidying up as they embark on this new phase of their lives. But 'anticlimax'? What could we say? I am lost for words. To be fair, my twin does try to speak some encouragement into the situation.

"Of course, Isaac," he says. "It's inevitable. You can't spend thirty-six years of your life in a place and not feel a massive sense of dislocation when you come home."

"You've given so much of yourselves to those people," I tell him. "It has to be hard…"

"Those people?" he says, smiling but abrupt. "Those people became our family. Every bit as important as our own children."

'And a fair bit more important than those of us back here who are your family, and who have been supporting you with money and prayer for all that time', I am thinking. Instead I say, "Of course, that is understood…and those people's lives have been changed for ever because of what you've done."

"Many of them wouldn't even be alive if you hadn't been caring for them," twin adds.

Our brother is silent. Lisa holds his hand, stroking the back of it in a comforting manner.

"Now it is time to lean back into retirement," she says.

"I can't even utter that word," he confesses. "I don't see any sign of the word in the Scriptures. There is a lot to be done here on this farm, and even more to be done in the church."

"Patience, honey," Lisa tells him. "Your health and recovery is the first thing."

Twin and I look at each other. His health? Of course we have noticed the tired, dark rings around his eyes, his listlessness and the fact that he has lost some weight.

"I'll be fine in a week or two," he says.

"Malaria stays in your system," his wife reminds him. "Any fatigue or any illness at all, and you know it is going to recur. You will be no use on the farm, or in the church, unless you learn to look after yourself."

I get the impression she is using our presence as a platform, taking courage from us being here to give him this lecture. She is glancing from twin to me, a small plea for support in her eyes. Given the kind of super-hero that Isaac has always been, it must be so difficult for him to surrender to rest and recuperation. Even in his next words I sense exactly that dilemma.

"I have never felt God call me to look after myself," he says stubbornly. "Only to look after other people."

"Fair enough," twin responds, "but you won't be able to do that if you're dead, will you? Nobody is invincible. Surely Jack dying is proof enough of that."

This little gem of truth puts an end to the argument, and we move on to other things, details of matters to do with what has been happening on the farm and in the community... the kind work of our neighbour, the letting of land, the sale of stock and the like.

My mind wanders off again to my own private preoccupation, the uncovering of brother Jack's secret life all those years ago. I look at the three faces opposite as twin describes how well his local business is going; how I would love to be able to share this load with them. But equally I know that I cannot. It is too intense; it's my private obsession. The rabbit hole I find myself in is too tight to be accommodating any more than one person. I must be allowed to dig to the bitter bottom of this saga before I make any of these revelations public to my brothers. Maybe I have no right to be thinking this. Maybe it is entirely selfish of me to be wrapping myself so tightly around the story's unfolding, to be inserting my own interpretations, anticipations and fears into the whole weave of the tapestry. How on earth am I ever going to be able to unpick myself from it, these twisting threads of fascination and dread? It all feels such a personal crisis. Existential almost. But it is not my story alone. Twin, and maybe his wife, Judith, deserve to be in on it, whatever the response is. So too does Isaac, albeit to a lesser extent.

After my chat with Jimmy McGrath, I had come home and read the next pages of brother's journal; a couple more episodes of nervous courtship in the cellar, both of them clearly fearful of being caught again, (but at least they seemed to have been faithful to their commitment regarding their level of intimacy, according to my brother's journal at any rate); the detail of how he had passed on Jimmy's address to his Josie, her delight at this clever plan on his part; the painful description of their parting that last week of August before her departure to Scotland. My heart went out to both of them. He described how they had pledged themselves to each other. It was a poignant account, and I couldn't but wish the girl well.

Her first letter back from Glasgow included an address where she was staying, some sort of residence attached to the Royal Academy. She was quite descriptive in her account, trying, I suppose, to give my brother a clear picture of the 'big city', and her particular environs.

"The Academy is a very grand, imposing, four story building in an area called St George's Place. It seems to have dozens of rooms and halls, very easy to get lost in. To my mind it looks not unlike the well known 'Bank Building' in Royal Avenue, Belfast, if you have ever seen it."

She had met all her tutors, and felt welcomed, if a bit intimidated, by the high standard of musicianship and singing she was encountering. There was definitely a nervousness about how she would live up to these expectations. It was a happy letter though; this was her big break, her great 'life opportunity', and she was determined to grasp it with both hands. At the same time the letter finished up very sensitively, in that she asked Jack many questions about how he was, and how things were around the farm.

"Do not feel that anything is too mundane to share with me," she said. *"I want to know all about your life. I want to feel that I am there with you, that we are one."*

Very sweet; clever of the girl to be trying to make Jack feel that the humdrum of his dull farming life was every bit as important as her more glistening one. It is a good beginning, but I cannot help wondering how on earth they ever thought they were going to manage to sustain this level of loving commitment and letter writing for the three years that she planned to be at the Academy, never mind the possible musical career thereafter. There are many more letters attached to the inside of the painting, and I look forward, once we have got Isaac settled back into his original home, to continuing the quest of finding out.

Chapter 28

Devastation

10th September 1959
My Darling Jack,
I love you. I miss you. I need you here with me right now. I am so afraid. (I am sorry about these blobs on the page, but my tears are flowing and I cannot stop them. They are tears for you, as well as for me, my love.) My news is very disturbing.
You know how a girl has her bleeding every month, her menstrual cycle. Well, I never have a problem with mine. Not until now. My period did not come in August like it should have done. I thought perhaps I had got my dates wrong. I was beginning to worry. But I thought perhaps it was just a freak occurrence, as can happen. That is why I did not mention it to you before I left, not wanting to concern you about something that might only be a fear in my head. But this month it should have come again, around about the 7th. It has not come. Instead I am feeling a very strange physical sensation in my body, as if I am changing in a way that has never happened to me before. Mainly I feel this in the morning. I believe it may be what I have heard called 'morning sickness'. I am scared out of my wits by what may be happening to me.
Darling Jack. We only did it once, I know, but I fear very much that I may be carrying your child inside me. While that is something I would always wish for my future, it is a very frightening thing to have happened to me at this time, just as I am starting my career in Glasgow. Jack, what am I to do? Who shall I go to, for help, for advice? I know nobody well enough in this place, this college, indeed this town. I cannot tell my father. He would go berserk. Please,

please Jack. Think for me and tell me what to do.
I am so sorry, Jack. I love you more than ever and need you more than I could ever have imagined!
XXX Josie
P.S. There is a public phone box on the ground floor of the academy. If I can find out a phone number for it, do you think you could phone me at a given time so we can talk about this. I so need to hear your voice right now. Please pray for me.

Oh Dear God In Heaven!
I burst into tears. I cannot help it. This happened forty-something years ago and I am feeling it as strongly as if it were current news, as if the letter had arrived in today's post. But this is my…this was my brother!

There are no words.

I hear myself shrieking in a mixture of grief and despair, then I am curled up in a foetal ball, sobbing like I haven't cried for years.

Maybe she's wrong! Hardly though. I should have seen this coming. He should have….

How crazy of my brother, to have landed this poor girl in this terrible mess! My heart goes out to her, across the years. I feel as viscerally involved as if it was myself in this position! My heart aches for her. The loneliness she must have been feeling. How would anyone cope with a situation like this?

Her father? Will he disown her? Her parish? What on earth will her priest say? I know how condemned she will have been by her own church, the institution itself, and probably many of the parishioners. It would have been the same in my own denomination; I needn't sit on any pedestal in that regard. Having a baby outside of wedlock in those days seemed to be up there with the worst of crimes.

The poor, poor girl. She is so alone, so far from home. Far from Jack.

I am interrupted by a knock on my door.

"Are you all right?" My husband has heard me from his study downstairs. I must have been very loud. What should I tell him? It isn't any of his business; not much has been any of his business recently, but I certainly cannot bring him into this pain. This is my purgatory right now.

"Yes, I am all right. Just thinking about Jack."

It's not really a lie either.

"Can I get you a cup of tea?"

"That would be kind, but keep it for me down in the kitchen."

I hear him descend again. My body goes back into a paroxysm of dread for a bit until I get myself pulled together, tidy away the 'evidence', and head to the kitchen.

Chapter 29

Aftermath

There is no record of my brother's first recorded thoughts after this announcement from Josie. Perhaps he's not been able to write down anything of his immediate reaction. I can understand. It was likely beyond his power to put words around his feelings.
   Instead this.

Sept 1959

Today I managed to have a telephone conversation with Josie.

She had sent me the number of a public phone-box and suggested a time. Wild horses would not have kept me from calling her. I did have an argument with my father over it. He could not understand why it was so urgent for me to go to the village at exactly 3.00pm today. How could he? How could he imagine that the love of my life was pregnant and wanted to talk to me? I would be there, should the sky fall down on me. I cycled there without incident, several loose coins in my pocket. I had no idea how much a trunk call to Glasgow would cost. It wouldn't have mattered if I'd been asked for £20.

As it happened, I was lucky that this particular operator was very nice. I explained that this was my first time to use a phone box to make a long-distance call, and she talked me through it helpfully. I think she could tell from the pitch of my voice that I was wound up like a spinning top. Into the wee slot I inserted all the shillings and tanners she asked of me, and kept the rest handy just in case I needed more time.

How great it was to hear Josie's voice on the line, crackle or no crackle. The poor girl cried a lot at the start of the conversation. I just had to keep reassuring her that I would stand by her, and that everything would work out all right. I may even have convinced myself of the truth of it!

What was she to do, now in the immediate present?

Get to a doctor, I told her. She needs to make sure whether or not she is with child, first and foremost. Once she has done that she needs to speak to her tutor or a chaplain or someone…some senior person in the institution who has wisdom. This kind of thing must have happened before, surely, and there will be solutions.

"Solutions?" she said. "There are no solutions. I will have a baby in seven months time. What am I to do about my course? What are you and I going to do about our baby?"

I told her not to be worrying about that. I said, "As soon as I can, I will come over to you, and we will get married somewhere."

"It is not as simple as all that," she told me. "Our parents will have something to say about the idea of us getting married, never mind having a baby that was conceived in those circumstances. I am dreading having to tell my father."

I was feeling exactly the same fear myself. All I could do was try to calm her down, assure her that I loved her, and I would never leave her…but practically speaking, I was as lost as she was. We needed good advice from someone who had a bit of life experience.

"Look," I told her, "if the worst comes to the worst, I will go and tell your father. How do you feel about that?"

"I feel…I have no idea how or what to feel," she said. "I just wish it would all go away. I am supposed to be starting this course, but all I can think about is what to do about this baby. I am not coping with anything, Jack. I just can't think straight. I wake up at night in my new bed, and tremble at the thought of what is ahead of me….and I can't get back over to sleep again. Then, when I do, I sleep in, and miss the start of my lectures."

"You really need someone there to talk to," I tell her. "It is very important and urgent that you do, Josie, with me so far away and not able to do anything. Promise me you'll go to your chaplain, or ask your doctor who to talk to about it."

She agreed to do this. But she said for me not to go near her father until she is sure, and until she has figured out what she wants to do. Her dilemma seems mainly the choice between leaving the Academy and coming home to me to be a family, or trying to complete as much of her course this year as she can, maybe making up for it later, and trying to see it through to get her qualifications....but in that case what about the baby? She can't surely do the course and be a mother.

Well, that is all up for thought and conversation as time goes on. In the meantime, I think I got her calmed down a bit. We promised to talk again at the same time next week. And of course I asked her to keep writing to me; putting stuff down on paper is a great way of straightening out your thinking.

All very wise on the part of my brother; it's very late to have discovered some wisdom in himself, but at least he has. I want to teleport back to 1959, take the boat from Larne to Stranraer and go to support Josie in Glasgow. She needs someone to lean on right now. Her not having a mother is a terrible reality in these circumstances. The poor girl. How does she communicate with her older and extremely religious father, and her in this very modern, yet age-old, predicament? I want to put her in a car, drive her back to her own home, mediate between her and her dad, bring Jack into the discussion and try to work out a way for them all to come to peace about the situation. After all, girls have been getting pregnant before marriage since Bible times. And, in this strange little country, I am fairly sure there has been the odd example of a Catholic girl falling pregnant to a Protestant boy, and indeed vice versa.

Surely in the slightly more enlightened circumstance of the late fifties…but I catch myself on. The late fifties in N Ireland, in Ireland as a whole, was every bit as difficult a scenario as the seventies, or the eighties….or any time in our twisted history. We have all heard the stories; read them too.

I well remember a few years ago being really moved by the sad story of the Cloney family. My husband and I had gone to see the movie, "A Love Divided" in the cinema; the tale was a tragic one, of a Protestant girl who was married to a Catholic man in Co Wexford in the mid 1950ies. The community was ripped apart when the woman ran away with her children, resulting in a boycott of Protestant businesses in the town.

The fact that this true story happened only a few years before the dilemma faced by Jack and Josie, albeit in the Irish Republic, underlined how serious a problem they faced. This is, this was, real life. It was happening in my own family. And sadly, the brother at the centre of it was gone and could offer me no clarity, no solace other than the words in his increasingly precious journal.

Chapter 30

Confirmation

13th October 1959
My Darling Jack,
I have just returned from my second visit to the doctor recommended to me by the Academy. Yes, my love, I am afraid it is definite now. I am to have a baby. How incredible it feels for me to be writing those words, and me only 18, and here in a strange city, so far from home and from you. But I suppose girls have been having babies, some at even younger ages, since the beginning of time. It hardly seems fair, though, that I got caught on my first and only time to have sex. Our love making was very wrong and very crazy, but it was so precious as well; our baby will also be very precious, but right now I just cannot imagine how it is going to be.
To say I am terrified, Jack, is the understatement of all time. I am sure you gather that when we have talked on the phone, although I do try my best to hide it from you. If I could think of a way out of this mess I think I would jump at it...but there is no way, no way that a Catholic girl like me could ever countenance. I hope you feel the same.
It has been very difficult for me to have any friends here. There are plenty of girls in my classes, but every time someone tries to make friends I find myself clamming up, unable to make small chat when the only thing on my mind is the terrible situation I find myself in. This is not like me, as you know. I like to be sociable, I like to have lots of friends and to make conversation...but I am so self-absorbed just now, and I cannot pretend to be enjoying people's company. I am sure the other girls are noticing this and are starting to give me a

wide berth.

I want to tell you that I really appreciate the strength and understanding you give me when we talk on the phone. You are so brave and so wise. I depend so much on you. I just wish you could be here with me to hold me in the waves of fear that sweep over me like a relentless sea-storm.

You mentioned that my father needs to be told. How on earth am I going to do that? I cannot imagine the pain this will cause him. He is as much on his own as I am. If only my poor mother were alive to support him. He has nobody else, so far as I know. He will not want to make it known in the parish, although I suppose he will try to lean on Father Maguire.

I have one idea about how I might tell him, or rather how we might tell him. You suggested this yourself, I think. If you could bring yourself to go to my house and meet my father at a set time which you and I can agree, you could perhaps begin the process of preparing him, or telling him, and then I could phone and try to explain to him. It is a dreadful situation to be imagining, but I have thought about other possibilities and this seems the best. I really appreciate that you had this idea yourself, and that you are brave enough, and responsible enough, to want to do this. You have no idea how much it means to me that you want to stand by me, darling Jack. Will you please give this some thought before we chat on the phone on Saturday again. We can decide then the best course of action, and then I will have a better idea of what to tell the Academy concerning the future, whether to pull out of the course now, or stick with it for as long as my pregnancy will allow me.

I love you with every fibre of my being, dear Jack,
Josie XXX

Chapter 31

Conflicted

I need my head showered, as we say around here. I need to be alone, and far away from this house, this town-land. I take the car, and head to the coast. It's quite a drive, but I have always found solace in the rhythms of the sea, the crash of wave after wave, the scrunch of pebbles underfoot, the cries of seabirds. Solace, if not answers.

Today the shore is showing the results of the recent storms. The river is in spate, swollen, beer-brown, relentless. I am almost afraid to venture across the wooden bridge to get to the strand, so intimidating is its dark power. Where it collides with the incoming tide, an explosion of frothing foam is created, an angry, boiling cappuccino. Beyond it, the river looks like a slew of gravy as it curves out into the longshore current, dissipating itself in the unruly ocean.

I drag my feet across soft, damp sand, a fresh deposit that hasn't had time to bed down into what you'd normally expect of this beach. To my right, a deep ridge of tangled seaweed has been piled up, kelp stalks as thick as my arms snaking through each other as if to hold on against the sucking draw of the next high tide. A few leafless branches litter the shoreline, torn from riverside trees further inland.

Gusts of wind slam against me with the force of a barn door.

I take little notice of this, or of my surroundings. I am in another place, a different time.

Wouldn't it be great if you could counsel someone through a time-tunnel? I want to be in my nineteen year old brother's life; I want to be in Glasgow and Castlecuinn simultaneously, to tell the two lovebirds that everything will be all right. I want to take my brother by the hand, put him in the car and drive him to this widower in town, the father of Josie whatever-her-name-is. I want to give him the courage to face up to this dilemma. The father will see that he is a good, sound young man who has just made a terrible mistake with his precious daughter. He will face up to the challenge of his faith and his church's teaching; he will see the sense in these two getting married as soon as possible, despite the barriers. If the worst comes to the worst, and they have to move to a place far away from here for their own safety and peace of mind, so be it. It won't be the end of the world, will it? But I can do nothing other than shout in frustration across the intervening years, the words being whipped off my lips by the onshore wind, silenced in the swishing marram grass of the sand-hills beside me.

I try to pray as I walk. Then I catch myself on. What is the point in praying about something that happened forty-eight years ago? It is not going to change anything. In some ways, though, I am praying less about the events of the past, and more about how I am receiving these revelations, that and how my twin will take this news about our brother's secret past.

I begin to think about the unborn baby in his story, in Josie's womb. What is to become of it? What has become of it? In my church's teaching, this baby is created by God, in the likeness of God….somehow. But it is illegitimate. How does this 'bastard' status square with the notion that it is made in the likeness of God, a God who is so Holy? I cannot get my head around that.

In the Psalms, I recall, it speaks about the early origins of the child. I remind myself of the verses; I think we must have had to learn them in Sunday School back when I was young.

"For you created my inmost being; you knit me together in my mother's womb. I praise you because I am fearfully and wonderfully made; your works are wonderful, I know that full well. Your eyes saw my unformed body. All the days ordained for me were written in your book before one of them came to be."

'All the days ordained for me'. For this poor baby. Even those early days. Written in the book before one of them came to be. I can almost hear my husband's voice reciting this. We are very much in his theological home turf here.

Everything has been planned….even this unplanned pregnancy. Yeah, I think, that's all very well, but what if our daughter had come home from England with a huge bulge around her waistline, and her not yet married? He would find that difficult to reconcile with his beliefs in predestination, wouldn't he! I can just hear his voice rising in righteous annoyance, his puritan sensibilities trumping the logical extension of what he claims to believe.

So, if the Psalmist is correct, Josie and Jack's baby has had its days written in God's book, even before it is born. That being the case, why should there be any issue with it, any tarring of its innocent little life with the label of illegitimacy? Why are the churches so hung up on this? Sure, they can preach against fornication, but if someone, like my wayward brother, fails to listen and a child is the result…as seems to be the case here…why is it so hard to accept it all as God's ordained plan? If not one sparrow falls to the ground unnoticed by him, how much more wouldn't he be interested in the conception and birth of a human child, made in his image?

Questions, questions. I have no answers. My inclination is to try to protect Jack. Him and his Josie. I feel his pain. I feel the despair of them both. I would do anything I could to bring them some peace…across the years. I think that is part of my frustration.

The sea, the restless sea. It has matched my mood today, rather than lifting my spirits. I return towards my car as a shower sweeps in across the strand. I get drenched in no time, but somehow it doesn't matter. I feel like I deserve it. I even imagine that I can somehow be cleansed by it.

'Soak me to the bone,' I hear myself cry, as I open my arms wide and throw my head back to let the water pour over my face. 'The sky is crying', someone sang, and I am receiving its anointing. The rain mingles with my tears, or vice versa, I don't know. Either way I am a mess as I finally open the car door and sit inside. Dripping hands grip the steering wheel, and I blubber away like a lost child.

"Oh Jack! My dear, lost brother. I want you back, even for an hour. I want to hold you, comfort you."

When I get myself under control the windows have all misted up. I am alone in my fogged-in world; deep doubts and crazy fears are beginning to distort my vision.

Eventually I settle, and begin my drive home.

Out of habit, more than anything else, I turn on the radio. Classic FM.

'Lacrimosa'!

Would you credit it? Even Mozart is on my case.

Chapter 32

Owning Up

24th Oct 1959

One of the most nerve-wracking things I have ever had to do, or will ever have to do. I am glad it's over, but the shaking has barely stopped, although I have been home and back at the milking since. Even the cows seemed to sense something wrong with me, turning their heads in the stalls to stare into my soul with their big, sorrowful, plum eyes. I interpreted their doleful moans as some sort of sympathy, beast to man.

Josie and I had arranged a 1.00 pm phone call. That worked well for me, as I had to be in town in the morning for a package of drugs from the vet. I went good and early, saw the vet, and then went in search of Josie's father's house. She had described it well. I found it far too soon.

My heart felt like a Lambeg drum as I rang the bell and waited. 12.30 on my watch. Was I not way too early? How was I going to fill half an hour before Josie rescued me?

He stared down at me from the top of the steps. Quite a large man, bulging waistcoat, well-greyed hair, half-lens glasses, neat moustache; my first impression was of a strong but kindly gentleman, at least twenty years older than my father.

"What can I do for you, young man?"

He had waited for me to speak first, but I couldn't muster the saliva to say a single word. Eventually I did though.

"I need to talk to you, sir," I said. "It is very important."

"What about, may I ask? Is it business or personal or what?"

"It's personal, sir, but it concerns you yourself...very much so."

He must have been able to discern my nervousness. I was shaking, my voice quivering. I have never felt such a wimp.

He stepped back from the door.

"You'd better come in," he said.

Into his study. He went behind his imposing desk, business-like in bearing; the oppressive bookshelves with their solemnly dark spines seemed to press down on me like the bars of a prison cell. I sat in the chair he pointed to.

He asked for my name. When I told him he smiled, and reached out over the desk to shake hands. This took me by surprise, the warmth. I think he said something like, "Ah I know your people, I believe. The Castlecuinn Shaws, am I right?"

I nodded. How in heaven's name did he know my family? That threw another cat into the pigeon coop.

"And how is your father?"

For a moment I was struck dumb. I opened my mouth, but all I could think was about how this would complicate things. Eventually I managed a squeaky response.

"You know him...my father?"

"Of course. A good sound man. Is he doing well?"

"He's fine."

That was all I could bring myself to say, a bit stunned by this disclosure, and by this man's friendliness. That's not going to last much longer, I thought. How was he going to react to my news? The warmth will go out of him like air from a burst tyre, I am sure. I started to wonder if he might get rough with me. I had no idea how a father might respond to such a bombshell.

"So what can I do for you, Mr Shaw?"

Mr Shaw? First time I've ever been called that. I am nineteen. I am about to confess to him that I've left his only daughter in the family way, and he is showing me nothing but professional respect. Lord but I was so far on the back-foot I felt horizontal!

"Sir," I began, "this isn't easy, but there is no other way than to tell you the truth."

"Go on!"

"Josie."

"Josie? Josephine, you mean. What about her?"

My courage dried up…but my eyes made up for it. I started to dissolve inside. The tension in me was too much. The tears just squeezed themselves out of me, and my shoulders shuddered and heaved. I held back the emotion as best I could, and tried to resume my story. I had only been able to say one word. Her precious name. My breathing had all gone to pot.

"Settle yourself now," he said gently. "How do you know my daughter?"

After a minute I was able to begin again. Very shakily, with stifled gasps punctuating my speech as I struggled for air.

"I met her at the Colonel's place…she was coming for music with…we got talking."

"And?"

"Sir, I am sorry…we talked a lot…then we fell in love."

"Oh dear," he said. A long silence. He stood there, then bent over, his hands gripping his desk. I think he began to guess where this was going. After half a minute he looked back up at me.

"You fell in love, you say? And…what have you to tell me?"

"Josie, Josie is the best girl in all the world. What I am about to tell you, sir, is entirely my fault. None of it should be blamed on Josie."

"You'd better spit it out, young man," he said, his cool deserting him a bit at last.

"You daughter is expecting our baby, sir."

He sat down abruptly, his face gone ghostly pale. I barely heard his whisper. "Sweet, suffering Jesus!" I waited as long as I could; I needed to give Josie some more defence before she came on the phone.

"Sir, I need you to know that it was not Josie's idea; it is not her fault. I take full responsibility. We only... sir, we only did it once. It was on my birthday when yous had come back from down south. It was a terrible mistake. We didn't do it again, I promised that to her....and we kept our promise. So please don't be too hard on Josie. She loves you, sir, and I know she would never do anything to hurt you, especially with her mother..."

I stopped. I had said enough. I had bared my soul, filled the space with my words of regret. It had all spilled out.

His head was in his hands now, muttering to himself. I was waiting for him to come back to me, but he was a long way away. In a world of tortured silence.

Then a mumble from his bowed head. "My poor darling girl! What were you thinking Josephine?"

"Sir, if I could just say....before Josie phones....she is going to phone you now at one o'clock, while I am here, if that's ok. What I want to say is that I will stand by her, you don't have to worry about that. We can get married as soon as possible...."

"Stop!" He held up both his hands in a very decisive gesture. "Stop... your....rambling. And don't tell me anymore."

I waited. He got up sharply, moved towards me. I cowered, unnecessarily so; he was only going to stare out the window. After a while he spun around to me again. His voice was still controlled, only just though. It had a harder edge than before.

"Marriage, you say? Marriage? Are you out of your mind? What age are you anyway?"

"I am nineteen, sir."

"And Josephine is eighteen. She's little more than a child. She has just gone to study at the Academy in Glasgow, just setting out on her career as a musician. And you have the temerity to talk about marriage! Are you mad altogether?"

"No sir, I am not mad...and I know all that," I said. "But circumstances have changed. We can't just wish this baby away."

He returned to his desk, as if hoping for some answer there. I watched him thinking deeply, shaking his head at times, and drumming his fingers on the desk.

"Marriage," he growled. "Did it never occur to you, or to Josephine, for that matter, that a relationship between the two you is impossible? A relationship! A courtship? Impossible! Never mind marriage! This is Northern Ireland. This is 1959. I cannot see your folks agreeing to you becoming a Catholic. Your father is a well respected Presbyterian, as I recall. He won't countenance you turning, and Josephine will certainly never turn her back on her faith."

"But sir...in this position Josie needs to be married. So do I. And we have promised each other that. All we need is your permission...."

He interrupted again. Hands in the air.

"Permission that will never come, young man."

"But sir...what is Josie to do? What am I to do?"

"I don't think there is anything for you to do, unless...unless you are prepared to abandon your parents, and your church and your whole family circle and be baptised into the Catholic faith. Are you willing for that? Because that is what it will take for this to happen."

"I'd have to think about that. I'd have to talk to my folks," I told him.

Another long silence.

"Can't you see it's hopeless? You cannot ask my daughter to choose between you and her father, can you?"

"No sir. It's not hopeless. I will stand by Josie, always. She doesn't have to choose between us."

"But she does. And she has lost one parent already; you wouldn't want her to lose a second. Josephine is my life. She will not disobey me. She will not desert me. Do I make myself clear?"

"You do, sir, absolutely, but... Josie needs to be married..."

The phone on his desk rang at that point. Before he picked it up he pointed me to the door.

"Wait in the garden," he said. "I haven't finished what I need to say to you yet."

I was out in his wonderful garden for a full twenty minutes. I wandered about between rose-beds and fruit bushes. I walked to the far end of the lawn and looked down over the spread of houses. This property of his was situated on a hillside; the view below me stretched out over the grey rooftops and across the valley below. I could just about pick out the distant forests that surrounded the Colonel's estate. I was in no mood for admiring flowers or landscape, however. Why, why, why had I not had a bit of common sense and resisted my basic urges? Beautiful and all as Josie is, thrilling and all as the love-making was... surely I should have foreseen such an outcome? It is not as if I am unaware of reproduction; the farm depends on it; my life is steeped in the cycle of it. What possessed me to imagine there was no chance of pregnancy happening to Josie that day? Her life changed forever by fifteen minutes of bliss... mine too. But, I told myself, it is all redeemable, if only, if only her father can climb down from his religious hobby horse and see the sense of letting us marry. It is all I want to do now to make this situation right. I see no other way for Josie and me.

He came looking for me in the shrubbery at the end of the drive. I waited, quaking every bit as much as at the start.

"I have talked to my daughter," he said quietly. His self-control was back, the *daddy in charge.*

"How is she?" I asked.

"She is as well as might be expected," he said, "but thank you for asking. And, might I say as well, thank you for having the decency to come to my house and make your apology in person. It says something for your character, but I would expect nothing less from a son of Jacob Shaw."

"The least I could do, sir," I said.

"Indeed, but you must now put the thing behind you and allow Josephine and I to think through the best way forward, you understand? I have promised her that I will travel to Glasgow to see her at the earliest opportunity, so that is…"

I interrupted, "Sir, I need to come too. I need to come with you. I need to see Josie…"

He held up his hands in that same dismissive gesture as before. "No question of that! The matter is now between me and Josephine. You have done your worst and I do not want you to have anything more to do with her. The matter is now inside my family. It has nothing more to do with you."

"But sir," I insisted, "Josie and I love each other. It has everything to do with me. The child is my child too."

He turned away and began walking back towards his house. Then he paused and half-turned. Over his shoulder he threw me a few final words.

"You made a dreadful mistake with my daughter. Once is enough. You will not have the chance to make another. Leave her alone. And do not breathe a single word about this debacle to a single person you hear me! Not a word. Good day to you, Mr Shaw."

With that he went inside and the door was slammed in my face. I was totally rebuffed. To say I was hurt, angry, frustrated….understatements of the greatest degree.

I drove slowly home, contemplating how to tell my parents and how to proceed.

Chapter 33

Parents

My wayward brother has gone up in my estimation. Such courage to go to the girl's father, and in his 'castle'. This brick wall that he finds himself up against will be difficult to deal with. How he manages it, and how he tells my parents…now that will really test his resolve.

I find a short letter from Josie which seems to fit chronologically into the story at this point. It is uncharacteristically brief; perhaps this is the result of something her father has said to her on the phone, or perhaps she is short of time, and wants to get this communication in the post as soon as she could. Another possibility, I suppose, is that she is just so troubled by the pregnancy, and by her conversation with her father, that she cannot express what she is feeling in the way she has been doing up until now.

25th Oct 1959

My Darling Jack,

I hope you are well and not too concerned about everything. It is only 24 hours since I had that conversation with my father. He was pleased with your courage in coming to tell him, but very, very angry about what has happened. Angry and disappointed in both of us, I suppose, me especially. He blames you, of course, which is what any father would do in these circumstances, but you and I both know we are equally to blame.

He will come to see me in the next few days, just to comfort me and make sure I am all right. He will also want the biggest say in what we decide to do, which again is probably what we might expect of any father. Already I am aware that he will not countenance any idea of marriage. He tells me he has seen so many other such marriages end in disaster. But I will work on him. It cannot be impossible.

I am feeling well, although the mornings continue to be times of nausea. This is to be expected, but may pass, my doctor tells me. Study-wise I am doing my best to stay afloat in the course. I have caught up on most of what I missed, although understanding everything is difficult. The practical sessions I have missed cannot be repeated apparently, which is too bad.

I look forward to our Saturday phone call at the usual time. (My father has forbidden any more contact between us, but what he won't know will do him no harm.)

I would love to be a fly on the wall when you talk to your parents. I hope that is not too hard for you. I miss you so much, Jack.
All my love as usual.
Josie xxx

Short, but very loving as before. She would love to be a fly on the wall for his encounter with the parents…that is exactly what I am thinking as well. In the absence of a Tardis, I turn again to Jack's journal.

Sunday 25th Oct 1959

Tonight I sat my parents down in the good room to explain everything that had happened. I started at the beginning, and talked them through it, as honestly and sensitively as I could. Even before I mentioned who Josie was, their reaction was every bit what I expected.

The disgrace! The sin! The shame on the family! Father's reputation! Our Church! The poor girl, whoever she was! The absolute astonishment that I had used the Colonel's time, and the ruins of that ancient place, to do the 'dirty deed'!

The thing only went nuclear, however, when I answered mother's question as to who the girl was. A Catholic, and daughter of this acquaintance of my father! This was the final straw. It seemed to drive him up the walls entirely. The religion issue seemed to put everything else into the shade.

"You have no idea what you have done! You stupid ejit! Nothing but a filthy brute, you are. My own son bringing me into such humiliation…me and the whole family. Everyone of us tainted. God have mercy on you. You have crossed a line here that you do not even begin to understand."

It was a vitriolic attack. I couldn't quite get my head around it.

"Why, what is the big deal about her father?" I asked.

My father got up and stormed out of the room at that point. I was nearly scared he was on the verge of a heart attack. I looked at my mother for an explanation. She had said nothing, just sat there on the settee, crying quietly. She eventually lifted her head and gave me the full stare from very hurting eyes.

"That man has been very good to us in the past."

"How so?"

"When we were buying the upper farm he lent the money to your father. This is the thanks he gets."

Dear God in heaven, I thought, a huge sigh exploding from my lips. That was a turn-up for the books. Who could have seen that coming? I couldn't think of a word to say. So, in the past Josie's dad had played a part in our whole farming enterprise, the farm that I would most likely be inheriting in the future. How incredible. The thought suddenly struck me that maybe this was all meant to be, that if I get to marry Josie she will be with me here on the very land that her father had a hand in securing for us. My wife will have an unexpected stake in this our farm. In my head it seemed so logical.

My father returned to the room, a bit calmer looking, the fiery red having drained from his cheeks. Glass of water in hand, he plunked himself down beside mother again.

"She's told me about the loan," I said. "I knew nothing about that; not that it would have made a difference to me falling for Josie or anything."

"You have been so foolish, Jack," he said.

"I know that, of course I know that now. I didn't mean for any of this to happen, but it has. Still, if I can marry Josie…at least she will be coming into a farm that her father…."

"Will you stop!" he interrupted.

I watched the side of his mouth twist up into a wince of derision, his eyes piercing, his head turning rhythmically from side to side.

"You have no idea what you are talking about. There is no question of you marrying that girl."

"But why? Just because it would embarrass her father?"

"Embarrass? Embarrass her father? I am not even thinking about her father. I am thinking about your father. Have you not been listening when I have been preaching, son? Have you not been paying attention over the years?"

"Of course I have, but that is all sort of theoretical stuff, isn't it? I have got my Catholic girlfriend pregnant, and now I have to marry her. It's only right. It's the only thing to do."

"Look Jack, you are young and innocent. You forget the reality of living in this community. It is simple, son. There is no way you are marrying that girl. For my son, to marry a Roman Catholic is absolutely not going to happen. I won't have it. Her church won't hear tell of it either, nor her father. He wouldn't stand for her turning."

"But why, daddy? It is my duty…"

"Your duty was not to fall for Satan's temptation. She was sent to trap your soul…"

"Agh, nonsense, daddy. I won't listen to…look, Josie is very devout in her faith. She is a good Catholic, a good Christian girl, far better than me."

"A good Christian girl, you say? Not very Christian to… to land my son in this mess. She is obviously a bit of a temptress…"

"No, daddy!" I interrupted, more vociferously than I intended. "I am not having you say anything against her. It was not her fault. We are both as guilty as each other. Josie is the best person I've ever met, Catholic or no Catholic."

"She may seem like a good person to you, but her church...look son, you say she is a good Christian girl. Such nonsense. Her religion is anti-Christian. The Westminster Confession of faith says it, clear as a bell; the pope is the Anti-Christ. I signed up to that when I became a Presbyterian elder. So don't ever start to think you can marry into that.... You would be turning your back on everything we have stood for as a family. You'd be turning your back on this farm."

I sat quietly for a minute; then I had an insight into his hypocrisy. I took a risk; I said it out loud.

"It didn't stop you accepting a loan from her father....and him a member of such an anti-Christian church."

From the look he gave me that barb hit home. He spluttered something about the two things being completely different. They were different, of course they were, but it seemed to me this was all about protecting the purity of the Shaw name, the tribal loyalty. I wasn't going to win the argument, not there and then. But I did appeal to my mother.

"Mum," I said, "do you not think I owe it to Josie to marry her? I don't have to turn, but surely I can't leave her in the lurch. I can't leave her bringing up our child as a single girl, and her in the middle of her studies, can I?"

My mother was a pitiable sight, hunched there against my father. She said not a word, but I knew she would have great sympathy for Josie. I knew she would love my girl whenever she got to meet her.

"What is she studying?" father asked.

I explained her situation, and how vulnerable she felt in Glasgow, with no support. I said that her father was going to go to see her soon, and that I felt I should be doing so as well.

"You'll do no such thing," he said. "Leave it to them."

So cold, so unfeeling.

"Look," he added, "I will go and have a chat with him; he must be wild with worry about her. I'll see what he plans to do about it all. It's only right."

"What he plans to do?" I said. "It's not just about him and her. I have a stake in this as well. Whatever happens, I have a right to have a say in it, and you tell him that."

So ended our first argument about it, but there would, I am certain, be many more.

Chapter 34

Absence

I have decided to take today off from work. I seem to have reached the point where I just cannot whip up the emotional energy to handle it. Operating in a school environment, probably like any work environment, demands that you put on that professional costume; not just the clothes and make-up… that whole facade of confidence, the smilingly efficient persona that you slip on when you are playing the role. I feel so low, so drained at the moment, that I shudder at the thought of having to fit my damaged and distended self into the artificial shape of that outer shell. There are too many cracks in this Russian doll right now.

I phoned in sick last night. The Vice Principal wasn't particularly sensitive in his response. I suppose I have been off school for a considerable period of time recently, compassionate leave, as they call it. The school even cancelled this year's spring show, guessing early, and correctly, that I would not be able to give it my full commitment in the circumstances. I have appreciated this decision, and their generosity over the past few months. Nevertheless, the VP wanted to understand my situation, being the person in charge of bringing in cover teachers.

"Are you feeling under the weather physically," he queried, "or is it just everything coming in on you, after all that's happened?"

"It's maybe a bit of both," I told him. "I am just not in the right frame of mind to be handling school at the minute."

"Is there anything we can do? How about maybe a chat with a grief counsellor or something?"

"Maybe," I said, noncommittally. "I'll see how I am after tomorrow. Maybe I could make it back in then and have a go, see how I manage. Even half a day."

He hesitated. I understood. If he was to bring in a sub for me it would be cleaner to do it for the whole day. I bailed him out.

"Look, I will do my best to get my head cleared and be back in by Thursday. I'll let you know in good time….and thanks, I hate doing this, but I just can't seem to concentrate at the minute."

"Maybe have a chat with your doctor," he suggested, "and, like I say, we could get a counsellor to see you; might help. Just say the word. It takes time to get over a death like this; you were close to your brother, I know."

Close to my brother? He has no idea. I hadn't really been, if I am honest, but Jack is living non-stop in my head just now. In some ways, he is more alive to me at the minute than he has been in years. I feel I am getting to know the man I only half knew. The hidden other half is being revealed, and, fascinating to think, this is the half he now wants me to know. He has been introducing me to his alter ego. And this is why I do not feel I want to be in school tomorrow. It is not grief. It is certainly not any physical illness. It is not a psychological thing, I don't believe… except in the sense that I am absolutely fixated on this saga of his. I am driven to read on, to get to the end of it, to uncover the truths of what happened. There is a subconscious fear beginning to rumble, like an awakening volcano, deep in my heart.

I cannot leave it another day. I must know.

My husband is worried about me. He hovers around me in the morning like a sparrow hawk, seemingly not quite content that I am telling him the whole story about why I am determined to be away from work, locked in my bedroom all day.

"It's hard to explain," I tell him. "You wouldn't understand. You've never lost a brother."

"But this is irrational," he says. "Jack has gone. No amount of crying or worrying about his soul's repose will do anything for him now. You have got to let him go."

I am not letting him go until he has told me the full story, the whole truth, I think to myself. To my husband, however, I parrot a more acceptable reply.

"Yes, I know all that, but it doesn't mean I don't think about him. "

"Of course," he began, "but thinking about…"

"You know, when he was alive, I never really appreciated him for who he was. I was always judging him. I think we all were, you included. It was like something implicit in our home…to criticise Jack. Jack was always to blame, for near enough everything. Always the black sheep. Whatever was wrong, it was always tempting to blame Jack. He was the fall guy, always the unhappy scapegoat."

He shrugs his shoulders. "Jack was his own worst enemy though. He could never seem to rise above his resentments."

"Maybe so," I say, "but have you ever wondered about that resentment? Like…why he was always seeming to be so down about things? Always deeply sad? You ever wonder about that?"

He shrugs his shoulders. "I would have thought that was obvious," he said.

"Obvious how?"

"Well, he had turned his back on God, for a start. He didn't have the peace that passes all understanding in his heart."

So glib. The trite, unthinking, party line. I should have seen that platitude coming. 'The peace that passes understanding'. I find myself thinking that if we had had a bit more understanding ourselves of who he was, and why he seemed to live under some dark cloud, we might have been better able to connect with him.

"Maybe he just thought it was God who had turned his back on him," I hear myself saying. It's close to heresy, I know, but I am not thinking straight right now.

Husband is shocked.

"You're not yourself since he passed, that is obvious. I am worried about you."

"Maybe I just mean that we all turned our backs on him, and he took it that, if we were doing that, and we were supposed to be God's people…well, God was likely doing that too? Turning away from him. Know what I mean?"

"In my opinion you are over-thinking all this," he says. "Look, go back to bed, and I'll bring you a coffee in a wee while."

"Me, over-thinking?" I say, leaving him. "I would have thought that was your domain."

"What is that supposed to mean?"

The original, row-starting question. I'm not taking the bait today. Not when I have so much to read through.

"Doesn't mean a thing," I say, heading to the stairs. "But no coffee, thanks. I just need to be alone for a day."

"No change there then!"

"Exactly."

"Do you mind if I go for my walk?"

"I don't mind at all. Suit yourself," I tell him.

I lock the bedroom door behind me, pull the curtains wide, and open the window….briefly. The raucous splutter of our neighbour's ageing tractor assaults my ears from across the fields. He must be carting silage to his animals further up the mountain. The window gets closed again. I need some tranquility here.

The valley spreads itself out below me like an elaborate guide-map of the area, the kind visitors pick up from the Council's Tourist Information Office. The Colonel's big house is almost hidden behind the winter-stripped trees, ghostly-looking in the emaciating morning light. I can't make out the old castle beyond it, though I do see the river worming its way into the estate grounds from the flat land beyond. I owe that castle ruin a visit though, I think to myself.

To the south I see thin pencil-lines of smoke curling up from the chimneys of Castlecuinn village; the incense of the turf-burners, kneeling in reverence before their early morning fires. I love our home here. It is my sanctuary, my high place on this elevated site. This upper farm of ours, with its rabbits and hares, its warbling larks and hooded crows, its spreading whins and rushes, its watery hollows and mounds, its erratic rocks and stubborn stone walls. Now to think that this is the land bought and paid for with money loaned by Josie's father to my father years ago! I recall Wally Brown mentioning something to me about a solicitor being very generous to our father back in the day. How strange to think of this twist in that particular strand of the story. His reward, a pregnant daughter and a bastard grandchild. So undeserved, so ironic.

I must speak to Wally further about the subject.

A sudden pang for my daughter. Christine is so emotionally-intelligent. I miss her today, in this aloneness that I have chosen. She would listen; she would understand the tremors that are shaking my foundations right now.

I set the fateful painting on the bed and remove the back panel once again, for the final time, I hope. I would love to reach the end of this quest today.

I begin in my brother's journal.

Chapter 35

Plans

Mon 9th Nov 1959

My recent phone calls with Josie have been very difficult. It is so hard to hear her distressed, far away, lonely and feeling abandoned. How I wish I could go to her. I have said this to her, but she would be horrified if I went against her father's wishes and arrived over there to surprise her.

She was to phone again on Saturday. I waited for her to call, but nothing happened. I felt very exposed, standing by the phone box in the village for half an hour. I am sure people passing were wondering, 'What's he doing waiting there? You'd think there wasn't a phone in his own house.' I even started to imagine that the more discerning of the villagers would be able to guess what I was up to. 'Ah, he's waiting for that wee catholic lass to phone him again!' I have to talk to myself about such stupidity.

Maybe Josie couldn't get through. Something may have cropped up. I really missed talking to her. The very sound of her voice is a calming music to me, despite her mood.

I find my sense of frustration growing by the day. The space between us; these gaps between our communications; the seeming impossibility of jointly solving our problems.

If only I could be with her. I long to see her, to fold her in my arms, smooth out any misunderstanding.

Christmas is coming, I have been thinking, but it is still six weeks away. It can't come soon enough.

13th Nov 1959

Josie's latest letter has contained some worrying thoughts. It arrived this afternoon, Jimmy McGrath slipping it into my pocket not ten yards away from where my father was laid out on the mucky concrete yard, attacking the under side of our temperamental old grey Ferguson with a spanner. He saw and heard nothing down there of course.

"There's a wee letter to brighten up your day, Jack," Jimmy whispered. "She must still love you, eh?"

Little did he know just how significant the contents of this latest letter would be.

·······

Mon 9th Nov 1959
My Darling Jack,

    I hope this finds you in good health. I am feeling fairly well, physically, at least, although I am very down just now. I wish I could have you near me. I need to be comforted by you. This is all too hard to bear alone.

I am sorry I could not phone you on Saturday as planned. My father had arrived over, you see, and he spent almost every moment with me, as if to let me out of his sight again might bring me further risk of disaster.

I have never seen my father like this. Obviously I have no memory of when my mother died, but I have the feeling that he is revisiting that long-buried grief, and compounding his distress about me with a resurrected version of what he went through then. He was very tearful. His normal self-control deserted him; I found it all very disturbing. While this is a big deal for me and you, I get the feeling it is something even more of a threat to how he sees himself. He kept going on about how he has failed me as a father; about how much I needed and missed a mother's guidance. He regretted that he should have counselled me about relationships, explained more fully to me the facts of life; I couldn't very well say that I had no need of such explanations. So I just had to play the innocent child. What a hypocrite I was. I felt bad about that afterwards. He quizzed me over and over about whether or not you had forced me. I assured him that you had not; the pressure got so intense I nearly told him that it was me had forced you! I told him it was an act of mutual love. Neither of us was to blame more than the other, which is completely true, although I do blame myself for being more foolish than you. I should have been more aware of the risk.

Jack, I am so sorry to tell you that he absolutely insists that we cannot be married. He said that, even if you agreed to become a Catholic, (which I would never ask you to do), he would still refuse his permission. He uses my career plans as an argument against me. Am I prepared to throw away every chance of success because of one mistake? When I said that I would always choose you and our baby over my career he became very angry. Was this how I wanted to thank him for everything he has put into my expensive education? Was this how I wanted to taint my mother's memory? She was a great star of the music world, he said. It is my duty to fulfil the potential, indeed the inheritance, that mother did not get the chance to. After all, her death was as a result of having me, the complications of child birth. (I had never realised that I was so much to blame for my mother's death. What a thing to learn at a time like this! I am so troubled about this Jack, and so worried about how giving birth to our child may affect me. Please hold me in your prayers, where you cannot hold me in your arms.)

So I am afraid, dear Jack, that I cannot see us getting married at the moment. Perhaps marriage will be possible for us in the future, but not right now. That being the case, my father has been making enquiries here about how we might handle things. You are not going to enjoy any of these ideas, I know.

He does not want me to return home to N Ireland for Christmas! My bump would inevitably be seen in the town. (It is beginning to grow large already and I am only in my 16th week. By Christmas it will be my 22nd week, more than halfway through the thing!) Instead he will come here and we will travel somewhere to a nice hotel, perhaps by Loch Lomond he says, to have Christmas together. After Christmas I will not be able to return to the Academy. They have firm rules about this; indeed after my father went to see the head of my school, there was a suggestion that I should leave straight away. My father used his charm and legal nous to persuade him that I might stay on until Christmas. I will therefore forfeit my first year of the course, returning in September of next year to take it up again. That was the deal between father and the Dean. In the meantime, however, I can have private lessons.

The second part of the arrangement is that my father has organised and paid for me to stay in a mother and baby home in Edinburgh, from January until after the baby is born.

Dearest Jack, the saddest news of all is that our little baby will have to be put up for adoption

Adoption!
I get no further!
Edinburgh?
Adoption in Edinburgh?
My head is spinning. Literally I fall off the bed.
Gather myself up and say, "Catch yourself on. It could never be!"
My heart is pounding in my ears.
Oh please, God! Let this not be true! Let this be some crazy coincidence of a mistake. Is this why he….?
Let me do the sums. When had they made love? It was Jack's birthday, wasn't it? July 26th.
I grab my diary, count on forty weeks from then.
30th April. Phew!
My date of birth, twin's as well, of course…5th April 1960.
But could it be?
I have been drawn along in this story with growing dread, I know I have. I have not been able to admit it to myself. It was an ephemeral

wisp of fear that had ghosted around the recesses of my mind, and could never quite be grasped. Denial? Was it even possible? How, in the name of my Father in heaven, could this be?

But wait! Josie is only carrying one child, isn't she? Not a mention of twins anywhere. As yet!

I grab the remainder of her letters, rip them apart looking for any mention of twins. How early could they tell back in those days?

I am searching, reading frantically.

Nothing…as yet. She had said she was large, hadn't she? But sure she has no experience of this. Maybe she was just…oh, come on! Rip another one open. Scan the small, neat handwriting. January. February. No mention of anything to do with twins. I am off the hook. But am I scanning too quickly? Could I have missed it…if it is there at all? I re-read, more carefully.

Oh Lord, let it not be so! Please!! February again. Another note. Nothing. Well, just a mention of 'feel like I am going to burst!' But I remember that feeling myself with my second child, my boy.

Into March. Only a few more weeks to go.

Surely she would have known by now if she was carrying…what was her doctor doing if twins had been missed in the scans? But of course there was no ultrasound then, was there? I don't recall when…

Surely, with a first timer like this, an eighteen year old girl on her own, vulnerable…surely twins wouldn't have been missed by this stage?

I start to content myself. I was imagining things.

It could never have happened, that Jack was not my brother at all, that he was actually my father, that he had somehow managed to bring us into his family, surely not? I was getting stressed for no reason. Relief begins to flow through me. What a crazy fear that was…

Then…

17th March 1960

My Darling Jack,

Happy St Patrick's Day, my love.
We are missing you, me and our babies! Yes, you read that right! Me and our babies. Would you believe it? I am carrying your twins. My doctor is astonished that he missed the double heart-beat until now. Still, everything will be all….

I see no more. Everything spins, dizzily.
Breath leaves me. Darkness!
Thump of pain. Jagged flash of lightening in the black sky.
Asleep, half-dreaming, nothingness. Slowly the darkness brightens.

When I come round I see everything at an angle. The mirror on the wardrobe door is all wrong. Horizontal instead of….I need to get that fixed. What is going on? I seem to be on the floor of my bedroom. I cannot understand why I am here. What happened me? Why is my head so sore? I put my hand up to my temple. Feels wet! Look at my fingers. Goodness. They are red. Ketchup red. I must have cut my head on…on what? My eyes focus slowly on the corner of the dressing table. Could I have fallen against it? Maybe, but why? I prop myself up on one elbow. Did I faint? Jeepers but this blood is dripping down from my head. Falling on to the floor…on to…drops soaking into a small piece of paper below. Red splodges decorating it randomly. I smear one of them back and forward. What is this page? I struggle to pick it up and bring it to my eyes. I can't make it out, my glasses seem to be missing. Where? On my knees, crawling. I find them by the waste basket. Stick them on. The letter again. Neat writing below the smudged red spots. 'My Darling Jack', it begins. What was this letter? The blood is creaming down my nose now, like tomato soup. Maybe need help. Who? How? I have a husband. No, not him, surely not him. I couldn't bear his help just now. Why this terrible pain in my head? Why am I so mixed? Confused. Throbbing. Dizzy still. My phone is on the bed surely? Where? Find my phone. See if Jack will answer it…he usually does. But…Jack? Jack is gone, isn't he? Jack is gone. I start to wail. Yeah, Jack is …my brother is gone. Gone forever. I don't have that brother any more. But I have twin. And twin needs to come. He needs to see this mess. Read this letter, whatever it was for. Oh yeah. Phone him, I think! I scroll to his number; try him. Is he answering? At the shop maybe?

Buzz, buzz. A few times.

Not picking up. Likely busy. Click.

"Sarah, what's up," he says.

"Not much, but I cut my head." I sound far away from myself.

"Oh right. Is it bad? How'd that happen?"

"Not sure. Bleedin' bad, I think. I need you to fix it."

"What? What d'ya mean fix it? Is it bad? Are you not at work?"

"No. Home."

"You're at home? And you've cut your head? Is Calvin not there?"

"He's likely here somewhere. I think he's away…think he's out. But he'll not understand. I need you."

"I'm in the shop. I can come like, but….you don't sound at yourself at all. Is everything all right, apart from the cut head."

"Not really," I say. "I need you. Will you come up now? Please?" I hear somebody crying, sobbing. Oh, it's me!

"Sarah, settle down. It's all ok."

"No it's not. It's not ok. There's stuff you…stuff you need to read, I mean…to hear."

"What stuff? You are worrying me here, sis."
"Stuff. Just stuff. Stuff like…."
"Like what exactly?"
"Like why you are called Joseph."

Chapter 36

Revelation

Three stitches on my temple. And a big duck-egg of a bruise. They keep me in for observation; some medication to settle me. Seems I was in a side-ward, overnight. No-one understands what I am rambling on about. My precious twin brother thinks I have lost the plot entirely.

"No Joe," I say, "I am just after finding the plot."

He doesn't have a clue.

I have tried to explain earlier as he drove me to the hospital. I know by his reaction that he is worried about my sanity.

"Did you leave a note for Calvin?"

"I did, on the kitchen table."

"Did you lock my bedroom door?" I asked him.

"I locked it….look, you've asked me that twice already. Why is the bedroom door so important?"

"You'll understand in a wee while. I just don't want him finding out."

"Finding out what?"

"Finding out…all those letters you saw. Finding out everything. Like why you are called Joseph."

"Aye, what's that all about?"

I was holding a swab to my brow to collect the bleeding.

"Your mother was called Josie," I told him confidently.

"You're talking nonsense, Sarah," he said. "Our mother was called Bella. Isabella, if you want to be exact."

"Yes, of course; our adoptive mother was Bella. But I mean our birth mother, before we were adopted."

We nearly drove off the road at that with his long stare across at me.

"How do you know that? Have you been researching this secretly? I thought…."

I tried to explain the journal and the letters to him. It didn't work all that well. My own confusion about what had happened all those years ago had been exacerbated by whatever the bang on the head had done to my senses. Even if I had been clear-headed, how could I explain to the brother who shared Josie's womb with me that the Jack we thought of as our older brother was no brother at all. He was our father, or so, in my tangle of a mind, it would seem.

Poor Joseph became very quiet. I wasn't sure whether this was because I was making sense to him, or because he thought I was losing my mind. I think he leaned towards the latter. Eventually I stopped rambling on about it. No bad thing, for I couldn't remember what I had already said in the conversation, and what was new info.

The order of what I had been reading in those letters and diary entries had become all jumbled up...and, anyhow, I have not even reached the end of the thing.

I need to go back to Josie's earlier letters, and to Jack's account, just to get the sequence of events straight in my head. I have to remember that, by the stage I have reached in my reading, neither of them know anything about twins as yet. They are well short of that revelation. I am in the bizarre position of knowing more about the outcome of everything than they are, back in real time. That much I am clear about, even if my brain seems to have slowed down since my fall. In my head, the 'now', the 'then' and the 'earlier' have entwined themselves, like ivy on a lattice.

There are still massive questions about how, if it is true that we were the twins born to Josie and Jack, we ended up being adopted by our parents....well, by Jack's parents. I could appreciate why Joseph was skeptical about my convoluted account.

****

The medication worked so well that I have slept all of last night and most of this morning. No desperate dreams. The confusion has started to clear. A very worried Calvin comes to pick me up after lunch from the hospital. He quizzes me gently about how I hit my head, about why I phoned Joseph instead of waiting for him.

"I came back from my walk. No sign of you. Your door was locked, and you weren't answering from inside. Then I found that note, signed by Joseph."

"I'm sorry," I say.

He asked about 'all this nonsense' I had been spouting off last night when he came in to see me.

He had come to the hospital to see me? I hadn't registered that...but of course he would have.

I tell him that I cannot answer him until I have rested some more, until I have straightened out matters in my own mind. The last thing I need is for his perspective on my dubious origins.

When we arrive home, Joseph is back in our yard waiting. He looks very concerned as he stands beside his car, his wife too.

"Oh dear," I say to my husband, "bring them in. Can you entertain

Judith while I talk to Joseph. It could take a while though. Maybe make her something to eat."

I bring Joseph up to the bedroom. I take the key from him and lock the door behind us, as I usually do. He observes this with a disbelieving look on his face. Clearly he is seriously worried about my strange behaviour.

"Why are you doing that?" he asks. "What's all this on the floor?"

"It's evidence."

"Evidence? What are you talking about, Sarah?"

"Wait, be patient. You'll see. That's why I lock the door."

"I don't follow. What is the threat you fear?"

"No threat, I have just become very conscious of my need for privacy at the minute. Sit down on that chair and let me begin to talk you through all that has happened."

So he does.

"Do you remember how Jack was very insistent about this painting? He went on about wanting me to have it, even mentioned cleaning it. Remember?"

"I do remember, but I never thought much of it. I thought he was just going a bit strange as he neared the end."

"Well, what he was doing was guiding me to the real story of his life…his life and ours. He had written it all down in a journal. It was hidden in the back of the painting."

I show him the notebook, and he takes it in his hands like it is one of the Dead Sea Scrolls.

"This explains how we were born, Joseph. It explains who our mother was. It tells us who our father was."

"Who? How?"

"Jack, our brother…he was actually our father."

His reaction is to sit there in a completely dumfounded silence. Other than 'Nonsense' at the start, he hardly said a word for the next couple of hours as I talk him through the details, using Josie's letters and Jack's diary. When we reach the point about Josie's school his hands go to either side of his head, almost in disbelief, I think.

"So you're saying our mother was a Catholic?"

"She was."

"And who is she, this Josie?"

"That I do not know yet. But I will find out, trust me."

Poor Joseph looks shaken to the core, elbows on his knees, head in his hands. In a weird tone of voice he tells me to read on. I do, until I reach the part where Josie tells of the fact she is carrying twins.

"This is the last thing I remember reading. It's what convinced me that we were those babies," I tell him.

"It doesn't necessarily follow," he says.

Clutching at straws, I think.

"Our parents could have adopted another pair of twins at a later stage..."

"Our birthday! Our place of birth!" I tell him. "Too big a coincidence. This is Jack's declaration to us, don't you see?"

He knows. He sits there quietly, defeated, the fragile shell of his identity crushed like an egg under a sledge hammer in a matter of a few hours.

"Remember all those times in our childhood when strangers thought we looked like our mother, or our father, or even Jack...I remember some woman saying that!"

He is shaking his head slowly, a wretched expression in is eyes. "It's just impossible to take this in, Sarah."

Weirdly, at that moment I have a sudden flashback.

Jack's wake!

Jimmy McGrath's wife! What she had said as she was offering her condolences.

I had thought, "Silly woman! She's starting to dote!"

"Sorry about your father," she had said.

That had made me so angry.

My father had been dead for twenty-two years, I had thought. She was talking nonsense. But she was right. I was wrong.

How had she known? The letters maybe? Had she steamed Josie's mail and read the contents? I couldn't believe so. Maybe Jimmy had spilled Jack's secret to her? I will have to find out. Maybe it's worse than that. Maybe our family secret has been common knowledge in the community, gossiped about in titillated giggles in the church car park? Whispers behind hands in the mission hall prayer meetings at the shame of the preacher's prodigal son?

I need to speak to Jimmy and her, and soon.

Joseph is asking another question though.

"Is that as far as you have got? If it is true, if we are Jack's children....him and this Josie girl...how come we were adopted by our parents? Lord above, what am I saying? They were actually our granny and granda. Incredible! Sarah, this is too much."

His expression has become very pained. The first sign of emotion. Joseph is a tough nut. Always has been; had to be, given what he had seen and come through in the police. But he is visibly rattled by this, uncertainty in his usually calm voice, a tremor in the hand that holds Josie's letter.

"They were our grandparents! They told us we were adopted. What a terrible half-truth that was!"

He almost loses control for a second, takes a deep breath.

"God above," he says, "why do we have to wait till this age to learn who we really are?"

I cannot think of an answer to that. I hold him for a while, my mind racing on to the question of how we ended up back here, in Jack's family in Castlecuinn, where we might have been anywhere. Might even have been separated!

"It is something that I never let bother me, this thing about who I really was. I didn't care. I was me. That was enough. Now that I am starting to know, for the first time...suddenly I am bothered," he says. "I nearly wish you had just kept it to yourself."

"How could I do that? Have we not suffered enough deceit?"

"Yeah, I'm sorry. Of course you had to tell me. I have to carry all the pain of this with you."

"Are you up for reading on... to figure out what happened?" I ask him.

"To the bitter end," he says.

Chapter 37

Confrontation

Together Joseph and I open Jack's diary, find my marker.

"I can hardly take it in," he says, "him telling us this, and him in his grave."

"I know, it is crazy, isn't it?"

"A voice from nearly fifty years ago. He must have been desperate that we find out the truth, the stuff he wasn't able to tell us when he was alive. Do you think it was cowardice? Or was he just being faithful to some promise he made to her….maybe even with Jacob and Bella?"

"I can't work that out either."

"Maybe a bit of both. Read on anyway; see what happens with these twins."

"Ah, but wait," I tell him. "Remember Jack doesn't know anything about twins at this stage. Neither does Josie. Nobody does. As far as they are concerned it's just one baby. The twin thing only comes out way later, in March, when she is near delivery. This is still way back in, let's see…"

13th Nov 1959

Soon as I could, I got away from Jimmy and my father, and read Josie's letter in secret in the corner of the hay-barn. I was in shock when I finished it, devastated. How could her father not see the madness of trying to take away her baby: this child is his own flesh and blood. How could a father like him not see the damage this will do to his precious daughter? He is a parent himself. This was a daft piece of thinking. He needs to be told that too. I must do all in my power to stop this. Surely he will see sense. Josie's mental state must be very low at the minute. I am so tempted to run away to Scotland to see her. But, being more sensible, I need to talk to my folks again. That is what I will do, soon as I get a chance. Daddy must come with me to talk sense into this man.

15th Nov 1959

I have spoken to my parents about this. I have told them of my fears for Josie, my concern for the child, my anger against Josie's father.

"And it her first baby! God help her." That was my mother's concern.

"And then to have to give it up, after going through all that," I said to her. "Don't you see it's just so wrong?"

My father wanted to know how I knew all this. How was I still in communication with her? I had not listened to him, to Josie's father either, with their demand that I not to be in touch with her. To stay out of the matter.

"You might as well tell the man in the moon not to shine, Daddy," I told him.

"We'll see about that," he said. "Anyway, how have you been able to talk to her? Does she write to you?"

I was never going to betray the part that Jimmy has played in this, so I lied... just a small white one. "Never heard of a phone?" I cheeked.

"You're not using our phone to talk to this hussy?" he said.

"No, I'm not using your phone. There are more phones in the country than ours. And she is no hussy! Anyway, that's all beside the point. What are we going to do about this adoption idea?"

My father's advice was to stay calm. No point in getting angry with her father. He was a good man. It won't help to go shouting at him. I must try to see it from his point of view.

I have tried. And I did see it. But there were other factors here, I told him.

"A baby needs its own mother. And she needs it. Rearing the child is going to be some undertaking. She needs me beside her."

Daddy shook his head. "You've forgotten that this is all your fault. You don't have a say in the outcome."

"Wrong, Daddy. It was not all my fault. Even Josie said that. Anyway, you're my father. You are supposed to be on my side, helping me in this mess, backing me up. Will you come with me to challenge him?"

"I will not. You have made your bed. You have to lie in it," he told me.

I think he was scared to face his former benefactor.

My mother intervened, wonderfully so, angel of a woman that she was.

"Jacob," she said, "Didn't he do you a good turn? Now his daughter is in trouble, and it's our son; we are involved, like it or not. You have to go to talk to him, if nothing else just to shake his hand and say sorry. Go with Jack. Support him; take the high road in this."

"I'll think it over," he said.

24th Nov 1959

I have been mulling over our dilemma for days. I think I have come up with a way forward. It is a bold plan, and it may backfire on me. But I have to try something. Daddy often said that I am pig-headed, stubborn as a mule; if that is so, he will not be surprised that I won't give up. Tonight I'll write it down for Josie, so she can consider it. Then she can tell me on the phone on Saturday whether she approves or not.

28th Nov 1959

Phone call.

Josie was very tearful again. She is under fierce mental strain. I can do little for her. I did assure her that I am fighting with every bone of my body to do the best for her. I still think we could and should get married. She did not sound so sure this time. Her father has clearly worked on her. But she knows she cannot keep the baby if we are not going to be allowed to wed. That is really the biggest fear in her mind.

I told her that daddy and I are going to speak to her father next Wednesday. It has been arranged, after my father agreed and phoned to set up the meeting. Her reaction to this news was a bit strange. I suppose she does not want her father to get upset. I assured her that the two men were on good terms. Their friendship might help smooth a way for us to be together.

I hinted at my plan to persuade her father to relent. She wanted to know more, but when I enlarged on the scheme she became very annoyed. I could tell in her voice.

"Please, Jack. Do not threaten him like that. You are being far too impetuous. It's foolish. He is a lawyer after all. Just go along with what he says. He has my best interests at heart."

I was a bit taken aback, but I answered calmly.

"Of course, I know he has… but he has a grandchild to think about too."

Our conversation ended well, on good warm terms as usual. We love each other, it's just…

How different, I thought afterwards, our conversations now in the cold light of winter to what they were in those blissful days of summer love!

Wed 2nd December 1959

The conversation between Josie's father and mine was remarkably civilised; no harsh words were spoken.

The two men obviously had a good deal of respect for each other; no smiles, but a warm enough handshake before they went in together, leaving me standing outside on the steps for a bit first while they talked.

For me, though, things did not progress like what I wanted.

The unspoken presumption was that Josie and I cannot, will not, be married.

Both men were adamant, to the point of dismissing the idea as if it originated in the pit of hell. What could be worse? A shotgun mixed marriage! Over their dead bodies, it seemed. When I opened my mouth to object, I was met with twin frowns of disapproval, a Catholic one and a Presbyterian one, holding hands with each other. Metaphorically speaking of course.

I was rash enough to threaten one of my secret weapons.

"Well, if we run away and get married at Gretna Green you'll just have to accept it."

"Josephine would never do that to me," her father said.

"Are you sure?" I asked arrogantly.

My father played his trump card. "You do that son, and you can forget about inheriting the farm!"

There it was! The land card! Stark and brutal.

Josie's father chipped in his tuppence worth with a half smile. "Where there's a will there's a way!"

So witty. So needless.

I was knocked speechless. And I sat like that for a good fifteen minutes, the wee boy on the naughty step, slapped down into submission. I listened to them waffling on, mainly about adoption plans, until I could bear it no longer.

I interrupted.

"Sir, is it true you are not going to allow your daughter to come home for Christmas?"

He looked at me for a second before replying. "My family's Christmas plans aren't really any of your business, young man."

"I see what you mean there," I said, "and I agree, it is your right to have Christmas wherever you please. Probably safer over there in Scotland. It would be a shame if any of your friends, or your business clients, or your priest, like... if they ran into Josie, and noticed the bump."

This had the desired effect, even if it was what Josie had asked me not to say. He suddenly lost his cool, the red creeping up his neck and his cheeks as if looking for an escape valve.

"How insolent," he said.

My father protested too, but I hushed them, holding up my hands.

"I am sorry if that shocked you, and I apologise, sir...it was out of place, but it was called for."

"What do you mean?"

"I mean this. I have been listening to you two, staying quiet, like a good wain in the corner. Not once have you asked my opinion. But I have opinions, and I have more right to express them than you are giving me credit for. I am the child's father. I admitted that when I came to see you, sir. I have not tried to run away or hide. I have taken responsibility for my actions. So now I have a right to say what I want to happen."

They looked at each other. My father was about to launch into a tirade, I could tell, but Josie's father stopped him with a raising of his hand.

"You make your point well," he said, the lawyer in him, I suppose. "So, tell us now what you would like to happen."

I cleared my throat and began.

"Your grandchild, it needs good parents. Me and Josie, we're the father and mother. The natural order of things, in your church and in mine, is that we should be the ones to raise the child. To do that we need to be married."

They looked at each other for a while, both shaking their heads.

"The thing is," my father said, "you two have already broken the moral law, so your point doesn't count. Different maybe if you hadn't got her in the family way."

Josie's father took it a step further. "Even if Josephine wasn't pregnant, a marriage would have been out of the question...unless you had been prepared to convert...but I know your father would have opposed that. So, a wedding is not on the cards here."

There was no point in me arguing this further. I had known this would be their take, both of them equally so. I moved on to my next argument.

"If that is so," I said, "I am presuming that you, sir, would not accept Josie rearing the child alone?"

"Absolutely. She has her career to..."

"Yes, her career. But the baby? What about it?"

"It will be put up for adoption, soon after birth."

So blunt, so final. I had anticipated this. I made my next point.

"If my child is being put up for adoption, you would have no objection, then, to me adopting it?"

Both men were astounded by this. Neither had seen it coming. Josie's father reacted first.

"Out of the question," he said. "For a start, you are unmarried. You cannot adopt for that reason alone. No, no...Josephine's baby will be taken by a Catholic family, most likely somewhere in Scotland. I have spoken to the authorities when I was over there. Josephine will go into a mother and baby home, one run by our nuns in Edinburgh. She will have the child there, and it will be put up for adoption."

My father was still quiet at this point, but I knew I could drag him into the argument on my side. The idea of his grandchild being brought up Catholic, by total strangers, and in a different country, would trigger him.

"What do you think, daddy?"

He spoke briefly.

"It's very brave of you to suggest this, Jack, but the thing is, you'd never be allowed to adopt, with you being single."

"But you both see the injustice of this, don't you?" I continued, speaking slowly, deliberately. "The child won't be reared by its mother, despite the fact she could rear it in her faith. This family that it goes to might turn out to be Catholic in name only, maybe turn out to be a dreadful home. Our child might end up being abused. Neither of you would ever know, of course, but your hands wouldn't be clean in the matter. You'd be carrying the guilt of abandonment...and neither Josie nor I, the two actual parents, would be able to do a thing about it."

Josie's father thought for a minute and then smiled wryly at me. "You'd have done well in my profession, lad. But your point falls down. I, as an active member of the church in this town, could never countenance, my grandchild being adopted and reared as Protestant. It would undermine everything we stand for."

I actually jumped up off the chair.

"Sir, think about what you are saying here. You would prefer to keep everything smooth to the eye here in your own parish. The child doesn't really matter. Just get it off your hands, out of sight. As long as nobody gets to know about Josie being pregnant. Hide the sin. Dispose of the evidence....let some unknown persons, of unknown moral character and class, in some unknown backstreet of a Scottish city...let them rear your own grandchild? Don't you see how hypocritical that sounds?"

I was quite angry by this stage; my own words were making me even more so, now that my mind was out in the open. Nobody was replying, so I kept going.

"It is just about the most unChristian thing I can think of. If I get to adopt the baby, then at least you will know it will have a good home, it will be well cared for, it will be taught the faith...I accept that it won't be your church's tradition, but as I say, it would be genuine. It could choose to be Catholic later on if it wanted to. And nobody need ever know that it is Josie's wain. Nor indeed mine, for that matter. I could just have gone to Scotland and adopted a kid."

"But you cannot, that's the point. You are a single man. Regardless of the religion question," he replied.

Fair play to my father. He had been listening to me with the strangest expression on his face. I had never seen that look before.

He came through for me.

"We could adopt it, Bella and me."

Silence. Utter silence. I was astonished at him. Josie's father too. He sat there for ages, stunned, saying nothing.

My father making such an offer. Unbelievable! What possessed him to say this? Had he been thinking about this all along? Why would such a crazy idea even cross his mind? Had he considered my mother? Maybe he had already talked about it to her?

"Does mammy know about this?" I asked.

"No, she doesn't."

"But...don't you think it's a bit much to...to just volunteer to adopt another child...without even considering how she might feel about it?"

"Your mother is a great woman."

What an answer, I thought. The man has no idea.

"Aye, I know she's a great woman," I said, "but she already has her hands full with Miriam, with all of us. She's not going to be able to raise a new baby."

"You don't know your mother as well as I do, son," he said. "She might just like the idea. Especially after her losing.... you know what I mean. God would give her the strength to cope with it. It might be a real blessing for her."

"But....you volunteer her without even asking her about it?" I protested.

"Ah no. Of course I would talk to her about it before we decide. You never know, she might be delighted to be rearing your child."

I shook my head.

"How is the child going to feel? Two fathers in the house? It's crazy," I told him. At the same time, my mind was running ahead into this new territory; a fantasy world where I could...

My imaginings were interrupted.

"The wain would have to think me and Bella were its father and mother, you'd just be a brother," my father said.

Josie's father had eventually found his voice.

"That can't happen," he said. "The church won't ever countenance it, Jacob. It is a nice idea, but my grandchild, illegitimate or not, must be reared in the context of the church. I could never lift my head in this parish if it was ever know that it was being brought up in a Presbyterian household."

"Nobody need know that the child we adopt is Josephine's," my father said.

"The news might get out," he argued.

I stepped in again.

"Yes, but the news of Josie having an illegitimate child to a Protestant, and it being adopted in Scotland somewhere...that news might get out as well. In fact, I am fairly sure it would get out."

Phew! I thought. That was brave of me.

Her father was thinking, his brow furrowed into a frown. "Do I read you right, young man? Are you threatening me? That sounded like blackmail."

I held my hands up against his accusation.

"I am not threatening. I am just saying...look, I don't want anything to spoil my child's life; certainly not the taint of being illegitimate. And I love your daughter, sir. I would never want anything to be known in the community that would blacken her name."

"If you truly loved my daughter you would not have left her in the lurch like this!"

"I do love her. And I haven't left her in the lurch, have I? I'm sure we are not the first in the history of the world to make this mistake and have to face these consequences. This might be the best answer to the problem. The child will be loved and cared for. It will have a good, local family. Josie will get to finish her training. Nobody has to know she has anything to do with the wain. Later on, if she wants to, she can see her child; you might want to see it too."

He thinks for a long time before speaking. His wise old head is shaking slowly back and forward.

"Can I say one more thing, sir?"

"Go on," he said wearily.

"I think Josie will really welcome this solution."

"I am guessing you have spoken to her about it?"

"I have, sir, I'll be honest. We are in touch."

More head shaking. From my daddy too, I noticed.

"If I am to consider this, it would be on the basis of one condition."

I waited as he stared me in the eye, a steely look like a judge passing sentence in a courtroom drama.

"You would have to swear to me that you would have no further contact with Josephine."

Goodness, I thought. That is a step too far.

"I could not do that sir. She and I are in love..."

My father interrupted.

"Jack," he said, "he is right. There can be no future for the two of you. If I am to do this....and we'll need time to think it all through...I will only agree to it if you promise to let this girl go and have nothing more to do with her."

There you are, I thought. Two against one. The polar opposites agree against me.

"It's just as well Mary didn't live in Northern Ireland," I said.

They looked at me mystified.

"Mary?"

"Aye, Mary, the mother of Jesus."

"Why are you bringing our Blessed Mother into it?"

I gave him a wry smile.

"If she'd lived here the chances are she wouldn't have been allowed to marry Joseph. She'd likely have been stoned. Jesus would never have made it to his Bar Mitzvah, never mind to the cross."

Both faces looked horrified. My father rebuked me for my blasphemy.

"Anyway, they were both Jews," he added.

"As opposed to Christians, you mean.... like us?"

Silence. Not even a glance at each other.

They knew!

"Josie and me are both Christian and..."

"That's enough, Jack. Leave it," my daddy said, getting to his feet.

Before we left, Josie's father suggested that we all need to step back for a week or two, talk to Josie, to my mother as well, and think through the implications of the suggestion. We agreed on that. It would be a massive decision, for all of us. But inside I was happy. Happy that at least I was being taken seriously. I was being listened to. The only cloud attaching itself to the silver lining was this idea of having to promise to have nothing more to do with Josie. That cloud hung over me for days, its billowing blackness blotting out every hint of sunlight.

Chapter 38

Developments

Judith knocks the bedroom door.

"We need to be going, Joey," she calls. "The kids."

I can see my twin is struggling. With what he has learned today; with the need to hear the end of the story; with his wife's concern to go home to their children.

"We can drive you back," I say, "if you'd rather stay and see this through."

"Thanks; think I'll stay. I can't leave it here," he says, getting up and going to speak to Judith on the landing.

When he comes back he has a question; same one that I have.

"Have you any idea who this Josie is? I can't recall ever hearing of any woman with that name; nor Josephine."

"Same here," I tell him.

"What was this solicitor's name? Her father? Does Jack never mention his surname?"

"Not so far. Maybe he was sworn to secrecy."

"Maybe we will read to the end of this, and still not know," Joseph says. "That would be even more strange. Knowing our birth mother was local, but never knowing who she was…if Jack kept to some promise or other. Maybe she never returned from Scotland."

Interesting to see how his mind is now running away with itself, just like mine had been doing all along.

"I think I know how to find out though," I tell him.

"Find out the name? How?"

"Wally Brown next door. It was Wally told me about that loan daddy got to buy the upper farm. He seemed to know who the solicitor was. I just remember that he was Catholic, and he lived in the town."

"Goodness. We need to talk to him quick," brother says, standing up from the bed, as if now would be a good time. I pull him down again.

"Let's see what else we can find out from these letters and his journal first," I tell him.

We continue. Following the trail.

The Christmas period…a blank, as far as communication from Josie is concerned. Of course. Her father was with her. Radio silence then.

Plenty of soul searching by Jack though. His journal is full of questioning around those weeks. Scepticism, to be honest.

The whole frivolity of Christmas was wearing him down. He could see no joy in it.

At one point he wrote a very brief note. I am guessing it came straight from his original diary into this summary journal.

24th December 1959

What I would give tonight, just to be heading to the stable! There would likely be no room at the inn for me either. Hear my heart, Josie.

What a poignant sentiment from him in the loneliness of his Christmas Eve night. Alone in his private cavern upstairs, while the parents buzz around doing festival preparations. He is missing his Josie, would love to be by her side.

Writing on Christmas night and Boxing Day he had little to say. There was a reference to Miriam, and how restricted her handicap left her, in terms of appreciation of this, our special feast day.

Her poor mind remains taped up in its parcel and will never, ever be able to enjoy a time like this. I should be counting my blessings, but the blessing my heart longs for is denied me. All these traditions are meaningless to me. The tradition that marches through my head today, brash as a brass band, is the one that trumpets our Ulster version of the Ten Commandments. We've taken 'Thou shalt not commit adultery' and added, 'Thou definitely shalt not do it with a Catholic'.

While I am enjoying Jack's poetic side, Joseph is losing patience with the slow pace of the story right now. He starts to rifle through Josie's letters again, and holds one out for me to see.

"Read this," he says. "She's arrived in Edinburgh."

I know this, of course, having delved through these when trying to find confirmation of 'twins'.

I haven't read the detail though.

Nazareth House Children's Home
Lauriston Rd
Edinburgh
22nd January 1960

My Darling Jack,

I am writing a brief letter to you in secret as I am not supposed to be doing this. My father forbade such communication, and left instructions with the nuns that I should not be allowed out of the home unaccompanied. One of the other girls has promised to get this posted for me, (for a small fee), and I can only hope this will reach you.

Let me tell you first that I love you as much as ever, and that I am so inspired by your courage in talking to my father. He may resent you, Jack, because of the pregnancy, but he has a good regard for your character, and for how well you put across your point of view. The idea of you volunteering to adopt our child is an absolutely fabulous plan. How on earth did you ever think of it, never mind having the courage to suggest it in that meeting with the two fathers? I am so proud of my boy.

As you know, however, it is impossible…because you are not married. I did say to my father, "And guess who is stopping him from being married? You are, daddy!" Very bold of me, don't you agree? He was not happy with me. Anyhow, when he told me of your father's offer to adopt the baby I could not believe my ears. What a great solution. That way, I immediately thought, I could see the child whenever I wish. Eventually, at some time in the future, you and I might be able to get married and bring it to live with us. It solves so many problems, I thought.

But I thought too soon. My father was still refusing to allow this. He is adamant that the child be reared as a Catholic.

I argued as follows. The child could maybe be baptised in the Catholic Church here in Scotland, raised in your home, and later in its life it might want to convert. That was a no-go argument for him as well.

Could you accept that? I would jump at that solution. I have argued this idea with him. At this moment in time he insists that we have nothing more to do with each other. He wants my promise on that point, yours too. If we made that promise, might he consider allowing your family to adopt the child? Oh I do hope it will work out.

By the way, in my opinion a promise made like that, under such duress, and with my hormones so heightened…such a promise would hardly stand up in a court of law. Might not such a promise be easily overlooked, do you agree? (You must never let anyone else see this scandalous suggestion, my love; I just cannot envisage the rest of my life being spent without seeing you. I have a feeling you will share that opinion.)

I don't have time right now to tell you about this institution that I find myself in. (The girl is waiting outside the door of my dormitory to take this letter.) Just let me tell you this; be very happy that 1. You are a Protestant and 2. You are not a girl and therefore, for both reasons, you are never likely to have to be in such a place. It is a tough regime; the point being it's a sort of penance for getting ourselves pregnant. The irony of it, for all those fathers are wandering the streets without responsibility, free and looking for other lasses to have their fun with. (I don't include you in that, by the way.) Oh I must stop…

All my love as usual,
Josie XXX

"Good for her," Joseph says. "My word, she was a feisty one, wasn't she?"

"I wonder is she still alive? Or where on earth she went to? And where she is now?"

"She's likely still alive; she'd only be mid-sixties…say she was nineteen when we were born…"

He stops, and, for a beat, struggles to keep his composure. I take over, bailing him out.

"Sixty-six-ish, I'd say."

"Good grief, Sarah, but I never thought I'd be having to deal with all this new information. It is mad."

I agree with him, silently; I am further down the road of realising the possible implications than he is, and it is 'mad', as he says. He continues.

"I sort of feel undermined, know what I mean? I was living in a misty half-light; only knowing partial truths about myself."

I know what he means. I tell him, "Yeah, it's as if….you and I…our existence has been like the negative of a photograph up until now, and that is all changing. Something like a development process is happening to us, and we are slowly having a colour version of ourselves revealed."

He nods. "Except that I don't like the colours I am seeing. I think I prefer the black and white. Safer. I kinda wish you had kept this all to yourself."

"How could I do that? Sure it has always been an unspoken curiosity for us. Who are we really? Or who were we at the time of our birth? But we could never find out. Now we are closer to knowing our roots."

"Maybe," he says. "But what if we don't like these roots? It's so unsettling. In some ways, this whole idea of 'the family tree'…it's a misnomer, isn't it? A tree is what you see above ground, but we aren't content with the 'above ground' bit, we have to go digging down into the earth, uncovering these all-important roots, with their twists and blemishes."

"But surely…"

"I just wish Jack had left us in our innocence," he says. "I think I'd prefer to have been left in the dark. Bad enough to discover that our brother isn't our brother, he's actually our father! Then the notion that our mother was some random Catholic girl he bedded in a dingy cellar. Lord above, what a sordid story of origin."

'Some random Catholic girl'! I am a bit taken aback by this dismissive line. The girl carried us for nine months! She is our mother, our flesh and blood. We carry her DNA, like it or not. Surely he could show her a bit more dignity in his comments. It's a very shallow response, in my opinion; very misogynistic as well. I am annoyed at him, and it probably shows in the abrupt way I pick up our brother's journal again to resume reading.

"When can we go and ask Wally about this solicitor?" he asks.

"He'll be at his milking now," I say, checking my watch. "Maybe tomorrow, if you have time to call up?"

Chapter 39

Disclosure

I drive over to Brown's.

Spring has been recolouring the landscape. The lifeless sepia is being transformed by the glaring yolk-yellow of whins, the pastel pink shades of cherry blossom, the bluebells along the lane side fighting back against the shadows. Over the greening hedge, the slope of a freshly rotovated field is mottled with a range of earthy tones.

I wander around the side of Wally's farmhouse looking for the farmer himself. The sleepy quietness of the yard is disturbed by a few welcoming yelps from Wally's black and white collie; it comes limping in my direction, its backend twisted from some old injury. Working dogs like this one don't get put down; too valuable around the farm. They are given time to heal up, maybe with the vet's help, then it's back to duties. I pause to ruffle the shaggy hairs around its neck, looking about me for any sign of the farmer himself.

Joseph has decided not to bother coming up. I think he fears this potential piece of news, either that or, as he said, it might look a bit suspicious, the two of us arriving as a delegation to ask an apparently mundane question about a solicitor from way back over sixty years ago.

"We don't want to be getting Wally suspicious about why we need to know that sort of detail," Joseph had said on the phone last night. "Just you go on your own, and sort of casually drop it into the conversation."

He has a point. Wally is no fool, and it wouldn't take long for him to puzzle out some answer to the riddle. To that end, I have needed to come up with a cover story, so he doesn't think I have arrived unexpectedly in his yard simply to find out the identity of the solicitor he'd mentioned to me weeks ago. That query I need to slip into the conversation with subtlety, as if by afterthought.

Wally emerges from behind his old, low-built piggery, the last remaining building from the farm's earlier history. All the other sheds and animal houses are much more modern, a credit to his foresight, investment, and general orderliness of character. Why he hadn't knocked down the pig house probably only he knew. It stands out like a sore thumb at the end of his street, but I am guessing it has a story in its architecture or its history that demands it stay in situ, and unaltered. Maybe it is right to have such a reminder of how farm buildings were in bygone days, before everything had to be modernised, standardised and made energy efficient. At least that old-fashioned out-house, with its uneven walls of dark field-stones and corrugated roof of rusting zinc, has a bit of character from another era.

He is surprised to see me, standing there in the middle of his farmyard talking to his dog.

"Are you coming in, daughter," he says, bustling past me. "It's just myself. Margaret is in the town still."

It was less a question, more an assumption. Of course I was coming in, but I remind myself to make sure I didn't get stuck behind a table or something, and so become a captive audience.

I turn down his offer of tea. "It's too near lunchtime," I tell him.

He ladles himself a bowl of thick-looking vegetable soup from the saucepan on the cooker, and cuts a wedge of soda bread.

"How's things over there? Is him and her settling in all right?"

It is the kind of question I am hoping to hear; I have my answer on the tip of my tongue.

"They seem to be," I say, "but that's why I called."

"What's on your mind?"

"Well....you know the way…if I was to suggest anything to him that I think needs attending to…well, with me being the wee sister, and a teacher who knows nothing about farming, you'd think…."

"Aye, I can see where you are going with that," he says with a half grin. "He mightn't be too keen to take guidance."

"It's not that I want to advise or anything," I say, "but there are one or two things that need attended to before they get any further out of hand. Things that affect the farms on either side of us, yours included."

"Oh, don't I know that," he says.

"I know yous did your best to keep the basics of the place going, but, now he's back and in harness, there are a fair few tasks he'd need to be getting into….if he could only see it."

"Aye. The sheughs are sitting full. The drains in those low fields must be blocked up. He'd need to either get at it himself with the JCB or get in a contractor. Has he said anything about it?"

"Not a word to me. He's too busy," I tell him.

"What's he too busy at? Sure he has nothing else to be doing."

"He's still only half-home, if you know what I mean. Part of him is still in India, I think. I see him sitting at the window as I drive past, just sitting looking out as if he's wondering where all his patients have gone. He doesn't even see me. Miles away. Then he'll be away taking a missionary service somewhere, or attending some committee meeting. I can't say a thing to him."

Wally gets my point. We waffle on about it for another ten minutes. He promises to call over, and gently raise some of the concerns, which will be a bonus to add to the more important detail….the answer to my next question. I thank him and casually get up to go.

I turn from the door to bid him goodbye, but pause in my step, as if trying to recall something I'd meant to say. As I do, the back door bursts open and Wally's wife bustles in, two carrier bags of shopping in hand. I am caught between several options. Inevitably I have to converse with the woman, and in doing so I lose my chance to quiz Wally about the solicitor in town. He slips out past me with a raising of those famous eyebrows, as if to say, 'You talk to her, for I am away back to work here'. So I am no further forward.

As I drive away from Browns I turn to plan B. I won't be beaten in this. What could Jimmy McGrath tell me about Josie's father? He had said he knew the man. A 'big man' in the church, I think he told me. Hopefully he'd remember his name. I drive to the gate lodge.

Jimmy brings me into his little kitchen. It's cramped and cluttered, and a pile of junk, magazines, flyers and newspapers, has to be lifted off the one decent armchair for me to get a seat. It's a room that has changed little over the years, I feel, a relic that has survived like a museum display in a folk park, little altered from what it might have looked like well back in the last century. Certainly the red-box radio and small screen television both look antique. Yet again the presence of the wife makes things a bit awkward. Mrs McGrath makes tea, whether I like it or not. I know better than to turn her down. I realise I am going to have to ask Jimmy the question in front of her; there is no alternative. Maybe her knowledge of the situation will be useful too.

"Jimmy," I say, "I need your help. I am trying to discover who the father of Jack's girlfriend was, all those years ago. Remember you told me you knew her father; a big man in the parish, I think you said? Would you recall his name?"

They look at each other, a brief, knowing glance. The woman diverts her gaze immediately back to the teapot. Jimmy's eyes follow his slow spoon as it stirs around in his teacup, then rise to stare at me, something in his gaze that I cannot fathom. He is slow to reply. When he does, I am the one to take cover in silence.

"Ah, Sarah," he says softly. "The time has come, has it?"

I am at a loss to understand what he means.

"The big questions need answering," he continues.

I wait. He is very solemn.

"You have to understand, lass…there's things we know, and there's other things we are only guessing."

"Go on," I tell him. "What do you know first, then whatever it is you are guessing."

"Well, the first thing is…the solicitor who was Josie's father…. he's dead years ago, you understand. Good man he was; the whole parish looked up to him."

"They did," says Mrs McGrath in support. "Everybody depended on him. 'Specially the fathers."

"The fathers?"

"Aye, the priests."

"Oh right. How did they depend on him?"

"Well, his law firm was always helping them out if there was a problem, like a claim or a dispute…or anybody needing advice."

I realise this backs up what Wally Brown had told me.

"I believe he even helped my fath…he even helped our family out in the past…with money and so on," I say.

"That could be."

"And what was the firm's name?"

"'Quigley and Quinn', it was called. "But Jerome seemed to have been the main man in it for a good while."

He drones on, but I am not listening.

Quigley and Quinn. My mind is racing.

Quigley? Jerome Quigley? Neither of those names mean anything to me.

In my mind I flick on to the Quinn bit. Mr Quinn? Jerome Quinn?

Nothing.

My face must look as blank as my mind.

Jimmy reads it though.

"Aye," he says, "Jerome Quinn was a gentleman. You never met him?"

Me meet him? What is he angling at here?

I shake my head.

"Whenever you went to his house for your piano lessons? Agh no…he was likely dead and gone by that stage. You just met the daughter."

****

Absolute and utter astonishment!

In a hundred years I could never have foreseen this.

Josie! Josie was Josephine Quinn?

Back then I had only known her as 'Miss'. Miss Quinn…yes. But her first name was never disclosed. She was my teacher… of course her first name never came into it. Miss, and only ever Miss.

I am in shock. I feel stunned, like somebody has just punched me in the chest and taken my breath away. My thoughts are whirling like a murmuration of frightened starlings, and every bit as darkly.

My mind leaves Jimmy's kitchen. I am back at Miss Quinn's piano.

My music teacher! She was….she is my mother? She was the beautiful girl that my brother Jack had seduced in the cellar….No! That my father, Jack, had…. The woman who sat by my side as I played my first scale of C major…she sat there as my mother? She sat beside her own daughter at the piano for next to ten years? She never gave anything away, never said a word about….What could she have said?

"Practice those pieces really well for next week, for your grade 3 exam is only a fortnight away…oh, and by the way Sarah, you and I are related…really closely related! Go on, have a guess!!"

That pious face…like the Virgin Mary herself! Innocent as a new…

Those moments when she turned her head away from me, got up from beside me to stare out the window at her garden.

That final hug when my last lesson was over and we were saying goodbye. I remember her tears…I just thought….

Oh, my Lord in heaven! This is too much to take in. I feel a familiar faintness creeping up my neck.

Mrs McGrath is fussing around me. Trying to get me to drink some more tea.

I am slowly aware that old Jimmy is hugging me, swaying me back and forward, doing his best to comfort me. I have a grubby tea towel in my hands, and it is wet, from my tears, I think. My heart is doing very strange things, painful, constricted.

"How could she have done that?" I hear myself sob to them, to myself. "She could have told us."

"It's all right, it's all right, Sarah. Just take a deep breath…"

"She should have…" I cry.

"She was sworn to secrecy, that's what I believe happened," Jimmy says. "Nobody ever told me that, but it must be what was settled on when Jerome agreed to allow the pair of you to be brought up as if you were Bella and Jacob's wains."

"She was a lovely woman," I tell them. "But she must have been going through torture every time Joseph and I came for a lesson."

"Likely enough."

"No wonder she was so hurt when Joseph gave up. I thought she was going to cry. It's years ago, but I still recall how upset that made her."

"Now you know why."

"And you two knew all this?"

It is a question without criticism; at the same time I am very troubled by the realisation that our farm labourer and his wife have known far more about me than I did myself. Who else might know? How long have they known? How did they work everything out?

"It's not so much that we knew," Jimmy says. "More that we joined the dots and…well, when your folks went off to Scotland for a few days, and came home with two babies…we couldn't help thinking… I was doubtful about it all at the start, but Rosie here, she was curious about it. She worked it all out, and it made sense."

"My parents went…Jacob and Bella, they went to Scotland?"

"They did. And Jack as well. It was all a bit strange. Like, usually some of them would have stayed behind for the work when the others went away. But not that time. The three of them set off in the big car, and I was left to look after the whole place for a few days. Isaac was still at school at the time, but he was able to help me in the evenings."

Isaac? Did he know what was going on, I wonder. Did he have any notion about who these babies were? I am sure he must have wondered why Jack had to go as well…why, if babies were being adopted, would father and mother not be enough? I have a feeling he must have had his suspicions, if not outright knowledge of the affair. How does that leave me now in my relationship with him?

"What about Miriam? Who looked after her?" I ask.

"Rosie went over and stayed with her till your folk came back."

I look at Rosie with gratitude.

"I thank you, Rosie," I say, "and I thank you for accidentally giving me the clue about all this."

She looks a bit mystified. "The clue?"

"When you sympathised with me that night at the wake."

"Why? What did I say?" She looks a bit mortified.

"You told me you were sorry about my father. You said 'father', not 'brother'. I was angry with you at first, then I thought you were starting to dote, and I forgave you. But you were right."

She has her hand to her mouth, her eyes staring like a child who has been caught out in a misdemeanour.

"Lord save us," she says. "I never knew I said that. I never meant…"

"It's all right," I tell her. She watches me from in front of her range, and there is quietness between the three of us. So silent that the tick of the mantlepiece clock seems rude. I start to think about how my twin is going to react to this incredible news.

"Well, now to find Joseph and tell him."

"How do you think he'll take it?"

"Not great, I imagine. It's just the shock of living till you're forty-seven, and then finding out that you're not who you thought you were, then finding out that you knew the woman who was your mother, but didn't realise it. And that she knew you, but never let on."

"It's hard to take in, I'm sure," Jimmy says.

It is. It's also hard to take in that our family skeleton has lain, buried in the stillness of this humble kitchen for a generation, that these two simple folk, in the late winter of their lives, have kept custody of our shameful secret through earlier seasons. I am so thankful for them both; I owe them so much.

I am about to slip away to my own company, and to a host of deeper thoughts, but it occurs to me that they might know what has become of Josephine Quinn. So I ask if they know anything about her.

Not a thing, I am told. They wouldn't be around the town so much nowadays. They have no memory of the last time they might have seen her at Mass.

"But you know where the house is. She might still be there if you were to call," Jimmy suggests.

Now there is a challenge, I think. Could I face that? There is some processing to be done before that….and there is a twin brother to be told of this incredible missing piece of the jigsaw! Not to mention a husband. And after that, the whole question about how and what we tell Christine and Jonathan. The next generation deserve the truth, not some redacted version of it either.

The whole truth, and nothing but!

Chapter 40

Grief

3rd May 1960
My Dear Darling Jack,
    There are no words to describe the pain of my loss, no colours to paint how darkly I feel in the depths of my soul. This is anguish, both emotionally and physically. As a man you cannot possibly understand the grief in me. I am utterly bereft, almost to the point of wanting to end everything and escape to my eternal destiny. The one single thing that I hold on to so tightly, and which keeps me from the act, is the knowledge that our babies are safe with their father, and that I will see them again…even if that must be in anonymity. But such a thought does nothing to ease the pressure in my breasts, as they flood endlessly with the milk that should be feeding Joseph and Sarah.
When I watched you from my upstairs window as you walked across the car park, your head bent forward, your shoulders sloped in dejection….horrible! You followed your parents at a distance, the twins swinging by your father's side in their little carry-cots. He was already usurping you; he was the father, the solver of your problems. Then when I saw your car disappear out the gates and fade away into the city traffic…at that point I wanted nothing else other than to die. The anguish was too great to bear. I didn't want to keep living. I wanted to tear out my heart, so badly did it hurt. I think my carers must have sedated me for a period, because the intensity of the feeling seemed to give way to a numbness of spirit which, to some extent, I suspect is keeping me sane.
I cannot help but wonder how much worse my despair would be if the twins were being taken away from us, and given to a random

family somewhere in Scotland, never to be seen again. How do these other girls cope? Days after giving birth they yield up their baby to a complete stranger, never more to see, to hold, to feed? At least we still have a measure of say in what becomes of our two…and it is my most earnest prayer that in the future we can be together in rearing them. I know that we both promised to your parents, (and especially to my father), to have nothing more to do with each other. It was hardly a fair request, I feel. I had to vow to have nothing more to do with my own children, a vow which sears my very soul, whereas you will see them every day. I know you had to promise never to reveal the truth of their birth to them, but still, my surrender is the greater. I am certain you will agree with this opinion. My promise was made, I will always argue, in the face of the pain that otherwise the children would have to be put up for adoption in the normal way. It was dragged out of me yet again, by the sisters in this institution, at a time of my greatest vulnerability. For these reasons, but mainly because I cannot countenance a future in which I never see you again, I do not put too much store on that promise. I think you and I agree on that…I hope so anyhow.

Thank you for being here with your parents when the twins were handed over. I think they are very nice people; your mother was especially kind and sympathetic to me. She held my hand longer than a normal handshake and whispered soothing words to me. I remember every word she said. "I feel your pain, Josephine, but this is for the best…for both of you. And be assured, Jacob and I will do our very best for the children."

Those words were much appreciated, as was their compromise regarding naming the children, and of course regarding the baptism. It was very necessary, in view of my father's insistence.

This will be my final letter from this address, as I will be leaving the home in a week or so. When I find out exactly where I will be staying I will let you know. It will only be for a few weeks anyhow, and then I will return home for the summer. Do you think we can

see each other then, before I return to Glasgow to continue the course? I would give up my entire inheritance just to have the twins in my arms, even to look at them again.
Love you forever,
Josie xxx

Joseph and I have again been sifting through Josie's letters and Jack's diary notes. We are nearing the end of the record. The details in the journal which Jack wrote are becoming more stark, more brief. There are only a couple more letters remaining in the frame to be opened.

Joseph's reaction has been very difficult to gauge. His silences are almost driving me up the walls just now. I need to talk everything out, explore the motivations, the rights and wrongs of those decisions, the implications for our futures. I want us to be thinking of how we together can come to a place of being reconciled to the truth of our origin. I want a plan of action for how we try to find our birth mother, for dealing with what we owe her, in terms of forgiveness and friendship and care. She is the only parent we have left, if indeed she is still alive. There are myriad considerations to be working through together. We lay beside each other in Josie's womb…we need to be beside each other going forward on this.

Joseph is silent. He is not ready to take anything forward, it would seem, not ready to even discuss all the implications of what he has read with me, heard from me. When I told him that I had learned from Jimmy who our mother actually was, his reaction had been bizarre in the extreme. I was surprised by the degree of anger that spewed out from him. I don't think I have ever seen him like that before. It was an anger that he couldn't get words for, so he took it out on me, as if I was to blame for the past. His language wasn't the best either; I am not judging him here, but he was using expletives I've never heard from him before.

His annoyance found a target in me because I had told him; I had opened the whole can of worms by insisting on investigating Jack's painting, by wanting to know about these letters and diary entries, by talking to Jimmy McGrath and so on. I should just have let the whole matter lie undisturbed. He would have preferred never to have known why he was called Joseph, never to have heard of Jack's affair with this Josie, never to have learned of the mother and baby home in Scotland, never to have known that our actual birth parents had been so close to us during the course of our lives. Oblivion would have been far easier, he said. My fault for spoiling his happy delusion, for presenting him with these unpalatable truths.

"Is it because our mother was a Catholic?" I want to know.

His answer follows a silence so long that I have almost forgotten the question. He sits rotating his head as if in awful and hopeless misery.

"I just wish I never knew that. It's not so much the religion thing…well, maybe a bit; it's just so unreal. That prim, wee woman with the sickly perfume! I didn't even like her. How could she do that to us?"

I want to defend Josie. She has my understanding, I think, and my sympathy, but then I've had longer to digest all this.

"You think this is hard for us," I tell him. "How much harder was it for her back then when she was trying to hold it all together, trying to teach us piano? The two of us sitting there like scaredy-cats in her grand room, not a smile from us, just sour-puss faces…and all the time she is dying to hug us and tell us she is our mother. How on earth was she able to keep up the firm teacher act?"

"I don't remember much about it, except that I didn't enjoy it," he says. "All those holy pictures, and the holy water, and the smell of the place. It just gave me the creeps, probably even more than she herself. Like….how could she go through all that pretence with us? I never sensed anything from her other than, 'Use your right hand for that note, Joseph! No, no, wrong finger Joseph!'"

"You're complaining about her," I tell him, my voice rising. "The woman who bore us! The worst you've suffered in your life is a bad back. She gave birth! To us! To twins! Double pain! You can't blame her when she was sort of blackmailed into silence! Our own brother…what I mean is… Jack! He was our father, yet he never even gave a hint of it until his final breaths. He is even more to blame than…"

"What do you mean, 'his final breaths'?"

"I mean….look, when he was nearing death, that time when we were both by his bedside. Remember he kept saying, 'Forgive me, forgive me!' You ever wondered what he was asking forgiveness for? It was for the lie he had lived. He wanted forgiveness for his silence."

"I suppose you are right," he says. "Neither him nor our parents…well, his parents, none of them got around to telling us. They lived the lie too. How do you do that, and go around preaching to the countryside? 'The truth will set you free'…but here, buried right under his hearth, there is a great dirty secret. It's crazy. I just can't get my head around it. I'm not sure if I can forgive any of them!"

"You have to forgive them," I insist. "The alternative is to hold it all to your chest and breast-feed it like a new-born, suckle the bitterness."

"Not a great choice of analogy, don't you think," he says. "You and me, we were sacrificed so that everything would stay nice and sweet in our community. Her's too. The appearance of respectability. One religion is as bad as the other when it comes to hypocrisy."

"It would be hard to argue with that."

Joseph gets up from the bed and goes to look out the window. I cannot help but notice the slight slump of his shoulders, clasped hands behind his head nestling his dejection.

"What was that about baptism…in her letter there? Read that bit again," he asks me.

I scan Josie's neat handwriting. "This bit? '…their compromise regarding naming the children, and of course regarding the baptism…?'"

"Yeah. What is she on about there?"

"I have no idea," I tell him. "That's another reason I would love to talk to her. Just exactly what was agreed with her father back then? And who decided the names?"

"Unless maybe there is reference to it in these final letters, or in Jack's story?" Joseph says, coming back to the bed and picking up the last two envelopes from the frame. "I hope you are going to throw this excuse of a painting in the skip after this."

"Maybe," I say, placing it against the wall.

"I wish to God you'd done that weeks ago. I could've lived happily without any knowledge of this sordid history," he persists.

"Sorry, Joseph," I tell him, in a tone more obdurate than I intend, "but that is not how I feel about it. Jack and Josie are our parents. All right, they made a mistake, but we are the result of that mistake. If they hadn't had sex that day in the cellar we wouldn't be here, would we?"

He looks at me for a beat, then laughs. "And that is just the weirdest thought of all, isn't it?" He is right. It absolutely is!

Chapter 41

Contrition

The thing about these last two envelopes is that they do not have the usual address written on the front. No mention of Jimmy McGrath. The only thing inscribed is our Christian names, on both envelopes.

Joseph & Sarah.

In one case, the writing is the same unmistakable, neat script as Josie Quinn's letters; the other looks less refined, more jagged and functional… the handwriting of our brother/father.

I realise that this is a significant departure from the material we have been perusing so far. The penny starts to drop that what we have in our hands…. well, my hands….are two letters, one from either parent, and written to the pair of us, possibly in a mutual pact… most likely an apology, or at least an explanation. My heart begins to do its butterfly impersonation again. But now it is excitement; the dread has been replaced by a feeling like warm, scented oil being poured over my head, somehow entering my blood stream as well, bringing a soothing sensation, comfort, connection.

I ask Joseph which one he wants to read first.

"It's immaterial," he says. "Why don't you just read them out loud."

I don't like that idea. I have a fleeting suspicion that he actually doesn't want to touch Josie's letter, the most physically intimate connection to her since she took his right hand all those years ago and guided his finger to the black F# key on her piano. Does he dread some sort of contamination from holding something so personal, so immediate to the woman whose womb he inhabited…her acknowledgement of him as her abandoned offspring? Is this another tiny signal of denial?

"No," I say, "you read Jack's. I'll take Josie's. Then swap over."

He takes it, reluctantly. It is a larger envelope than Josie's and feels much more bulky. I watch him open it slowly, with some solemnity. He fishes inside, and first of all produces a small piece of jewellery. A green-stoned Celtic cross. It dangles from his hand. His eyebrows lift, mystified. Straight away my mind goes back to Josie's account of her trip down south; hadn't she brought him back such a cross as a present?

"Josie's gift to him." I take it from him. "He has kept it to pass on to us. Likely had to keep it secret and hidden away from his father."

Instinctively I put it around my neck, turning to my twin for help in fastening the strange, antique clip. Yet again there is that flicker of hesitation before he aids me, but he does, and I have another echo of linkage back to the woman who gave the gift, the mother who bore me. I do my best to hide the emotionality of the moment from Joseph, but it's unnecessary. His eyes have fallen back to the letter.

"Do you mind if I keep this?" I ask, fingering the little cross.

"Suit yourself," he says. "I don't want it."

Then we read silently.

The first thing I notice about Josie's letter is that it is written on sheets of special notepaper…with a hotel brand printed at the top. It appears she must have been in this hotel in County Galway when she decided to write this letter to us, or at least had picked up the notepaper there. Whatever…it is what she says that is more important here.

O'Mahoney's Hotel
Clifden, Co Galway

March 1986

Dear Sarah and Joseph,

My dear darling children, by the time you read this letter you will already know the secret of your conception and birth. You will know that Jack is your father. You will have learned that I, that strange lady that you used to come to for piano lessons, am your mother. I am so sorry that you have had to wait so long for this realisation.

How I loved those days. How I grieved when they passed. If you knew the tears I shed every single time when you left my door. Precious memories for me, but probably not so much for you; I am sure I was unduly harsh as a teacher, but it was all to cover up my churning torrent of emotions. I had no right to have had that unique privilege of being your teacher, but Jack made it possible. Despite the promises we made never to see each other again, and the commitment I gave to have nothing to do with you two, Jack somehow worked it that your folks agree to me being your music teacher. Of course I had to swear that our secret would remain secret, and it did. My father by that stage had passed away, God rest him. That did make it easier.

Sarah, you have no idea how proud I am of you, and your musical achievements, and your career to date. You are a star, and will be a much better musician than I ever was. Joseph, I was disappointed that you gave up the lessons, but I am equally proud of the young man you are becoming, by all accounts. And you are so like your father, in many ways. I pray every night for your safety.

In a sense, I share with you both the fact that you did not know your real mother. My own mother died after giving birth to me, and so I lived my life in the absence of her love and guidance. I think I have probably missed her more than I realise, although my father did his very best for me. I suppose I have always felt that I owed him extra honour, and that very fact meant that, when I fell pregnant with you two, I felt duty bound to do as much as I could to protect him from the scandal. But of course, in doing that I equally have caused untold hurt to my own dear children. I was caught on the horns of an impossible dilemma. I always wanted to be the perfect girl for him, the best Catholic in the parish, a model for all the other families who so looked up to my father. Instead I found myself yielding to temptation on that one occasion. My sin found me out, and I have lived ever since with the punishment of having to give you up. I beg you both to forgive me, as I beg God and His Holy Mother to forgive me.

Jack and I were determined that, even though we have been locked into secrecy about the past, we should find a way to tell you the story of your conception and adoption, so that you learned it from us rather than someone else. It was Jack's idea to record his account, more or less as it happened. He had kept all the letters I had sent to him, just so you would eventually be able to know who you are.

I am sorry beyond words for the circumstances that led to your unique passage in life. I have loved you both from a distance with every bit as much intensity as if I had been your constant carer.

I must tell you that your father, Jack, has been amazingly considerate to me in keeping me informed about your lives. He wrote many letters to me when I was in Glasgow, and sent many photographs of the two of you when you were tiny babies. How I loved those pictures. I still treasure them. Jack's descriptions of the little changes in you as you grew into toddlers, and then becoming school children, were priceless to me. He has always been a talented writer, but of course his letters and pictures were no real substitute for being present in your lives; nor indeed were they much consolation.

Can you please find it in your hearts to forgive me, and your father, my beautiful Jack, for what we have done to you; forgive us for the lie we were forced to live; forgive me for the abandonment of my two darling babies all those years ago in Edinburgh....please.

How I wish we could live our lives again. In any place other than Northern Ireland, Jack and I would, without doubt, have already married. (I would love to think we still might in the future, though there are so many obstacles, now as then and we are both a bit set in our ways.) We would have reared you, and loved you as much as any normal parents would. But wishing such a thing is pointless. You were well looked after and reared by Jack's parents, and I am glad of that. So many other poor girls I saw in that Edinburgh home did not have such a good outcome. I think of them often. You have been brought up in the Christian faith, albeit not the denomination of your mother...but in my view, it is more important that you are good people than to be Catholic or Protestant. That is my opinion anyhow, although many in my church would think it heresy.

By the time you get to read this letter, (and Jack's letter too, because we have both decided together to write in this way,) one or both of us may have passed away. We do not know what the future holds, nor when and how you will come into the knowledge of your story. All we ask, and I ask you now, from the bottom of my heart, is that you try to accept this apology, and try to find it in your hearts to

grant us absolution for our failure to be what we always wanted to be, that is proper parents to you both, our darling twins.
God bless you both,
Josephine Quinn

Joseph has finished reading first, and has his head in his hands. I pass Josie's letter to him, but he doesn't offer a hand to take it.

"You need to read this one too," I tell him.

"You know what," he says without looking up, "I never realised until now how much Jack had to endure in his life. He always came across as having a chip on his shoulder, sour and discontent…it's only now I am starting to understand him."

"Me too."

"Like…the farm. It should have been his to pass on. But he had no say in that, with the way the will was left. He was kinda left working it for no real purpose other than to pass it on to Isaac. He had no stake left in it, after him being the main man working it all his life. Labouring away, day in, day out…it was like he was doing penance for his mistake back then."

"Ironic, isn't it?"

"Yeah, and I am only realising it now."

His voice cracks a little. I glance at him. Goodness, there are tears in his eyes. I put my arm around his shoulders.

"I'd love to have him back for ten minutes…just to tell him I understand what was hurting him," he says.

"Me too. He must have been so lonely in his thoughts. He had nobody he could talk to. He was sworn not to tell us his secret. He had no relationship left with his father; nor Isaac, whether he was at home or not. He had no close friends about the place, maybe a few farmers he knew…but the chat with them would have been just mundane, work stuff. The loneliness of the bachelor farmer, eh!"

"But he still had her," Joseph says.

"How do you mean?"

"Well surely you see they must have continued their relationship? Does she not mention that in her letter?"

"Not really," I tell him. "Not a relationship as such. He just wrote to her sometimes."

"He tells us in this," he says, handing me Jack's letter. "There's a lot more in it that is going to shock you, Sarah."

"How do you mean?"

"Just read it and see. But they definitely kept seeing each other. Sure even the fact that he has this letter of hers, written…let me see, March 86, yonks after they were supposed to have stopped all contact. And it was him arranged the piano lessons long before that...I'm fairly sure they were still seeing each other for years."

I can barely wait to read Jack's letter now.

Same hotel notepaper, I realise. Now there's a story in that fact alone.

> **O'Mahoney's Hotel**
> **Clifden, Co Galway**

17/03/86

Dear Sarah and Joseph,

If you are reading this you know our story, your story. Forgive me please for living the lie for so long. Forgive me for what I have done to you. Forgive Josie too, for she did nothing wrong. She was blackmailed into silence, just like I was. Your mother is a great woman. How I wish I could have married her and raised you two as my family. Instead I had to agree to yous being stolen from us. Stolen is maybe too strong a word, but your grandparents stepped in at the thought that you might be lost to an anonymous family in Scotland, and adopted you as if you were strangers, never telling you the truth, all to protect their good name in the area. Fair enough, they did their best to rear yous, but if I didn't agree with something I had no say in it. I had to keep silent, and go along with their decisions. The only thing I was able to do was to get yous to Josie for piano lessons. That was a hard battle, but I won. That meant the world to her. The price I had to pay for that was huge and very hurtful, but worth it, just to hear how she loved yous both.

You see, despite our promises to never see each other again, Josie and I did meet. Just the odd time. And I would sometimes take her away for a wee break, just a day or two here and there....well, mainly 'there', for we couldn't risk being seen about this country.

But because of all that, because of my misdemeanours, my sin with Josie back then, because I refused to 'repent' and stop seeing her, my father has changed his will. I have been done out of my inheritance. The farm is the next thing stolen from me, and it will go to Isaac when he decides to come back from being a missionary. It should be going to my son, to Joe.

But that's the price you have to pay as well, for having the gall to be born on the wrong side of the blanket, and to a Catholic mother.

In this envelope there is a wee Celtic cross that Josie gave me way back when we were courting. I want you to have it, Sarah, and I want you to wear it with pride. If you think it looks a bit Catholic then hold it to your heart all the closer. There's a reason I say that.

You see, back when yous were born there was a lot of negotiating with Mr Quinn. He was a good man; even my father liked him...but once he knew Josie was carrying twins he insisted that one of you be baptised a Catholic. It was a compromise for him, and was the condition he laid down before agreeing to let my parents adopt you. It didn't seem to matter so much to him that they'd be rearing you in the Presbyterian church, so long as one was baptised Catholic. So when a boy and a girl arrived, it fell to Josie to decide which one that would be. She chose you, Sarah, and Jerome Quinn was somehow able to arrange it that a priest he knew in Scotland came and baptised you. I don't know how that makes you feel. Maybe nothing at all, for I know your faith is strong and it may not make a pin of difference to you.

The other thing that we agreed on was that I name one child and Josie names the other. So I picked 'Joseph', after your mother, and she picked 'Sarah' after her own mother. That's how you got the names.

I have no idea when or in what circumstances you will get to read these admissions. They will be hidden somewhere for you. Please know that you are both loved by me and by your mother. Have mercy on us, for not too many others have had.

One more thing to say. I have struggled to forgive my parents. I am sorry about that too, for it eats away at me and destroys me from the inside out. If I have seemed dour and resentful to you, and I confess that I must have been a horrible brother to live with, then this is what lies behind it. But understand that it has been so hard. When you graduated, Sarah, and when you joined the RUC and had your passing out parade, Joseph, I did not get to see either of you. My parents had to go...because they were 'your parents'. On both those days I sat at home with a bottle of Bushmills. And when you married Calvin, Sarah, I was your sibling watching on from a distance, while my father walked you up the aisle and gave you away and made that hypocritical speech at the reception, with all his standard jokes and bonhomie...and I had to leave the dining room in a hurry, if you remember, to go to be sick in the toilets.

What I am telling you is not to ask for pity, just understanding and forgiveness...and I realise that this is me being the pharisee now, for I cannot forgive and forget what was done to me and to Josie. I don't pray any more, but if I did I would be asking God to help me get over this and to forgive Jacob and Bella and everybody else in this judgemental Christian land that time forgot, these folk who seem to believe that dogma is more important than people. So please, you two, don't be like me. Don't hold on to bitterness. Try to forgive me, and forgive Josie, and the parents; forget about these ghosts and move on with your lives. I hope I can do the same before the grim reaper comes for me.

Your father,

Jack

    Good grief! What an incredible thing to be reading. Our...our father speaking so passionately to us in his death. My twin stands up and hugs me very tightly, for a long time. We are entwined together, back in the womb again, but slowly, very slowly, struggling from the uterus, emerging painfully from the birth canal into a new reality, into a new light, a new colour of truth. It is traumatic, and tears flow from both of us. There is, among the myriad of emotions coursing through me, this resonant sense of rebirth, of open-eyed freedom, of truth, deep and brand new. Still in the clutch of Joseph's arms, I sense his suppressed shuddering sobs slowly diminishing, and I hear his voice, a high-pitched whisper as he struggles for control.

"Poor Jack," he says. "Poor oul Jack."

He releases me and fumbles for a tissue. I haven't seen my twin in such an emotional state since childhood. It feels nice to realise he is prepared to be so vulnerable with me, a bonding thing we definitely needed to go through together in handling these discoveries. He takes me by the shoulders and peers closely at my eyes. His still look a bit damp, but I see the hint of a twinkle there.

"I always knew there was something different about you, Sarah."

"What…haha." I know what he's getting at.

"So I have a whole range of new nicknames to call you now. Let me see…which one do you think you'd prefer? How about….?"

"Don't you dare!" I interrupt, but his melancholy seems to have morphed into a suppressed chuckle which, as I start to tickle his weak-spot ribcage, quickly becomes a paroxysm of laughter, a hysterical duet, with both of us squirming about on top of the bed like a pair of rollicking toddlers. In circumstances like this, there is such a fine line between anguish and hilarity.

I just want to have him back, even for two minutes. Long enough to call him 'Daddy'!

Chapter 42

Search

The piano teacher's house at the top of the town hasn't changed much in the near thirty years since I used to come here. I'm sure I must have driven past it on occasions during that period, but I don't recall paying much attention to it. I turn in through the grand gate pillars and ease between over-grown rhododendrons and azaleas to the front door.

I am alone. It's a Saturday. Joseph is in the shop.

Calvin decided against accompanying me. Why should today be different? He is not best pleased at my determination to find my birth mother. I had asked Joseph to stay with me that day last week when I broke the news of our origins to my husband. The whole story astonished him. Watching his reaction, I could almost see buyer's remorse swell up in him. He said very little, but I was imagining what might be going on behind those widening eyes. Was he thinking something along the lines of 'This is not who I thought I was marrying! I was cheated all those years ago. I've been sold a pup! She was baptised Catholic, she's a covert apostate.'

I may have been wrong, probably was. He didn't say much. If he was annoyed, it may have been as much due to the fact that we had interrupted him at a critical moment, just as he was almost finished tying a particularly intricate fly. His eyes kept falling away from mine, back down to the sheen of the tiny Delphi Blue he was working on.

I climb those well-remembered steps and ring the doorbell. I don't recall the door being painted in this shade back then. It looks like a brash postbox red. The house may be Victorian, but the door looks twenty-first century now. Through the side panel I see a man arriving, opening the door, staring at me as welcomingly as if I was a Jehovah's Witness evangelist. I counter the indifference with a bright, school-teacherish smile.

"Sorry to disturb. I am looking for a lady who lives here.... Or maybe used to live here?"

"Ah, yeah," he says. "Used to live here is right. I'm taking it you mean the previous woman, a Miss Quinn?"

His accent is not local, maybe Cork, or the west, somewhere down there anyhow. I am no expert. It's quite musical, not unlike the lilting of a person from Wales.

"That's her," I say. "So she has moved, has she?"

"Indeed she has so. We've been here… what? Must be coming up on five years now."

"Ah ok, sorry," I say. "Do you happen to know where she has gone… like, where she lives now?"

"I don't, sorry, no. No idea. But whenever post comes for her, which it still does…these nuisance mail people never learn, do they? Waste a fortune. Anything that comes for her we take over to the Parochial House so."

"The Parochial House? Oh yes, to the priest, you mean?"

He looks at me as if I am stupid, or maybe just a Protestant, and nods. "Father McCartan might be able to help you locate her," he says, with the tiniest hint of sympathy. "The Parochial house is the big house beside the chapel further down the road."

I know that. I'm a local!

I thank him and drive back down the hill.

Father McCartan invites me in, which is nice, for there's a real bite in the shower that has just begun to splatter on me as I wait at his entrance.

"Come in outa that cold," he says, leading me into his study and pointing to a chair. "Can I get you a cuppa tea?"

"Not at all, Father," I tell him. "I'm only going to take a minute of your time."

"Ah, that's a pity now," he says, almost a bit too jocularly. He's mid fifties, I am guessing, balding, fairly handsome of himself, with something between a two-day stubble and a beard adorning his face. "I was hoping for a bit more distraction than a minute. What can I do for you?"

I mention that I have been at Quinn's old home, and that I'd like to get in touch with Miss Quinn.

"Yes, yes; Josephine Quinn; of course Josephine, one of our organists, wasn't she?" he says, looking up at the ceiling as if to find a remembrance of her face up there. "I didn't know her well. She was in the process of leaving as I was arriving, so to speak. I only came to this parish in 2002. As I recall, she was selling the house and moving on elsewhere. We crossed over by a matter of months."

"So you don't know where she's gone, where she lives now?"

"I don't, I'm sorry. My predecessor might have known more about her now, but, short of a phone call to heaven…hopefully to heaven, ha… we can't really contact him."

"Ah, he's passed away," I say. "But the man up in Quinn's old house tells me that any mail that comes for Josie…for Miss Quinn….he delivers it down here, for forwarding on, I gathered?"

"Is that so? Well, you may be correct. Maybe our parish secretary does that. Monique…she's not in today; just works Mondays, Wednesdays and half day on a Friday. If you could maybe call one of those days?"

I must look disappointed for he makes another suggestion.

"Maybe I could phone her for you, would you like me to do that?"

The smile gets him, and he takes the mobile from his inner pocket. I watch him find the number and call. From what I hear of the conversation, this isn't going to be as straight forward as I had imagined it would be.

"Ah right. I see. Right. Yes. I understand. Ok. Yes, I can do that, Monique. Shouldn't be a problem....seems a nice...Certainly. OK. See you at Mass. Yeah. Bye. Bye. Bye. Bye."

The Northern Irish goodbye. Once isn't enough. We can make a serial out of a 'goodbye' here, whatever creed we adhere to, I think.

"Right, not quite as easy as we imagined....I'm sorry. What did you say your name was?"

We get that bit reinforced, and I wait for his explanation as to what the impediment is. Seems Miss Quinn has left instructions that her mail be forwarded to a particular address, but that that address is not to be given out to the public. So would I leave my name and email address with him, he will pass it on to Monique, who will in turn forward it to Miss Quinn, and she can then decide to contact me if she wants to. OK, that all makes sense...I am used to such procedures within the education environment. I jot down my details, email and mobile number, and push the page across the desk to Father McCartan.

He scans the address.

"Do you want to maybe say what it's about, Sarah...like, does she know you?"

How tempted I am to say, "Yip, she's my mother," but I hold back, of course I do. I go with the simple truth that she is my former piano teacher and that it has been on my mind for ages to get in touch with her, see how she is and so on. Nothing any more sinister than that. He seems happy enough. I shake hands and leave him.

How I hope that the message gets to Josie, and soon, and that she gets back to me. I still have no idea what part of the world she is in, but the signs are that at least she is alive...somewhere.

****

I don't have too long to wait.

I'm on a non-teaching period in my music department office on Tuesday morning; I'm marking mock GCSE papers, in some despair. What were these kids doing when I was teaching them? Ah, maybe I wasn't though...I was absent quite a while. I hear my phone ping. A number I don't recognise. I open the text in a nervous fumble.

> Sarah Sarah Sarah I cant believe it. Just got call from Monique at St Johns. You came looking for me! Fantastic. Phone me soon as you can. Josie.

I am bawling my eyes out.
Thank you God.
The deepest prayer of my heart is answered.
I'd better not phone now, tempted and all as I am.
It wouldn't be fair, to either of us. It will be a long call.
Oh I wish I could though. I wish I could see her. Hug her.
Still don't know where she is; maybe nearby; or miles away.
I'll reply to her text, if I can dry my eyes and focus on this screen.

> Oh Josie! I am crying like a baby here. In school at the minute. Will phone you when I get home, 4.30-ish if that's ok? Thank you for text. I will never get a more precious one. XXX Your daughter Sarah

I am not a great one for sacred objects, fetishes, icons and the like. I've always had a sound skepticism about superstitions, and relics, and moving statues. That being said, just now I have fished up from my bosom an old and very small Celtic cross which has hung around my neck since we found it in that envelope. I press it to my lips, and kiss the little emerald stone in its centre.

The bell rings.

I am immediately transubstantiated back to the mundane rituals of my day job by the shrill, insistent sound. A gang of two dozen rumbustious fourteen year olds is assembling itself at my door. I very much doubt if a single one of them will notice the tear streaks on my cheeks, or the smudged mascara, but I take out my wipes just in case. In my hand mirror I see the face of a sad panda bear gawking back at me. 10A2 will think they're at the zoo.

Chapter 43

Contact

"Are you sure you want to do this, Sarah?"

The question is from Joseph. I have called into the shop after school. It's the day following my phone call with Josie. We are locked in conversation in the back storeroom. I have been trying to bring him up to speed about our chat. His handbrake seems to be firmly on, however. My exuberance is being dragged back to a disappointing halt.

My phone call with Josie had lasted three quarters of an hour. It ranged from past to present, from the time of the piano lessons right up until my discovery of Jack's secret hoard of letters. She wanted me to talk her through all the details of Jack's final months, at which point she seemed to shed a load of tears. She had heard from him a few weeks before he passed. Even though they hadn't seen each other since 2002, they had kept in touch by email, frequently at first, but less so as time went on and she became more involved in her new life in Edinburgh.

I wanted to know what had taken her back there, to a place of cruel memories. Apparently she had been struggling with life here, with the mundanity, the endless cycle of stupid politics, the pointlessness of everything, maybe with a delayed mid-life crisis. Beyond all this, though, she had a growing inner conviction that she needed to do something to 'atone for herself', in her words, make some sort of restitution for the mistakes she had made in her life. So she had gone back to Scotland to work as a volunteer in a residential home for young people who had gone off the rails and needed help to get their lives back together…that is what she told me anyhow.

"I felt a growing vocation to do it," she told me. "I was too old at sixty-two to go into a convent, and anyway the religious life would have been too safe for me, too cloistered. I needed some place where I could make a difference, especially to young girls who had ended up in trouble and could see no way out. I looked online and I found a Trust that was working with the homeless and destitute in Edinburgh. They were advertising for a house keeper, someone who wouldn't mind doing a bit of caring and counselling as well as the practical stuff. I felt that this would be a better way to spend the latter part of my life than sitting up on the hill there, looking down at the town, minding my father's garden and playing Chopin."

My first reaction to that news was to ask about her piano. What had she done with it? I should have known. When she sold the house, most of her furniture and personal possessions had gone to charity shops; the piano, however, the thing that more than anything else defined her, in my opinion, she had shipped to Edinburgh.

"It's in the common room here," she told me, "along with the pool tables and TV. At least it's doing something useful, even if it's only to set their coffee cups on!"

I can't believe her precious Bechstein is ending its days performing such a role.

"I do play for them as well," she says. "The odd one likes to do a few songs of an evening. I play for them; some of the time I actually know the song, but not often. Then I make them sit and listen while I play a sonata or something. That pacifies them for a while…they do listen too."

I'll bet they do!

She had wanted to come to see Jack before he died; then she heard he had passed, but too late to come to his funeral.

"But, for all sorts of reasons, it just might not have been a good idea. People would have wondered who I was, and what I had to do with him; it might have caused talk, and I didn't want to complicate the period of mourning. But I grieved for him," she told me. "I grieved for him in death, but, to be honest, it was just a sort of extension of how I grieved for him in life. Death was yet another barrier being erected between us. During our lives we had fought against every obstacle; we had ignored them, climbed over them, sneaked our way around them…just to be with each other. I suppose we even took a form of pleasure in cheating the system. We enjoyed the thrill of the deceptions, you know, the games we played to be with each other. It only served to make our times together more precious. And believe me, we had some great adventures, Jack and I. But then his health lets him down and he passes away…and that is the one barrier we cannot get around. For a while I felt I didn't want to continue to live in a world that he wasn't alive in, even though we had stopped seeing each other as we got older. It was very strange to have to accept counselling from the very kids I had gone to help, but that is what happened, and it showed me that we were all equal, that I needed them as much as they needed me. I still need them, for I am still grieving for Jack; every night I pray for his soul."

I believe her; even talking to her I could sense the intensity of her emotion. There is so much I wanted to ask her, but a phone conversation about such deep matters, without presence, without being able to read body language, without the physical support you get from a look or a touch or a hug…it's just not a great idea.

She wanted to know all about Joseph, and I told her as much as I could. It wasn't difficult to sense that she would love to have a good relationship with him; we both understand, without needing to verbalise it, that it is so much easier for us to talk to each other as women than it is for Joseph to come to terms with everything. Even the far distant fact of him packing in the piano lessons so quickly may be something that stands between them. Both of us hope for some sort of healing in that, I am quite sure.

One of the weird little things she told me was that back during those years when Joseph was in the police, (which Jack, needless to say, had kept her informed of), she had had such an obsessive desire to meet him in his uniform. Apparently every time she had been stopped at RUC checkpoints, which of course was an extremely frequent occurrence in the eighties and nineties, she would be looking closely at the faces of the officers to see if one was Joe. The same when she had seen policemen in our local TV news bulletins, or when she came across patrols in the street; whereas most civilians wouldn't be paying too much attention to them, trying to act as nonchalantly as possible around these cops, she would be staring at the them to see if one was my twin.

"I could've gotten arrested," she laughed, "I was so brazenly in their faces. But sadly I never saw my Joseph."

Incredibly, she told me that she had seen me as a bride on the day of my wedding. She had bought a wig, specially for the occasion, and a pair of clear-lens glasses, and had turned up at our local church, joining the crowd of neighbours and well-wishing congregation folk who usually stand around the front of the building to see what everybody looks like, especially the bride and her mother.

"I didn't speak to a soul," she told me. "Just floated around in my disguise; not even Jack recognised me. We had some laugh about that afterwards. The next time we met he was showing me his photographs, and there I was, in the corner of one of them, along with the other spectators, looking like Marilyn Monroe in my blonde wig. He laughed till he cried at my get up. And the brazenness of me. But I thought I had as much right as those Presbyterians to be enjoying my daughter's wedding, didn't I? I was mother of the bride, but nobody was paying me an ounce of attention."

I had no idea of course. What a character she must have been back then.

"Fair play to you," I told her.

She asks about Miriam, about my husband as well, about my job in school, about the farm and what will happen to all Jack's work now that the place has passed on to his brother. She knows so much more about us than I could ever have imagined. From how she puts her questions I can sense she carries the guilt of knowing that he lost his inheritance because of her, and that this is something that has impacted Joe and me. That is a subject to be talked out more fully when we get face to face.

Because we must get face to face. We absolutely must!

I told her this and she was saying the same to me at exactly the same moment in the conversation. The question is whether I go across to Scotland at half term or she comes to me.

I could do either, but if I go to Edinburgh, it cuts Joseph out of the loop, yet again. I don't want that pattern to continue. Josie took my point. I asked her when she has had time off in the past twelve months. She hasn't taken any, none at all. I told her that she needed to, for the sake of her health, and of her role there. She sort of agreed. I got the bit between my teeth at that point. Basically I talked her into committing to come back here during the next school holiday. It's not too far away. I can pick her up at the airport, or off the boat in Larne or Belfast. She can stay with us.

"Won't your husband mind?" she wanted to know. A question that hadn't occurred to me. I told her he might not even notice, but I was being facetious of course. Anyhow, I persuaded her to think about it. She is to text me and let me know. I hope she gets a move on and books flights.

But now telling Joseph about my plan, he isn't so sure it's a good idea. I want to know what he has against it. I have a fair idea that he just doesn't want to face the fact, the tangible reality of his biological mother, doesn't want the hassle of dealing with his emotions when they meet, even sorting out in himself what those feelings are. He had said to me once that he would rather focus on the future, that he doesn't feel this compunction that I have to redeem the past, not even to come to understand it, deal with it, come to a place of peace about it all. I have a feeling that this pattern sort of mirrors his feelings about his time in the police, and the whole betrayal that he and so many of his colleagues feel about what happened to them after the Good Friday Agreement. And if you can't come to terms with something, you bury it deep and move on out of the graveyard, so to speak. It's a parallel response to the whole 'fight or flight' thing. In this case, the 'flight' is simply a blocking out, an ignoring, an interment. I haven't been in his shoes, in terms of what he experienced in the police, or how his career there had ended, but I am walking in the same moccasins in the matter of this winding trail of reconciliation with our birth mother. I feel an almost missionary zeal to bring my twin with me on this journey.

"Yeah, I'm sure," I tell him. "Why, what do you have against the idea of her being here?"

He tidies boxes of confectionary, his back turned to me. It's all a bit symbolic.

"I just don't see the point. We have lived forty-seven years without her in our lives. We can manage the rest."

"Don't you feel you owe her anything though? It wasn't her idea to give up being our mother."

"I can't get over that she was able to sit there beside us and teach piano, without ever…"

"I understand that," I say, "but she couldn't. We didn't even know we were adopted then, did we? What could she say?"

"She could have said something. Or at least she could have been more kind, more mother-like."

"What do you want her to say? 'Now be sure to practice that wee piece for next week, Joseph…and never forget, dear son, that you used to live inside me'?"

He visibly shudders at that and moves further down the line of shelving to gather up empty cartons and bits of cardboard. Then, as he bins these, he turns to ask a question that is bothering him.

"Anyway, what story are you going to go with if she comes to stay with you?"

"Story? What do you mean?"

"Who is she when she is here? Just some random lady who once taught us piano?"

"No, of course not. She is coming as our mother. Why should I try to hide that?"

"What about Isaac? And your kids?"

"They will all know it. Eventually. It's not something I feel I have to keep to myself."

"And the folk in the church? Are you going to bring her in there? 'Look brothers and sisters! This is my long lost mother. She got pregnant to our Jack in a cellar, and she had us in some mother and baby home in Scotland, and now she's turned up in our lives again looking for forgiveness. Oh and by the way, folks, don't say anything outa place, for she's not…ah, she's not one of us, like…'"

Wow, I think, this is going to be tougher than I imagined. Not so much the idea of having Josie with me in this my community… as my mother, and I as her proud daughter. More the fact that Joseph, my dear twin, has issues in the deep sewer of his soul that need dealing with.

I am remembering his attitude to Saoirse Coyle, my friend from university days. He had been so sensitive about that friendship. Fair enough, it wasn't the most auspicious time for me to be bringing her over to our home, nor me going to hers. The Troubles were at their height back in the summer of 1981. That summer had been one of the worst periods, with hunger strikers in the H-Blocks dying, violent protests in the streets, police and army under attack and several civilians killed in Catholic areas. It was the closest we came to all out civil war. Joseph was on edge the whole time. You never knew who was going to be next. Those fears left an indelible stain on someone's psyche. My twin was not immune to such a stain. His trust in humanity had been shot to pieces, literally. So Saoirse, given her background, was always going to be 'suspect'. Maybe I am expecting too much of him to suddenly have purged himself of those feelings. While he probably can have no suspicions about Josephine Quinn's allegiances, the taint of association may still be there. She isn't 'on his side', so inevitably she must be closer to the other one.

I think I will risk a gentle challenge. Maybe it's picking at a scab, and maybe it will only make things worse, but I want him to know that I hurt for him, that I think he needs to talk this all out. My own views have been re-examined during this journey, and, as the person closest to me in the whole world, I think he deserves to know.

"Joseph," I begin, "I can see that you are challenged by all this. I am too. Or I have been. It's some journey, after the kind of upbringing that we have had, to have to admit that much of it was…I suppose 'phoney' is the word I'm looking for."

"How do you mean?"

"Well…so much of what we were led to believe has turned out to be fake, hasn't it? Way back, the first challenge was when we learned we were adopted. Then we discover that the story was far more complicated than that. Jack was not our adoptive brother, he was, unbelievably, our father! The people we thought had adopted us were actually our grandparents. Then, to top it all, we learn that our mother was a person we knew, a woman we had visited on a weekly basis for piano lessons, and….horror of horrors in your mind at least, she is a Catholic."

He winces in disagreement at this last bit.

"And so?" he asks.

"And now that I have talked to her, and I have sensed her warmth towards us, well it has given me a different perspective."

"I get all that," he says. "And I get it that, as a girl, as a woman who has given birth to children of her own…yeah, I can see that that is a big deal for you. But not for me. We may be twins, but we don't have to have the same feelings about everything, do we?"

"Of course not! But what I suppose I am saying is….look, we were both reared as Bible-believing Presbyterians; we were both brought up to think that we, as Protestants, had the truth, right? We were the only ones who were right. From the cradle on, we imbibed the idea that 'Catholic' equals 'bad', that they are deceived, that their priests have them deluded. That's what we came to believe, right? It may not have been spoken about much in our home, but it was the constant agenda in so many of the meetings we were dragged to; the sermons in the various halls, and the lack of any counter-balance in our church's teaching. You never heard any clergyman suggest that Catholic was Christian, did you? That would have been regarded as heresy. And that sort of became our view of things; it was maybe unspoken, but it was just how we thought."

"Go on."

"The version of faith we were reared with underlined our attitudes. It gave a kind of divine stamp to our sectarianism, rather than challenging it."

He frowned, examined his nails, said nothing.

"You agree, so far?"

"Go on."

"But the very people who told us the 'truth', they themselves were living a lie, and leading us to believe a lie. We were the ones being deceived…certainly about who we were. So…"

"Hang on, hang on. Are you saying you don't believe the gospel that we grew up with?"

"No, I am not saying that. I'm saying… look, you have to admit that we grew up with a lot of very narrow-minded thinking."

"Of course, but no more than most folk in this country," he counters.

"Surely ours was more extreme. I sometimes think I grew up seeing the world through the mist of my father's hot breath. His attitudes coloured everything. We were fed clichés with our cornflakes, know what I mean? It was a gospel of catchphrases and platitudes, most of them meaningless to people outside our tight evangelical lexicon. And the key point of it all was that only we were right. We had this superiority complex sort of hard-wired into us. I see this at its most extreme in my own husband. He totally blocks out any alternative view other than his own theologies and opinions."

"And what has this to do with Josie? The idea of bringing her into our lives?"

"It has everything to do with it. Look, here is a woman who has lived an unfulfilled life, mainly due to the circumstances she found herself in, because of our Jack, and because of her church, ours as well. And because of the attitudes of our family, and the bigotry of this strange society of ours. Our brother…. Lord, what am I saying? Our Jack, our father…he was the biggest part of her ruination."

I pause for breath; he says nothing. Am I getting through? I try again.

"Look, Josie is a very good person, I believe. It so happens she is Catholic, she's very religious, she believes in the sacraments of her church…"

"Didn't stop her screwing Jack on a hay bale. And plenty of times since."

"Yeah, she's not perfect, and she has been trying to atone for that all her life."

"Her own works won't atone for it."

I choose to ignore his recourse to evangelical dogma.

"Maybe, maybe not, but look at what she's doing at the minute, what she's been doing for the last five years. Working as an unpaid volunteer in a shelter for homeless kids in Edinburgh. Serving the kind of girls she met when she was in the mother and baby home. Does that sound like the actions of someone who is deceived by her church?"

"Just because she does that doesn't mean a thing. Look, there's a bit of good in everybody…."

"I agree, there's good in everybody, but there's plenty of bad in everybody as well. Like Christian parents who could have explained the truth of your birth to you, but were too embarrassed by the circumstances to talk about it. Those age-old obsessions with illegitimacy, and with the Catholic thing. Particularly the obsession with building a boundary wall between us and anybody who wasn't our version of 'Christian'. It's made us blind. We only see what we have been conditioned to see. Everything was distorted for us. We saw people through an evangelical lens…always 'them' and 'us'. Still do, if we're honest."

I think I have really shocked him with this outburst. Maybe it is no bad thing. It has to be said. He has to be challenged.

"Goodness," he says with a cynical half-smile. "Tell a woman she is carrying Catholic genes, and her whole world turns upside down!"

He gets a slap for that comment, facetious or not!

When I think about this conversation afterwards, I have a sudden urge to write an email to Saoirse. How amazed she will be by my story. I can just imagine the surprise on her face, her delight at the irony of this plot-twist in the arc of my life. I can just hear her, in that sing-song Derry accent of hers.

"Ach Sarah, sure I always knew you and me were like blood-sisters, d'ya not think?"

Chapter 44

Arrival

In the history of Aldergrove Airport there has never been a more emotional reunion, of that I am absolutely certain.

I am as nervous as a kitten as I stand by the exit bay. The kaleidoscope of faces flowing towards me seems to turn into some sort of collage of colours and features, a sort of fluid 'Where's Wally?' I have been staring so intently and for so long that I feel like a case of vertigo is happening to me. I have almost got to the point of grabbing some random elderly lady and saying, "You'll do. Come with me to the car."

The blue screen on the pillar above confirms for me that the Edinburgh flight touched down twenty minutes ago. Security checks slow everything up these days. Maybe she has a mobility issue that she hasn't told me about. I am trying to be patient, but it's not easy. People continue to throng towards me. Some connect happily with folks waiting to greet them. Others skip purposefully past me towards the car park or the buses. I had thought of creating a small sign, a piece of card with my name emblazoned in thick Magic Marker. 'Suggested names', as some comedian had joked; 'you can be anyone you want in an airport arrivals hall.' I thought better of the contact card idea. Surely we will recognise each other, mother and daughter? It's a weird ambivalence, that possibility. Maybe, maybe not. It's been almost thirty years since that final piano lesson.

The crowd thins out a bit, and suddenly she is there, beyond the thick blue cord, the barrier rope which fails in its duty to hold me back. No mistaking her face and form, and that delights me. I drag the rope forward with me, and it clings to my legs, between us as we wrap ourselves around each other.

I hear again the same mantra as on the phone; "Sarah, Sarah, Sarah."

I hesitate. Is it to be 'Josie'? 'Miss Quinn'? Hardly! Is it to be 'mother'? 'Mummy'?

No, you can't really bring yourself to say 'Mummy' when that had been the only thing you ever called your late mother/grandmother.

So 'Josie' it is.

The initial conversation is a splatter gun of quick-fire banalities.

"Welcome home".

"So good to see you."

"You too, you too."

"God but how I have waited…longed for this day!"

"Me too. I can't believe it."

"I was late getting off the plane; got myself at the back of the crowd."

"No problem. Better late than…than too late, I suppose…in the other sense!"

She smiles at my silly attempt at a joke.

"Sorry, that was bad," I say. "As bad as it was tasteless."

There's an eloquent silence between us for a few seconds. Except for the eye-to-eye stare.

"Aye, my poor Jack. I'd love to have seen him before….but…"

"Here, let me give you this handkerchief."

"No it's ok. You need it."

"You think?" I can't stop these tears.

"My goodness, how well you look."

"You too. How was the flight?"

"Fine…oh Sarah. Come here again."

And so it went on. We made it to the car eventually. We just sat and looked at each other. So much to say. No idea where to start. So we just sat and stared, and cried some more.

"Will we ever be able to stop these tears?"

"I hope not," I reply. For me, if not for her, it's been a forty-seven year separation. Nearly forty-eight. That's a lot of crying to catch up on.

"Isn't it incredible, Sarah….this? Just a miracle."

"Absolutely. And it's our crazy, real-life story."

"Indeed. Nobody else's." She reaches across and takes my hand, half confidentially, more in jest. "Unless….do you think we could sell the rights to some movie company?"

"You haven't lost your sense of humour anyhow."

"How would you know about my sense of humour? Sure back when I was teaching you I never even cracked a smile, never mind a joke. I had to wear that mask all the time, incase I'd lose control of my emotions."

"Yeah, I remember that," I tell her, "but don't forget I've read all of your escapades in Jack's journal, and your letters. I know you when you were eighteen."

"Eighteen, eh? Was I ever eighteen? I don't know. Who was I when I was eighteen?"

"What I want to know is what you looked like then? This girl that swept my brother…sorry, my father…I still can't get used to that. Have you any photographs?"

She gives me a wry smile. "I have, but not with me. Not the originals. Maybe just as well. I think you'd be disappointed. I was no oil painting."

"Away on with you! Audrey Hepburn! Jack's movie star."

"Ha! Jack had some imagination, I'll give him that. Actually, I do have one or two old pictures on my phone…I can show you those later if you can wait."

I can wait. Right now her real presence is enough.

I stare at my mother's face. The same proportions and the same fine bone structure as my old music teacher, but with so much more character. The pale translucence, the creamy blandness…now given definition by a subtle web of wrinkles radiating out from her azure eyes, like almost invisible sunbeams. Her make-up is minimal and tasteful, gently accentuating the eyes, defining the cheekbones. I don't really get the famous actress that Jack thought he saw, but I do see a pretty lady. The silver hair swept back from her brow, held by a simple green hair-band. She looks so well for mid-sixties, especially when she launches that smile, although I cannot help detect a spectre of heaviness hiding behind it. Her posture seems younger than her years, her neck thin and sinewy, and adorned with a simple chain and cross in silver. Her open suede jacket reveals….

Suddenly I notice the piano brooch that I gave her all those years ago. She's wearing it on her lapel. Instinctively I reach over to touch it.

"You're wearing my brooch!"

"Of course I am. You didn't think I would've lost it?"

"Well, guess what," I tell her, fiddling with my necklace. "Look what I am wearing."

"My word! I recognise that. I bought it for your father, in County Kerry, I think."

"He put it in the envelope, you know…with his final letter to us. I've worn it ever since."

"And so you should, Sarah," she says.

As we drive home, I turn off the ubiquitous Classic Radio, the unconscious soundtrack to all my travelling, and we talk incessantly. How wrong my impression was, back then when she was our teacher. Unlike that dull, rather prim and studious person, she becomes quite animated. It's all about context I suppose.

"I've put you in the guest bedroom," I tell her. "Calvin doesn't mind. He's cleared his stuff out to Christine's room. I couldn't put him in Jonathan's for it's so cluttered, and he might be home at the weekend: you never can tell when he is going to turn up, that one!"

Our first period of silence follows that comment. I can sense she is puzzled. Eventually she gets the question out.

"Can I be bold, Sarah?"

"Of course."

"I'm only with you fifteen minutes, and I'm about to ask a 'mother' question."

"Go on. Ask away," I say. "I've waited long enough, haven't I?"

She hesitates. How can I put her at ease again?

"…Or can I explain first," I say.

"It's ok. Your husband? He's in the guest room?"

"He is."

Another slice of silence. I have to clarify, but how? How can I explain what I don't understand myself?

"He moved out of my bedroom, our bedroom, a few months ago."

"Of his own volition?"

"Yeah….well, maybe it was my idea, but yeah. He didn't…"

"Object?"

"He didn't seem to mind too much."

"Was it a row?"

"No, not at all…unless you call boredom…"

"Look, maybe we shouldn't talk anymore about this now. I have no right to pry. I didn't mean to anyhow; it's just that I don't want to be coming into your house and disturbing the equilibrium."

"You won't be disturbing anything," I tell her. "There's nothing much to disturb. We are together, him and me…maybe just going through a phase. I think it started when I was up and down to Jack, you know….when he was ailing. I wasn't the best to be with around then, and I didn't find Calvin much of a comfort. It didn't help…"

I tail off. This is difficult. More difficult than what actually happened between us, to be honest.

"I see."

"I just couldn't take his words of wisdom any longer. It was all so discouraging, so condemning. He didn't mean it to be, I know he didn't, but… I'd be talking about Jack's medication, or should we be getting the doctor back in the morning or whatever….he wasn't listening. He wasn't on the same wavelength. He'd be reading me some passage of scripture, or something he'd read in his daily meditation notes. It grated with me that he had to have a theology for everything I was going through. I suppose he meant it to encourage me, but I knew about my brother…I knew he didn't have faith, but far more important right now was his sickness, and his depression. Calvin wasn't coming into that world. He was on some more elevated plane, a hyper-spiritual one. It wore me down. So I suppose I just moved his stuff one day…from our room to the guest room. When he noticed he didn't even argue. He just accepted it; maybe even welcomed it, I don't know. He headed to the guest room that night without a word, and we haven't been together ever since. I suppose neither of us are that interested. I don't really miss it, if I'm being honest. I have no idea if he does or not."

We turn on to the motor-way slipway. Goodness, I think; my mother has only been with me half an hour, and I am opening myself up to her like I haven't ever done with any other human being before; not my mother/grandmother, not my twin, not my husband, no-one. I begin to get emotional. Josie's hand touches my thigh.

"You'd better pull in for a minute," she says, and I do.

Parked on the hard-shoulder, we hug across the car. My Lord, I think, how I have missed my real mother. And I know it's mutual. I mutter my thanks. She pulls away, and we stare at each other. A smile begins to spread over her face, like a sunrise over the valley.

"You realise you have just turned me into your priest?" she says, her eyes sparkling with mischief. "I knew that getting you baptised Catholic would pay off at some stage."

I cannot help but laugh in response, but I protest.

"Ah now, that wasn't a confession. I wasn't talking about any sins there, just explaining our sleeping arrangements. You can't convert me that quick."

"No," she said, "and I'm glad you said that, for I will never try to convert you, Sarah. You are who and what you are, and so am I, and we should respect and accept that, all right?"

"Of course…mother," I say.

Later I tell her about Jack's car.

"His Saab is still in the shed at the farm," I say.

"The Saab? The beige coloured one? That's the car he used to take me away to the south in. Oh my word. I can't wait to see it. A piece of Jack."

I have my chance for revenge.

"Yeah….away to the south, eh? Like Galway and so on? And what did yous do there? Walk the beaches? Have a wee bite to eat together? A nice wee chat? Then off to separate bedrooms? I can imagine…"

The laughter between us sounds and feels like a joyous waterfall. When she gets herself under control she says, "So now you want me to be recounting all my misdemeanours to you, do you?"

"You probably haven't got time. Like, you're only here for a week."

But she begins anyhow. I feel like I am listening to a confessional ballad, the basic narrative of her journeys, but what I am hearing underneath is a countermelody of delight, as she recalls trips to Donegal, Sligo, all the western counties, right down as far as Kerry. It seems that she and Jack celebrated every St Patrick's Day together. They'd drive away on a Friday evening, stay in a grand hotel, walk beaches or climb mountains on the Saturday, talk and laugh, and have a drink, and enjoy each other's company…two proper, romantic, little lovers. Then they'd return to their sentences in the drab-grey enclosures of Northern Ireland, until the next bright adventure. I do not sense any great regret in Josie. She describes these holidays with a quiet rapture at what she is remembering.

"And did you only see each other once a year then?" I ask, a bit naively, I soon realise.

She laughs. "You will think I am the most immoral mother in Ireland," she says. "Yeah, we only escaped to the south maybe once a year, but sometimes, maybe three or four times a year, when he was lonely, Jack would appear at my house in the middle of the night. He'd ring the bell, or sometimes, if he was in a romantic mood, I would hear gravel spitting off my bedroom window, and I'd open the curtains and look down and there he'd be with a handful of flowers he'd pinched out of my garden, and a stupid grin on his big farmer face. What could I do but open the door to him?"

"But what about your father back then? Surely he wouldn't have…"

She holds up her hand. "My father had passed away," she says. "Not long after I came back from Scotland. I found him dead in his bed one morning. He was already gone by the time I was teaching you piano."

"I am so sorry," I say. "The grandfather I never knew. That must have been so tough for you."

"It wasn't easy; I'd be lying if I said otherwise. I was an orphan at twenty four. Do you know one thing I remember about that time? Both Jack and his father came to the funeral. I couldn't believe it. I don't know if they were in the church or not, but both shook hands with me at the graveside. It meant so much to me that Jack came."

"That is lovely."

"It really was. And of course…he knew I needed him after that. He understood my loneliness…and that's when he started to visit me. He was wonderful."

"So he'd drive to you in the middle of the night…?"

"He would. Sometimes earlier. He'd park his car away down the street in some car park and skip up to me in the shadows."

I shake my head in wonderment at this father I didn't know.

"The good sinner that he was!" I say.

"We both were, Sarah. But we were in love. It was a love stronger than death, stronger than the religious walls and the political divisions that box us in here in this part of the world. We loved each other, in mind and in body, believe me, it was powerful."

"I believe you," I say. "And I feel very, very rebuked."

"You do? How come?"

"There you were, not married, but deeply in love with each other, having to skip around in secret to be together, and not often either. Meanwhile, I am married, and I have a husband who loves me, I know he does, for all his oddness…and I put him out of my bed. Worse than that, I don't miss him, I don't miss the sex. What sort of cold person am I?"

"I don't believe for one second that you are a cold person. I think you just need to rewind the clock, and see the twenty year old guy that you fell in love with. Tempt him back to being that person. Go away for a romantic weekend...I'd recommend Westport. Have a drink. Two drinks. Seduce him again. You're married. You're allowed to, right?"

"Right," I say.

I was giggling at the idea of me getting Calvin tipsy.

"I always thought that as a Catholic you are supposed to have a complete taboo about this sort of thing. You realise that, don't you?"

"I know," she says. "I'm scandalous, am't I!"

"How did you get over...you know...all those feelings, the guilt thing? Like, were you not totally brainwashed about the evil of sex when you were at your Belfast school?"

"Of course I was. We all were. The teachers, especially the nuns, were on our case about it often. It was a sin worse than death to be even thinking about it, not to mention talking about it, never mind doing it! But there was more than one curriculum going on amongst us boarders. There was the official Catholic one in the classroom, especially Religious Instruction, and then there was a clandestine curriculum in the dormitory. It tended to be conducted in whispers, wee groups of girls, their heads together, giggling over pictures. The textbooks we had in the dormitories were sort of under-the-counter novels, magazines and comics. We were always torn, some of us anyhow, not all of us...torn between the official Catholic line, the church's teachings, you know, and the allure of that forbidden world. When I met your father, at eighteen...I hadn't much of a clue about sex. I should have been able to resist him and all, but that day of his birthday...resisting him was the furthest thing from my mind."

She pauses, and I glance across briefly to her.

"And here you are," she says. "You are the result. You and Joseph. And am I sorry? No, Father, I am not sorry. Not now, not ever!"

I glance at my speedometer. Dear goodness, I am doing close on eighty miles an hour. This mother of mine has me so excited, so alive. And this is only day one of her stay? How am I going to survive?

I slow down a bit. I have another question.

"So...can I ask you about marriage?"

"Ask me what?"

"Well, your father dies; you don't seem to have much family around here; you have Jack at your window, but only occasionally. Did you never look at other couples and wish you were married?"

She is slow to answer, looks away out the window at the distant hills.

"Wishing wasn't going to make it happen, was it? I came to realise that early on. I think I even developed a mind-set to take the edge of that natural desire...I told myself that marriage wasn't for me, that being single was a sort of life-time penance for what I had done."

"As if giving up your children wasn't penance enough?"

"Maybe; I don't know. I just came to accept that that was how my life was going to be. Maybe that seems strange to you..."

"It does. You were a beautiful woman, still are…but you never found yourself in a situation where some handsome man was making overtures to you, asking you out, or whatever?"

"There were a couple of times," she smiles, "but no. I could never have betrayed Jack by getting into another relationship."

"Really? You were so in love with Jack that you turned down all other possibilities?"

"That's about it, Sarah. In my mind you see, Jack and I sort of were man and wife already; I was his, he was mine, whether the powers that be wanted to give it their blessing or not. That is how it was, pretty much up until I retired and decided to go to Edinburgh."

I'm also curious about that retirement; even more so about her earlier career in music. Had she continue to teach after I had stopped lessons with her? What else had she been involved in?

"I would have been such a huge disappointment to my father," she tells me. "He had delusions of grandeur about his daughter's talent. I think he imagined me touring the world as a performer, giving concerts in the great halls, mixing with the elite. It was all a mirage. If I did have some ability back in my teens it didn't really develop. Maybe what happened to me undermined everything. Maybe the whole trauma of losing my two babies affected me emotionally and mentally, far more than I would ever have admitted. My confidence was shot, but, more importantly, I didn't have the ambition any more. I settled for teaching locally, so as to be near Jack….and as close as possible to you two."

"So you felt unfulfilled, creatively?" I ask.

"Not really. I did enjoy teaching, especially at the start. And music in the church was an outlet. I also got involved in theatre productions here and there, sometimes on stage, but more often as musical director. Quite enjoyed all that."

I tell her that I am glad to hear that. "I would hate to think you were musically unfulfilled," I say.

"Sarah, I would have happily never sung another note if I had been able to be a mother to you two," she tells me.

Chapter 45

Visit

The week together has been memorable, incredibly so. And that was the point of it, I suppose; to make memories for the future in the absence of any anthology of them from the past.

Calvin has welcomed Josie quite warmly. In a way, his attitude is a mild rebuke to me; perhaps I had expected some sign of resistance from him, but I am pleasantly surprised. He has appreciated the sacredness of this reunion as far as I am concerned, and is making a real effort to be the sociable host…this despite having to vacate his hallowed space in the guest bedroom.

Josie is great with him too, and I am delighted by the absence of any barrier or awkwardness. They chat away freely, all very accepting, harmonious even. She does poke a bit of quiet fun at me when he goes to the kitchen to organise coffee not long after we arrived.

"He's nice. You had me expecting him to be something a bit more…" She tails off.

"A bit more what?"

"I dunno; maybe I expected him to be wearing a T-shirt with Luther's 39 Articles on the front."

"Ah no," I laugh, "he only puts that on on a Sunday."

"He's quite handsome too," she observes.

I wince a bit at this.

"Don't you agree?" A follow up question to unravel me.

"I used to think so," I say, defensively.

"You need to look again," she says, and I notice she is grinning at me like the host on some TV couples show.

He emerges from the kitchen with a tray of coffee and biscuits, and proceeds to serve us.

Where has this guy been concealing himself for the past few years?

She's clever, this mother of mine. She has noticed several framed photographs around the house, those that have survived my attempted culls. Pictures of my husband, beaming proudly as he holds various specimens of salmon and trout. These poor fish had met their destiny at his hands, succumbing to the temptation of his famous flies. Not the first creatures to fall for Calvin's lure either.

So Josie could not fail to detect this fixation with fishing; she doesn't say anything on the first night; my guess is that she googles the subject in the privacy of her room later. Mid-morning I happen to emerge from the kitchen to find the two of them in the hall, studying Calvin's favourite photograph. It is a good shot too. Appropriately enlarged, there is himself knee-deep in a swirling river, holding up a large, silvery specimen. The shock still shows on its face, and the camera loves it.

I watch him now, arms waving about as he relives the conquest; Josie's eyes never leave his performance. I pass her, briefly placing a consoling hand on her shoulder, a gesture that says, "Do you want me to rescue you here?" But no! She seems engrossed in this animated account; how he landed this glorious fifteen-pounder, which river he'd been fishing, how long he'd had to play it, what fly he'd had on…the whole, tedious works. I knew exactly what she was doing. I was almost annoyed with her, so admonished did I feel at the warmth of her motivation, the skill of her subtlety.

Our visit down the lane to Isaac and his wife does not have the same vibe at all. They know, of course, who Josie is. Some time back I had spent a couple of hours explaining the whole backstory to them, Jack's affair with this woman who became mother to me and Joseph. Whether or not Isaac knew about any of this he did not admit. From the fleeting glances between himself and Lisa, I suspect they knew at least something of the scandal, but they weren't giving anything away.

It was a case of 'Mum's the word', as we say in this country.

What a bizarre circumstance, to have been sitting there with the man that for most of my life I had regarded as my brother by adoption, as opposed to my biological uncle, and not have any clarity if he was aware of my real origins, my identity. For all the blood connection, this unspoken question doesn't half put an extra layer of insulation between us.

We drive down to the farm. I knock the front door. That is weird in itself; gone are the days of entering what had been my childhood home by the traditional route, the back door. Lisa just could not get accustomed to the country custom of people walking into her kitchen unannounced, and without invitation. It had taken me a few *faux pas* moments to adjust to this.

The two of them arrive on the threshold and smile their welcome.

"This is my…."

Oh wait, I think. I hadn't planned to introduce Josie as anything other than 'Josie', but here I am, halfway through the process, about to own my daughterhood. I have to continue. It's the truth anyhow. I rewind.

"This is Josie, my real mother," I continue.

We stand in the hallway together. I sense a degree of holding back in both of them. It's pleasant enough, but just that bit stiff. Not a clue do they have as to what to say. All that wonderful service in India, dealing with indigenous people of many diverse languages and faiths, but it hasn't really done anything by way of preparing them for this kind of interaction. Sentences are staccato, the rests between passages longer than in natural conversation. More is being said in those awkward spaces than in the actual discourse. We have to be so good at sight-reading between the lines in this country.

I try to inject some common ground into the exchange as we stand between a potted Christmas cactus and the hall mirror.

"Josie is a sort of missionary herself," I say, trying to break the deepening ice. "She is a full-time volunteer in a care home in Scotland, working with disadvantaged young people."

"That is good to hear," Isaac says, and asks a few questions about it.

Josie turns the conversation quickly back to him, however, and on that stage he is more secure, Lisa operating as his prompt. It is an impressive story of the various medical initiatives he has been involved in over there. I am proud of his achievements, and delighted that Josie seems genuinely interested.

We get an invitation to come into the sitting room, which is nice, if not too insistent...a 'would-you-like-to' lukewarmness in the tone. I hesitate however.

"Actually," I tell them, "I want to take Josie down to the back shed to see the old Saab that Jack used to take...used to drive. You don't mind if we take a dander down there, do you?"

So that is what we do. At the shed I struggle to drag open the big door of corrugated iron; it is stiff and creaky, its hinges shrieking like the soundtrack of a horror movie. I undo the straps that keep the tarpaulin cover in place, pull it carefully from the body of the car. The surface is dusty, but not enough to stop Josie from running her hand along the bonnet. She tries the handle. Surprisingly, the door opens. I'd expected it to be locked, the key inside the farmhouse somewhere. Josie sits herself into the passenger's seat and inhales the musky scent of the leather interior, an aroma from a different era.

"Still there," she says. "All the memories. Oh Jack... what fun we had in this old bus."

"Well, it's waiting for you if you ever want to come back here and need a car," I tell her.

"That would be some craic," she laughs. "Would it ever start, do you think?"

The following morning we drive up past the chapel to visit her old home. I nose my car a fraction through the gate just to look from a distance. The profusion of shrubs near the entrance is tending to block a decent view of the house. I am tempted to continue along the driveway, but she stops me.

"It's all right," she says, "this is far enough. It's just a big museum of memories now. I don't need to go in there to be reminded. The new people will have changed everything, even if they have neglected this garden a bit."

"Ok, so where would you like to go now?"

"Would you mind if I spent an hour in my church?"

"Of course not, if that is what you want. And don't forget, I can drive you in to Mass at the weekend."

When I pull up in front of St John's Parish Church she looks across at me as she holds her door open.

"I want to visit my parents' grave first, then I'll go inside to pray. You are welcome to come with me…only if you want to."

"Ah…thanks but…look, I have something to do down the town, but when I'm finished I'll call back up and come in, say in half an hour or so."

"No problem, see you then."

I am not dodging the issue; I am not lying either. I want her to have some quiet time on her own, for prayer or confessions or whatever she wants. I do have something I must to try to find down on Main Street.

Our local Barnardo's Charity shop is renowned for its collection of all sorts and standards of second-hand clothing; it is where I deposited all Jack's stuff some time ago. The sentimental me wants to find and rescue one particular piece, if it is still there…and I imagine it will be. Sure enough, at the rear-end of one of the rails I discover it, hiding away in embarrassment at its age and condition. I take it to the counter, pay the £5.00 shamelessly demanded on the attached card, take it to the car.

While I am waiting to go into the chapel I text Joseph. I've heard nothing from him yesterday or today, despite the fact that he knows I was going to pick up our mother.

> Josie arrived safe. She's looking forward to seeing you. Call up whenever suits.

Inside St John's the atmosphere is utterly still and sombre, as it has been on every other occasion I have been in a Catholic church. Three or four times in my life I've been at a funeral or a wedding. The contrast with my Presbyterian church is very noticeable. Our churches, especially the rural ones, generally would have a lot more light about them, I have always thought. In the past I would have imagined that this difference had a measure of symbolism in it; today I reproach myself for allowing such an arrogant thought to flicker in my subconscious. If, in my mind, I am despairing of the insidious undertone of judgemental spirit that I hear within the circles I inhabit, I continually need to silence such echoes in me. Unlearning takes time, I remind myself; maybe as much time as the learning took. It is a depressing thought.

The silence is spacious in here. It's as if the background hum and clutter of life has been sucked away into the ether. Not a sound do I hear as I stand just inside the door, looking around for Josie. She doesn't appear to be in the nave, so I wander slowly up the aisle until I see her in the side transept. She is alone in the building, it seems. She sees me at the same moment, and rises from her kneeling position to come to me.

"Would you like to play the organ?" she breathes. "I think it is ok."

"No way," I say, "that would be very bold…"

But she is already leading me by the elbow to the narrow staircase at the rear that leads up to the balcony. I don't want to make a scene in the sanctity of this building. What can I do but follow?

The console lies open, twin manuals beckoning, but she hangs back.

"Go ahead and play something," I tell her.

"Ah no, no! It's been way too long," she says…but she is sitting down, unable to resist the temptation. She clicks the 'on-switch'; the red light glows; she pulls a few familiar stops, slips off her shoes.

Soon she is playing a slow, wistful piece that I don't recognise. It's beautiful, a real nostalgic moment for her, I sense.

"Now it's your turn," she says, standing up and taking my arm in case I try to escape.

I sit down reluctantly.

"Do you want music, or can you play something by ear?"

She is looking around for a hymnal, or some sheet music.

"See, way back I had this piano teacher," I say. "And she would tap my fingers if she thought I wasn't reading the score. She was a tough one, that woman! 'Follow the music! Follow the music!' she'd say."

She enjoys the humour of course. Despite my protestations, I launch into the familiar, *'The Arrival of the Queen of Sheba'*. The instrument has a majestic sound. I haven't played such a fine pipe organ in years. My feet are skipping around the pedal board as if they have a memory of their own, which they do of course. The first section I can play by ear, after that I would be struggling, but Josie sits beside me and together we make an absolute mishmash of Handel's *tour de force*. We finish up laughing hilariously on the organ bench, our arms around each other like a pair of giddy schoolgirls.

And that is how we are when the head of the Parish Priest appears at the top of the staircase, his face looking rather alarmed.

"What in the name of God is going on here?" Father McCartan's voice modulates quickly from shrill annoyance to a more mellow tone as he recognises me from our recent meeting. "Ah," he says, gently, "Mrs Moore. My apologies…I thought a bunch of kids must have broken.…"

He is giving my mother a long, curious look, no sense of rebuke in it either. Then, turning to me, "Looks like you have found your old music teacher, am I correct? How are you, Josephine?"

We are apologising for taking such a liberty, but he is waving us to silence. Josie is reminding him that she played for Mass on many occasions, explaining how she came into the church today to pray, then had fallen into the temptation to be playing the organ again, "one more time", as she put it. The conversation develops; I enjoy being a novice fly on the unfamiliar wall of matters ecclesiastical in St John's. The chat is mainly about bygone times, about her father, ('the legend that was Jerome Quinn', the priest says), who is still known by reputation, and about other parishioners she could recall. Father McCartan turns, sensitively, to bring me into the conversation.

"How nice it is, you finding your piano teacher," he says. Then to Josie, a little jocularly, "Do you keep in touch with all your former students like this?"

We glance at each other, she and I. She smiles, a confident, affirming kind of smile. I sense at once what she is about to do.

"Sarah is my daughter, Father."

His eyes widen and his mouth opens. I can virtually see the gears of his mind clicking round to process this.

'But she is 'Miss' Josephine, is she not?' he is likely thinking. 'What has been happening here? Was there an estrangement or something?'

It takes a second or two for him to find the appropriate comment.

"Really?" he says, with remarkably little alteration to the even timbre of his voice, "I didn't see that one coming!"

There follows one of those lovely moments of silence, almost a smugness, certainly a comforting boldness that at last you have climbed out of a shadowy valley onto high ground, that you cannot now be touched by an untimely revelation of scandal.

"Well, that's great," the priest says with considerable magnanimity. "And do I take it....I am guessing here, ladies....that you have only recently rediscovered each other?"

Together we recount our story, a confessionary duet in several stanzas. Sometimes I am the leading soprano in the piece, sometimes I am throwing in embellishing harmonies as Josie takes the lead, in her rich contralto. It's quite a joint performance for a first gig, I think; a fusion of tone, of perspective, of faith. When it is over we are almost chuckling with delight in each other. And, incredibly, Father McCartan looks very much like he appreciated the performance.

"I am delighted for you both," he says, 'utterly delighted. It is an amazing story. I almost feel like I want to bring a blessing to you both... in this new phase of your lives together. May I do that?"

Josie looks at me. Her face says, 'please?' I can tell she is yearning for this. I shrug my shoulders submissively; she nods to Father McCartan. They both bless themselves. "In the Name of the Father, the

Son and the Holy Spirit..." he begins. It is fairly brief and entirely painless, even from a theological point of view. It has meant a lot to my mother. To me too, if I am honest.

So that is another first, me being prayed for by a Catholic priest on the balcony of his church, in my own town. The man has impressed me yet again; sincere and compassionate, with a deep sense of humanity about him. The old stereotypes that have lurked in the musty wardrobe of my mind have been blown away by the warmth of his acceptance. I am listening intently to what he is praying, but I would have to admit that in the back of my mind I am wondering how Calvin is going to take the news of this benediction.

As we walk across the car park arm in arm, I tell her I have a special present for her in the car. I ask her to close her eyes. Taking Jack's old leather jacket from the back seat, I wrap it around her.

"Just a wee thing I picked up for you in a charity shop," I say.

She virtually swoons with amazement. She has it around her shoulders all the way home. I catch her bring the sleeve up to her nose on several occasions, drawing its stale scent into her nostrils as if to conjure a more intimate memory of my brother...my father.

Chapter 46

Grandchildren

How special to be able to forget all about school during my break this week. Usually I am mentally exhausted; I need the time to recuperate, but I find myself still thinking 'teaching'; I will be marking projects, worrying about results; I'll be planning a junior concert; sometimes I have even found myself having imagined dialogue with a talented student whose laziness has been bugging me for months, or with a tiger-mum who is taking it personally that her Olivia didn't get cast in the lead role in the school show.

Not this time! None of these things make it into my consciousness at the moment.

Instead, I am delighting in Josie's company. We take ages over our meals, chatting away at the table until it's almost time to prepare the next meal. We walk up the farm track behind our house into the hills, and explore places I haven't been in since childhood. I find myself lying awake at night, thinking of her and our conversations into the wee small hours, trying to make a mental note of particular questions I need to ask her.

I have wanted to ask my mother about the events surrounding our birth. When we get into the subject, she talks very openly about that period in Nazareth House. She found the sisters there generally kind and understanding, unlike the usual stereotype associated with such homes. Believe me, I've read those dreadful stories. Our Belfast press would not have been slow to emblazon the horror headlines of historical abuse in Catholic institutions in the Republic. It happened across the religious spectrum, of course, and in both jurisdictions, a stain on the national conscience of all concerned.

In Josie's case, however, she thinks that she may have been treated well because of her background. She was that bit different from the local Scottish girls who tended to be the home's normal clientele. She was Irish, she was refined, educated. As far as the nuns were concerned, she got the feeling they thought that 'poor Josephine must have just been very unfortunate to 'get caught''. The other girls seemed to merit much less sympathy; they were treated more harshly, the presumption being that their promiscuous life styles had landed them in trouble.

"What about the birth itself?" I want to know.

"I was in the local hospital, so I had a Caesarean, thankfully," she tells me. "I was slight in my body; my first pregnancy; and I was having twins. So it was logical. I didn't object, especially after what happened to my own mother."

I could believe that. I want to know about her recovery, about feeding, about how long we had with her before the hand-over happened. She shakes her head sadly at the memory.

"The whole thing was just crazy. I was so dopey for a while after the operation, I didn't know what was going on. Then I had so much pain, you know. I was not in good shape. So they had me on pain-killers. Everything was like a dream, well, more like a nightmare really. I was so drowsy. And of course, I didn't get to spend time with you two."

"So who fed us?"

"Well, you see…because the sisters knew you were going to be adopted, you couldn't be allowed to get attached to me. So it was bottle-feeding more or less from the start. That was one of the hardest things, I suppose. I really missed feeding you. After a couple of days it became very uncomfortable, the compression around my chest. I so wanted to nurse my babies."

"I can imagine," I say. "For me, with my two, that was one of the greatest feelings. I know some women struggle with it, but I found it such a pleasure. I am so sorry you had to be deprived of it."

"Well, when you think of it…that was just the first brick in the wall of deprivation I had to endure. It was very tough, I'll not deny it, but nowhere near as tough as saying goodbye to the pair of you when Jack's folks were leaving."

"Did you get much chance to talk to Jack at the time?"

She laughs ruefully. "I did, a bit. I wasn't supposed to, Jack wasn't even supposed to exist, as far as the sisters were concerned. 'Father unknown', and all that. But Jack, being the resourceful boy he was, he found a way. I had a ground-floor room, thankfully, so late in the evening I would hear him tapping at the window. He must have escaped from his folks, and he'd be standing outside, waiting for a chat. We would hug each other through the open window; it was lovely. It deadened the pain, but in some ways it made it much worse."

"And the baptism? How did that happen?"

"My father organised it, like he organised everything then. A priest he knew from before. You see, all that happened before Jack and his parents arrived on the scene. By the time they got here, my father had left. It was all very sterilised. No hassle."

"But why only me? Would the priest not have insisted on both being done?"

"I suppose that was what was agreed between the families earlier. The priest may only have been aware of the one baby. The whole affair was always about half-truths," she tells me. "Even the poor nuns were very confused, but they just had to go along with what my father had organised."

****

Understandably Josie is keen to meet her grandchildren. In Jonathan's case that is easily arranged; I have sent him a text and he promises to drive down from Queen's for a few hours. In Christine's case it is not really possible. A phone call will have to suffice.

I listen in of course.

Christine sounds a bit bewildered at first, and I can understand. Her responses are tentative, as this mysterious grandparent tries to get a conversation going. The randomness of the situation is not lost on me. A disembodied granny that you've never met, whose voice you've never heard, whose existence you've only very recently become aware of…and here she is, on the phone, trying to make conversation with you, probing about your course, your life in Bath, your boyfriend, your plans for the future! It is an incongruous situation, but my emotionally intelligent daughter makes it as painless and normal as possible. She skilfully turns the dialogue back around with thoughtful queries, and I hear a repeat account of Josie's story, patchy and somewhat sanitised for the sensitivities of the circumstance.

"And your mum tells me you are very musical as well," Josie says.

Christine laughs. "Yeah, she would like to think so, but I am nowhere near as accomplished as she is. I suppose that must be a mother thing, false pride in the talents of the next generation."

"Not this mother," Josie says, a little firmly.

Christine pauses. "How'd you mean? Sorry…"

"I mean…your grandmother is proud beyond words of her precious daughter, but unfortunately she cannot take an ounce of credit for it, see what I mean?"

"Ah, yeah," my daughter replies thoughtfully. Then after a pause, "But you mustn't forget the genetic inheritance surely? My mother is who she is because of you, every bit as much as because of Jacob and Bella…don't you think?'

Gosh, what a lovely thing to say in the circumstance, I think. The conversation finishes with mutually warm pledges to meet and get to know each other in the future, and as soon as possible. The end of the dialogue has been so much more affable than the earlier part.

Jonathan keeps his promise too. He drives in, meets his dad outside and we watch them chat for a few minutes; Calvin is heading out to a meeting, conveniently I think. Jonathan sidles uncertainly across the back yard and into his own home, stands by the back door, typically nervous, seemingly shy to cross the floor to this stranger who is beaming at him from the other side of the room. It is painfully awkward for a second. As Josie circles the central island to her right, so does Jonathan. For a brief second it looks as if it's going to turn into a chase around the room, a sort of musical chairs for the unwilling. Then they both stop at the same time, both giggling now at the craziness of the moment, both unsure of which direction to move next. My instinctive reaction is to grab my son.

"I've got him, Josie," I say.

"Hold on to him," she laughs, and eventually they manage to get close enough to shake hands. The delicacy of the situation has been trumped by the humour of this bizarre dance. Jonathan's face has loosened up into a broad grin.

"I wasn't running away from you," he says, "honest."

Over dinner the conversation moves in sync with the three courses; starters accompanied by banalities, much deeper topics to chew over with the steak, and funny stories with the apple crumble.

She wants to know about his course.

"Why sociology? Why philosophy?"

He scratches his neck characteristically, thinking, slow to divulge an answer that is palatable to his free-spirited Catholic granny and his… what is she…maybe 'recovering' evangelical mum?

"I was for doing Science," he says, "but it always seemed to me that Science was trying to answer the wrong questions, or at least ones that I was losing interest in. I had other questions."

We wait, neither of us sure what he means.

"Like…this place we call home, this country of ours. Why is it the way it is? I got into the history of it, but that only explains things up to a point. It gives us a set of background reasons. Every country has its problems, its divisions, and every country has its own unique history. But what is it in society that polarises people, rather than bringing them together? In so many societies?"

I've not heard my son talk about this kind of thing before. We two oldies flick a look at each other, hoping he'll continue.

"That's why I wanted to study…you know, society. The different groups and how they see each other. How they stay separate, how they develop myths about each other and pass them on to the next generation, how they end up hating each other, killing each other. Like why, for example, do the most religious societies end up being the most violent towards each other?"

"And have you any answers yet?" Josie asks him.

He smiles. "I've only started this course; give me time."

"I hope you can find them, Jonathan. I think you are asking the right questions," his grandmother tells him.

Jonathan pauses, bite halfway to his mouth, looking at her with an intensity I couldn't quite understand for a second.

"Actually," he begins, "I was hoping….my mum has told me a fair bit about you and Uncle Jack, and…"

He hesitates, his eyes still focused on hers.

"Me and your grandfather," she says. "Go on."

"I want to know…I hope you don't mind me being curious…but I am your grandson after all. I would love you to talk to me about how it was for you, for you and him back then. Like…how did the Troubles play into your lives, when you were coming from opposite sides of the fence? It must have been very difficult….I'd love to know about that, and maybe also…how it went down with….like, how did you feel about the rules in this place? And….why did you not…why did you not just get away out of here, and get married, or at least just get to be with each other without…." He fades to silence.

Josie sits back in her chair, dabs her mouth with her serviette and grins at him.

"You sound like my kinda grandson," she says. "How long have you got?"

Chapter 47

O'Cuinn

I take Josie to the coast one afternoon; we dander along the strand, deep in conversation. The freshness of the chill sea-breeze is blowing through us; we cuddle together for warmth, arm in arm like best party buddies. The ocean swell today has attracted a shoal of surfers in black wet-suits, their calls to each other combining with the cries of swooping seagulls above the rush and hiss of the sea.

I take the opportunity to revisit my emotions on my last visit here, which was just after I had read her letter telling Jack that she was pregnant. Obviously at that stage I had no idea that I was the foetus, or one of the two foetuses, that she was carrying. Nevertheless, even then I felt so absorbed by the saga of Jack and his girl that I recall crying like a baby at the drama of it all, the rain pelting down on me.

Then I get the courage to ask her a question that has been bothering me for a while, a query from the naive land of Protestant ignorance.

"Can I ask you about confessions?"

She smiles knowingly. "Go on. I think I can guess what's coming."

"So, when you and Jack headed off for…for a weekend together… Did you have to confess all that to your priest afterwards?"

"I didn't have to, I suppose, but I did."

"Really? Every last detail?"

"We didn't really do 'detail' in the confessional, just bland generalisations, sort of like a ritual formula."

"But he would know exactly what you were owning up to? Or would he question you, for more detail like?"

"If you mean, did he ever ask if I was sleeping with a Protestant….no, he didn't ask that. I don't think he knew about Jack. He probably just thought I was a bit of a loose woman."

That would have been the last thing I would ever have thought about Miss Quinn, piano teacher.

"And was he cross?"

She laughs at the innocence of my question.

"He wasn't best pleased."

"Would he have been even worse if he'd known the truth, that you were having sex with a Protestant?"

"Probably. Why do you ask, Sarah?"

Why indeed!

"I suppose because… I don't know. I'm curious. I want to know how it might have been for me, if I had been reared as a Catholic. I am trying to absorb all I can about…about you, about your faith, how it affected your life."

"I can understand that," she says. "And it is only right that you have an answer to what is really going on in your head."

"How do you mean?"

"I think your real question is… Jack and Josie broke their promises to their folks. They betrayed the churches that had succoured them from childhood. They kept seeing each other secretly. They loved each other, slept together. They were habitual sinners. Right so far?"

"Maybe. Go on."

"But, while your father sort of gave up on church, this sinner didn't. She must look to you like a hypocrite altogether. She kept going back. Jack might slip into her bed of a Wednesday night, and she'd be at confession before the week was out."

Quite a conversation to be having as the waves rolled relentlessly up the beach beside us, their rhythmic crescendos crashing into our chat.

"That must be a Catholic thing," I say. "I can't imagine confessing to my minister once, never mind the repeat performances. He'd have had a heart attack if he'd been hearing your story. 'Oops, sorry…I did it again, your reverence!'"

She laughs at me. "Just think what he misses."

"And the whole thing about absolution. Did you get forgiven, every time like? How does that work? Did you feel any…I suppose, did you feel any burden of guilt lifting off you?"

"Ah yes, of course. You see…confession is such a special thing in our church. It is a sacrament, after all. You definitely feel the benefit of it, the wonder of it…that you have opened your innermost heart to God and let him…it felt sort of like rebooting yourself, in the same way a computer needs the occasional reboot. I always felt like I do after a lovely warm shower; cleansed, but in a spiritual way."

"And this despite the fact that you knew you would go back to Jack as soon as he appeared, same as always?"

She just hangs her head, smiling a small smile of remembrance.

"The pleasure trumped the guilt?" I continue.

"Maybe it did, maybe it didn't, but, to be honest, eventually it didn't really bother me."

"How come? I thought that guilt was a big thing in…"

"Well, yes. It was. It is. And at the start of things…the relationship, I mean…I did carry terrible feelings of guilt; even worse was the self-hatred. I was letting my father down, disobeying my church. I was hurting God and His Blessed Mother."

"But you didn't break it off with Jack?"

"I didn't. I tried. I tried a couple of times. But I couldn't. Literally I couldn't. Those days, those weeks when I told him not to come back to me, when I tried to put him out of my mind...those were awful times. I felt like I had cut off a part of me, the part that most mattered to me. I just wanted him back, regardless of church and all that. Jack was all I had left in the world. At the end up I had to choose between him and a whole life without meaning."

"So, you chose Jack, but how did you manage your relationship with church, with your priest and all?"

She thinks quietly for a bit, reflecting on difficult times and choices. She is looking out to the horizon, seemingly shy of meeting my gaze until she gets these intricacies sorted out in her memory.

"Well....all right, can I tell you how I believe I dealt with these feelings, 'cause it was a big thing. I'd be sitting there in the confessional box, one on one with my priest, telling him of my misdemeanours...a single girl speaking in code to a single man, an older, celibate man...and I'd be thinking...right, I am about to make my confession to him, I am about to apologise. But when is he going to apologise to me for what the church has done to my life?"

I wait for that bombshell comment to be explained.

"But never once has anyone in the church asked me for forgiveness," she continues.

"Forgiveness for what?" I ask...but I can guess. I just want her to verbalise it, and in clear terms.

"Forgiveness for the fact that, if they'd known anything about it, they would have regarded my pregnancy as a terrible sin, an almost unforgivable one. And so the whole messy consequences of my secret sin had to be hidden from them. Neatly tidied away! All for the common good of the parish! Nothing to do with the good of me, the sinner. That's the first thing I'd like to talk to the hierarchy about."

"It would have been pretty much the same if you'd been raised in my church," I tell her. "What's the second thing?"

"The second thing is the whole business of control. Telling me who I could or couldn't marry. Jack and I could easily have been married, should have been married...but the church denied us that right, that privilege. To me that is a sin. Not an individual sin, like mine, or like Jack's. But it's a sin, nevertheless. A sort of social sin...to put religious barriers between two people who love each other, who want to be together for their whole lives...two people who are both Christian, for God's sake! I am still angry about that. I still go through the motions of my religion, and I know I'm not a very good Christian, but Jack lost his faith altogether over the head of it. If we'd been allowed to marry, I could have saved him from that."

"You absolutely could," I tell her, "and don't ever tell me again that you are not a very good Christian. I think you're a saint."

"I'm no saint, Sarah."

****

We pay a visit to Miriam in the nursing home. She is fifty now, my… my auntie. First time I've thought of her as that. However, I am careful to introduce her to Josie as my 'sister', and Josie as my 'friend'; you can never tell what level of understanding someone with her condition has, so it is wise not to risk needless confusion. It is lovely to see Josie's compassion as she holds Miriam's hand and chats away. We stay twenty minutes, then drive from the town, back through the village.

I point out Joseph's filling station and shop as we drive past.

"You think he'll come to see me?"

I'm glad she has asked the question. It must hurt a bit that she is in her third day here, and hasn't yet set eyes on her son. He had got back to my text, eventually, insisting that things are very busy in the shop right now, that he's had to fire one of the girls, and find a replacement. All sounds plausible enough, but surely he could have popped up for ten minutes after close-down.

"I hope so," I tell her. "If he can't persuade himself to come up, perhaps we can call to see him."

"Maybe he wouldn't like that," she says. "Maybe best leave it, if he thinks it is too awkward to meet me just now…"

"Don't worry about him. He'll come round to it when he gets his head in place. He's not going to let you slip away back to Scotland without seeing you. I know him. He'll be too curious."

"I hope so. It's been so good getting to know you, but it would leave a vacuum of wondering….if I didn't get to chat to him."

"By the way," I say, "do you see where I am driving now? You should recognise this road. You used to cycle it often enough back in the day…or so I have read in some old storybook, I think."

She peers out the window, a smile gathering itself around her eyes.

"Ah ha, I do recognise it….and I feel almost as much excitement in my chest now as I did then…well, that's an exaggeration…maybe not quite as much."

We are driving along beside the famine wall around the Colonel's estate, and soon I am pulling the car into the parking area at the western gate lodge. She looks at me questioningly.

"What? What are you doing, Sarah? You can't seriously be…"

"Why not?" I say. "I just thought you might want to revisit…"

A grimace and a hesitation.

"I'm not sure I do. Too many ghosts haunt that old castle."

"Come on," I tell her. "We don't have to go down to the cellar if you don't want to. Jack took me down there once anyhow. There wasn't much to see."

This surprises her completely; she gives me a long, doubtful stare.

"He did not? You shock me. Why would he want to do that? He didn't say anything about…"

"No, of course not. I was a kid then anyhow. No, I thought it was all just part of him showing off what he knew about the estate, the old castle and all his secret haunts," I say as we slip through the gates and begin to tramp along the inside of the wall towards the ruins. The grass is damp and mucky, and we pick our steps carefully.

"But maybe he did have a secret desire to show me where I was conceived….a subconscious idea to connect me with that time, with this place. It was weird. The place was spooky enough in itself…I'm glad I didn't know any more about things just then."

"What did he tell you about the ruins?"

"Far as I remember he said it had been where the original people who owned this land had lived, like way back in history."

"Do you remember who they were?"

"I should know this," I say with a rueful smile, "but remind me."

"They were the O'Cuinns," she tells me. "My people."

"How do you mean, your people?"

"O'Cuinn. An old Irish clan from these parts. It's my name, in Gaelic. It got anglicised to Quinn at some stage."

"Seriously? I never knew that. So, are you telling me that your ancestors were the people who lived here?"

She laughs. "I'm not entirely sure if it's a direct line of descent, the actual chieftains and all…but there's a fair chance; or at least that they are lurking somewhere in my family tree."

"Wow," I say. "That's quite a heritage."

We arrive at the castle ruin, but stop well short, just stand and stare. I watch her closely, her head gently turning from side to side. Is it a gesture of sadness, wonderment? I can't begin to imagine what these memories are doing to her. This was a risk, I think now; maybe too raw to be doing this, even after all this time.

"Yeah, the scene of the crime," she whispers. "Ah no, it was never a crime. But it was a place that changed my life. That's for sure."

"I hope you don't regret it though?"

She gives me a long stare.

"I could never regret giving life to a beautiful human being like you, Sarah."

"Yeah, irony upon irony, isn't it?"

"How do you mean?"

"Well, for a start," I tell her, "your deflowering happened in the ruins of the very building where your clan had been kind of kings of the castle…and it happened at the hands of a Protestant who was living on your ancestral land. In fact, the reason he was farming this land was because, years before, a solicitor called Jerome Quinn loaned his family the money to buy land, long before Jack was even born."

Josie stares at me as if I had started to speak a foreign language.

"What are you talking about?"

I recount the story I have heard from Wally Brown. "He knows nothing of you; he has no knowledge of you and Jack, nor of where Joseph and I came from….so far as I know. But he told me all this information one day just after Jack died."

"What a strange coincidence," she says. "I had no idea."

"So I owe you doubly; so does Joseph. Your father helped us get our land. You gave us life, with our Jack….and then you lost us."

After a bit she turned back towards the car.

"Take me to his grave, would you please?"

Chapter 48

Twin

Joseph and Judith arrive with us mid-afternoon on the penultimate day of Josie's visit. I will drive her back to the airport tomorrow morning. I am so glad that they accepted the invitation to eat with us this Saturday evening, and pleasantly surprised that the two of them have appeared so early. That is a good signal, even if it does throw me off balance a bit that my culinary preparations are way behind schedule. In contrast to my fluster, my twin and his wife seem to be reasonably at ease. Their introduction to Josie is more relaxed than I had envisioned it might be. Amid the smiles of greeting, when Josie offers her hand to Joseph, my twin seems to conquer his earlier reticence. He ignores the outstretched hand, opens his arms, and makes a jokey remark as they hug. Maybe it's a defence mechanism kicking in. Maybe he had thought long and hard about this moment, and had planned what to do and say.

"You have waited long enough to give me a hug," he says. I think he has judged the moment very well. I watch our birth mother beam through misty eyes.

"You can say that again," she says, as Judith comes forward and follows her husband's example.

The pleasantries continue, all bland, small-talk queries and answers. As they dry up, my husband comes to the rescue.

Calvin has been hovering uncertainly by the door of the sitting room, observing us in the manner of a nervous diplomatic advisor at a political summit meeting. His sensitivity has pleasantly surprised me during the past few days.

"Would you all like to come into the sitting room and have a seat?"

We move in his direction, but knowing what I have got to get through in the kitchen in the next hour or so, I make my excuse.

"Yous go on ahead, but, if you'll excuse me, I need to go back to check on the chef," I say.

Calvin holds the door for Josie. As Judith is about to enter, she has the sound idea that I might need some help, so she turns back to me... leaving Josie and Joseph in the hands of Calvin in the sitting room. To be fair to him, he makes his escape in a matter of minutes, having excelled in his unaccustomed role as facilitator, and the crucial *tête à tête* can begin.

Suddenly I want to be in that room. I desperately want to be observing, mediating if necessary. But I know I have to let the two of them come to terms with each other, and it may take time; it may take way longer than the half hour they are going to have in my front room. For me it has all been well-paced, the slow dawning of who I was from my birth, the growing acceptance of the weirdness of those circumstances, and of my upbringing. Joseph, on the other hand, has had a crash course. I realise I cannot begin to tell him how to feel, how to adapt to the trauma of these disclosures. Yes, of course I want him to love his mother as I love her…but slow steps towards acceptance may be the best I can hope for today.

That I have come to forgive, to accept, to be reconciled with, and yes…to love this woman, our secret mother, is to me a deeply cleansing experience, a sort of re-baptism. It is as if a tidal wave has swept into my life from some external source; its effect has been to wash away all those resentments against the falsehoods that we were reared with. And, in so doing, it has also swept away some of the walls of dogma that had been built into me as bulwarks against uncertainty. In a funny way I feel like I am carrying fewer weighty bricks around with me now.

This is what I would love for my dear twin…but I know I cannot prescribe anything for him. He must negotiate his own course through these floodwaters. Anything I think I can do for him will only be useless flotsam, a distraction at best, at worst something to argue with me about. If I am honest, I do fear a division growing between us. How ironic would that be, that in the whole process of conciliation with my birth mother I should provoke a schism with the twin who shared the space of her womb with me?

I am aware that I have not heard a word Judith has said since we began here. I apologise, and explain my distraction. She understands, empathetic lady that she is.

"I know he is struggling," she tells me. "But he just has to work through it."

I risk a question. "What do you think are his main hang-ups about it? The religious thing?"

"I don't think so," she says. "I guess it is just the whole shaking of his knowledge of who and what he is."

"But he is still the same guy he was before," I tell her. "Nothing really has changed. He is still Joseph Shaw."

"I know that, and you know that, but…that Jack was his father! That Jack named him after this woman he never knew….a stranger that he now has to have polite conversation with. That is hard. A woman he only ever met as the person who tried to teach him piano as a kid…."

The sound of the electric beater interrupts for a minute. The pause gives us time to think.

"What would you like to see as the outcome?" I ask her.

"Oh dear, that's a hard one. Just that he could put all this behind him, and come back to being the normal sort of person he was before. He just really resents that his story is such an abnormal one. Like…why could he not have had a normal father and mother, same as everybody else? Why does this woman have to arrive into his life now, and demand a mother-son relationship?"

"Is he seriously that hung up about it?"

"Sarah," she says, setting down her chopping knife, and turning to give me a glum stare, "I am worried that it might destroy him."

Goodness, I hadn't seen anything so drastic coming. My arm goes around her automatically.

"I am sorry if I have brought this on," I tell her. "Maybe he needs to talk to somebody…professional like… if you are that concerned about him."

"It's not your fault, it's nobody's fault….well, maybe the religious people in the past who…I suppose the ones who created this culture of despising…Oh I don't know. I just hope the two of them talking today will help. Maybe the start of it. You know, he really did not want to come. He was so nervous about facing her. I was working hard on him all morning. I thought I wasn't getting anywhere, he was so quiet. Then after lunch he suddenly says, 'Right, get ready. We'll go now, before the notion leaves me.'"

"Really? I thought he was dead on with her. He did the hugs and all…"

"That probably took more out of him than you can imagine," she says. "I'm glad they are having time to talk."

We are interrupted. I wouldn't say that Calvin storms into the room, but he gets as close to that descriptor as I've ever seen. He holds an opened envelope, and is excitedly waving some correspondence at me.

"Would you look at this, Sarah," he says.

"What is it?" I ask across the food-covered island.

He's laughing as he reads. "'Confirmation of your holiday for two, a tour of Germany in July. Berlin, Wittenberg, Augsburg and Munich… 'In the footsteps of Martin Luther', it's called. Ten day tour. Did you book this?'"

I do my best to appear mystified. Total denial, but my words don't match my facial expression. He smells a rat.

"Well, did you know about it?"

We've had enough lies. I confess.

"All right, if you must know. It's Josie's present to us. She thinks we need a holiday together."

"What? You are joking me?"

"No joking; she sat me down a few nights ago, asked me where I thought you would like to go for a wee holiday. I protested, I tried to put her off. She absolutely insisted, and she insisted that she was paying. So I just thought…"

My word, I have never seen Calvin react like that; not even after he has tied his most perfect fly! His eyes are wide in surprise, but he doesn't know what to say. He takes a step towards me, but glances at Judith, turns on his heel and scampers from the room.

We look at each other and laugh, Judith and I.

"I think he's well chuffed," she says. "What a class idea. Martin Luther will be delighted to see him, eh? Well done yourself."

"Well done, my mother," I reply.

Our evening meal sees the five of us around the table. Calvin has got himself under control again, and says a sober grace as we hold hands; I am holding his and my mother's. It's a perfect little metaphor. The conversation is civil, if not animated. As outsiders to the intensity of the family drama, Judith and my husband play their parts with consummate skill, filling in the missing lines, prompting new directions for the dialogue, and injecting just the right humour, in both tone and degree. My husband's gratitude to Josie for her gift to us is warm and genuine. I think it moved him far more than either my mother or I could have imagined.

"'In the footsteps of Luther,'" he whispers, not to anyone in particular. He cannot contain himself. It's either excitement at the prospect of the tour or sheer incredulity that his newly-discovered mother-in-law should have thought it a good idea to send him on such an adventure. "Oh man," he says, "I am so looking forward to this summer!"

The irony of his elation!

I know exactly what Josie is doing with this scheme…she doesn't have to spell it out for me. I see the devilment twinkling in her eyes, those same eyes that entranced our Jack. Her hope is that this trip, even the anticipation of it, will somehow be the lure that brings Calvin up from the depths of his disinterest, and that I will be ready and waiting to net him back into my bed. Generous; charming; Machiavellian.

Later, as my twin and Judith are leaving, handshakes and hugs on the doorstep, I am blessed to hear Joseph ask, "What time is your flight then, Josie?" When she tells him, I catch a quick glance between him and his wife; then he says, "Why don't we drive you up?" It is said in his matter of fact tone, very naturally, as if it were a sudden afterthought.

"You come too, Sarah," he says.

Josie and I look at each other in that whatever-ish sort of way, belying our secret delight.

"That would be lovely, Joseph," says his mother.

****

Josie and I spend the evening seated together at my piano, the one Jack bought back in the 1960ies. I am so glad I've had it brought up here to my home. It survived the move, and has responded perfectly to being rigorously tuned. We take it in turns to play various pieces to each other. It's absolutely not a competition, more a therapy of the memories. All those old tunes from her drawing room so long ago. She has lost little of her touch, I think, despite her protestations to the contrary.

"This piano is glorious," she says.

"I told you that it's the one Jack bought for Joseph and me right at the start, didn't I? Some investment."

"You did." She seems to hesitate over something, then speaks again. "What I haven't told you yet is that I have actually played it before."

"How come?"

I am confused. She couldn't have surely? Had she ever been in our house?

"He asked me to recommend a piano."

I wait for more explanation.

"Yeah, Jack told me one night that he intended to buy a decent piano for you two. Apparently the one your folks had was ancient and beyond repair."

"Go on…what happened?"

"Well, I knew the best piano firm in Belfast, so I went up, played a few of their selection and recommended this one to Jack. Good choice, don't you think?"

The surprises never seem to stop with this lady!

"Absolutely," I tell her. "Jack made a lot of good choices in my opinion."

She laughs, poised to play again.

"No wonder I love it."

"Must have cost him a wee fortune back then. Do you remember?"

She smiles. "I do as it happens, but you don't need to know."

Something about her body language triggers me, and I have a sudden realisation. My hand goes on top of hers to delay her beginning again.

"You helped, didn't you? It was your gift too?"

The half-stifled grin tells me I am correct.

"That's incredible, Josie. How much did…., look, you were just my teacher…"

"I was your mother, Sarah. Now please let me play this. Listen… soak it in."

She plays an ascending diminished arpeggio in a dramatic upward flourish, beginning with a sonorous, *fortissimo* bass and culminating in a high, delicate *pianissimo*. I still adore the instrument's power, that earthy quality of its timbre that seems to resonate in my very bones.

"Doesn't that sound just like him," she says. "So much character, such resilience and strength, and yet so delicate when you ask it to be."

"I think that's more about the pianist on this occasion than about Jack," I tell her.

An hour into this recital without audience she sits silently after a piece, eyes closed, two hands together at her mouth as if in prayer. I wait as she ponders something; she seems far away.

"Do you remember this one?" she says, and begins to play again, a tune I think I only ever heard her play once. A wonderful Robert Schumann piece…we usually refer to it as 'Dreaming'. Absolutely gorgeous piece of music and she plays it with such emotion. She has the phrasing perfect, a magically sensitive touch. I am hanging on every note, some of them so quiet you actually wonder whether she has played them or your mind has just imagined them. At the end, in the sacred silence as that final note fades, her elbows lean on the frame of the instrument and her head goes down to rest in her hands. I sense a deep stirring in her.

"You know why this piece is so special to me?"

I wait.

"Only once did I have the courage to play it to you as a child," she says. "Do you remember?"

"I think so. It is such a beautiful…"

"Don't you have any memory of what happened at the end?"

I am not sure that I do. I can't risk a guess. I stay quiet.

"I had to rush out of the room, don't you remember?"

"I do seem to recall that you did that once," I tell her. "I couldn't have told you specifically when that was, or what tune you had played. I likely just thought you had to get to the loo quick or something."

"Probably did as well," she tells me, "but not for the usual reason."

"So explain."

"You know what the piece is called?"

"Yip, *'Träumerei'* isn't it?"

"*'Träumerei Kinderszenen,'*" she says, "*Kinderszenen* means 'Scenes from Childhood.'"

"I thought…ah, right, I see what…."

"It was always a favourite piece of mine, even before I met Jack. My father loved it too. But there was real irony in the whole thing."

"How do you mean?"

"So, you know about the composer? Robert Schumann? He was in love with an amazing girl called Clara Wieck…she was to become a composer as well, and fantastic pianist. Thing was, Clara was his pupil; a lot younger than him. So Clara's father wouldn't allow her to marry Robert. He was dead set against it. Sound familiar?"

"Really? I didn't know any of this."

"They married anyhow, maybe in secret I think; and Clara had eight children to him, as well as being a concert pianist all over Europe. She was a force of nature, a hero of the romantic movement. So his *Kinderszenen* was written for her, for their growing family. I so loved those tunes; I can imagine her with that brood of children playing around her."

Ah, I think; the pain is always just under the surface.

She's not quite finished her reverie though.

"I wanted to identify with Clara, but I guess I was the reverse side of the coin. I was the girl who never did get to marry her guy, who never did get to enjoy those scenes of childhood. I was just *'ein Träumer'*, a dreamer. The dream didn't materialise."

"I am so sorry. But you're here now."

"Yeah, but it's 2007. I'm just forty seven years too late for your childhood."

Coda

May 2020

We did not see this coming.

This wicked COVID 19! So far as I was aware, nobody was predicting anything like this, or, if they did, they were very quiet about it. Yes, there have been novels on the subject, like '*The Andromeda Strain*'; there was the movie, '*Contagion*'; there were even the official Government plans way back, apparently… eventualities that had been thought about, plans that had never been implemented. And now there is plenty of hindsight, all over the place. Experts bravely putting their heads above the parapet to say, 'Yeah, we have been warning about possible new viruses for years'. Doom merchants rising from their misty swamps to lament the end of civilisation as we knew it. We have shed tears at the medieval scenes we have witnessed on TV, scenes of heartbreaking crises in places like Italy, mass graves being dug to hold hundreds of corpses in Brazil. Nowhere seems to be immune. Fear levels have risen across the country. Residential care homes in the United Kingdom are a new frontline battlefield.

How glad I am that we have my mother living with us here in Castlecuinn.

Josie had stayed at her post in Edinburgh until 2016. She was seventy-five when she came to us. She had slipped on ice, and had fallen down some stone steps at the rear of her 'place of work', breaking a few of her ribs. At the time, I had a long phone call with her boss over there, and, reading between the lady's very discrete lines, I got the impression that it had reached the time when Josie should be retiring gracefully. That said, there was a mountain of praise being heaped on her for her work there over something like thirteen years. Not only her practical role; she had, according to the centre manager, made very substantial financial donations to the place. I could believe it, and I am fairly sure many of the girls benefitted individually from her generosity as well.

Josie had wanted to come back to Northern Ireland, but her idea was to move into some form of sheltered accommodation. She had contacted a scheme in a town twenty-five miles from us. I wouldn't hear tell of it. Neither would Calvin. Between us we persuaded her to move in with us.

It has been a very blissful period. We opened up an exterior door into the guest room to give her more private access; the room was ensuite, of course, so all we needed to do was install a small work bench for a toaster and kettle, so she had her own mini-kitchen. She ate her meals with us. She had driven her little car over from Scotland, so she has had some independence, able to take herself off to Mass, and to various functions in the town, mainly to do with St John's Parish. She had renewed some friendships with local folks, and made new acquaintances.

All that has had to stop, however. We are all back in our boxes, our personal echo chambers, as this virus robs us of human contact. The choral has had to surrender to the solo. We all feel stripped of our essential instinct to talk, to be neighbourly...to see our 'selves' reflected in the eyes of another human.

Seems to me that this virus is actually reinforcing, even multiplying, the barriers that we have allowed ourselves to be hemmed in by, especially in this country. How ironic that a virus which has no respect for creed, colour or class, entrenches us more deeply into tribal boxes. We isolate in family bubbles, which makes sense. The family is vital. But the controversies around this pandemic tend to force us into camps. We become oppositional, angry at each other for having different points of view. We find rabbit holes to hide in, bunkered with like-minded folks.

In Northern Ireland, responses to COVID have even managed to reflect our sectarian divisions. Where else would there have been such distinctive reactions to, for example, the policing of weddings, funerals and wreath-laying ceremonies? Whose side is the virus on?

Josie and I talk about this often, Calvin joining in from his more conservative position. They argue, but always in good spirit. Josie's humour and lightness of touch is such a blessing to hear. She can disarm him with such gentle sweetness, poking holes in his conspiracy theories with an affectionate smile. How I wish I had known her all my life.

I am really pleased that Father McCartan has driven up to us a couple of times to give communion to Josie, through the open window, of course. I love having my birth mother in our bubble. I hate to think what might have happened had she been in a residential setting with a group of other pensioners. I've heard already of people we would have known who have lost their lives to the thing, mainly due to the crowded nature of their living circumstance. The herd instinct is challenged. The financially sensible idea of housing a group of people together, for care, for education, for catering....whatever, is completely overturned by a pandemic. Instead it manipulates us into living in microcosms, tiny units of isolation, a dystopian 'brave new world' which, until now, has really only existed in the imagination of novelists and film makers.

Our Miriam has been protected from the virus so far, thank God. At her age, and given her underlying health issues, I cannot imagine that she would be able to survive the infection. We take it in turns to call at the nursing home to see her. I say 'see her', but the reality is, of course, that all we see through the sometimes steamed-up glass is her rather rigid form, sitting propped up close to the window in her wheelchair. Communication, if it exists at all, is more spiritual than physical. Who knows whether or not she is even aware of our presence?

It is good to have Isaac nearby. His medical knowledge and wisdom has been so important to us all. He phones regularly to ask about Josie, and calls at her window on his frequent walks up the lane past our house.

My twin brother drives up to see us two or three times a week. His business is in difficulty of course, but government support will see him through this crisis. He has developed online services very quickly, and is now able to deliver essential groceries all around the countryside to more vulnerable people. He even has a group of villagers volunteering to do this for free, the pandemic bringing out the best in people, as well as the darker side.

When Joseph arrives in our yard he cannot, of course, come inside, so he chats through the kitchen window. He brings supplies, but he also carries local gossip, a social cross-pollinator on wheels. In that respect, I suppose he is just perpetuating the role of the village shop. We have learned that Wally, across the fields, has been admitted to hospital and has been placed on a ventilator. We pray for him to survive, a good man and a great neighbour, now in his eighties. In some ways I am glad that Jimmy McGrath and his wife are no longer around to have to face the threat of this evil plague. They lie together safely in the bosom of the chapel graveyard in the town.

From my kitchen, I watch as Joseph chats to his mother through the half-opened window of the guest room. Their conversations have become so important to her, and I appreciate that he takes so much time just standing there, chatting away as normal as you like. He shows great patience when she goes to play him a tune on the piano. I am so glad we didn't get rid of the Yamaha which now keeps her company in the guest room. My twin stands there, arms crossed, a smile on his face as he hums along with the theme from *'Love Story'*, then applauds generously as she finishes.

I love the final moments between them each time; the warmth of the smiles; the palm of her hand spread widely on the inside of the glass, his placed and held against it on the outside of the pane.

Transparency.

'Mother and son,' I think. 'Mother and son.'

Acknowledgements

In writing this novel I have drawn on advice and guidance from several friends. I thank the following for their candour in recounting life experiences and insights; Peter Quigley, Roisin Coll, Christine McKee, Brigene Dunlop, Robin and Janet Ruddock, Neil and Trish McGinley, Nancy Blanton, Claire Mitchell, Stephen McCracken, Stephen McAuley, Anne Morrison, Robert and Heather Montgomery.

May I also pay tribute to Kate Adie's book, "Nobody's Child", (Hodder & Stoughton, 2006), which was a tremendous help to me in trying to understand some of the emotions attached to the process of finding one's birth parents.

Once again, my deepest appreciation to my wife Mary who goes beyond the call of duty in an editorial and proof-reading role. She would, I suspect, know the text off by heart, but for the fact that I have altered it several times a week!

About the Author

David A Dunlop was born and raised in the north of Co. Antrim, N Ireland; he divides his time between there and his home in west Donegal. He spent many years in education, both as a teacher and as a school leader; in those roles he exercised his passion to bring together young people from across the various political and religious traditions in Ireland, north and south, so as to encourage a shared understanding of their history and culture. David's contribution to education was recognised by Queen's University Belfast in 2023 when he received an Honorary Doctorate, presented by Secretary Hilary Clinton. His six novels, as with a number of musical dramas he wrote and produced during his career in Limavady High School, have historical and cross-cultural themes, and draw on his experience of performance in various musical genres.

Other books by David A Dunlop

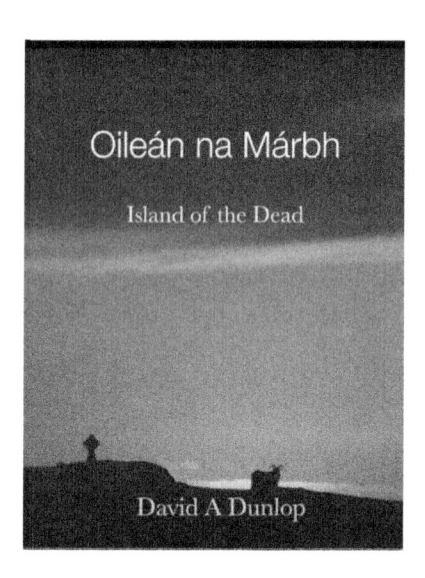

Oilean Na Marbh (2014)
When Sean-Bán Sweeney finds a body of a stranger washed up on a Donegal beach he can never imagine the hidden backstory that intertwines his simple life with that of the unknown youth, nor the connection to Annie, his mute, childhood sweetheart.

Set in 1898 when a new railway was being planned to link the impoverished regions of west Donegal to the centres of commerce and trade in the east, this is a story of tragic misunderstanding, but ultimately of the triumph of love.

The Broken Fiddle (2016)
As partition carves Ireland in two in 1922, Matthew Henderson, a young Protestant farmer in Tyrone's border country, goes to the hiring fair and finds himself a maid. Sally-Anne Sweeney is a feisty, Irish-speaking Catholic from west Donegal. As Matthew falls for her charms, his maid proves equally attractive to Joe Kearney, Matthew's friend and neighbour across the new border. Inadvertently this pretty, fiddle-playing maid causes a feud between the two friends, lads whose fathers had fought beside each other at the Somme, six years previously. No-one is immune to the political violence of the period and, in the end, a tragic set of circumstances leads to the maid leaving for home. As she goes, a distraught Sally Anne takes out her anger on a gift which Matthew had given her, his late father's precious fiddle. The broken fiddle haunts her over the years until she writes a letter of forgiveness to Matthew. Can there be any reconciliation of the fractured relationship?

A Maid Again (2020)
The concluding part of the trilogy.
The letter is dated 25th July 1945. The handwriting looks familiar, even after twenty three years. The signature confirms his guess. Sally-Anne Sweeney, his former maid, almost his lover, from all those lonely years ago. The warm tone of the letter stuns Matthew Henderson. It is a letter that reaches out across time, that transcends hurt and offers forgiveness, that tempts him with the possibility of reconciliation. But it is also a letter of farewell. She is leaving Donegal for a new life in America, and very soon. Matthew drives from his borderland farm in Co Tyrone to try to find her home in The Rosses before she sails away for ever.

We, The Fallen (2018)
"Without really meaning to I somehow found myself part of an All-Ireland study trip to the war cemeteries of the Somme, 100 years on from the infamous battle. This changed my life, for the simple reason that I met Magdalena. Lena, as she prefers to be called, is from Germany, though she is not exactly German. She has fascinated and frustrated me ever since. Most of my songs are now about her, about us. So is this book, but not only about us. With all that's going on in Europe, Brexit and all that, how could it be?"
Patrick McAleese 2017

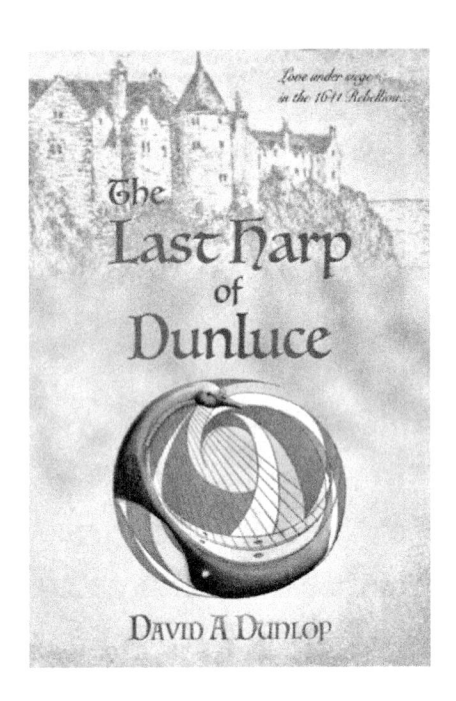

The Last Harp of Dunluce (2022)
The 1641 Rebellion was a seminal moment in Irish history. This story traces its course as it impacted the people of north-east Ulster, an area largely unaffected by the Plantation of 1607, a place where native Irish lived side by side with fellow Gaels from Scotland who had settled in the area over many years.
Harp-maker Darach O'Cahan witnesses the destruction of his beloved Dunluce and the demise of Ulster's last Gaelic chieftain, Randal McDonnell. His girl, Katie McKay, finds herself incarcerated in the little kirk of Ballintoy in a siege that lasts for three excruciating months. Can their love for each other endure and help them survive the terror and trauma of this troubled time in this beautiful place?

These novels can be purchased online through the usual websites, from selected outlets in Ireland and N Ireland or by direct contact.

email- dadunlop50@gmail.com   Twitter- @dadunlop50

Printed in Great Britain
by Amazon